big
NATE
HUG IT OUT!

Complete Your *Big Nate* Collection

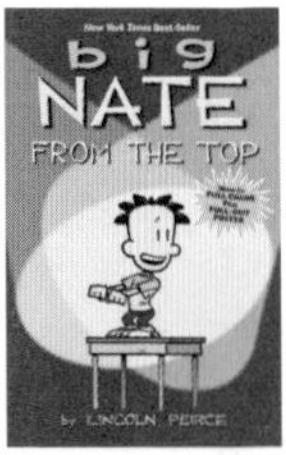
big NATE
FROM THE TOP
by LINCOLN PEIRCE

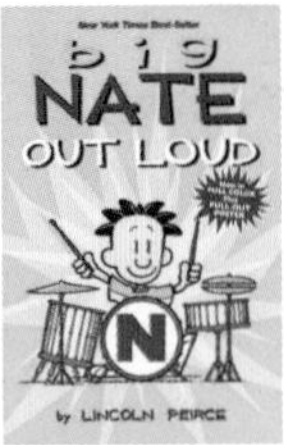
big NATE
OUT LOUD
by LINCOLN PEIRCE

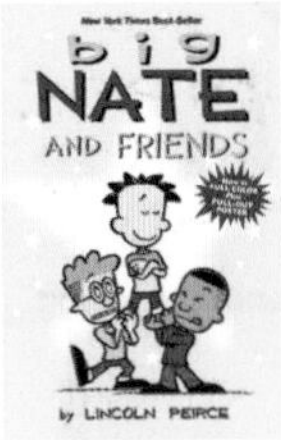
big NATE
AND FRIENDS
by LINCOLN PEIRCE

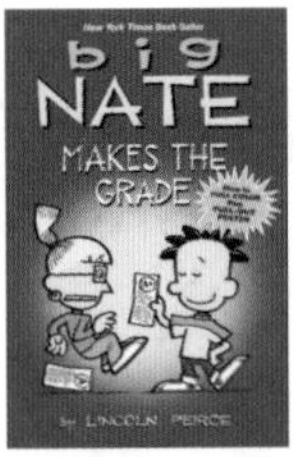
big NATE
MAKES THE GRADE
by LINCOLN PEIRCE

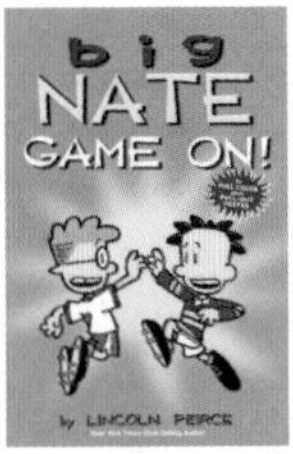
big NATE
GAME ON!
by LINCOLN PEIRCE

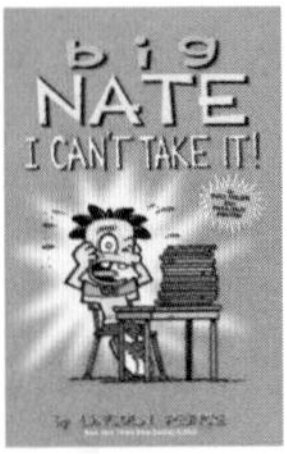
big NATE
I CAN'T TAKE IT!

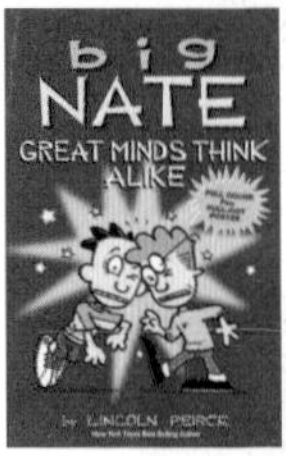
big NATE
GREAT MINDS THINK ALIKE
by LINCOLN PEIRCE

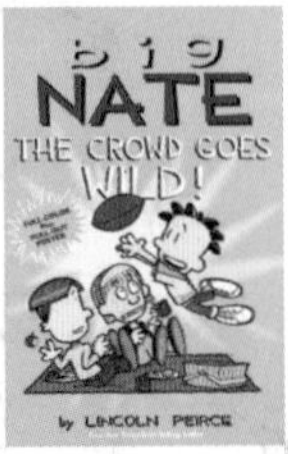
big NATE
THE CROWD GOES WILD!
by LINCOLN PEIRCE

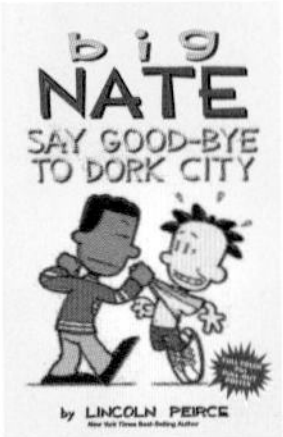
big NATE
SAY GOOD-BYE TO DORK CITY
by LINCOLN PEIRCE

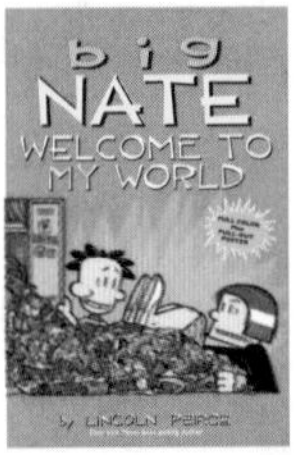
big NATE
WELCOME TO MY WORLD
by LINCOLN PEIRCE

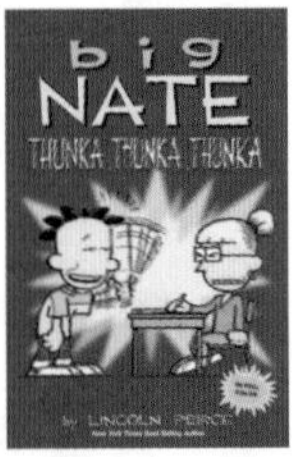
big NATE
THUNKA THUNKA THUNKA
by LINCOLN PEIRCE

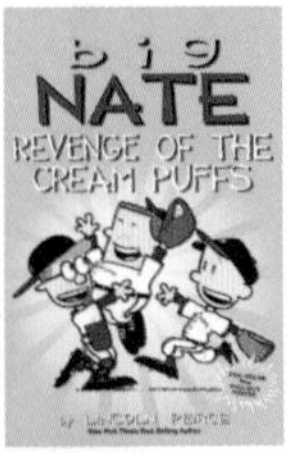
big NATE
REVENGE OF THE CREAM PUFFS
by LINCOLN PEIRCE

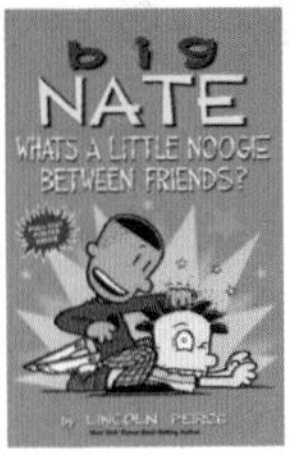
big NATE
WHAT'S A LITTLE NOOGIE BETWEEN FRIENDS?
by LINCOLN PEIRCE

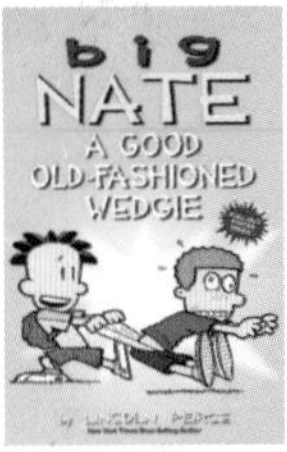
big NATE
A GOOD OLD-FASHIONED WEDGIE
by LINCOLN PEIRCE

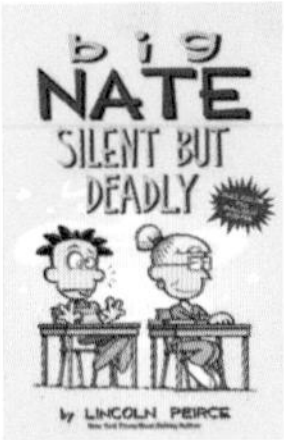
big NATE
SILENT BUT DEADLY
by LINCOLN PEIRCE

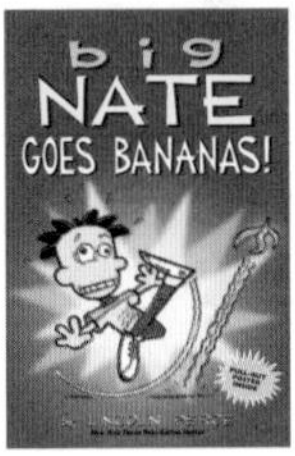
big NATE
GOES BANANAS!
by LINCOLN PEIRCE

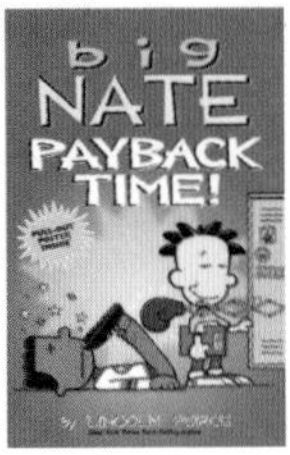
big NATE
PAYBACK TIME!
by LINCOLN PEIRCE

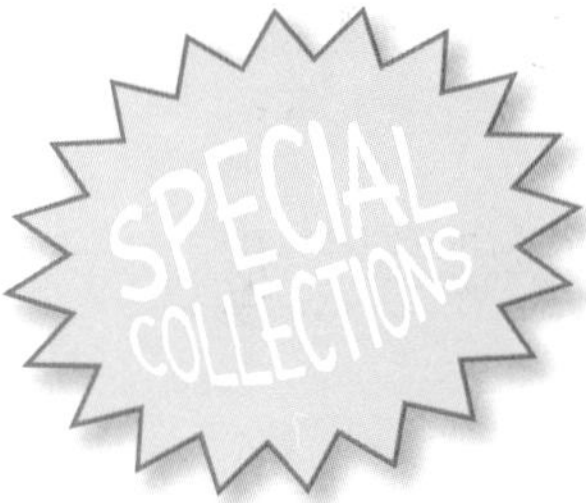
SPECIAL COLLECTIONS

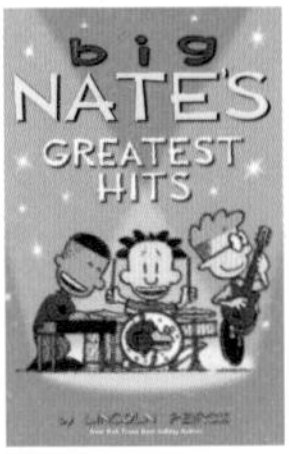
big NATE'S
GREATEST HITS
by LINCOLN PEIRCE

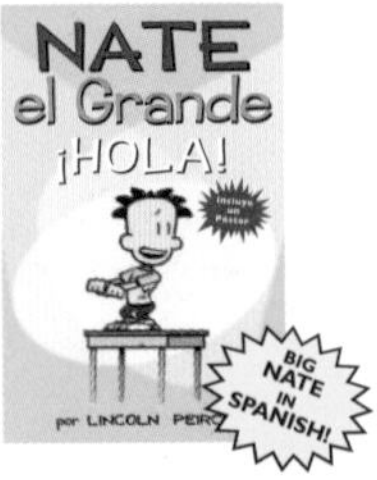
NATE el Grande
¡HOLA!
por LINCOLN PEIRCE
BIG NATE IN SPANISH!

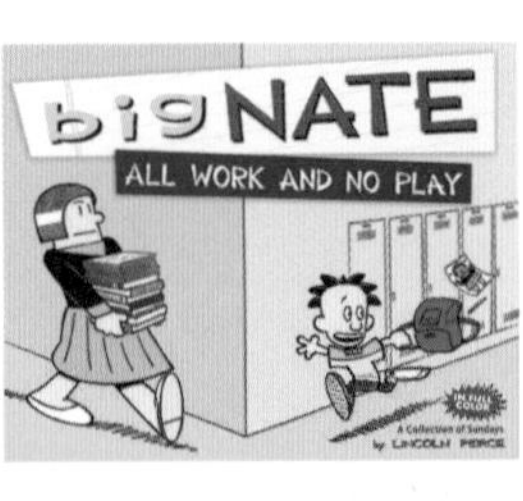
big NATE
ALL WORK AND NO PLAY
A Collection of Sundays
by LINCOLN PEIRCE

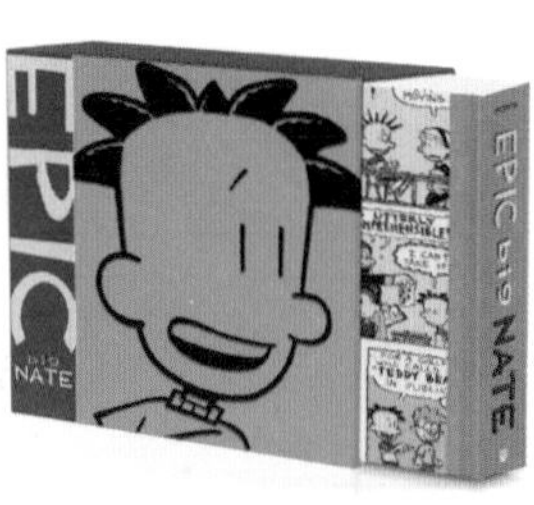
EPIC big NATE

big NATE
HUG IT OUT!

by LINCOLN PEIRCE

Andrews McMeel
PUBLISHING®

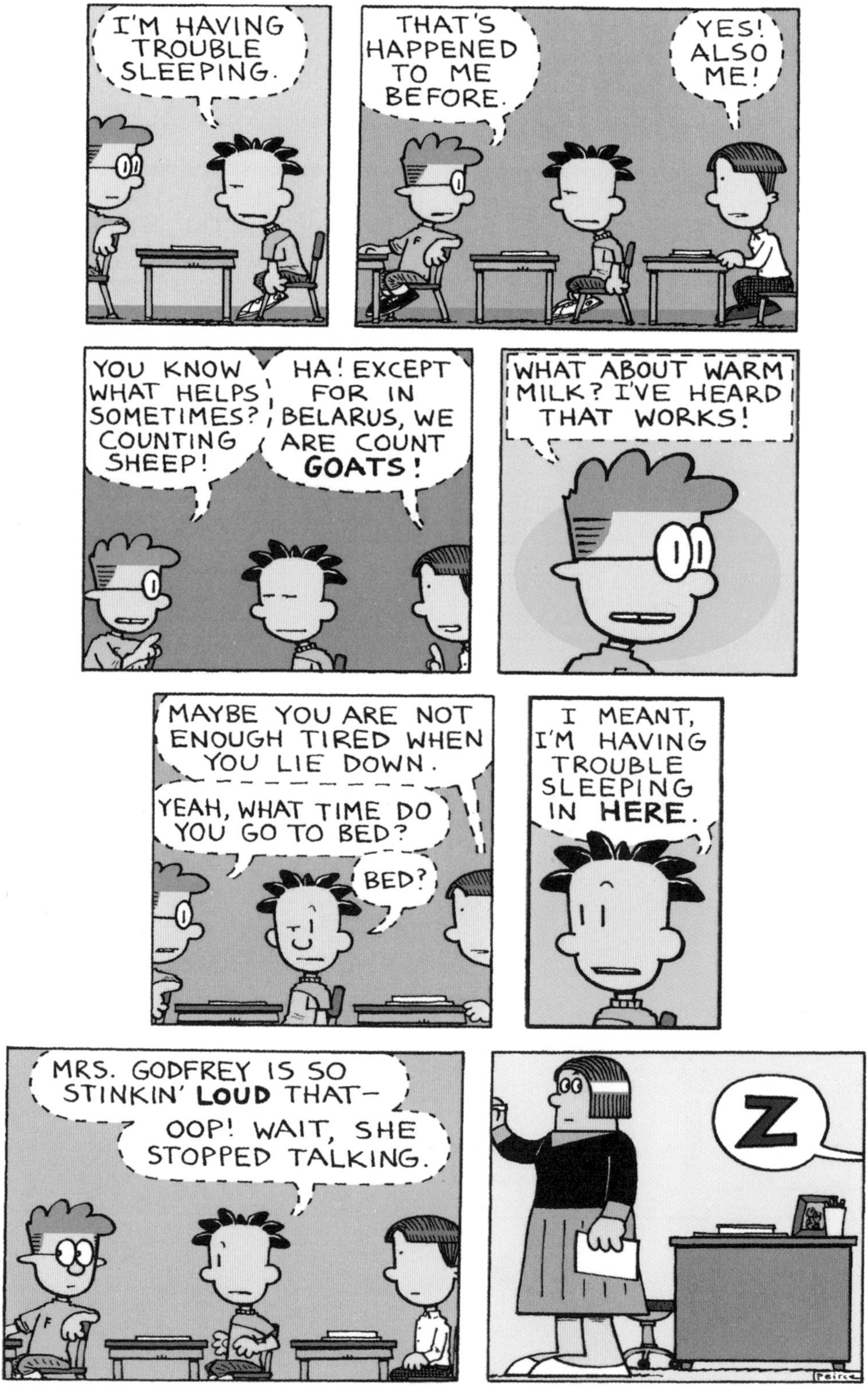
I'M HAVING TROUBLE SLEEPING.
THAT'S HAPPENED TO ME BEFORE.
YES! ALSO ME!
YOU KNOW WHAT HELPS SOMETIMES? COUNTING SHEEP!
HA! EXCEPT FOR IN BELARUS, WE ARE COUNT GOATS!
WHAT ABOUT WARM MILK? I'VE HEARD THAT WORKS!
MAYBE YOU ARE NOT ENOUGH TIRED WHEN YOU LIE DOWN.
YEAH, WHAT TIME DO YOU GO TO BED?
BED?
I MEANT, I'M HAVING TROUBLE SLEEPING IN HERE.
MRS. GODFREY IS SO STINKIN' LOUD THAT—
OOP! WAIT, SHE STOPPED TALKING.
Z
PEIRCE

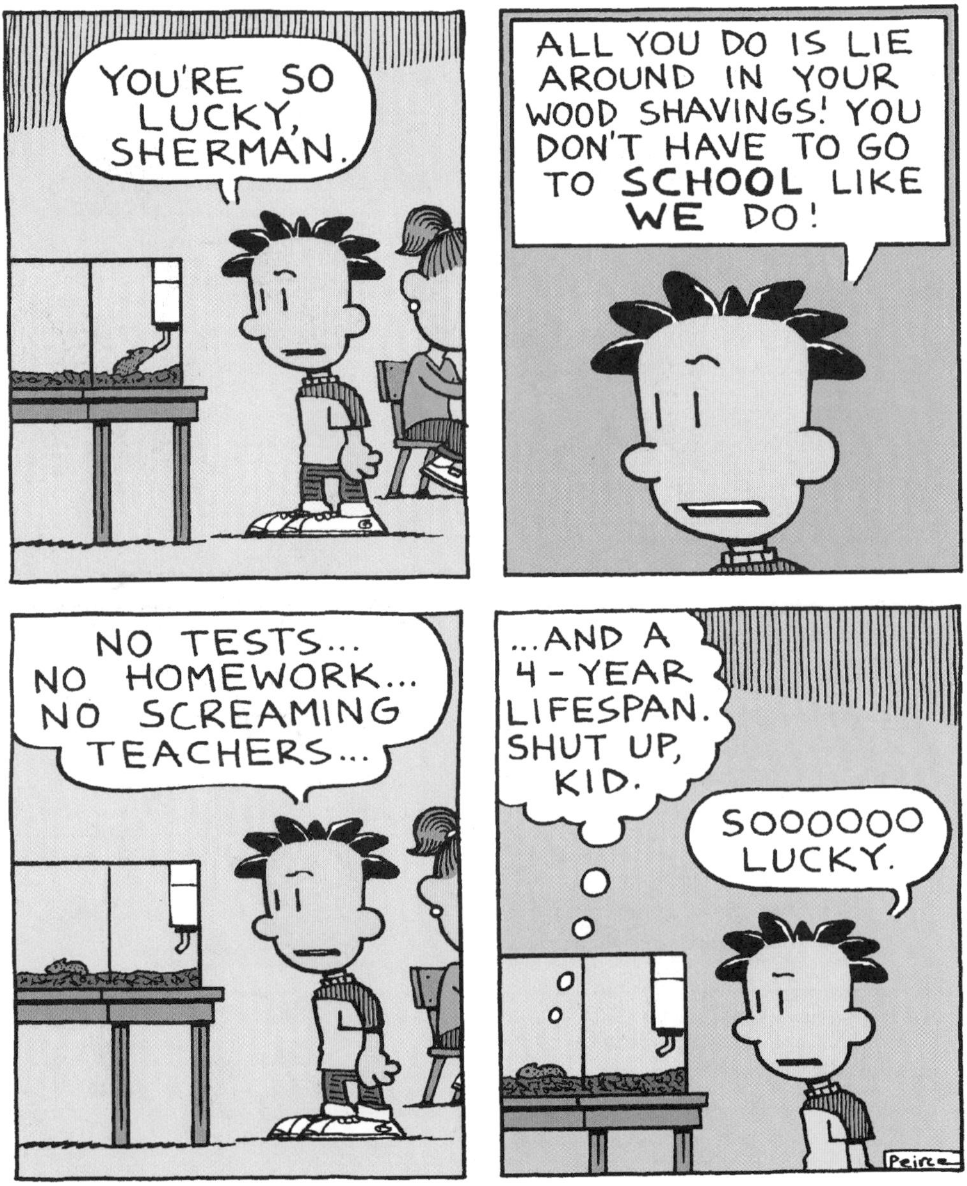
YOU'RE SO LUCKY, SHERMAN.
ALL YOU DO IS LIE AROUND IN YOUR WOOD SHAVINGS! YOU DON'T HAVE TO GO TO **SCHOOL** LIKE **WE** DO!
NO TESTS... NO HOMEWORK... NO SCREAMING TEACHERS...
...AND A 4-YEAR LIFESPAN. SHUT UP, KID.
SOOOOOO LUCKY.
Peirce

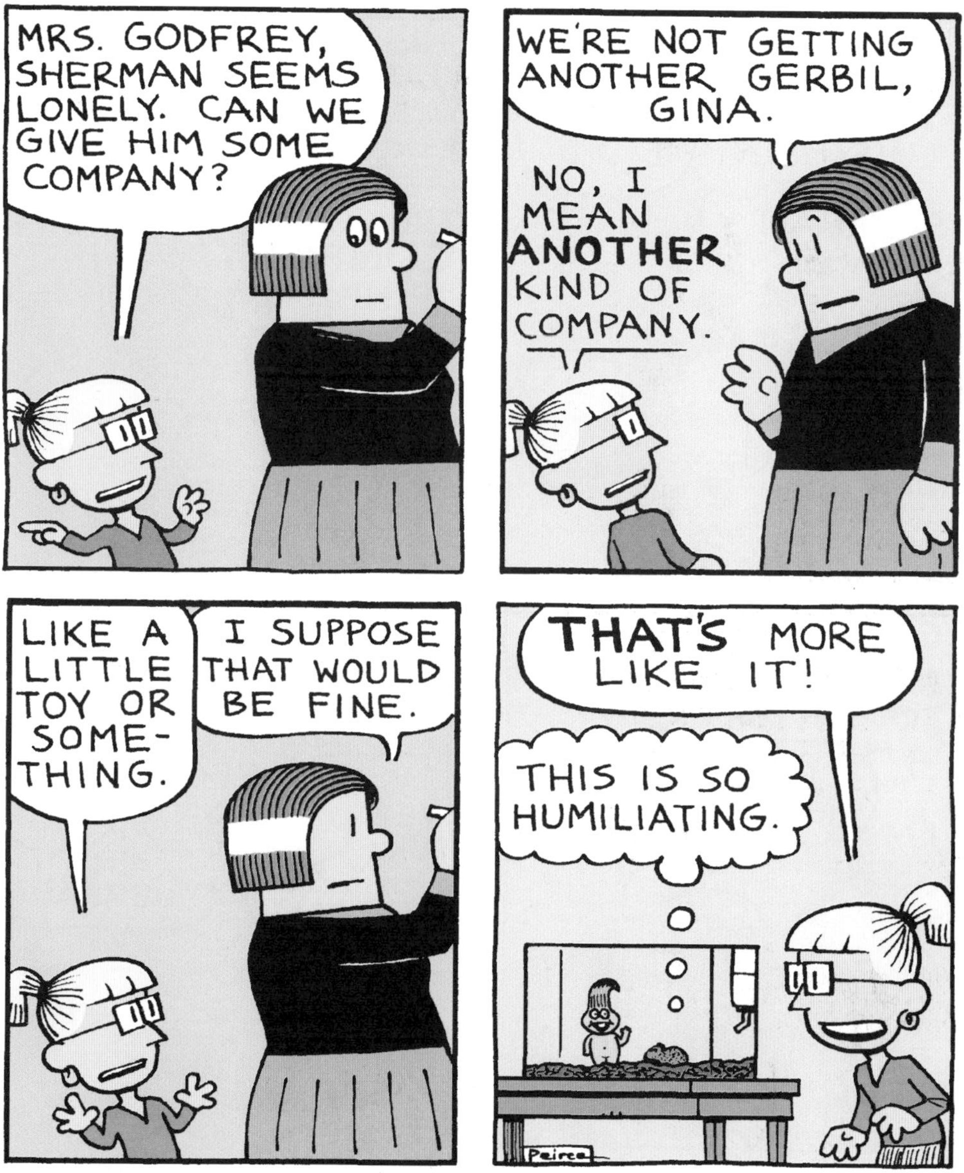
MRS. GODFREY, SHERMAN SEEMS LONELY. CAN WE GIVE HIM SOME COMPANY?
WE'RE NOT GETTING ANOTHER GERBIL, GINA.
NO, I MEAN **ANOTHER** KIND OF COMPANY.
LIKE A LITTLE TOY OR SOME-THING.
I SUPPOSE THAT WOULD BE FINE.
THAT'S MORE LIKE IT!
THIS IS SO HUMILIATING.
Peirce

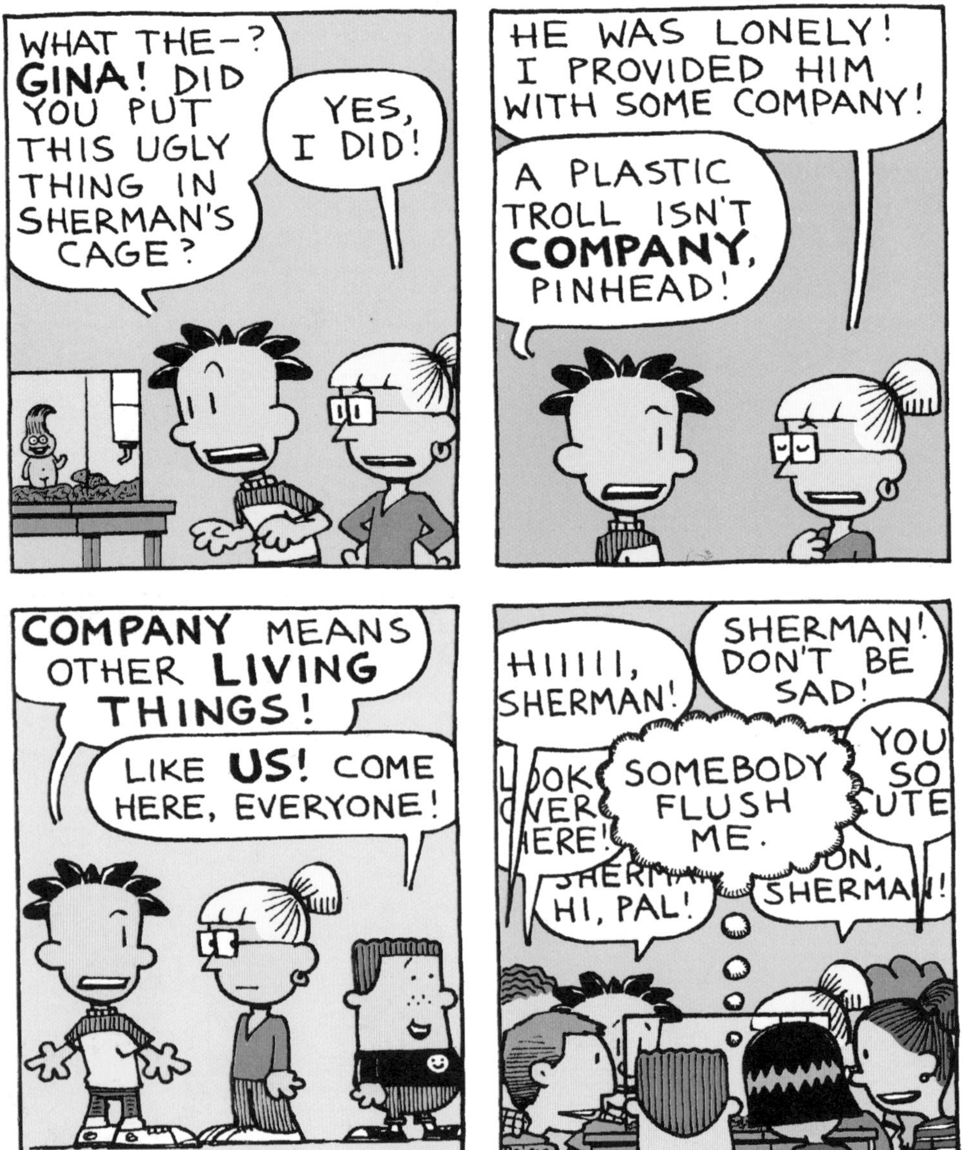

WHAT THE-? GINA! DID YOU PUT THIS UGLY THING IN SHERMAN'S CAGE?
YES, I DID!
HE WAS LONELY! I PROVIDED HIM WITH SOME COMPANY!
A PLASTIC TROLL ISN'T COMPANY, PINHEAD!
COMPANY MEANS OTHER LIVING THINGS!
LIKE US! COME HERE, EVERYONE!
HIIIII, SHERMAN!
SHERMAN! DON'T BE SAD!
SOMEBODY FLUSH ME.
HI, PAL!

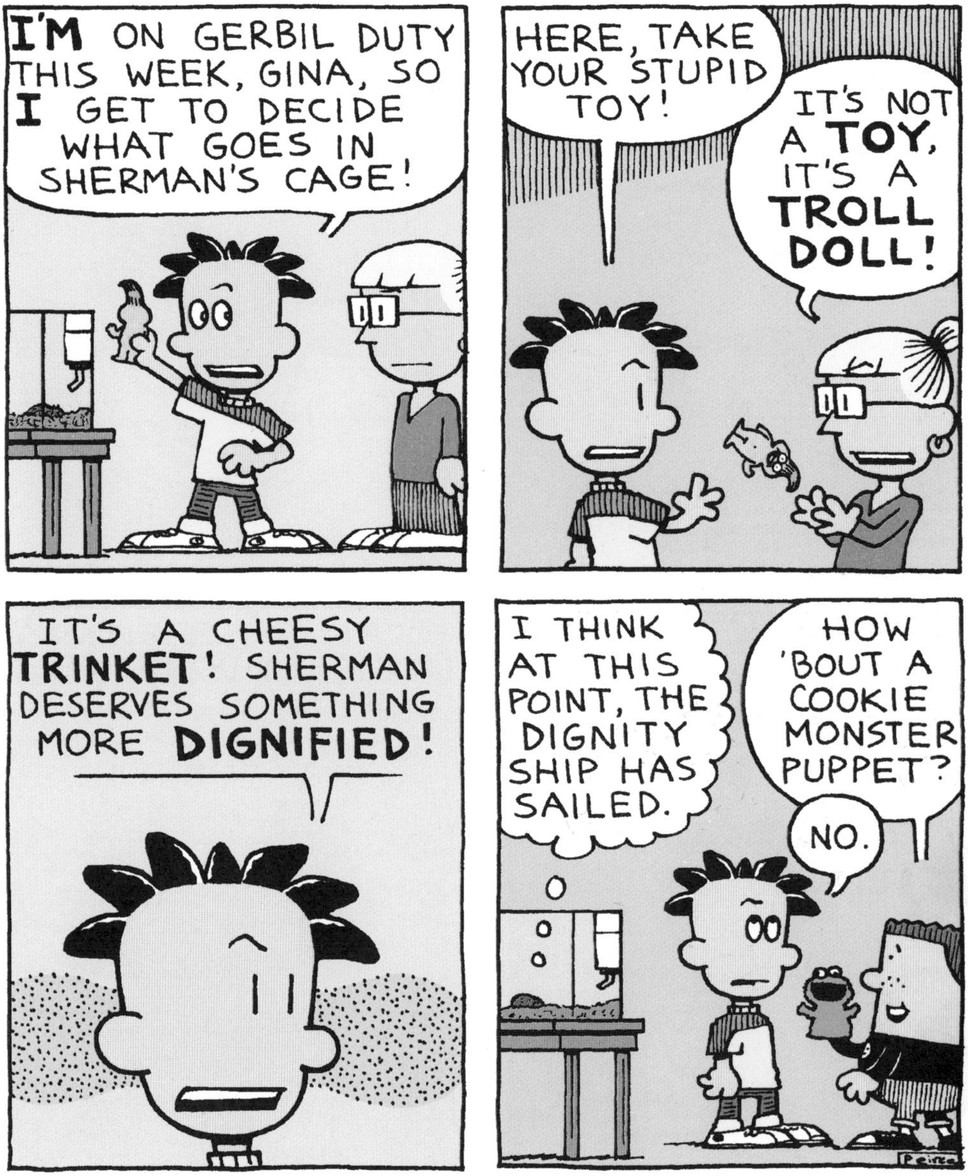
I'M ON GERBIL DUTY THIS WEEK, GINA, SO I GET TO DECIDE WHAT GOES IN SHERMAN'S CAGE!
HERE, TAKE YOUR STUPID TOY!
IT'S NOT A TOY, IT'S A TROLL DOLL!
IT'S A CHEESY TRINKET! SHERMAN DESERVES SOMETHING MORE DIGNIFIED!
I THINK AT THIS POINT, THE DIGNITY SHIP HAS SAILED.
HOW 'BOUT A COOKIE MONSTER PUPPET?
NO.
Peirce

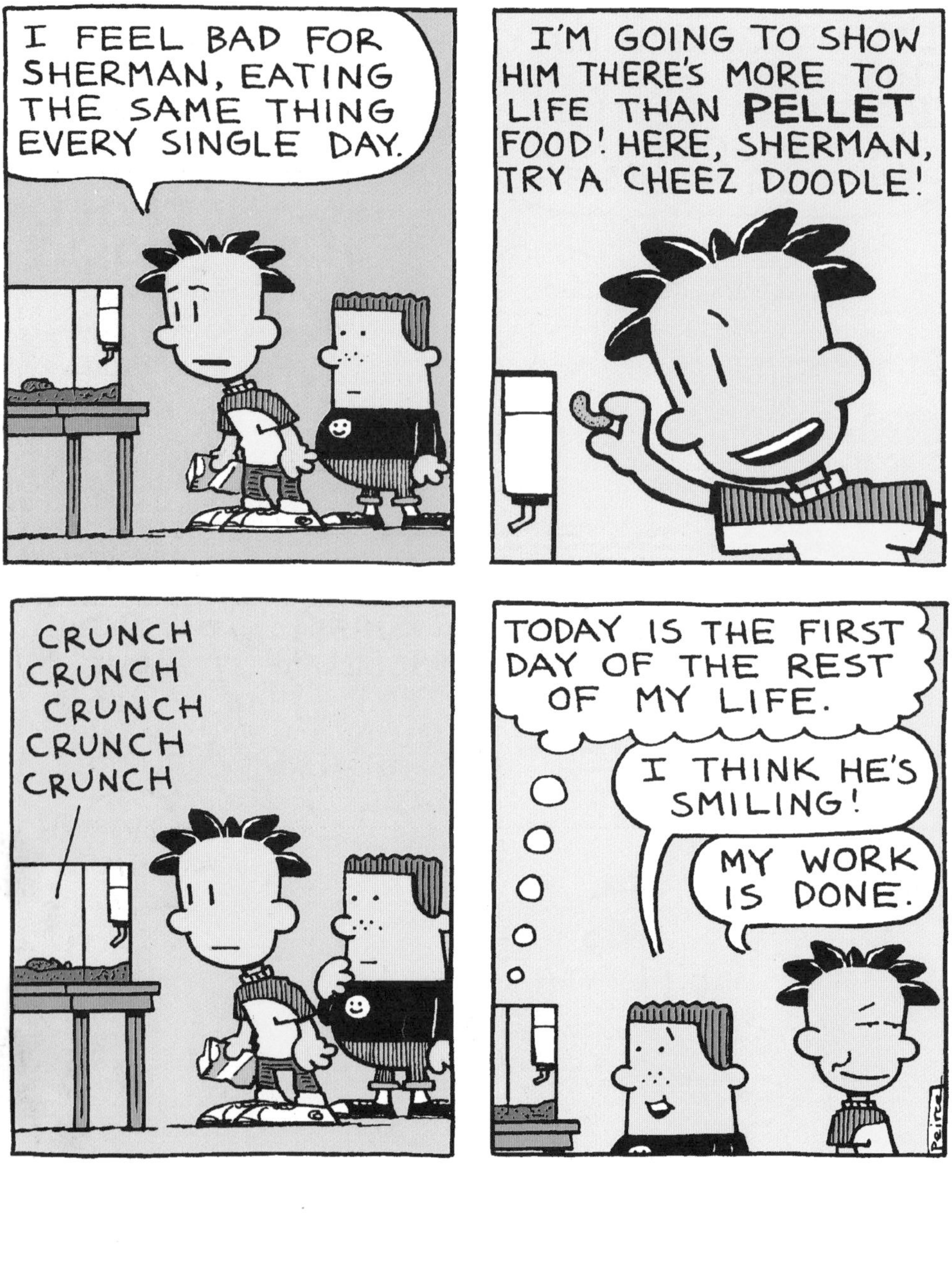
I FEEL BAD FOR SHERMAN, EATING THE SAME THING EVERY SINGLE DAY.
I'M GOING TO SHOW HIM THERE'S MORE TO LIFE THAN **PELLET** FOOD! HERE, SHERMAN, TRY A CHEEZ DOODLE!
CRUNCH CRUNCH CRUNCH CRUNCH CRUNCH
TODAY IS THE FIRST DAY OF THE REST OF MY LIFE.
I THINK HE'S SMILING!
MY WORK IS DONE.
Peirce

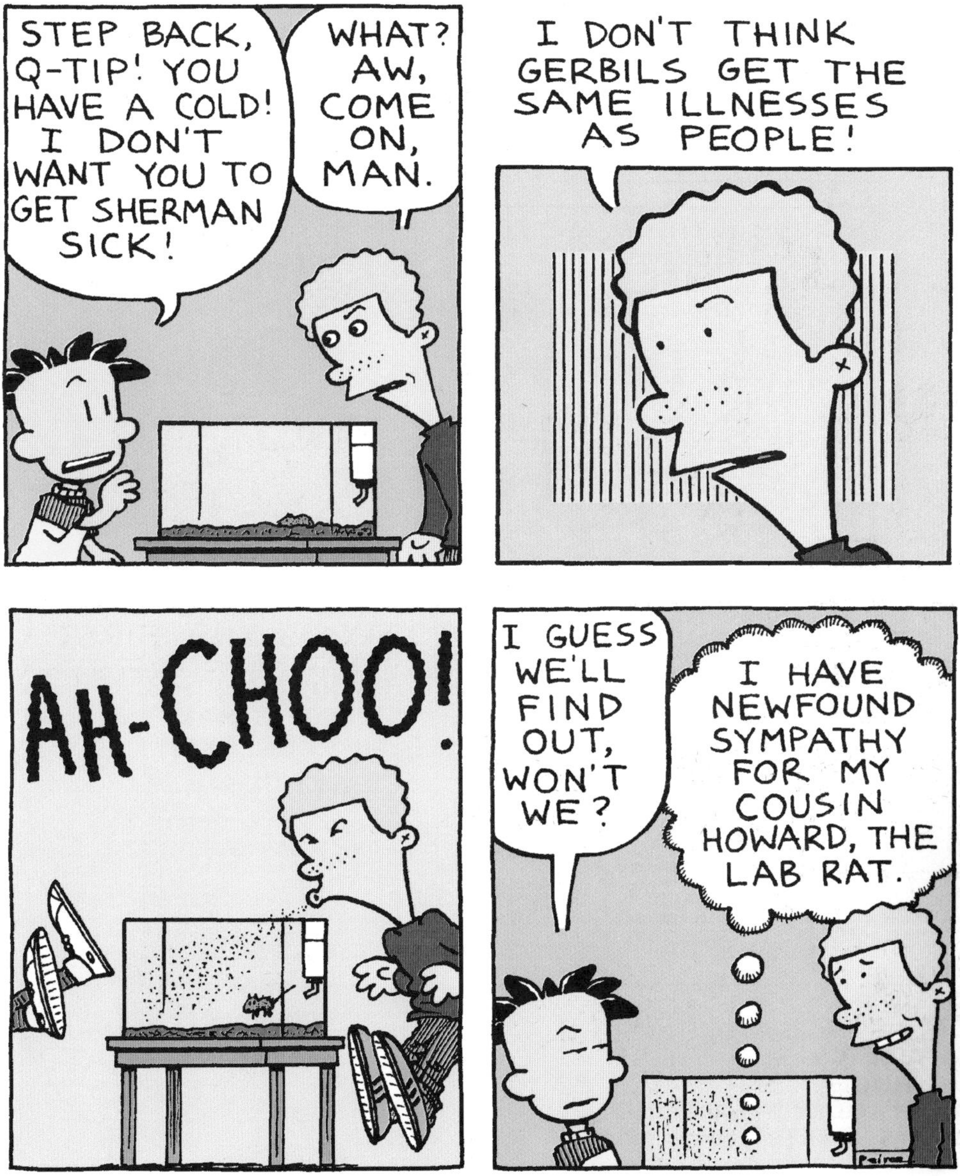
STEP BACK, Q-TIP! YOU HAVE A COLD! I DON'T WANT YOU TO GET SHERMAN SICK!
WHAT? AW, COME ON, MAN.
I DON'T THINK GERBILS GET THE SAME ILLNESSES AS PEOPLE!
AH-CHOO!
I GUESS WE'LL FIND OUT, WON'T WE?
I HAVE NEWFOUND SYMPATHY FOR MY COUSIN HOWARD, THE LAB RAT.
Peirce

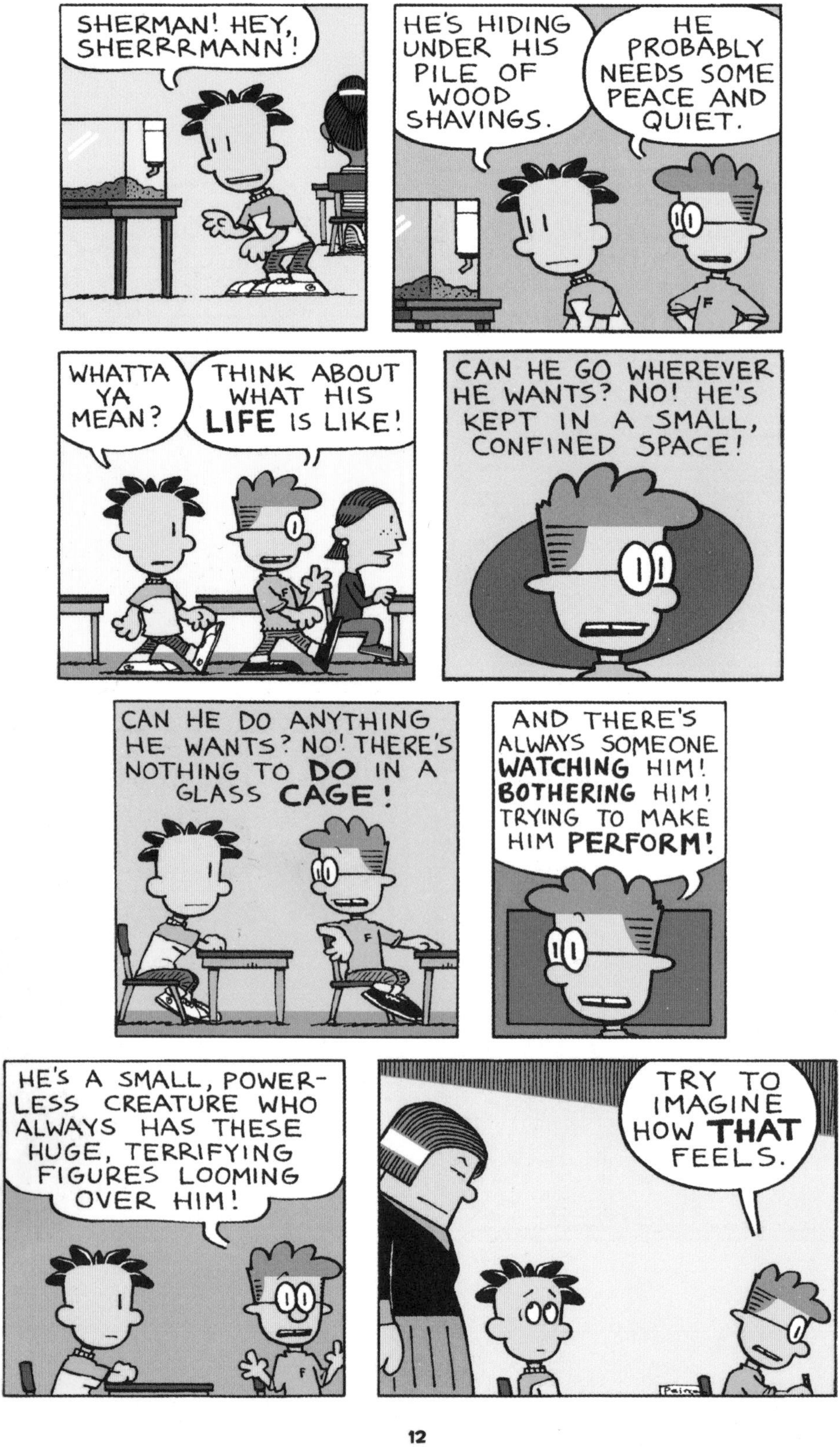
SHERMAN! HEY, SHERRRMANN!
HE'S HIDING UNDER HIS PILE OF WOOD SHAVINGS.
HE PROBABLY NEEDS SOME PEACE AND QUIET.
WHATTA YA MEAN?
THINK ABOUT WHAT HIS LIFE IS LIKE!
CAN HE GO WHEREVER HE WANTS? NO! HE'S KEPT IN A SMALL, CONFINED SPACE!
CAN HE DO ANYTHING HE WANTS? NO! THERE'S NOTHING TO DO IN A GLASS CAGE!
AND THERE'S ALWAYS SOMEONE WATCHING HIM! BOTHERING HIM! TRYING TO MAKE HIM PERFORM!
HE'S A SMALL, POWERLESS CREATURE WHO ALWAYS HAS THESE HUGE, TERRIFYING FIGURES LOOMING OVER HIM!
TRY TO IMAGINE HOW THAT FEELS.

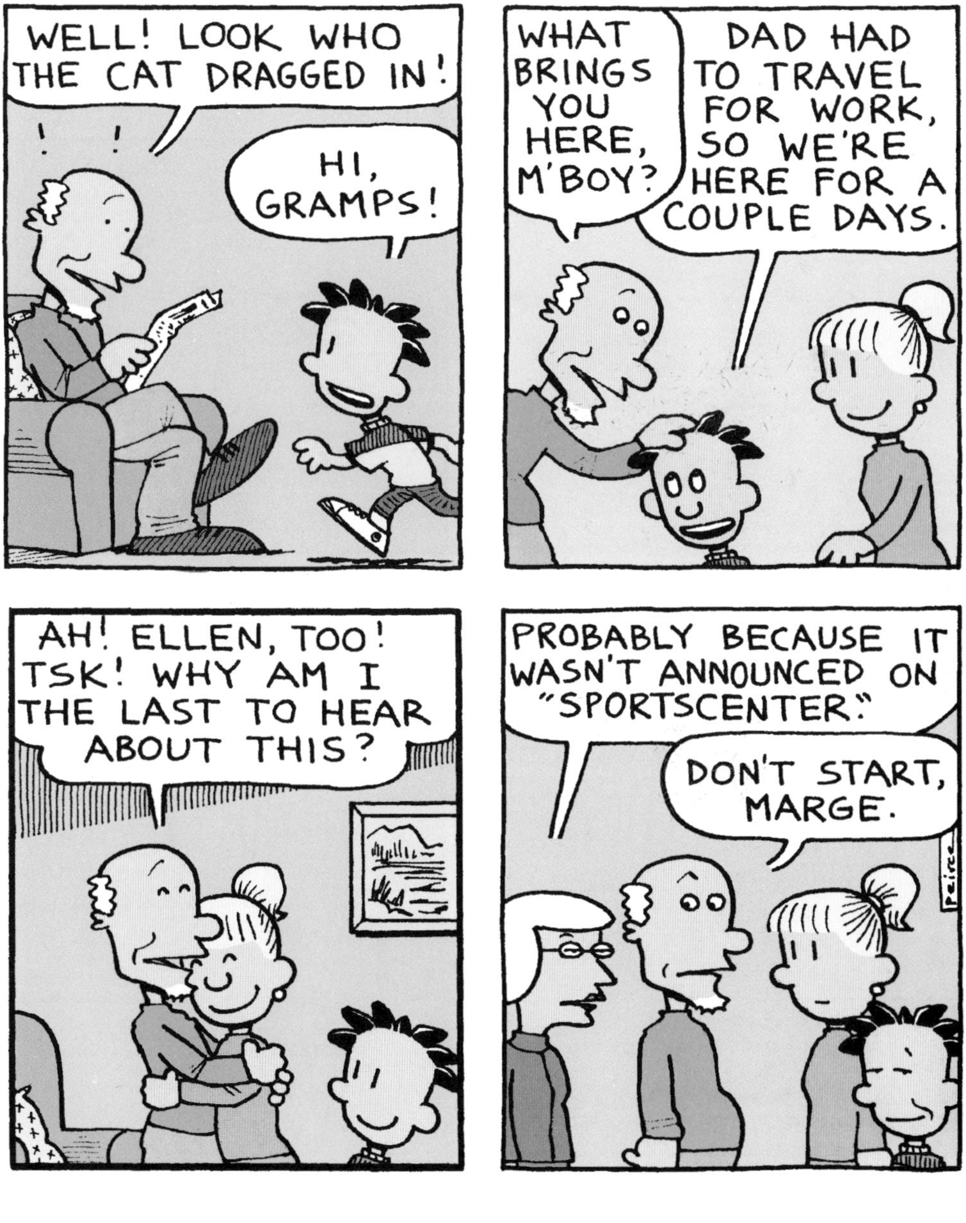
WELL! LOOK WHO THE CAT DRAGGED IN!
! !
HI, GRAMPS!
WHAT BRINGS YOU HERE, M'BOY?
DAD HAD TO TRAVEL FOR WORK, SO WE'RE HERE FOR A COUPLE DAYS.
AH! ELLEN, TOO! TSK! WHY AM I THE LAST TO HEAR ABOUT THIS?
PROBABLY BECAUSE IT WASN'T ANNOUNCED ON "SPORTSCENTER."
DON'T START, MARGE.
peirce

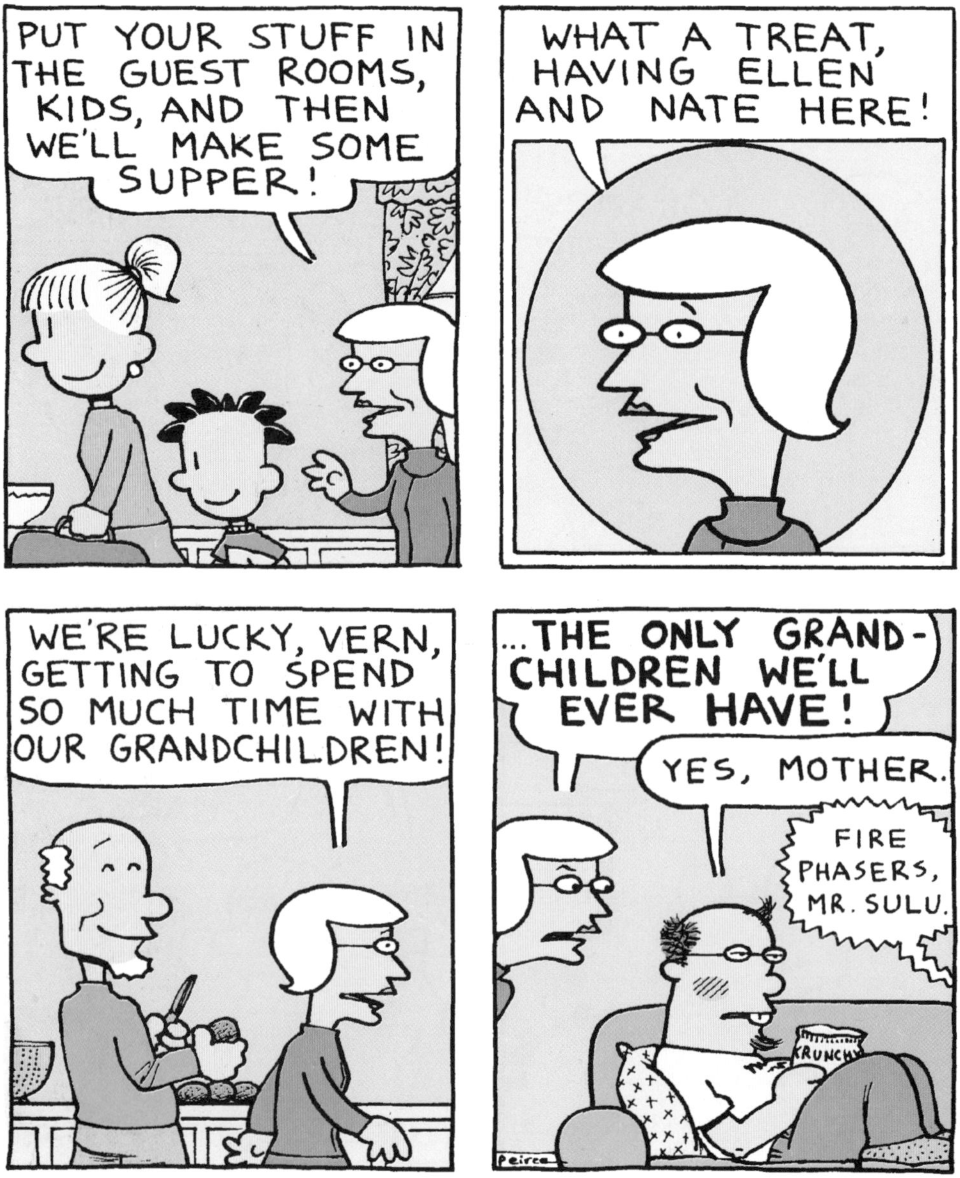
PUT YOUR STUFF IN THE GUEST ROOMS, KIDS, AND THEN WE'LL MAKE SOME SUPPER!
WHAT A TREAT, HAVING ELLEN AND NATE HERE!
WE'RE LUCKY, VERN, GETTING TO SPEND SO MUCH TIME WITH OUR GRANDCHILDREN!
...THE ONLY GRAND-CHILDREN WE'LL EVER HAVE!
YES, MOTHER.
FIRE PHASERS, MR. SULU.
KRUNCHY
Peirce

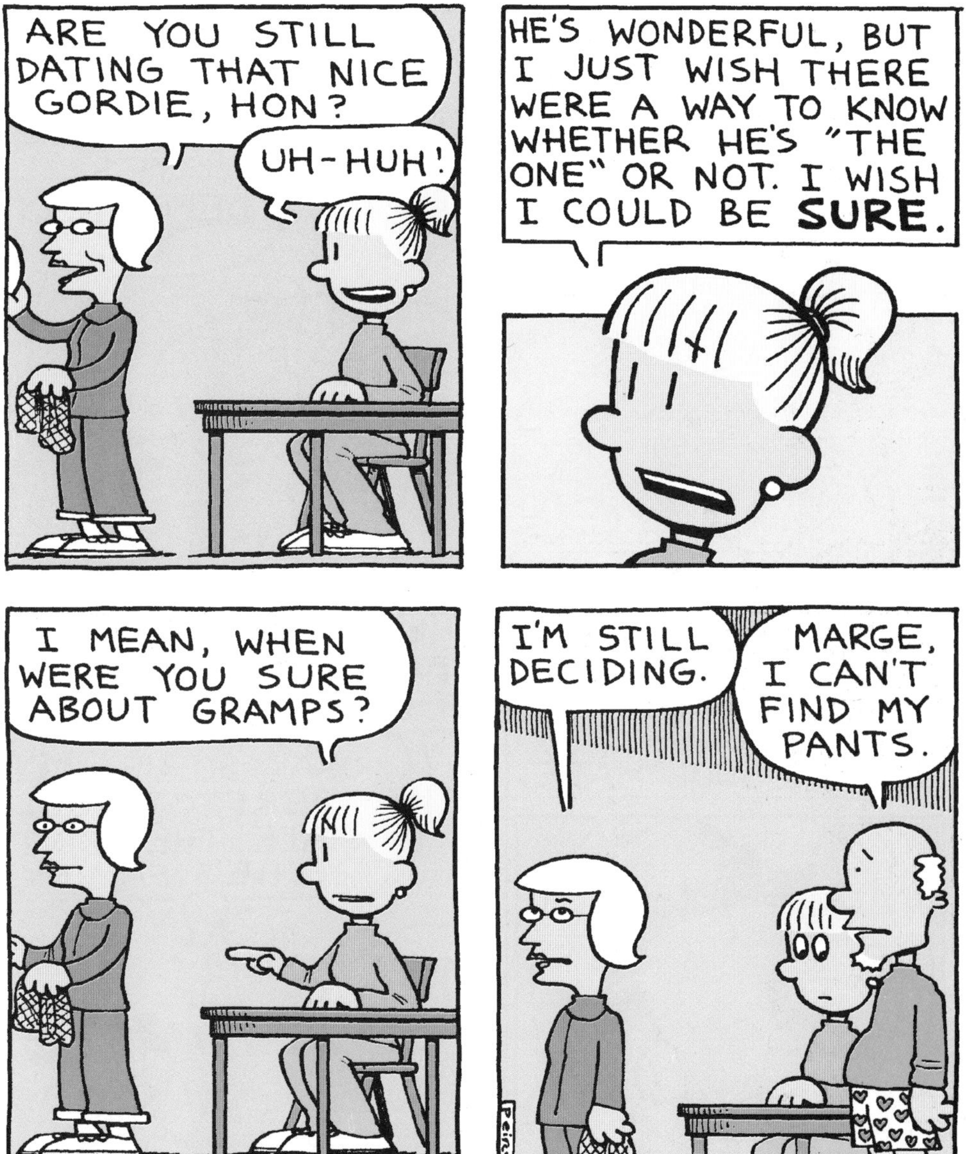
ARE YOU STILL DATING THAT NICE GORDIE, HON?
UH-HUH!
HE'S WONDERFUL, BUT I JUST WISH THERE WERE A WAY TO KNOW WHETHER HE'S "THE ONE" OR NOT. I WISH I COULD BE **SURE**.
I MEAN, WHEN WERE YOU SURE ABOUT GRAMPS?
I'M STILL DECIDING.
MARGE, I CAN'T FIND MY PANTS.
Peirs

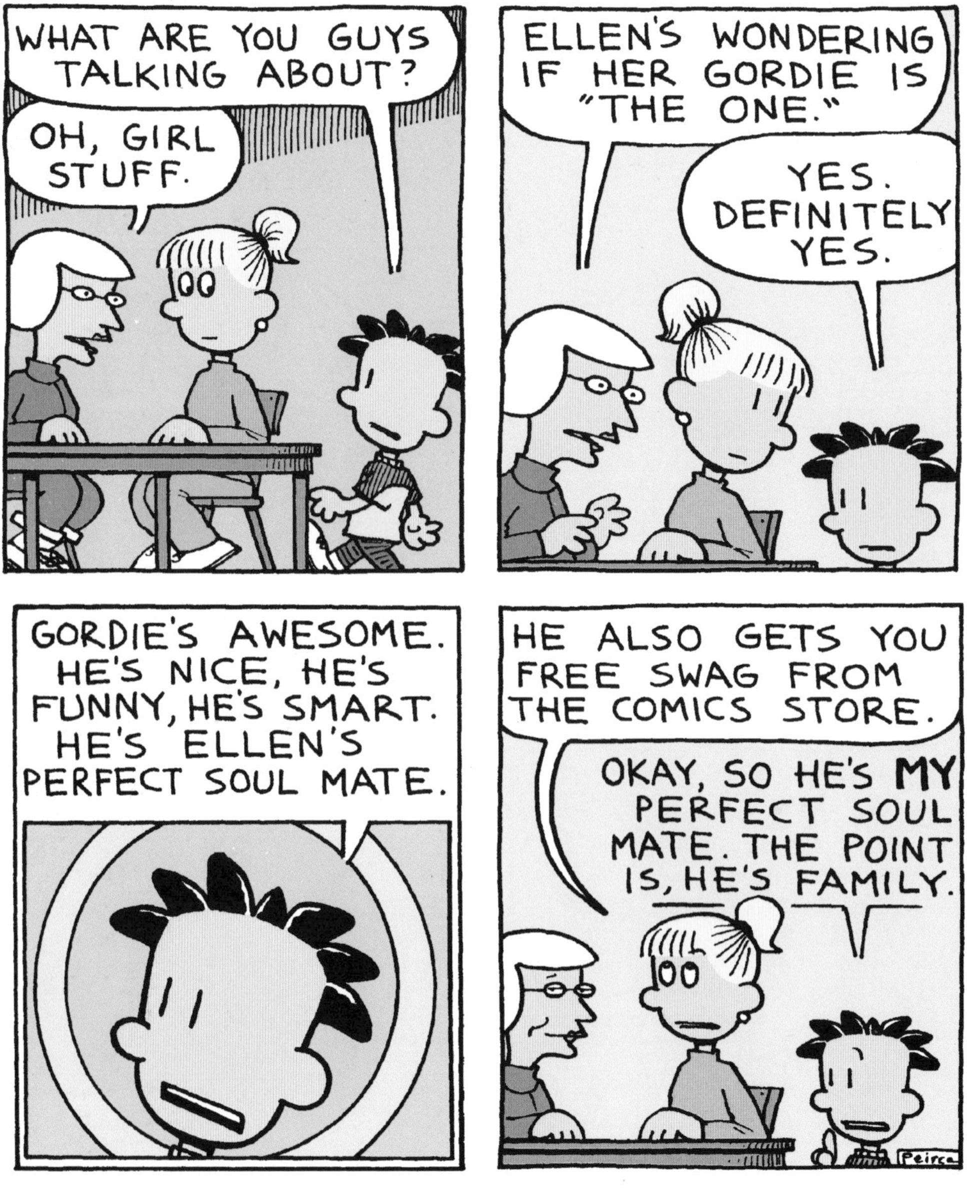
WHAT ARE YOU GUYS TALKING ABOUT?
OH, GIRL STUFF.
ELLEN'S WONDERING IF HER GORDIE IS "THE ONE."
YES. DEFINITELY YES.
GORDIE'S AWESOME. HE'S NICE, HE'S FUNNY, HE'S SMART. HE'S ELLEN'S PERFECT SOUL MATE.
HE ALSO GETS YOU FREE SWAG FROM THE COMICS STORE.
OKAY, SO HE'S **MY** PERFECT SOUL MATE. THE POINT IS, HE'S FAMILY.
Peirce

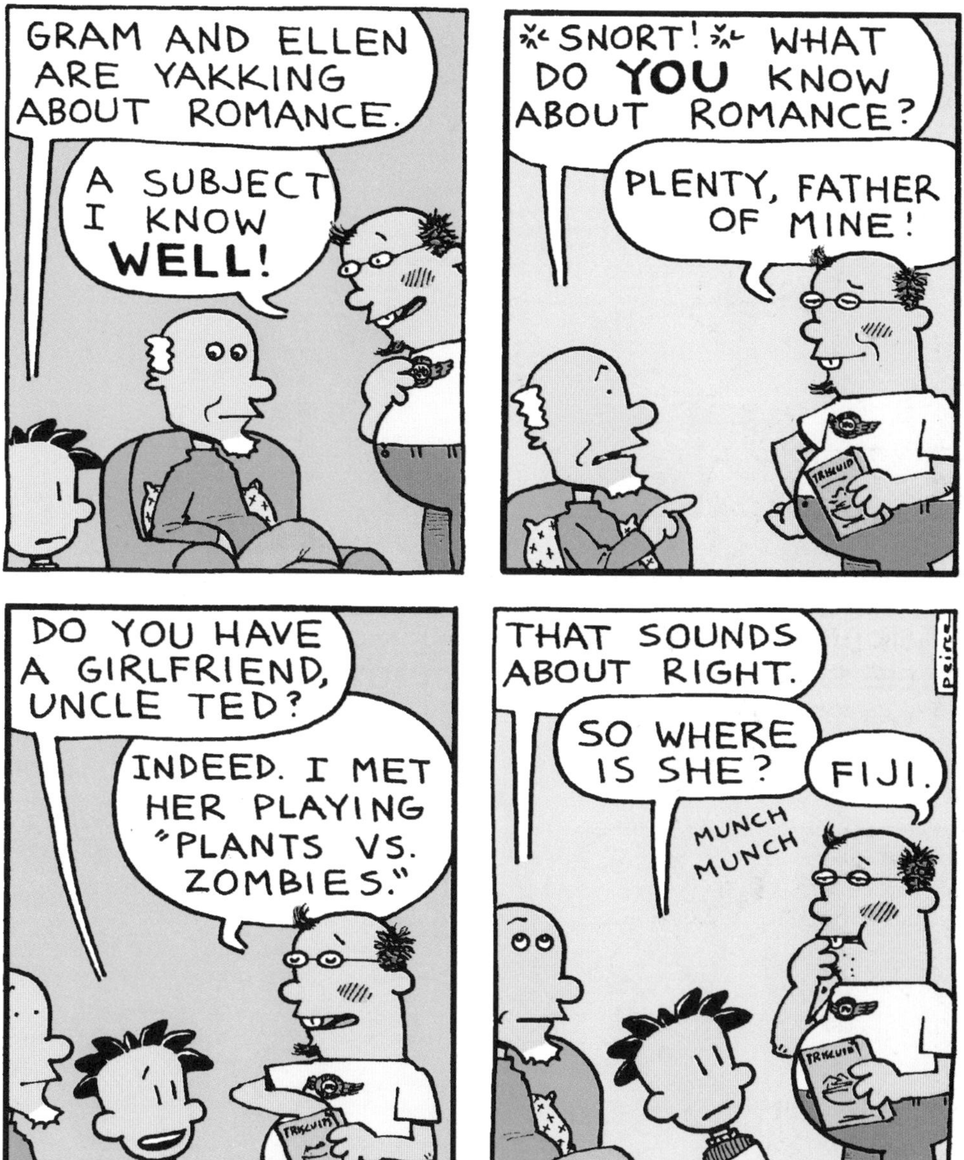
GRAM AND ELLEN ARE YAKKING ABOUT ROMANCE.
A SUBJECT I KNOW **WELL**!
SNORT! WHAT DO **YOU** KNOW ABOUT ROMANCE?
PLENTY, FATHER OF MINE!
DO YOU HAVE A GIRLFRIEND, UNCLE TED?
INDEED. I MET HER PLAYING "PLANTS VS. ZOMBIES."
THAT SOUNDS ABOUT RIGHT.
SO WHERE IS SHE?
FIJI.
MUNCH MUNCH
peirce

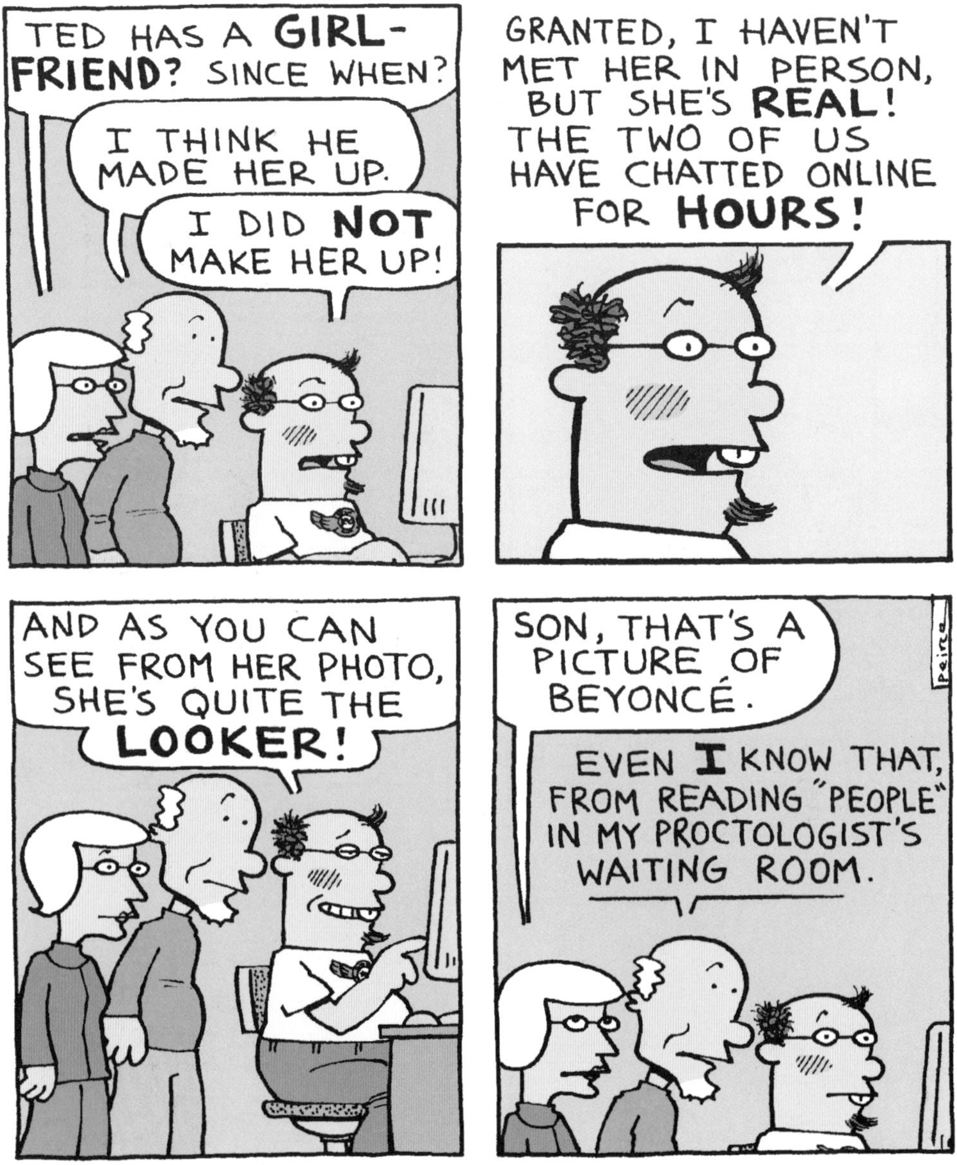
TED HAS A **GIRL-FRIEND**? SINCE WHEN?
I THINK HE MADE HER UP.
I DID **NOT** MAKE HER UP!
GRANTED, I HAVEN'T MET HER IN PERSON, BUT SHE'S **REAL**! THE TWO OF US HAVE CHATTED ONLINE FOR **HOURS**!
AND AS YOU CAN SEE FROM HER PHOTO, SHE'S QUITE THE **LOOKER**!
SON, THAT'S A PICTURE OF BEYONCÉ.
EVEN **I** KNOW THAT, FROM READING "PEOPLE" IN MY PROCTOLOGIST'S WAITING ROOM.
peirce

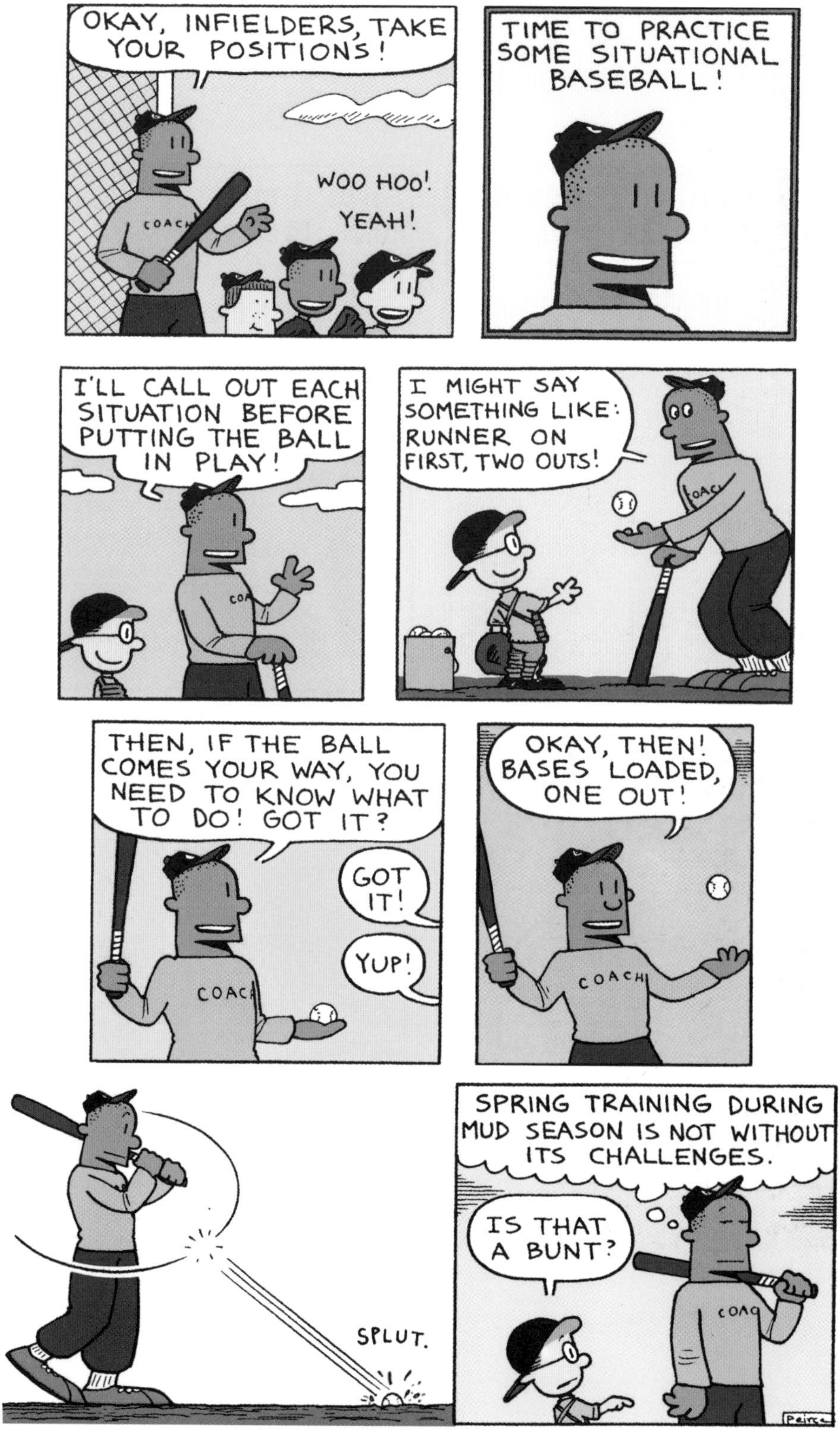
OKAY, INFIELDERS, TAKE YOUR POSITIONS!
WOO HOO!
YEAH!
COACH
TIME TO PRACTICE SOME SITUATIONAL BASEBALL!
I'LL CALL OUT EACH SITUATION BEFORE PUTTING THE BALL IN PLAY!
I MIGHT SAY SOMETHING LIKE: RUNNER ON FIRST, TWO OUTS!
THEN, IF THE BALL COMES YOUR WAY, YOU NEED TO KNOW WHAT TO DO! GOT IT?
GOT IT!
YUP!
OKAY, THEN! BASES LOADED, ONE OUT!
COACH
SPLUT.
SPRING TRAINING DURING MUD SEASON IS NOT WITHOUT ITS CHALLENGES.
IS THAT A BUNT?
Peirce

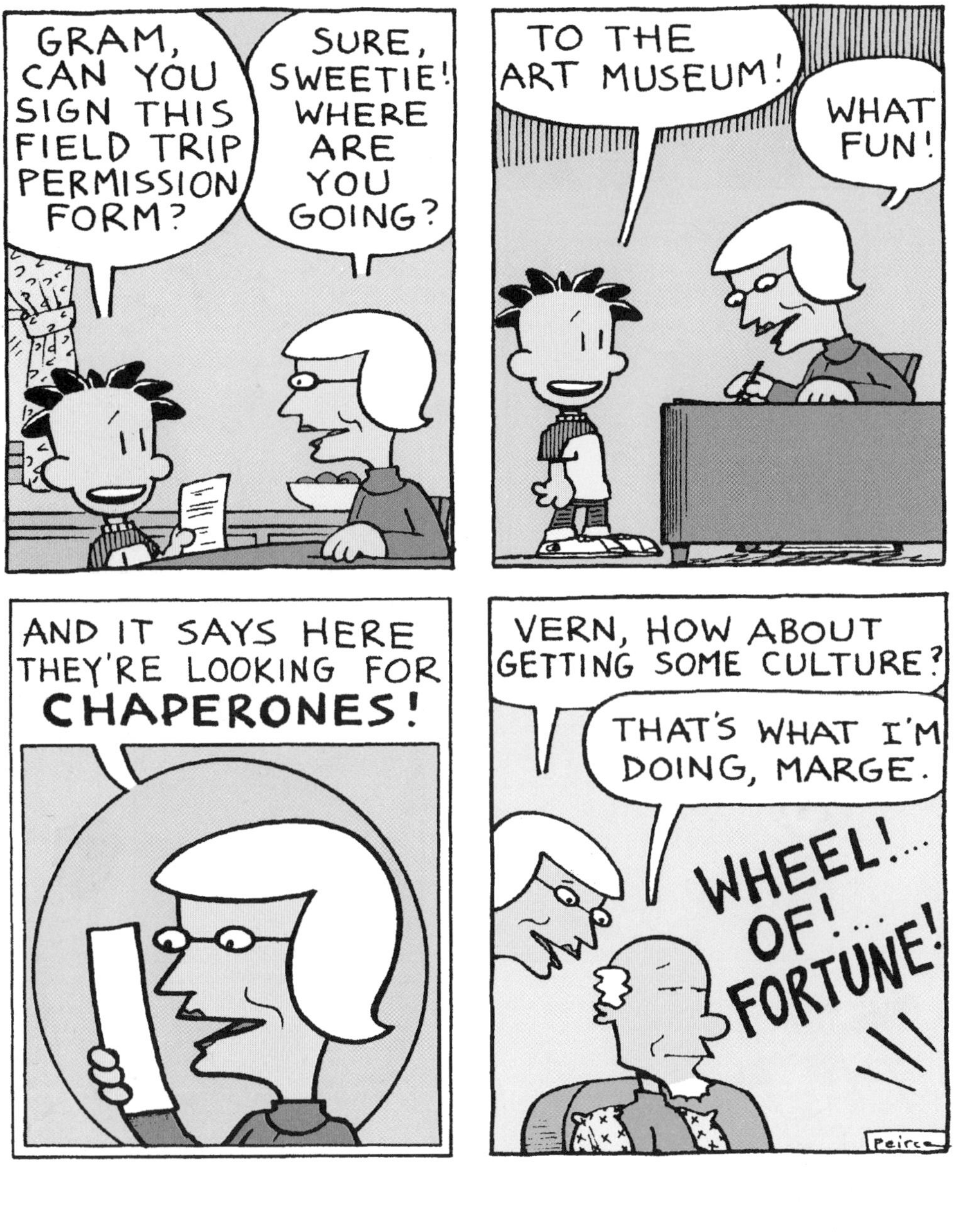
GRAM, CAN YOU SIGN THIS FIELD TRIP PERMISSION FORM?
SURE, SWEETIE! WHERE ARE YOU GOING?
TO THE ART MUSEUM!
WHAT FUN!
AND IT SAYS HERE THEY'RE LOOKING FOR **CHAPERONES!**
VERN, HOW ABOUT GETTING SOME CULTURE?
THAT'S WHAT I'M DOING, MARGE.
WHEEL!... OF!... FORTUNE!
Peirce

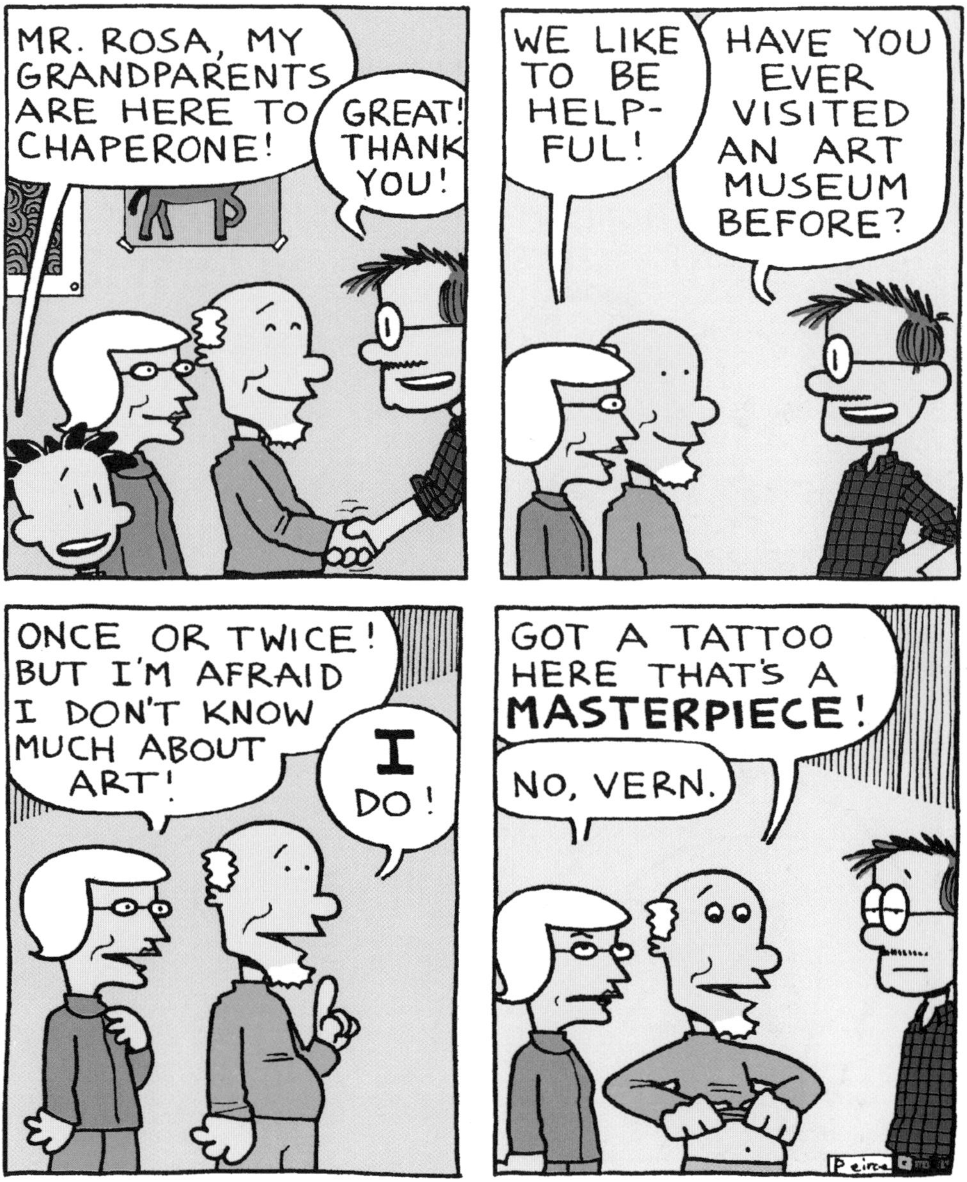
MR. ROSA, MY GRANDPARENTS ARE HERE TO CHAPERONE!
GREAT! THANK YOU!
WE LIKE TO BE HELP-FUL!
HAVE YOU EVER VISITED AN ART MUSEUM BEFORE?
ONCE OR TWICE! BUT I'M AFRAID I DON'T KNOW MUCH ABOUT ART!
I DO!
GOT A TATTOO HERE THAT'S A **MASTERPIECE**!
NO, VERN.
Peirce

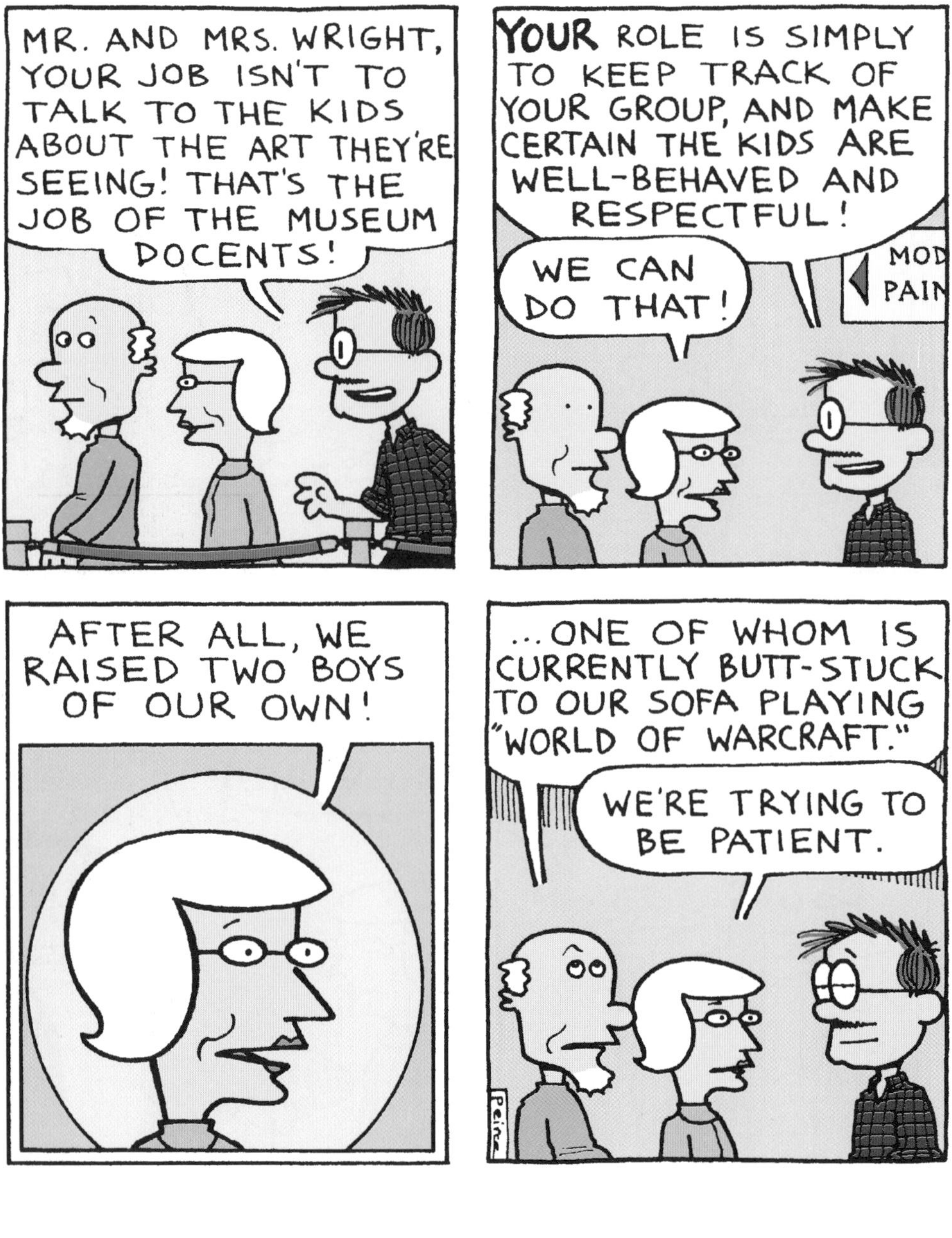
MR. AND MRS. WRIGHT, YOUR JOB ISN'T TO TALK TO THE KIDS ABOUT THE ART THEY'RE SEEING! THAT'S THE JOB OF THE MUSEUM DOCENTS!
YOUR ROLE IS SIMPLY TO KEEP TRACK OF YOUR GROUP, AND MAKE CERTAIN THE KIDS ARE WELL-BEHAVED AND RESPECTFUL!
WE CAN DO THAT!
MOD
PAIN
AFTER ALL, WE RAISED TWO BOYS OF OUR OWN!
...ONE OF WHOM IS CURRENTLY BUTT-STUCK TO OUR SOFA PLAYING "WORLD OF WARCRAFT."
WE'RE TRYING TO BE PATIENT.
Peirce

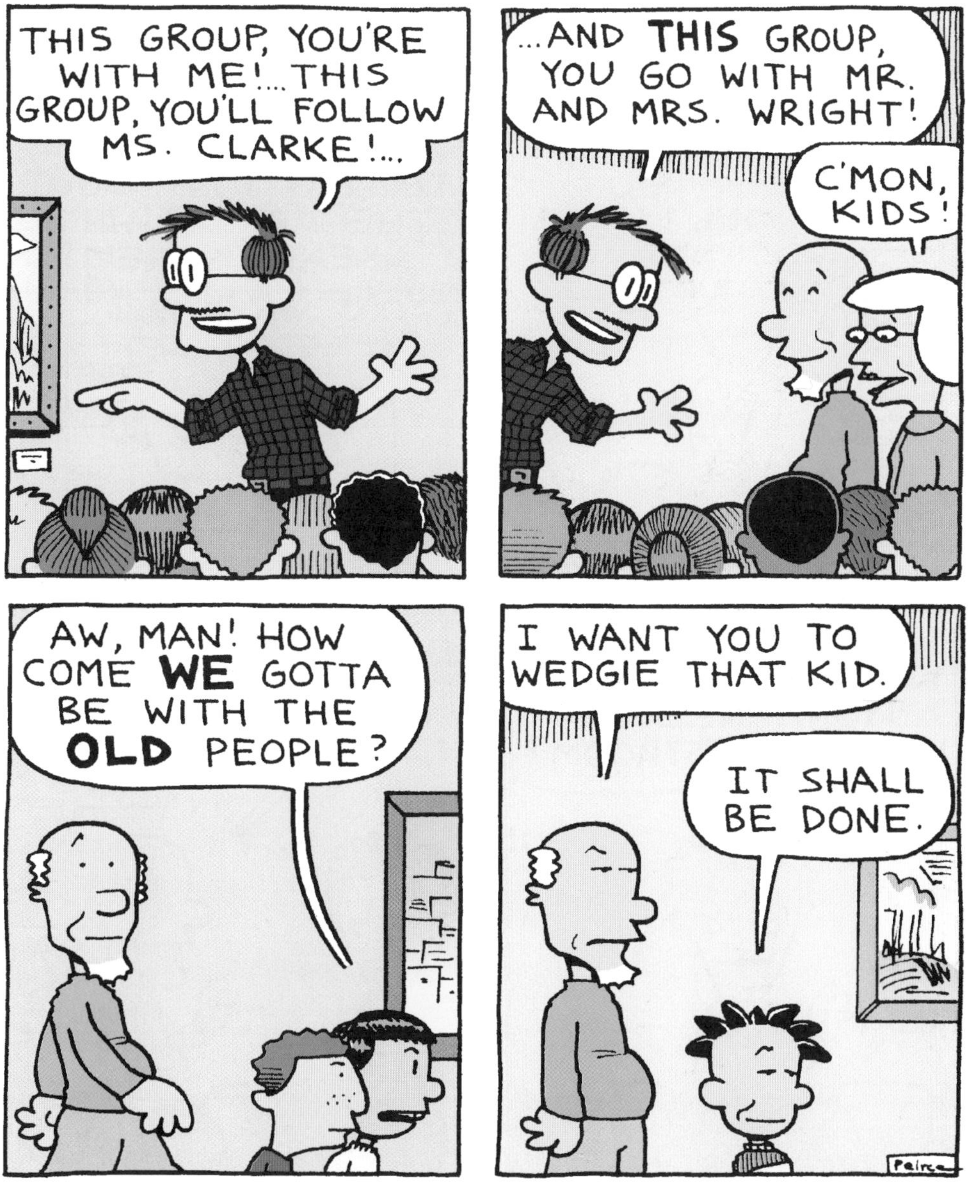
THIS GROUP, YOU'RE WITH ME!... THIS GROUP, YOU'LL FOLLOW MS. CLARKE!...
...AND THIS GROUP, YOU GO WITH MR. AND MRS. WRIGHT!
C'MON, KIDS!
AW, MAN! HOW COME WE GOTTA BE WITH THE OLD PEOPLE?
I WANT YOU TO WEDGIE THAT KID.
IT SHALL BE DONE.
Peirce

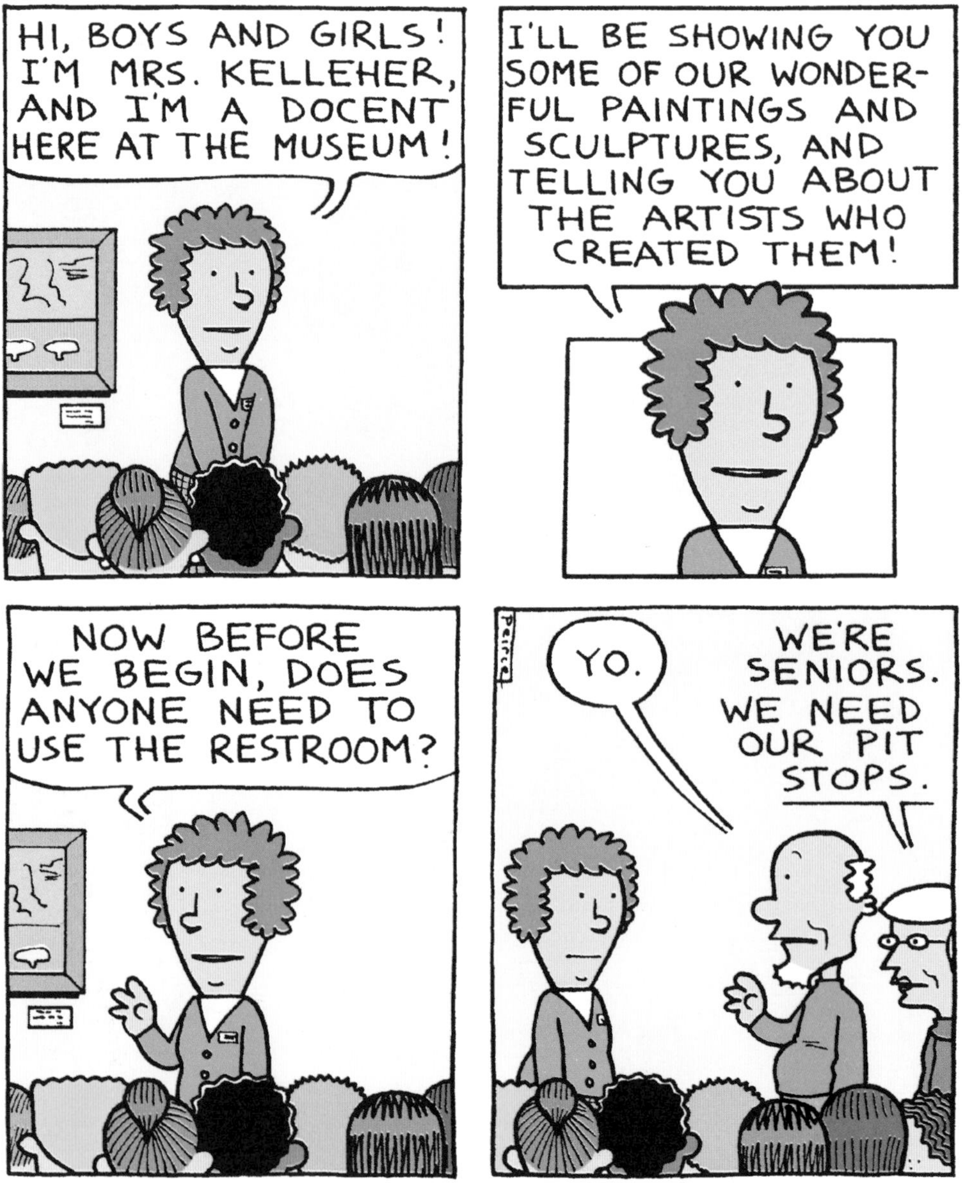
HI, BOYS AND GIRLS! I'M MRS. KELLEHER, AND I'M A DOCENT HERE AT THE MUSEUM!
I'LL BE SHOWING YOU SOME OF OUR WONDERFUL PAINTINGS AND SCULPTURES, AND TELLING YOU ABOUT THE ARTISTS WHO CREATED THEM!
NOW BEFORE WE BEGIN, DOES ANYONE NEED TO USE THE RESTROOM?
Peirce
YO.
WE'RE SENIORS. WE NEED OUR PIT STOPS.

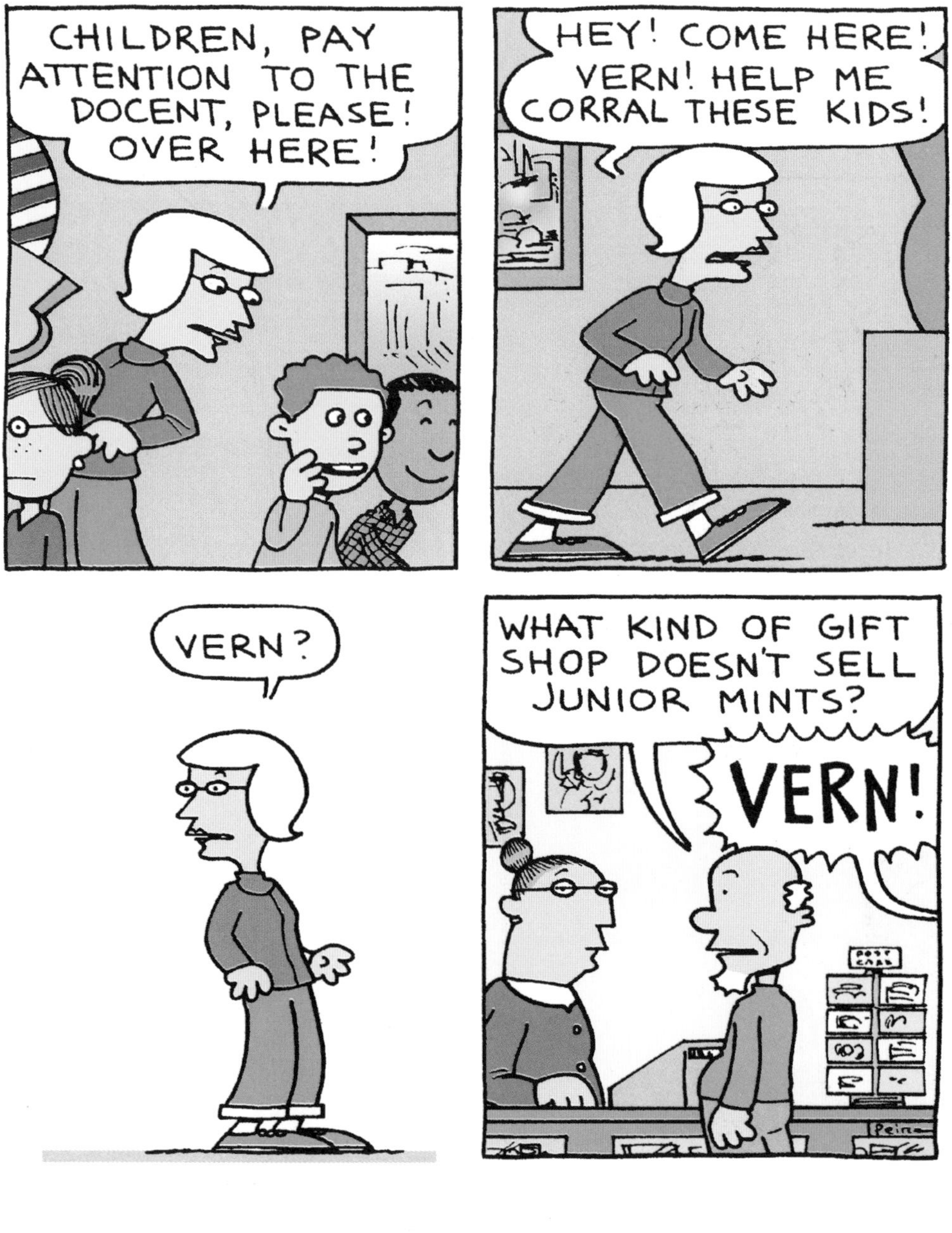
CHILDREN, PAY ATTENTION TO THE DOCENT, PLEASE! OVER HERE!
HEY! COME HERE! VERN! HELP ME CORRAL THESE KIDS!
VERN?
WHAT KIND OF GIFT SHOP DOESN'T SELL JUNIOR MINTS?
VERN!

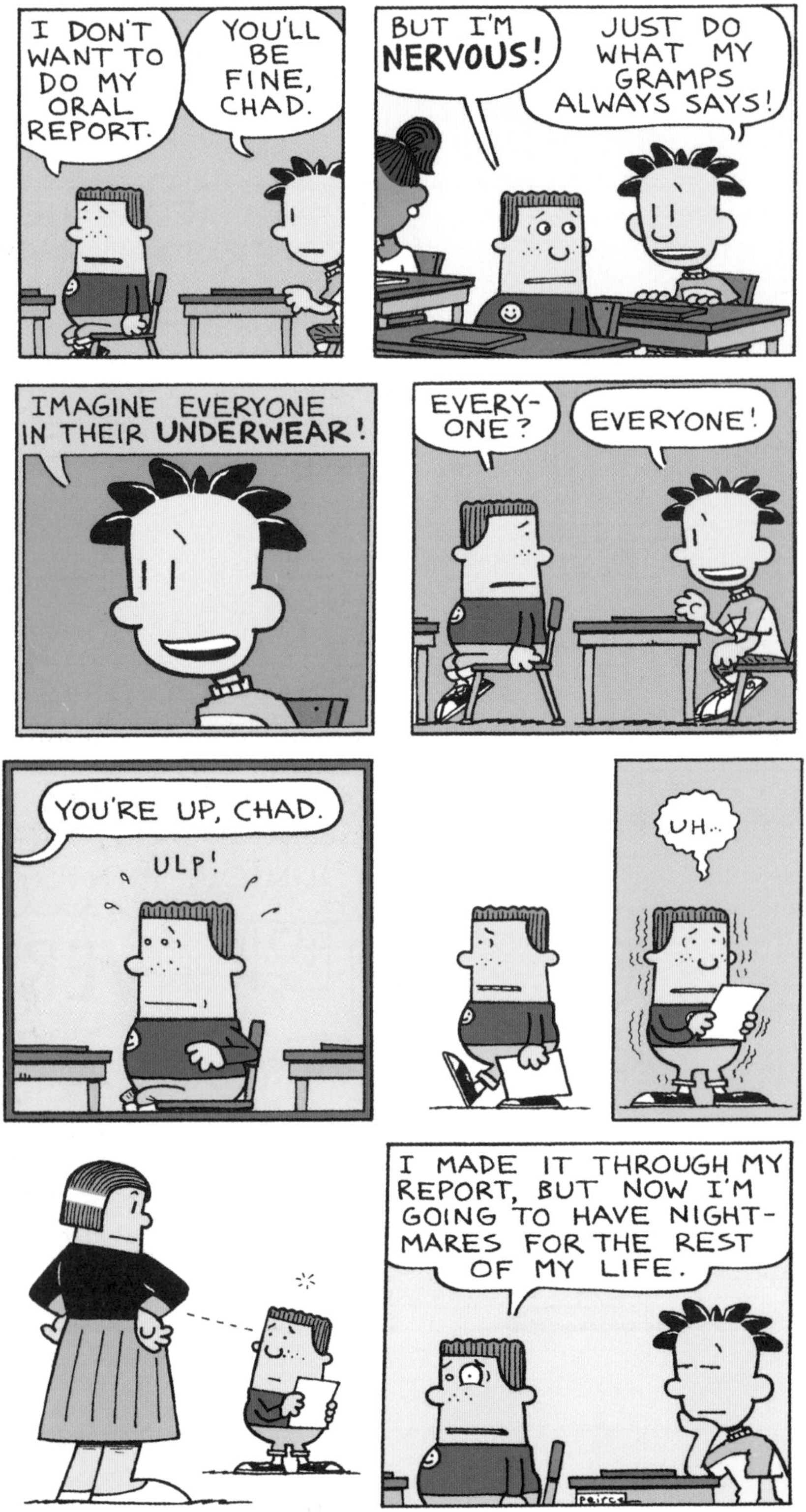

I DON'T WANT TO DO MY ORAL REPORT.
YOU'LL BE FINE, CHAD.
BUT I'M **NERVOUS**!
JUST DO WHAT MY GRAMPS ALWAYS SAYS!
IMAGINE EVERYONE IN THEIR **UNDERWEAR**!
EVERY-ONE?
EVERYONE!
YOU'RE UP, CHAD.
ULP!
UH...
I MADE IT THROUGH MY REPORT, BUT NOW I'M GOING TO HAVE NIGHT-MARES FOR THE REST OF MY LIFE.
PEIRCE

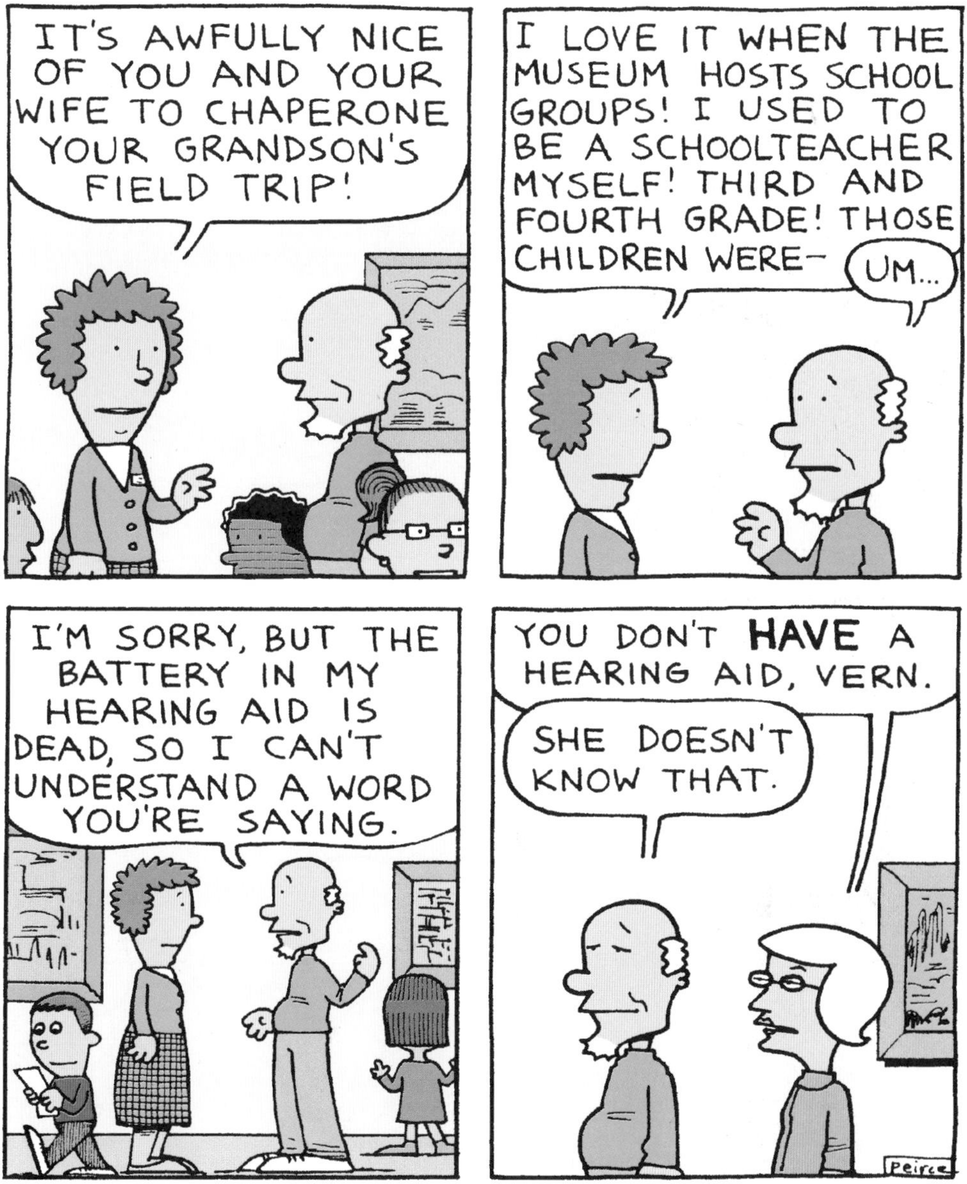
IT'S AWFULLY NICE OF YOU AND YOUR WIFE TO CHAPERONE YOUR GRANDSON'S FIELD TRIP!
I LOVE IT WHEN THE MUSEUM HOSTS SCHOOL GROUPS! I USED TO BE A SCHOOLTEACHER MYSELF! THIRD AND FOURTH GRADE! THOSE CHILDREN WERE–
UM...
I'M SORRY, BUT THE BATTERY IN MY HEARING AID IS DEAD, SO I CAN'T UNDERSTAND A WORD YOU'RE SAYING.
YOU DON'T **HAVE** A HEARING AID, VERN.
SHE DOESN'T KNOW THAT.
Peirce

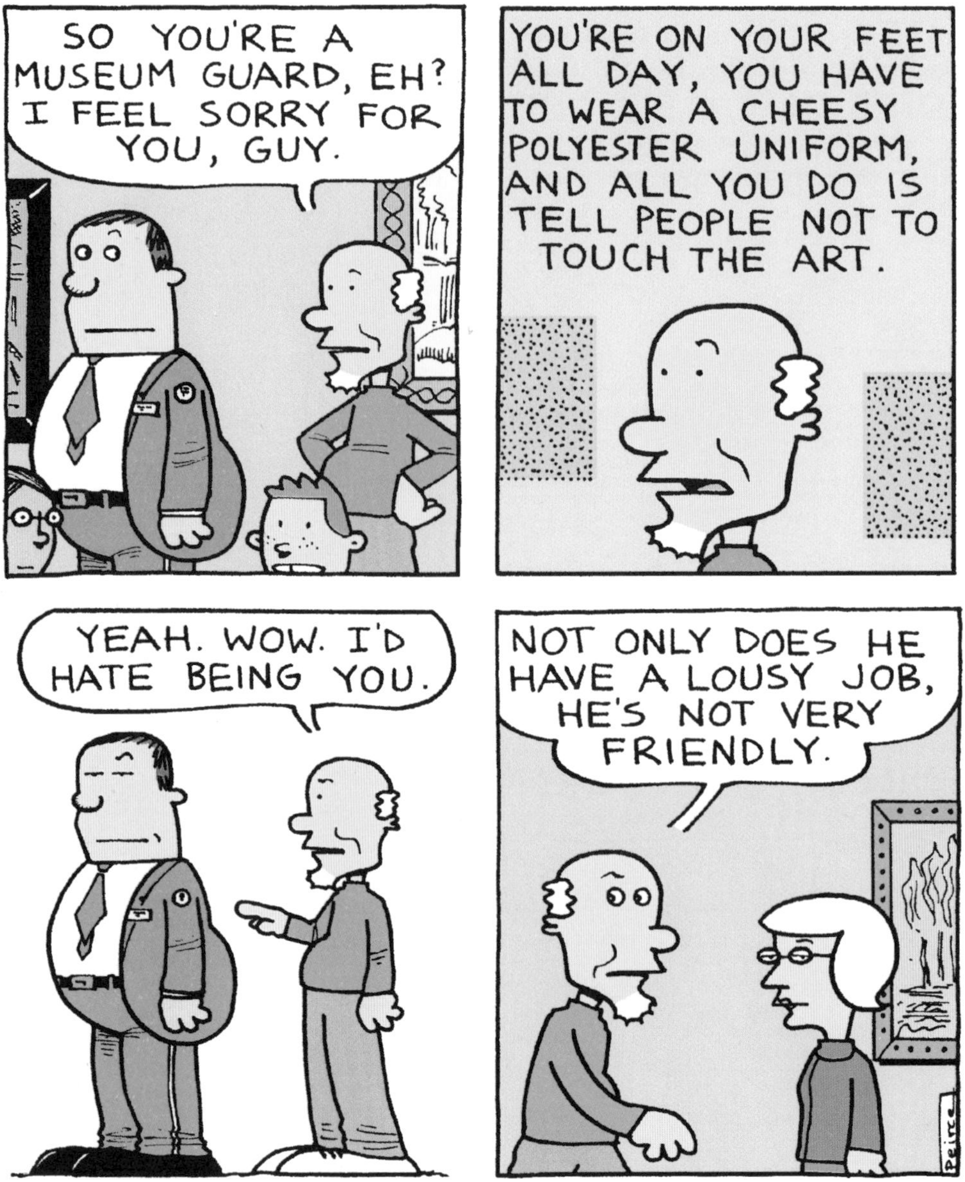
SO YOU'RE A MUSEUM GUARD, EH? I FEEL SORRY FOR YOU, GUY.
YOU'RE ON YOUR FEET ALL DAY, YOU HAVE TO WEAR A CHEESY POLYESTER UNIFORM, AND ALL YOU DO IS TELL PEOPLE NOT TO TOUCH THE ART.
YEAH. WOW. I'D HATE BEING YOU.
NOT ONLY DOES HE HAVE A LOUSY JOB, HE'S NOT VERY FRIENDLY.
Peirce

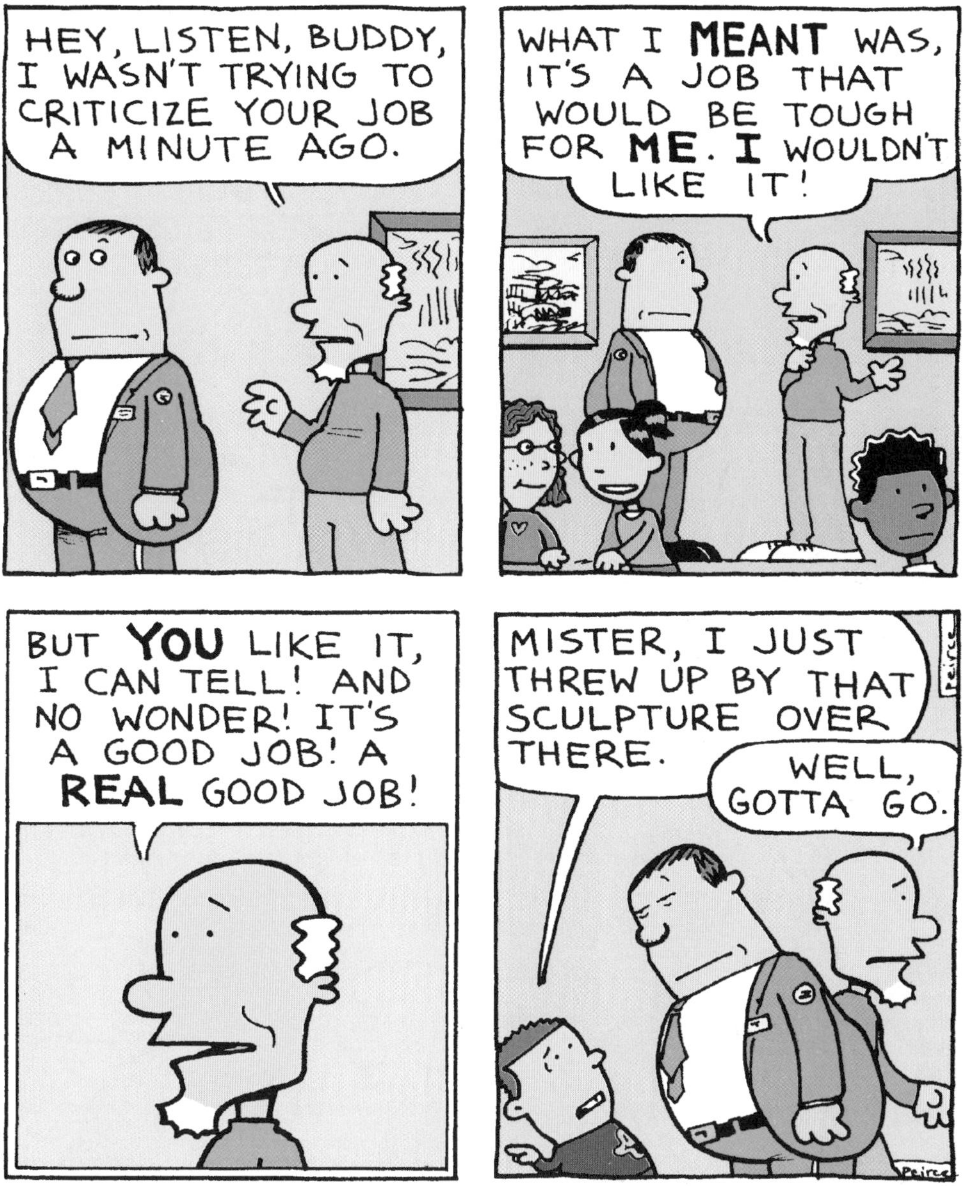
HEY, LISTEN, BUDDY, I WASN'T TRYING TO CRITICIZE YOUR JOB A MINUTE AGO.
WHAT I **MEANT** WAS, IT'S A JOB THAT WOULD BE TOUGH FOR **ME**. **I** WOULDN'T LIKE IT!
BUT **YOU** LIKE IT, I CAN TELL! AND NO WONDER! IT'S A GOOD JOB! A **REAL** GOOD JOB!
MISTER, I JUST THREW UP BY THAT SCULPTURE OVER THERE.
WELL, GOTTA GO.
Peirce

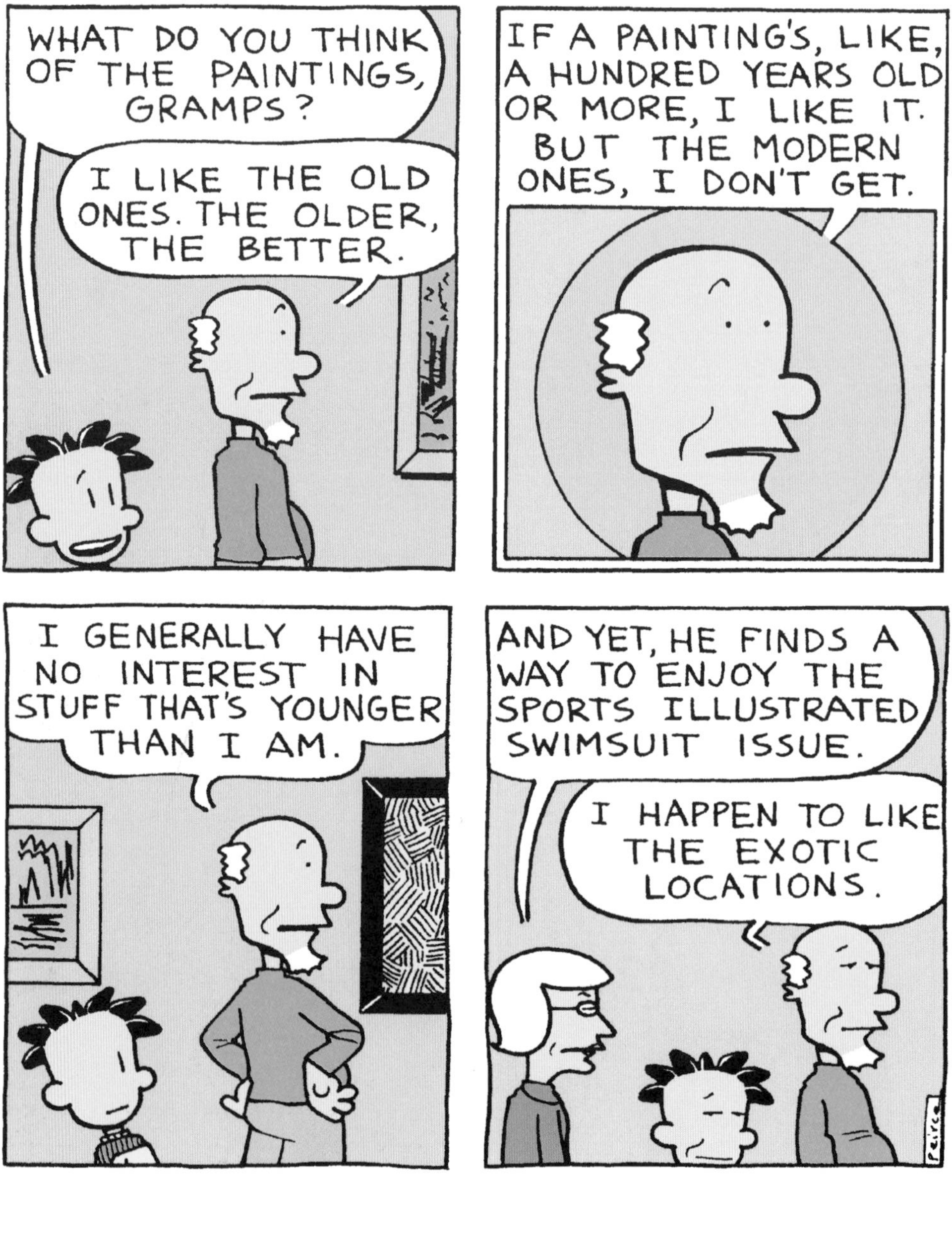
WHAT DO YOU THINK OF THE PAINTINGS, GRAMPS?
I LIKE THE OLD ONES. THE OLDER, THE BETTER.
IF A PAINTING'S, LIKE, A HUNDRED YEARS OLD OR MORE, I LIKE IT. BUT THE MODERN ONES, I DON'T GET.
I GENERALLY HAVE NO INTEREST IN STUFF THAT'S YOUNGER THAN I AM.
AND YET, HE FINDS A WAY TO ENJOY THE SPORTS ILLUSTRATED SWIMSUIT ISSUE.
I HAPPEN TO LIKE THE EXOTIC LOCATIONS.
Peirce

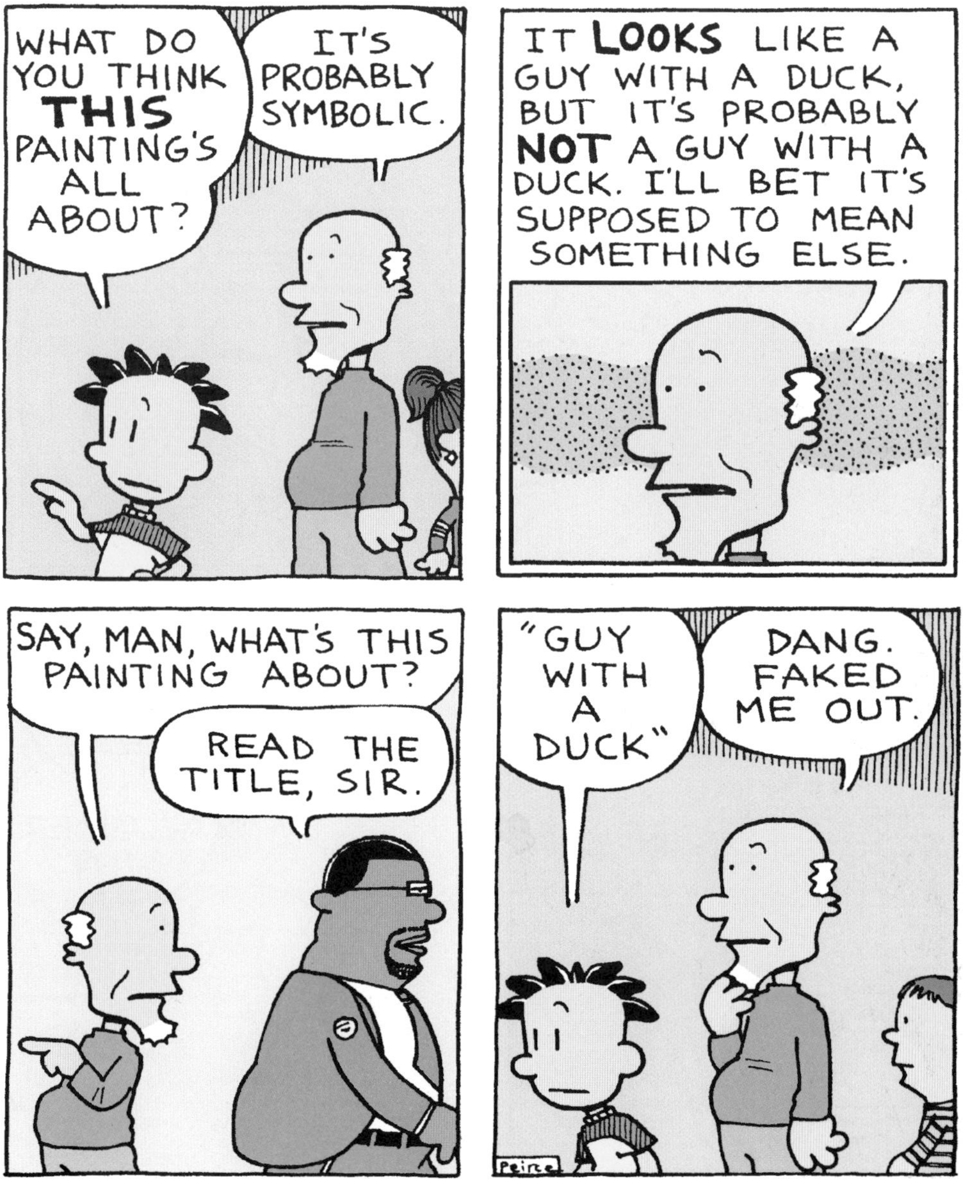
WHAT DO YOU THINK THIS PAINTING'S ALL ABOUT?
IT'S PROBABLY SYMBOLIC.
IT LOOKS LIKE A GUY WITH A DUCK, BUT IT'S PROBABLY NOT A GUY WITH A DUCK. I'LL BET IT'S SUPPOSED TO MEAN SOMETHING ELSE.
SAY, MAN, WHAT'S THIS PAINTING ABOUT?
READ THE TITLE, SIR.
"GUY WITH A DUCK"
DANG. FAKED ME OUT.
Peirce

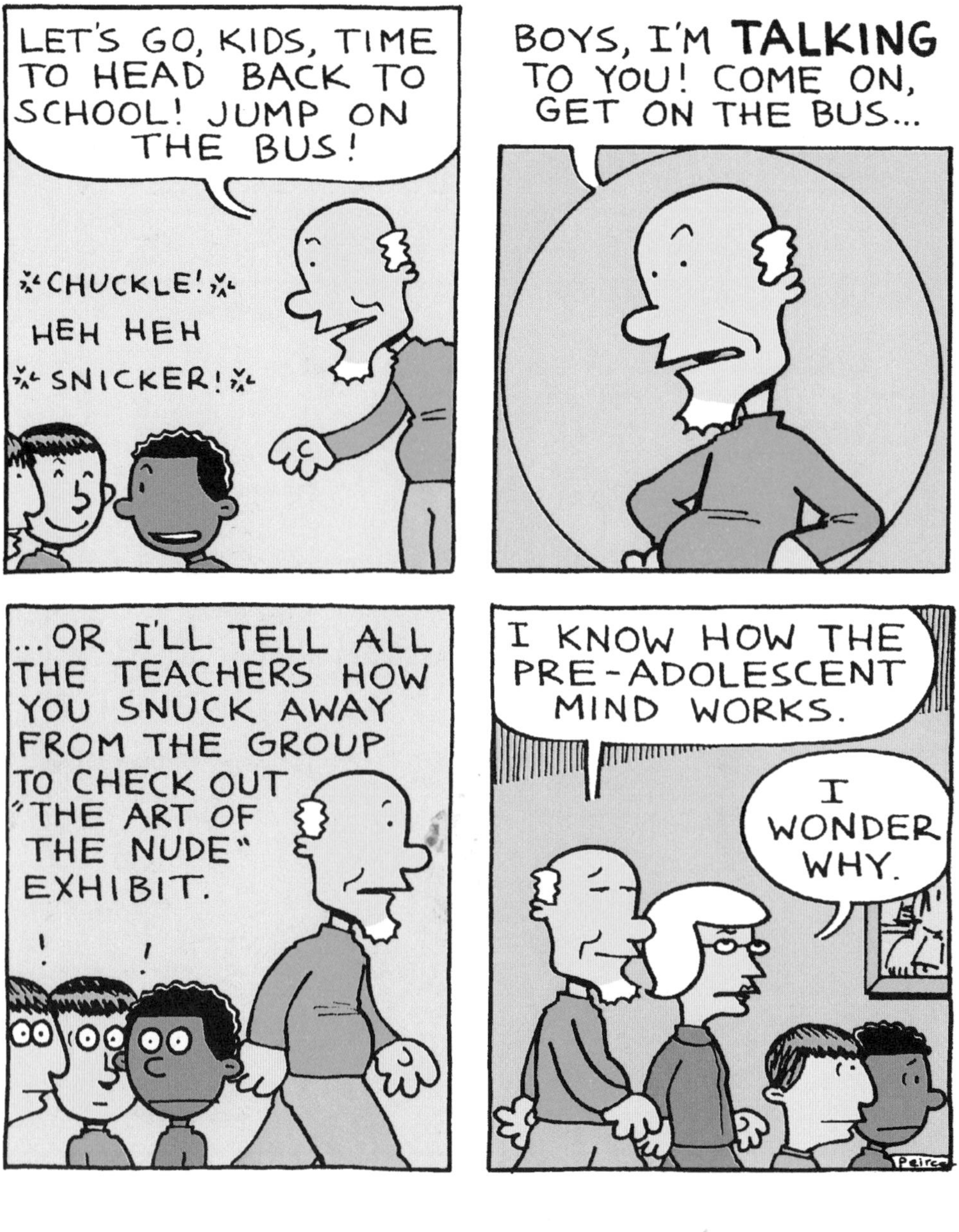
LET'S GO, KIDS, TIME TO HEAD BACK TO SCHOOL! JUMP ON THE BUS!
CHUCKLE!
HEH HEH
SNICKER!
BOYS, I'M **TALKING** TO YOU! COME ON, GET ON THE BUS...
...OR I'LL TELL ALL THE TEACHERS HOW YOU SNUCK AWAY FROM THE GROUP TO CHECK OUT "THE ART OF THE NUDE" EXHIBIT.
!
!
I KNOW HOW THE PRE-ADOLESCENT MIND WORKS.
I WONDER WHY.
Peirce

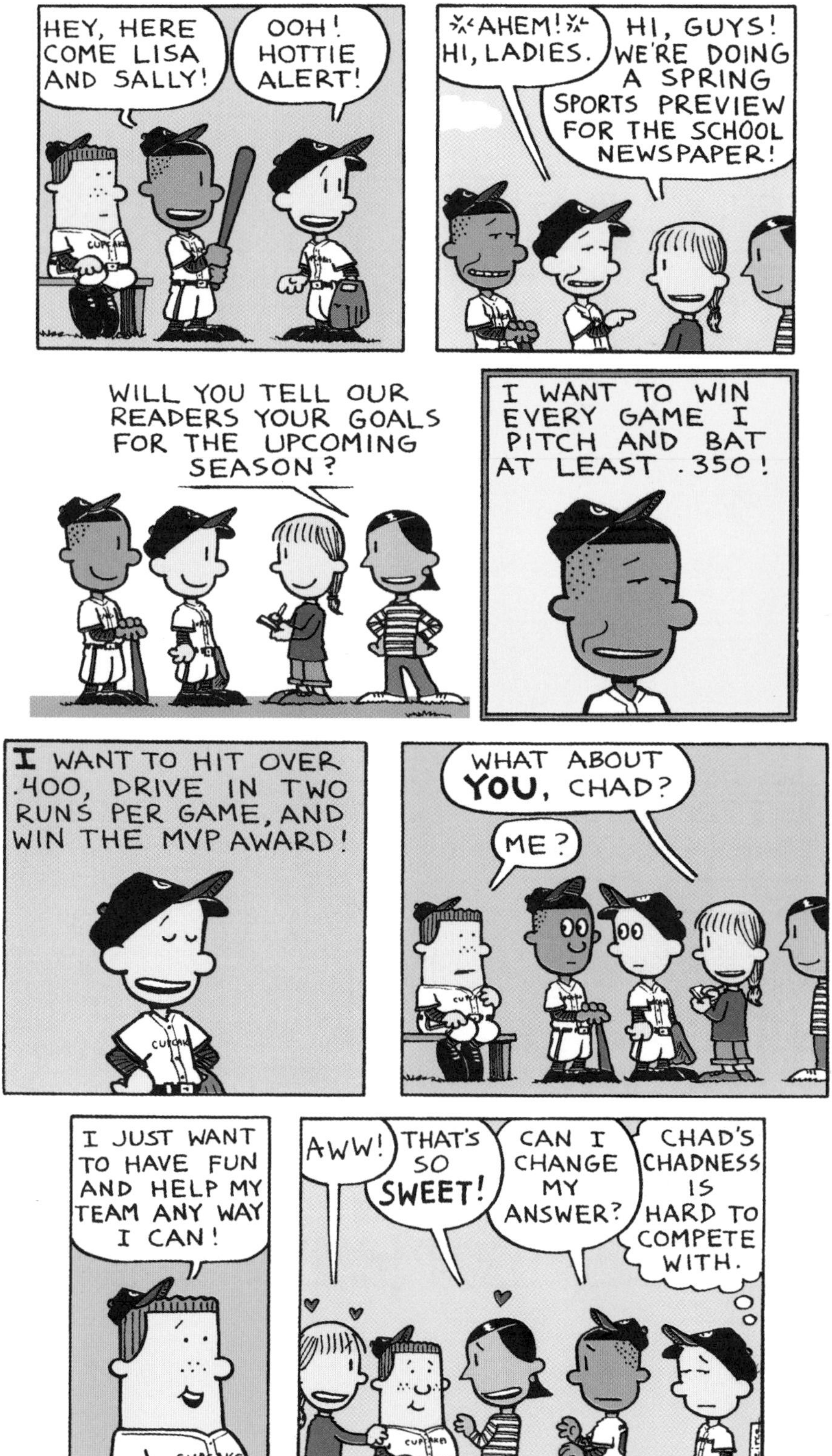
HEY, HERE COME LISA AND SALLY!
OOH! HOTTIE ALERT!
AHEM! HI, LADIES.
HI, GUYS! WE'RE DOING A SPRING SPORTS PREVIEW FOR THE SCHOOL NEWSPAPER!
WILL YOU TELL OUR READERS YOUR GOALS FOR THE UPCOMING SEASON?
I WANT TO WIN EVERY GAME I PITCH AND BAT AT LEAST .350!
I WANT TO HIT OVER .400, DRIVE IN TWO RUNS PER GAME, AND WIN THE MVP AWARD!
WHAT ABOUT **YOU**, CHAD?
ME?
I JUST WANT TO HAVE FUN AND HELP MY TEAM ANY WAY I CAN!
AWW!
THAT'S SO **SWEET**!
CAN I CHANGE MY ANSWER?
CHAD'S CHADNESS IS HARD TO COMPETE WITH.

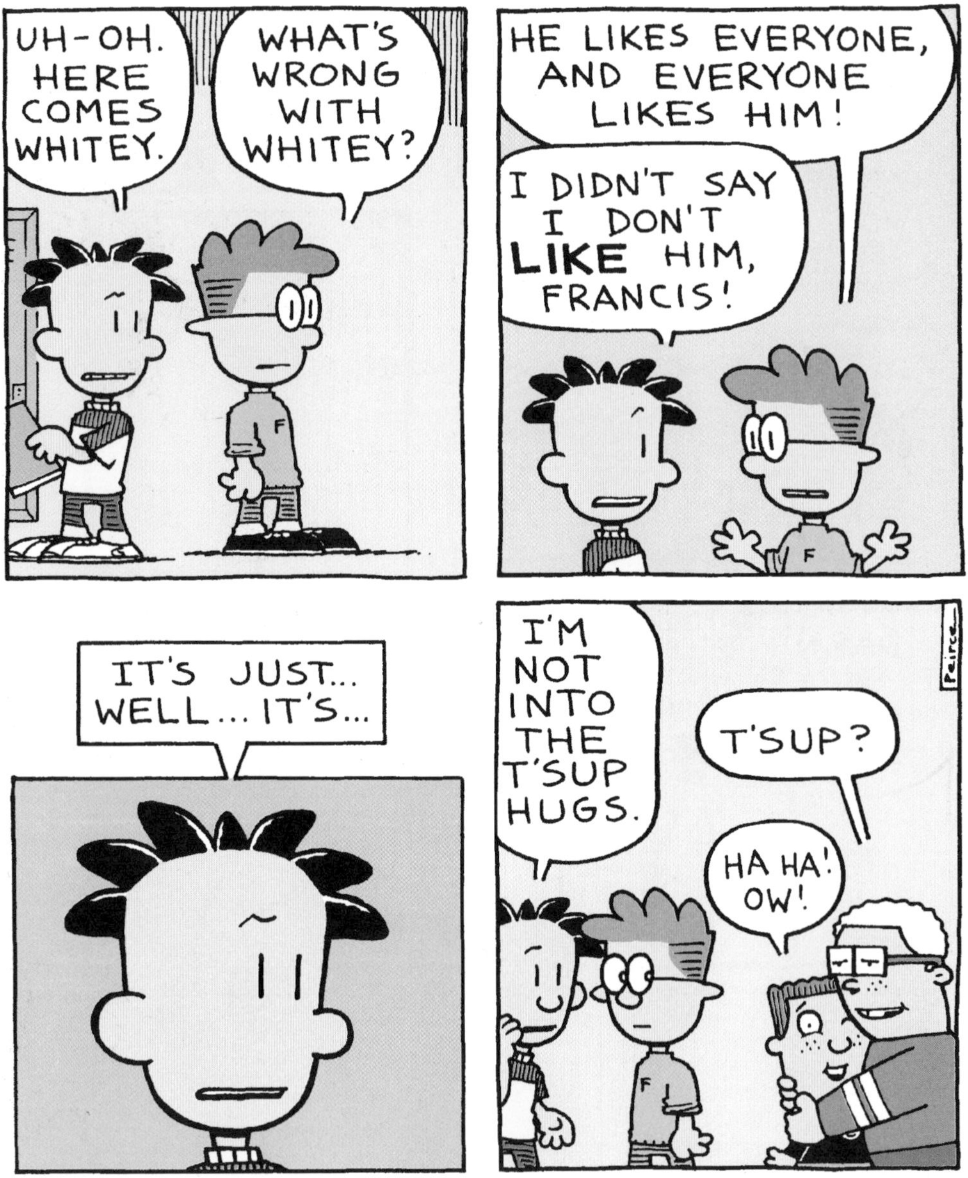
UH-OH. HERE COMES WHITEY.
WHAT'S WRONG WITH WHITEY?
HE LIKES EVERYONE, AND EVERYONE LIKES HIM!
I DIDN'T SAY I DON'T **LIKE** HIM, FRANCIS!
IT'S JUST... WELL... IT'S...
I'M NOT INTO THE T'SUP HUGS.
T'SUP?
HA HA! OW!
Peirce

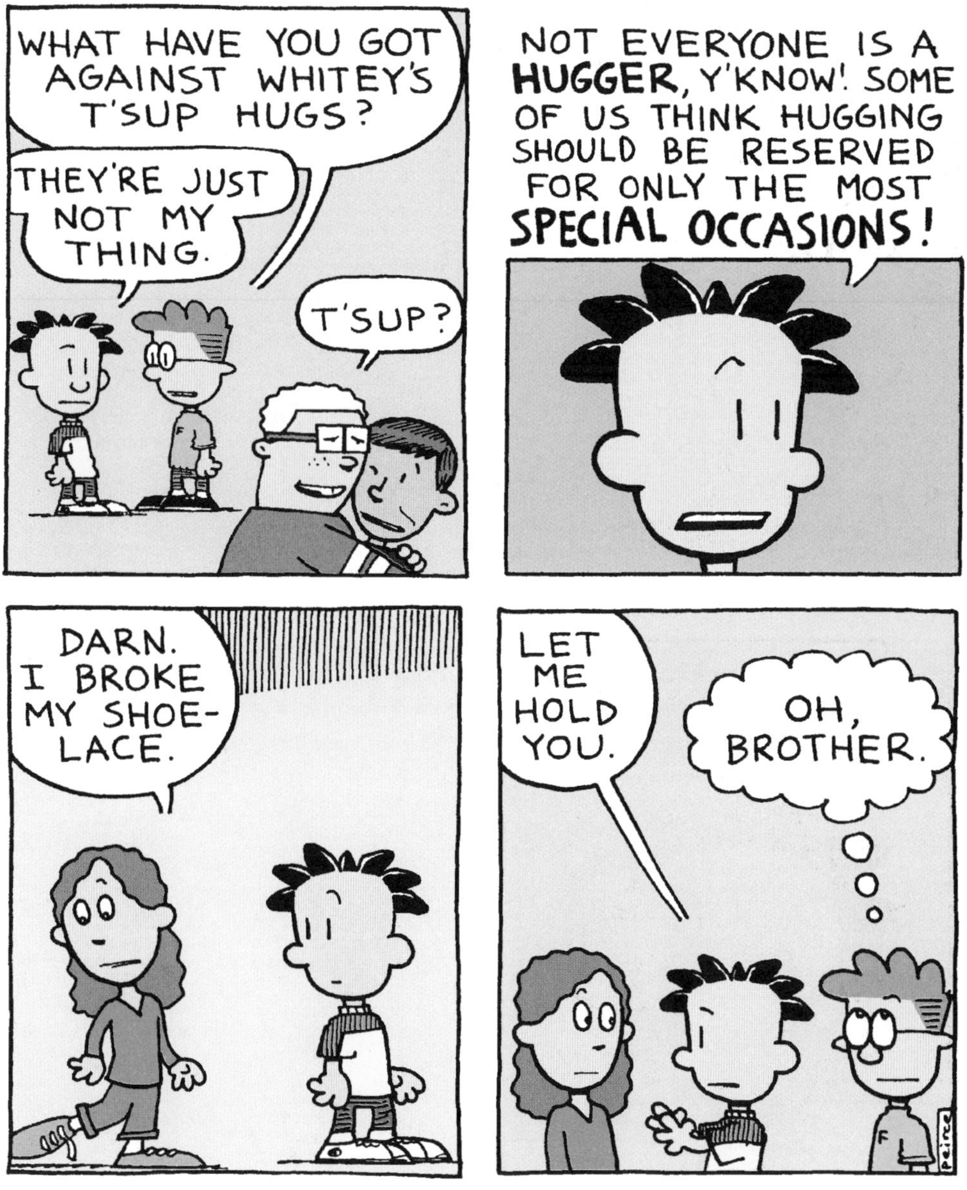
WHAT HAVE YOU GOT AGAINST WHITEY'S T'SUP HUGS?
THEY'RE JUST NOT MY THING.
T'SUP?
NOT EVERYONE IS A **HUGGER**, Y'KNOW! SOME OF US THINK HUGGING SHOULD BE RESERVED FOR ONLY THE MOST **SPECIAL OCCASIONS!**
DARN. I BROKE MY SHOE-LACE.
LET ME HOLD YOU.
OH, BROTHER.
peirce

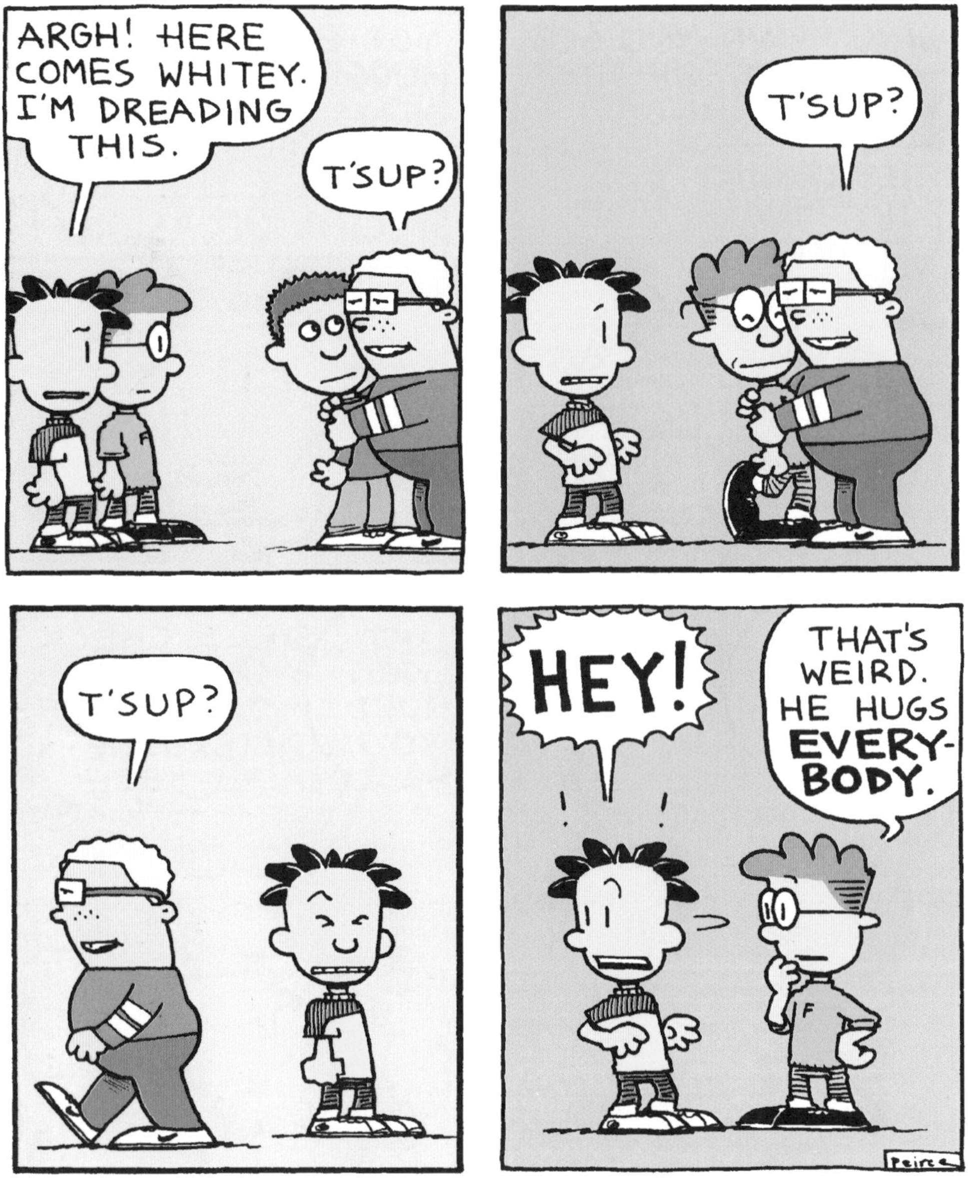
ARGH! HERE COMES WHITEY. I'M DREADING THIS.
T'SUP?
T'SUP?
T'SUP?
HEY!
THAT'S WEIRD. HE HUGS EVERY-BODY.
Peirce

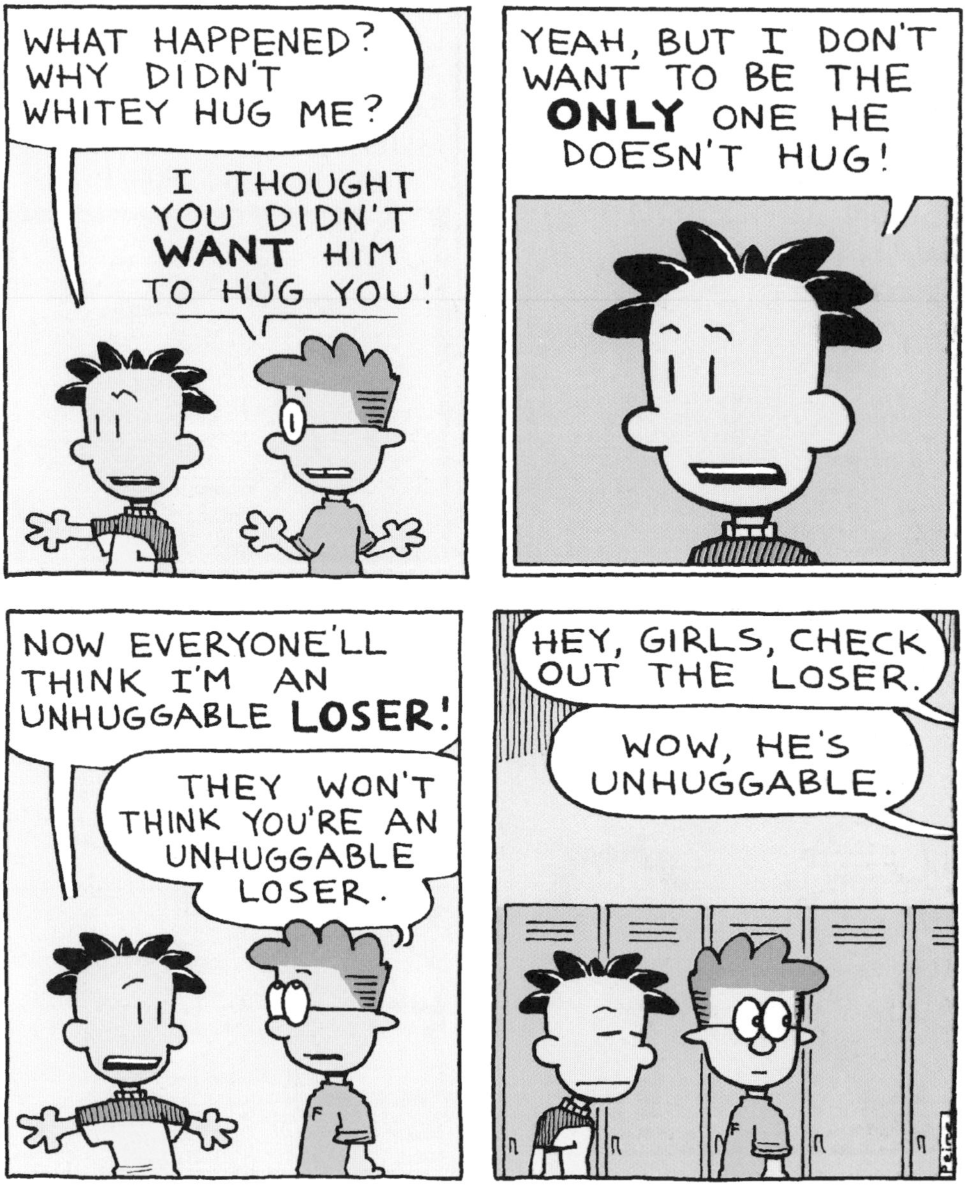
WHAT HAPPENED? WHY DIDN'T WHITEY HUG ME?
I THOUGHT YOU DIDN'T **WANT** HIM TO HUG YOU!
YEAH, BUT I DON'T WANT TO BE THE **ONLY** ONE HE DOESN'T HUG!
NOW EVERYONE'LL THINK I'M AN UNHUGGABLE **LOSER**!
THEY WON'T THINK YOU'RE AN UNHUGGABLE LOSER.
HEY, GIRLS, CHECK OUT THE LOSER.
WOW, HE'S UNHUGGABLE.

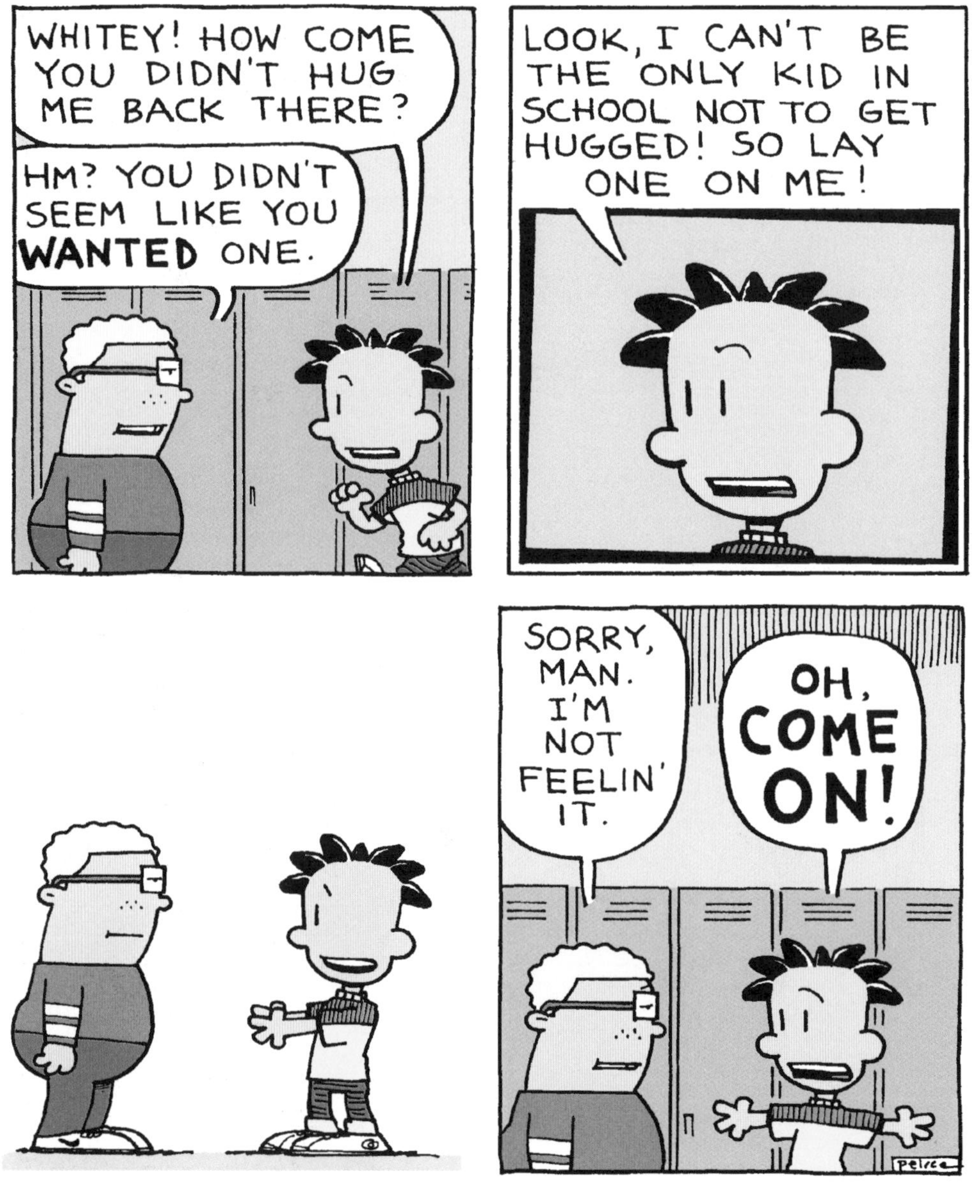
WHITEY! HOW COME YOU DIDN'T HUG ME BACK THERE?
HM? YOU DIDN'T SEEM LIKE YOU **WANTED** ONE.
LOOK, I CAN'T BE THE ONLY KID IN SCHOOL NOT TO GET HUGGED! SO LAY ONE ON ME!
SORRY, MAN. I'M NOT FEELIN' IT.
OH, **COME ON!**
PEIRCE

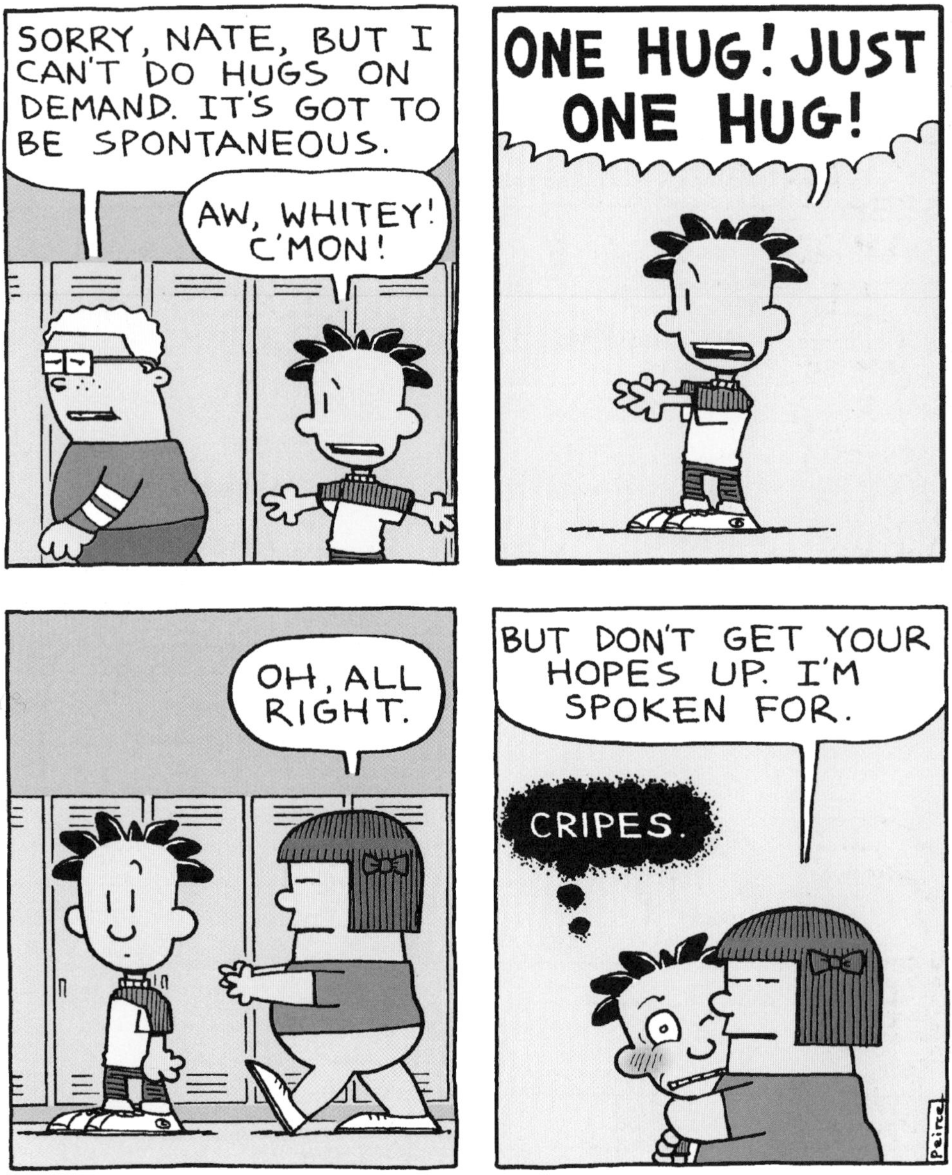
SORRY, NATE, BUT I CAN'T DO HUGS ON DEMAND. IT'S GOT TO BE SPONTANEOUS.
AW, WHITEY! C'MON!
ONE HUG! JUST ONE HUG!
OH, ALL RIGHT.
BUT DON'T GET YOUR HOPES UP. I'M SPOKEN FOR.
CRIPES.
Peirce

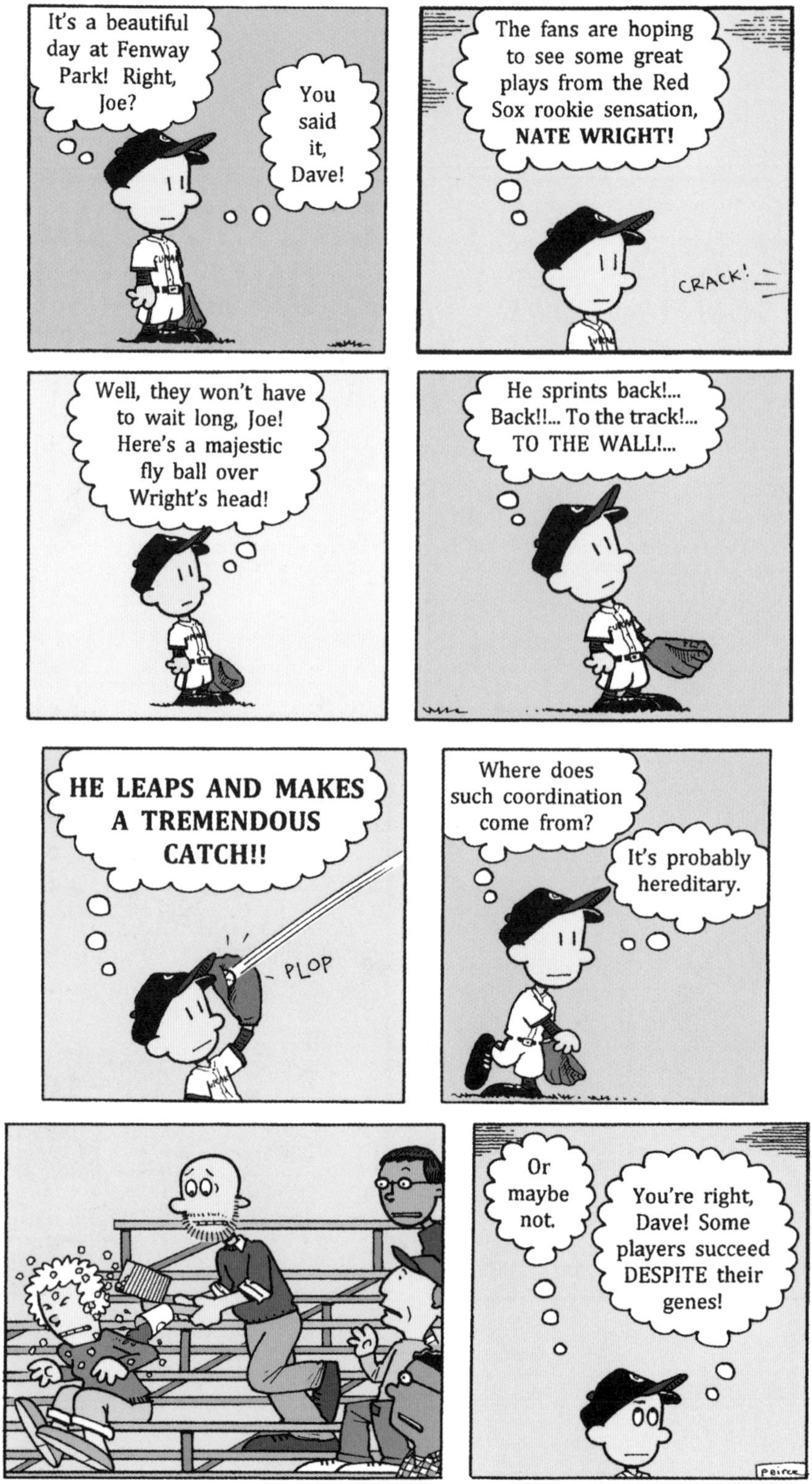

It's a beautiful day at Fenway Park! Right, Joe?
You said it, Dave!
The fans are hoping to see some great plays from the Red Sox rookie sensation, NATE WRIGHT!
CRACK!
Well, they won't have to wait long, Joe! Here's a majestic fly ball over Wright's head!
He sprints back!... Back!!... To the track!... TO THE WALL!...
HE LEAPS AND MAKES A TREMENDOUS CATCH!!
PLOP
Where does such coordination come from?
It's probably hereditary.
Or maybe not.
You're right, Dave! Some players succeed DESPITE their genes!
Peirce

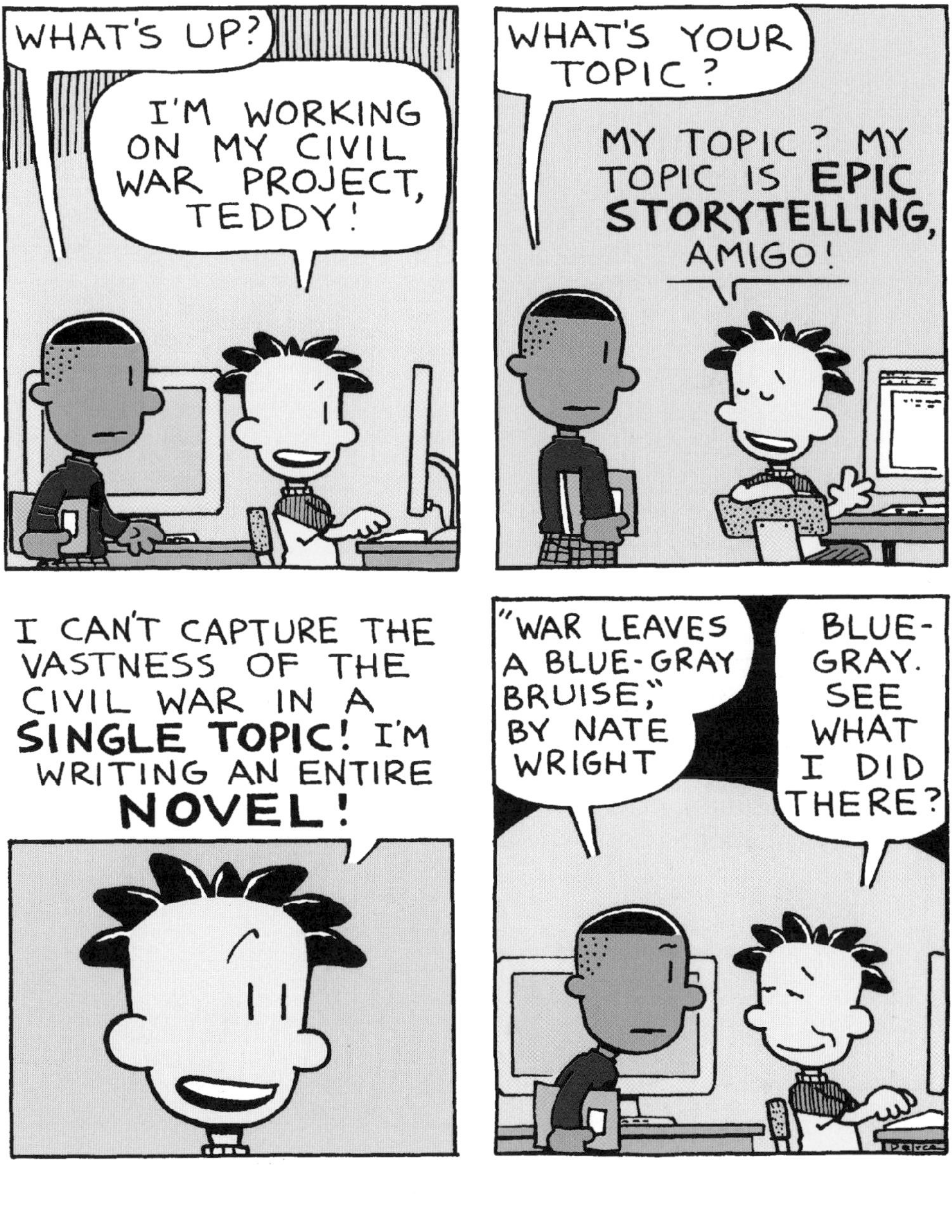

WHAT'S UP?
I'M WORKING ON MY CIVIL WAR PROJECT, TEDDY!
WHAT'S YOUR TOPIC?
MY TOPIC? MY TOPIC IS **EPIC STORYTELLING,** AMIGO!
I CAN'T CAPTURE THE VASTNESS OF THE CIVIL WAR IN A **SINGLE TOPIC!** I'M WRITING AN ENTIRE **NOVEL!**
"WAR LEAVES A BLUE-GRAY BRUISE," BY NATE WRIGHT
BLUE-GRAY. SEE WHAT I DID THERE?

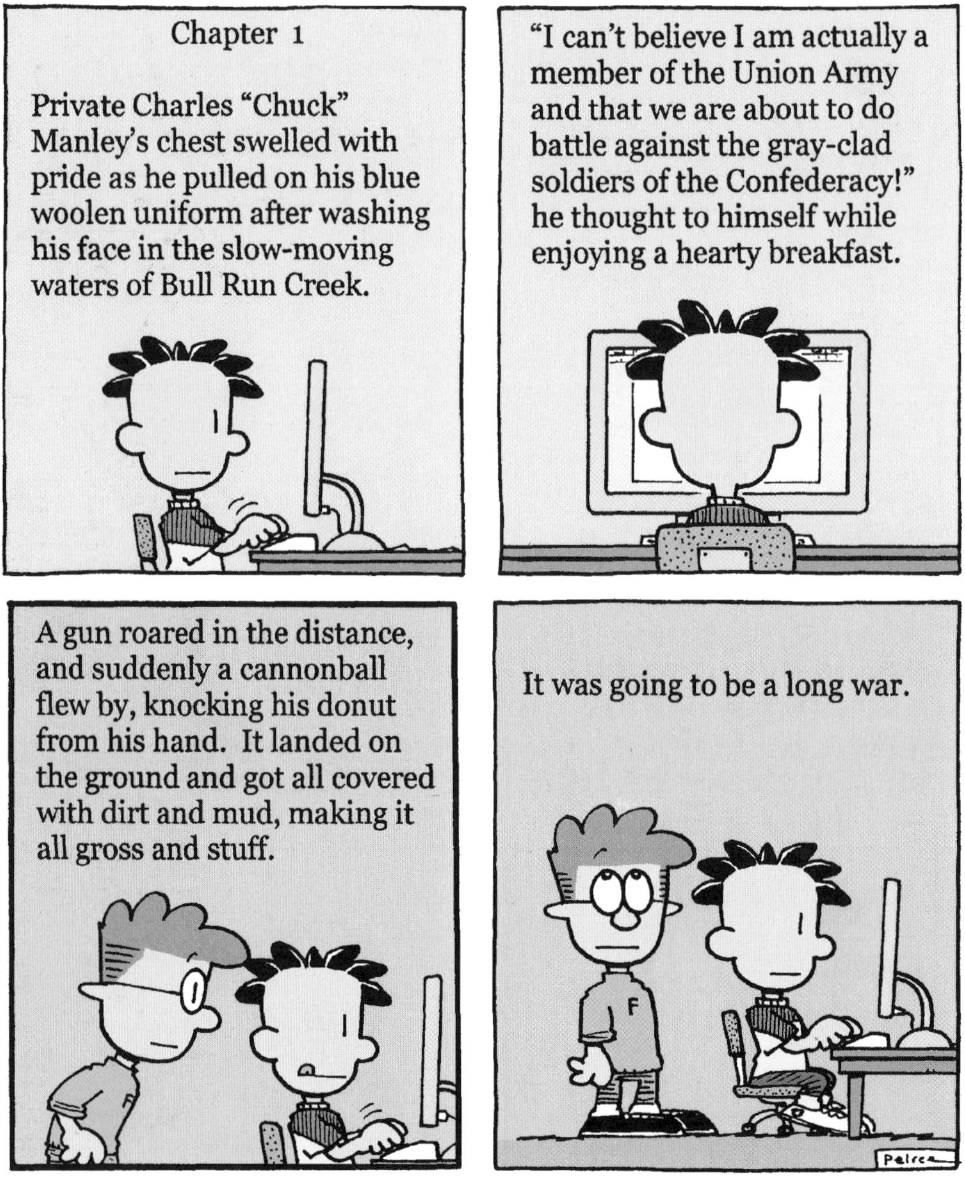
Chapter 1
Private Charles "Chuck" Manley's chest swelled with pride as he pulled on his blue woolen uniform after washing his face in the slow-moving waters of Bull Run Creek.
"I can't believe I am actually a member of the Union Army and that we are about to do battle against the gray-clad soldiers of the Confederacy!" he thought to himself while enjoying a hearty breakfast.
A gun roared in the distance, and suddenly a cannonball flew by, knocking his donut from his hand. It landed on the ground and got all covered with dirt and mud, making it all gross and stuff.
It was going to be a long war.
F
Peirce

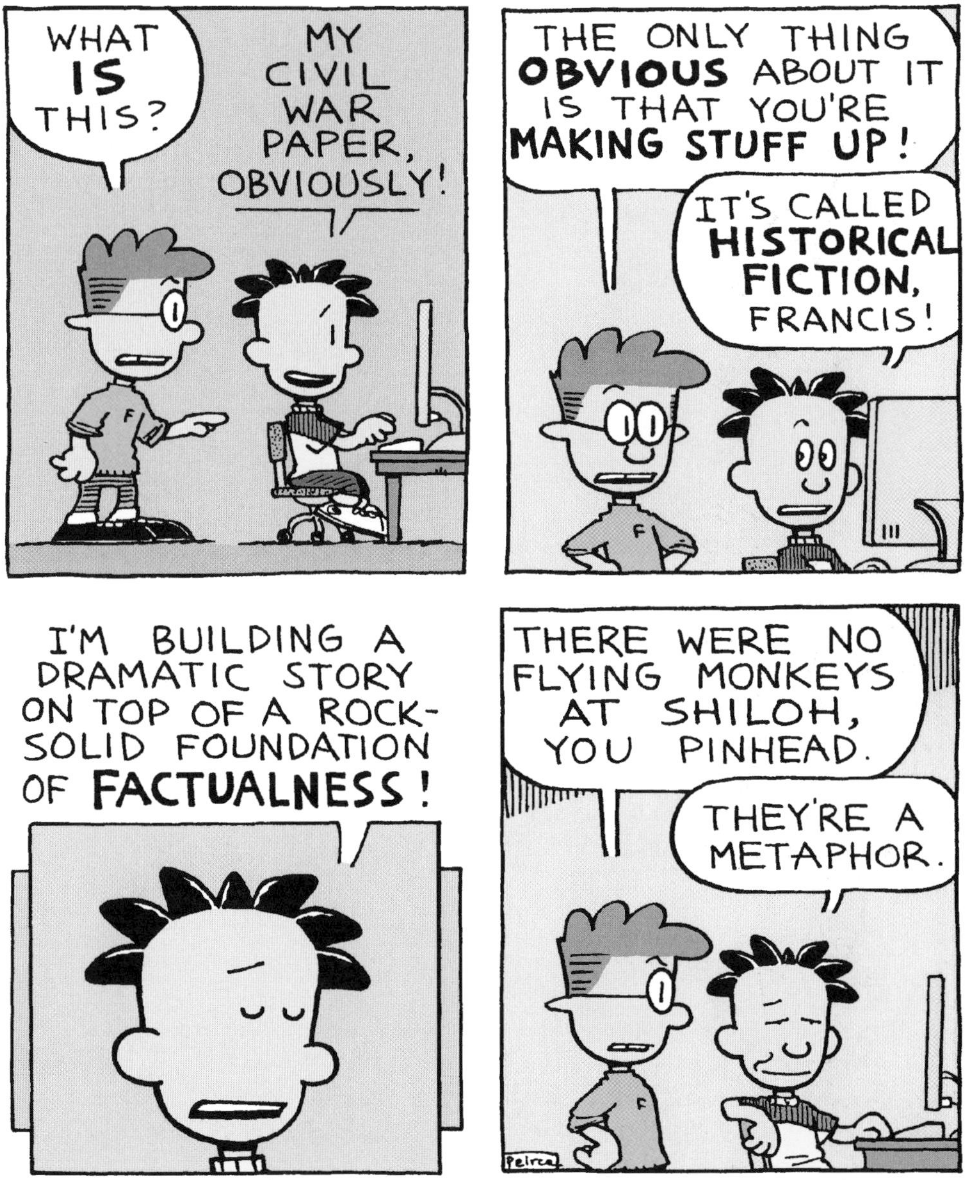
WHAT **IS** THIS?
MY CIVIL WAR PAPER, OBVIOUSLY!
THE ONLY THING **OBVIOUS** ABOUT IT IS THAT YOU'RE **MAKING STUFF UP**!
IT'S CALLED **HISTORICAL FICTION**, FRANCIS!
I'M BUILDING A DRAMATIC STORY ON TOP OF A ROCK-SOLID FOUNDATION OF **FACTUALNESS**!
THERE WERE NO FLYING MONKEYS AT SHILOH, YOU PINHEAD.
THEY'RE A METAPHOR.
Peirce

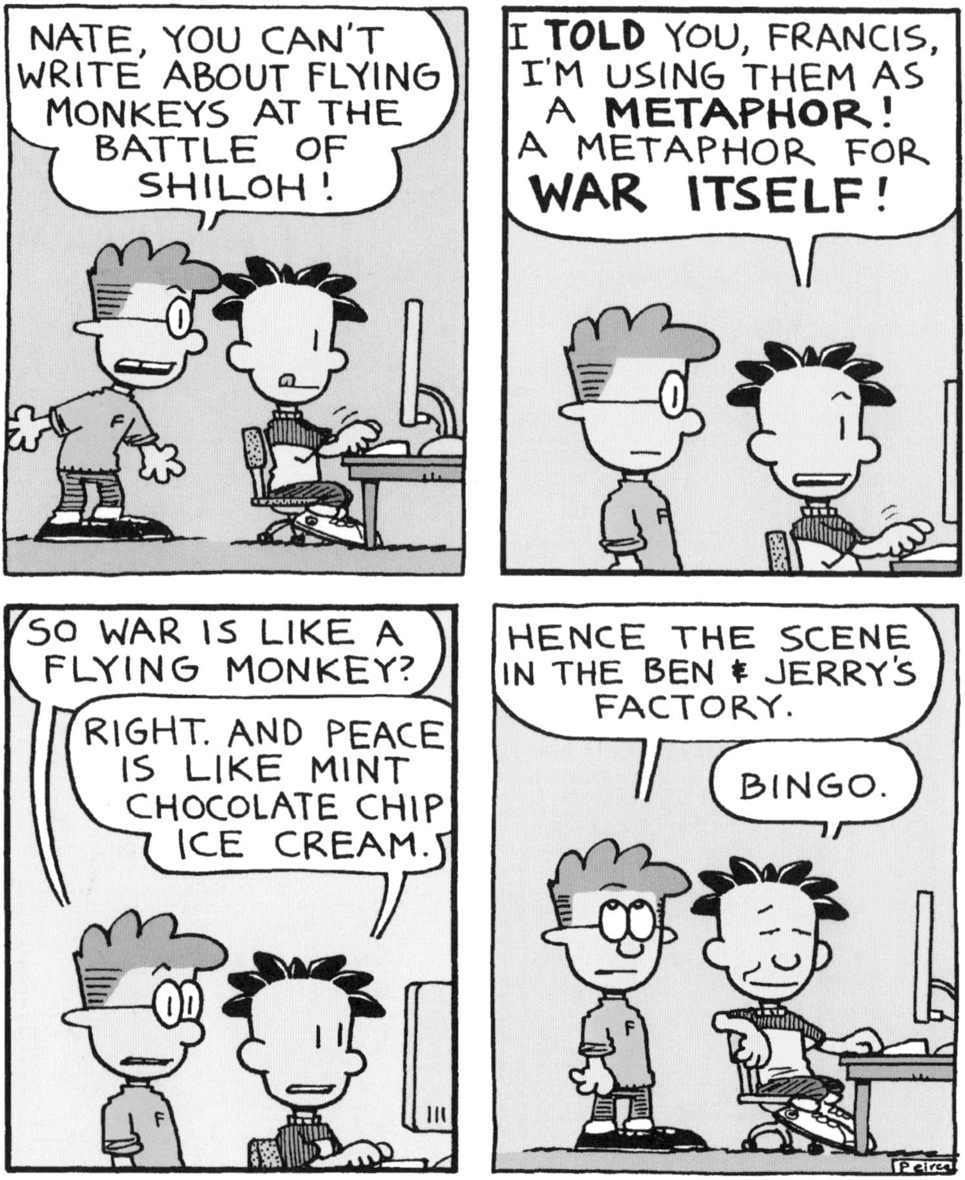
NATE, YOU CAN'T WRITE ABOUT FLYING MONKEYS AT THE BATTLE OF SHILOH!
I **TOLD** YOU, FRANCIS, I'M USING THEM AS A **METAPHOR**! A METAPHOR FOR **WAR ITSELF**!
SO WAR IS LIKE A FLYING MONKEY?
RIGHT. AND PEACE IS LIKE MINT CHOCOLATE CHIP ICE CREAM.
HENCE THE SCENE IN THE BEN & JERRY'S FACTORY.
BINGO.
Peirce

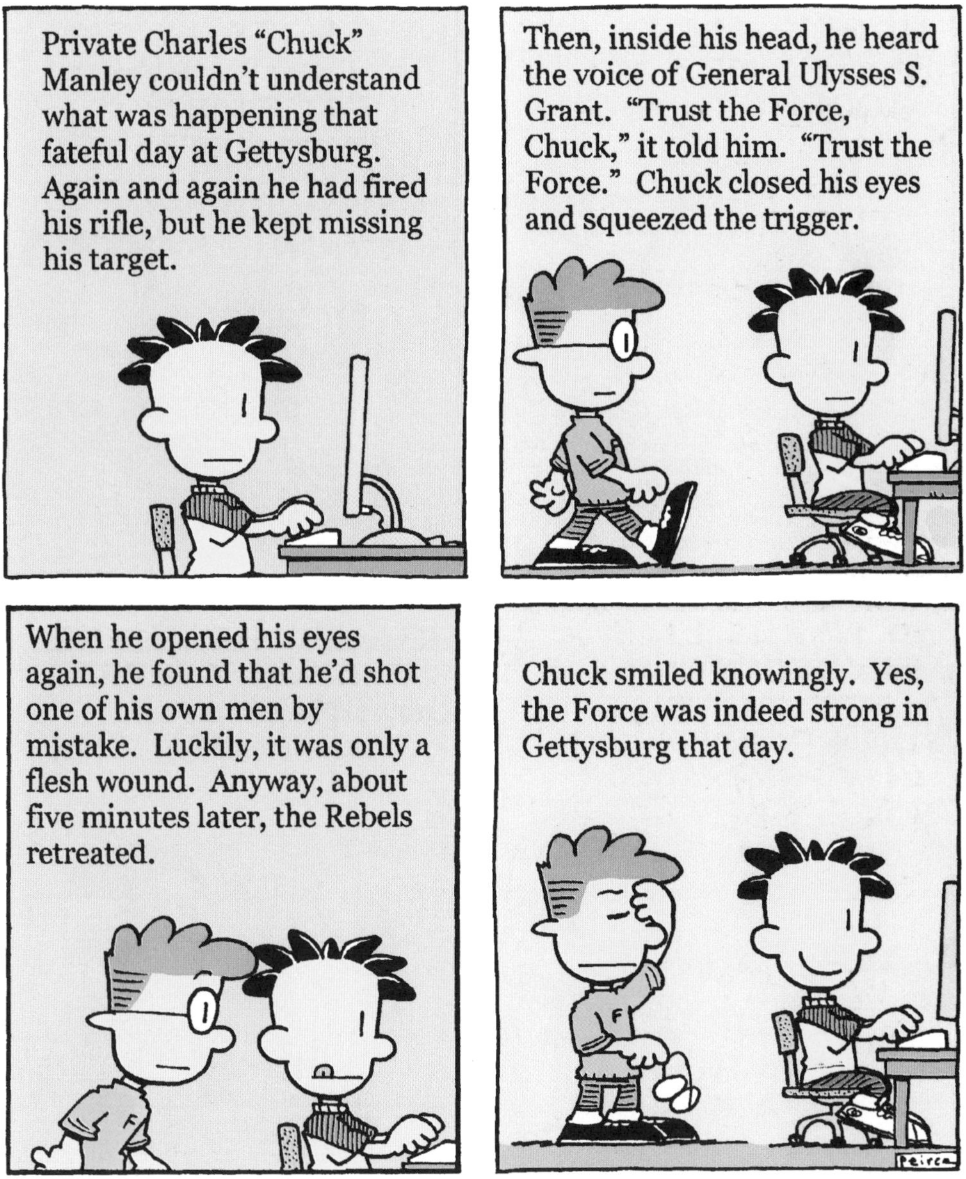
Private Charles "Chuck" Manley couldn't understand what was happening that fateful day at Gettysburg. Again and again he had fired his rifle, but he kept missing his target.
Then, inside his head, he heard the voice of General Ulysses S. Grant. "Trust the Force, Chuck," it told him. "Trust the Force." Chuck closed his eyes and squeezed the trigger.
When he opened his eyes again, he found that he'd shot one of his own men by mistake. Luckily, it was only a flesh wound. Anyway, about five minutes later, the Rebels retreated.
Chuck smiled knowingly. Yes, the Force was indeed strong in Gettysburg that day.
Peirce

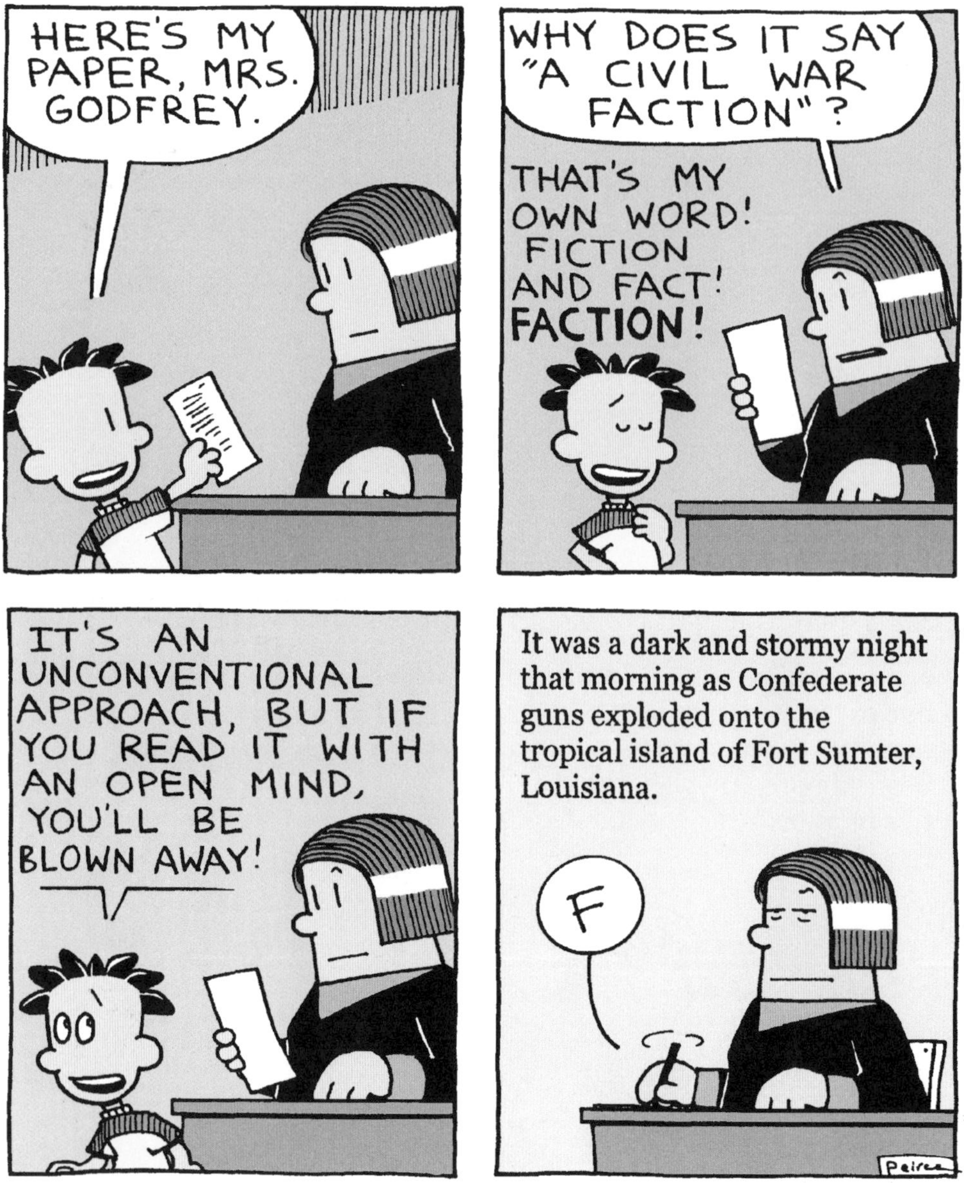
HERE'S MY PAPER, MRS. GODFREY.
WHY DOES IT SAY "A CIVIL WAR FACTION"?
THAT'S MY OWN WORD! FICTION AND FACT! FACTION!
IT'S AN UNCONVENTIONAL APPROACH, BUT IF YOU READ IT WITH AN OPEN MIND, YOU'LL BE BLOWN AWAY!
It was a dark and stormy night that morning as Confederate guns exploded onto the tropical island of Fort Sumter, Louisiana.
F
Peirce

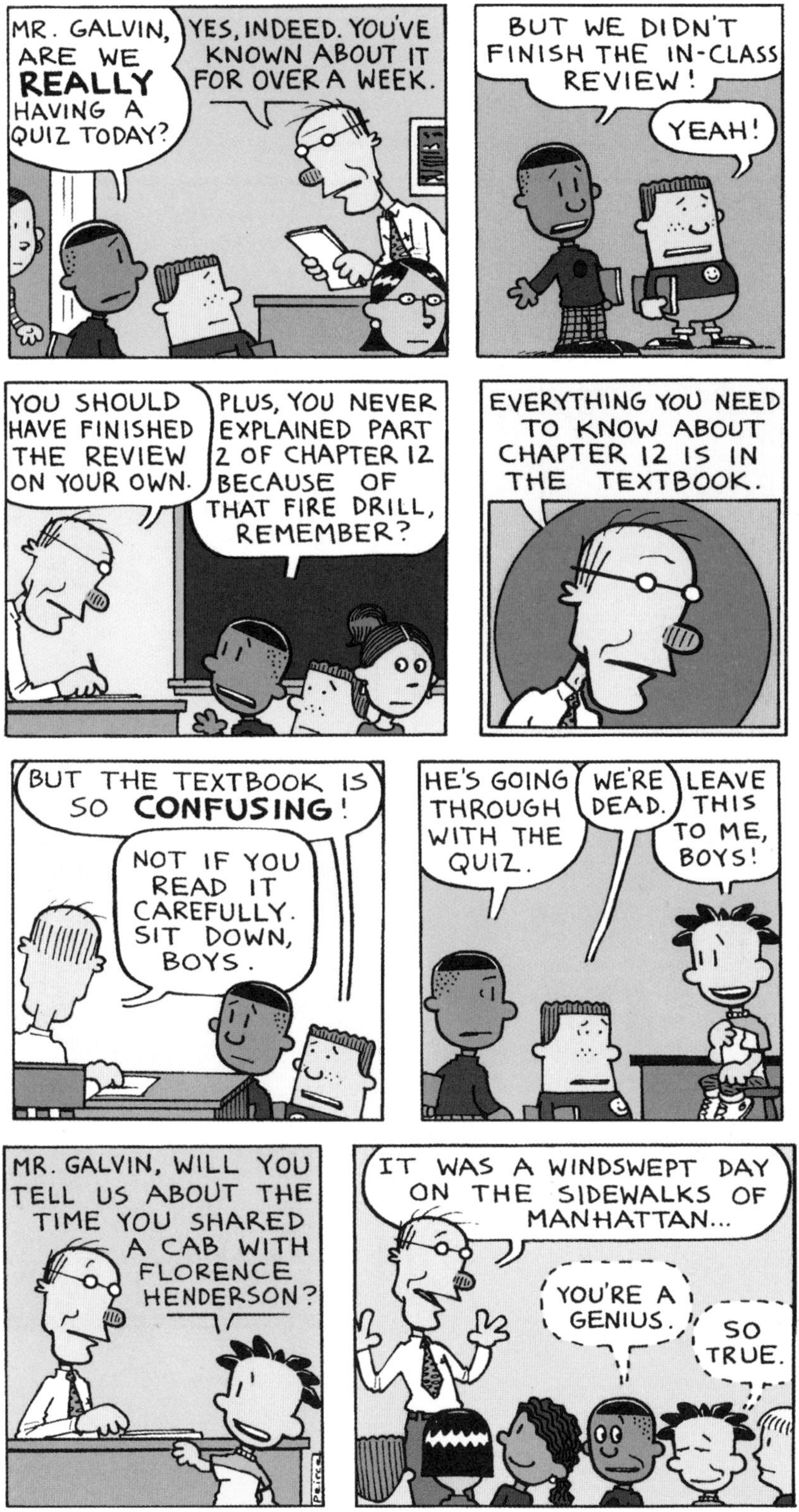
MR. GALVIN, ARE WE **REALLY** HAVING A QUIZ TODAY?
YES, INDEED. YOU'VE KNOWN ABOUT IT FOR OVER A WEEK.
BUT WE DIDN'T FINISH THE IN-CLASS REVIEW!
YEAH!
YOU SHOULD HAVE FINISHED THE REVIEW ON YOUR OWN.
PLUS, YOU NEVER EXPLAINED PART 2 OF CHAPTER 12 BECAUSE OF THAT FIRE DRILL, REMEMBER?
EVERYTHING YOU NEED TO KNOW ABOUT CHAPTER 12 IS IN THE TEXTBOOK.
BUT THE TEXTBOOK IS SO **CONFUSING**!
NOT IF YOU READ IT CAREFULLY. SIT DOWN, BOYS.
HE'S GOING THROUGH WITH THE QUIZ.
WE'RE DEAD.
LEAVE THIS TO ME, BOYS!
MR. GALVIN, WILL YOU TELL US ABOUT THE TIME YOU SHARED A CAB WITH FLORENCE HENDERSON?
Peirce
IT WAS A WINDSWEPT DAY ON THE SIDEWALKS OF MANHATTAN...
YOU'RE A GENIUS.
SO TRUE.

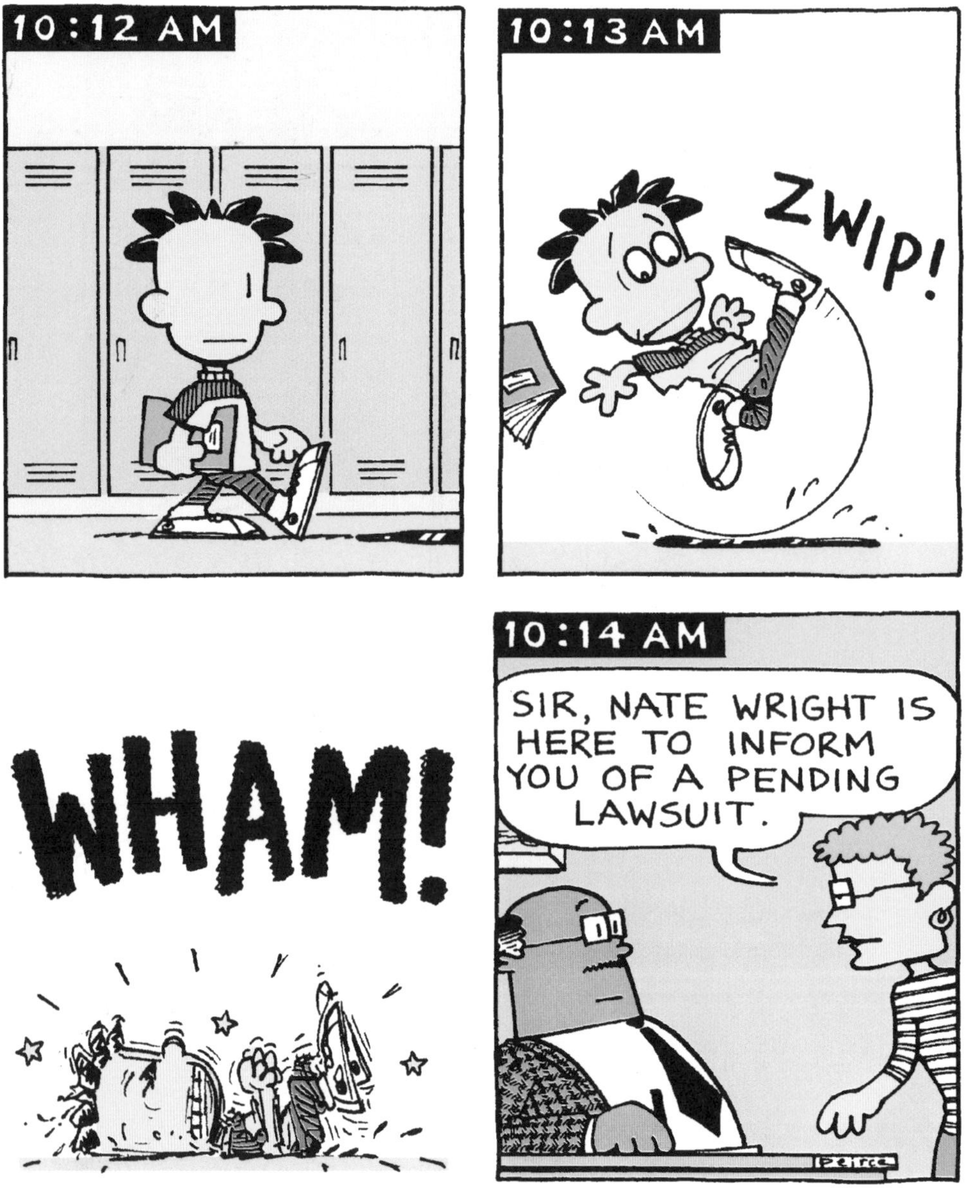
10:12 AM
10:13 AM
ZWIP!
WHAM!
10:14 AM
SIR, NATE WRIGHT IS HERE TO INFORM YOU OF A PENDING LAWSUIT.
Peirce

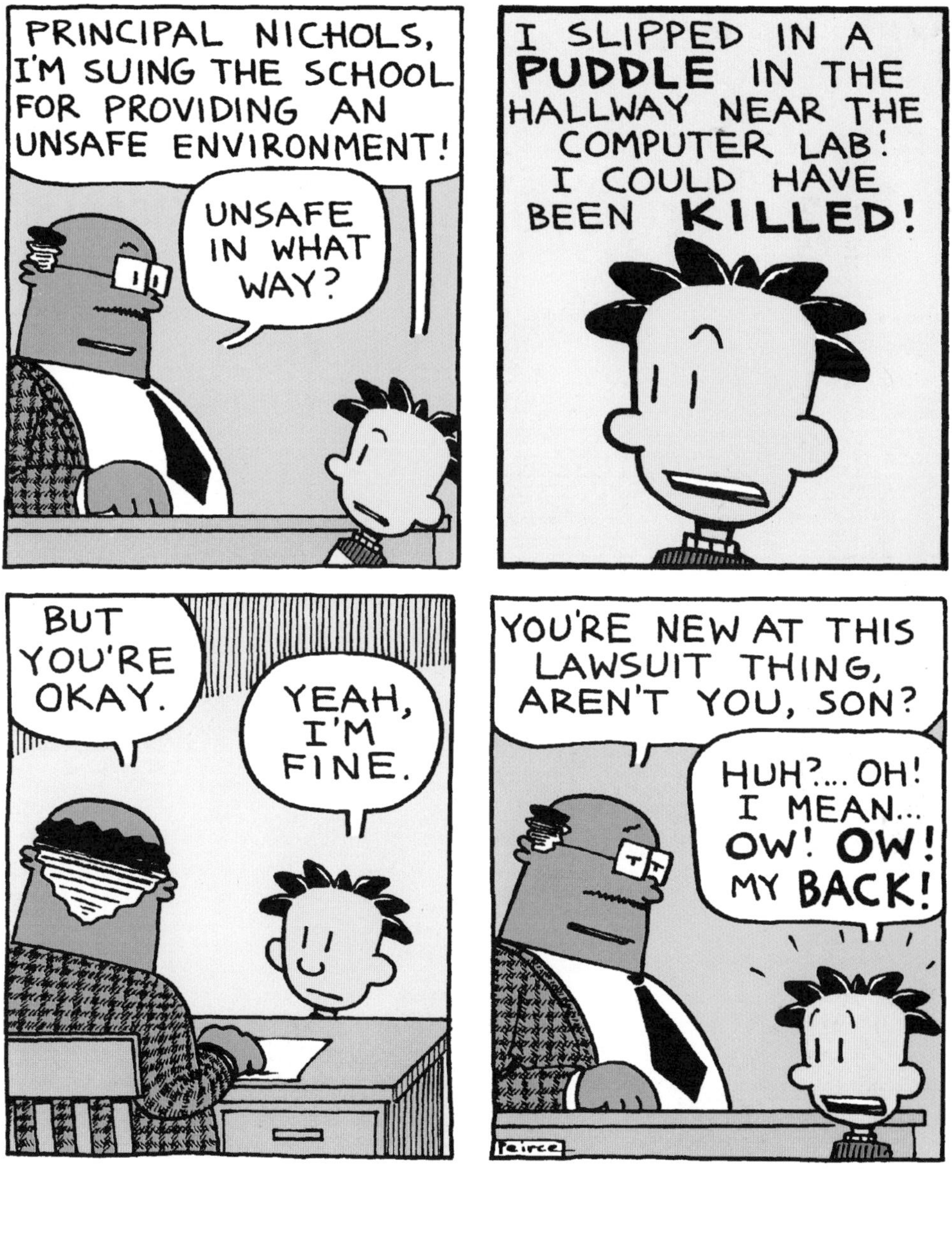
PRINCIPAL NICHOLS, I'M SUING THE SCHOOL FOR PROVIDING AN UNSAFE ENVIRONMENT!
UNSAFE IN WHAT WAY?
I SLIPPED IN A PUDDLE IN THE HALLWAY NEAR THE COMPUTER LAB! I COULD HAVE BEEN KILLED!
BUT YOU'RE OKAY.
YEAH, I'M FINE.
YOU'RE NEW AT THIS LAWSUIT THING, AREN'T YOU, SON?
HUH?... OH! I MEAN... OW! OW! MY BACK!
Peirce

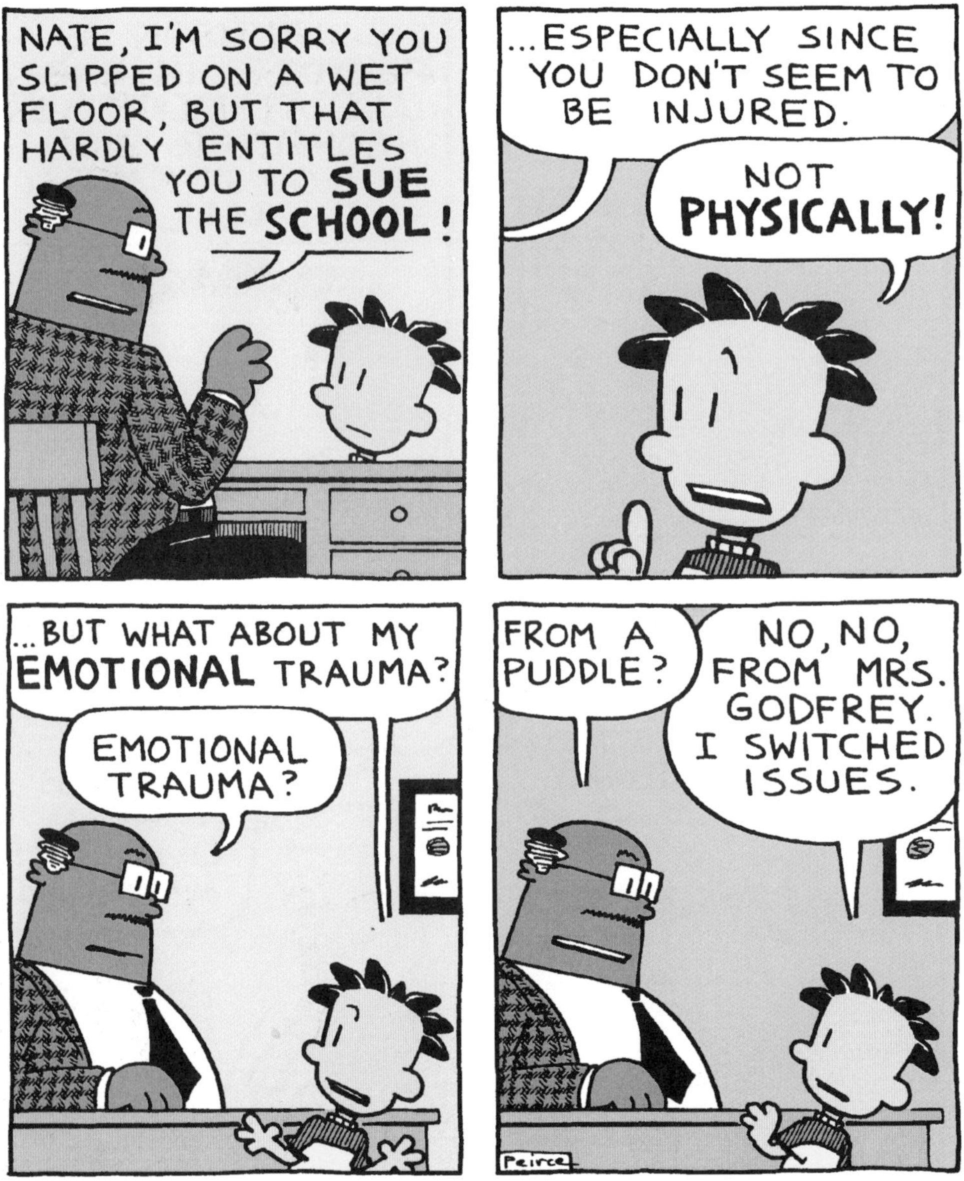
NATE, I'M SORRY YOU SLIPPED ON A WET FLOOR, BUT THAT HARDLY ENTITLES YOU TO SUE THE SCHOOL!
...ESPECIALLY SINCE YOU DON'T SEEM TO BE INJURED.
NOT PHYSICALLY!
...BUT WHAT ABOUT MY EMOTIONAL TRAUMA?
EMOTIONAL TRAUMA?
FROM A PUDDLE?
NO, NO, FROM MRS. GODFREY. I SWITCHED ISSUES.
Peirce

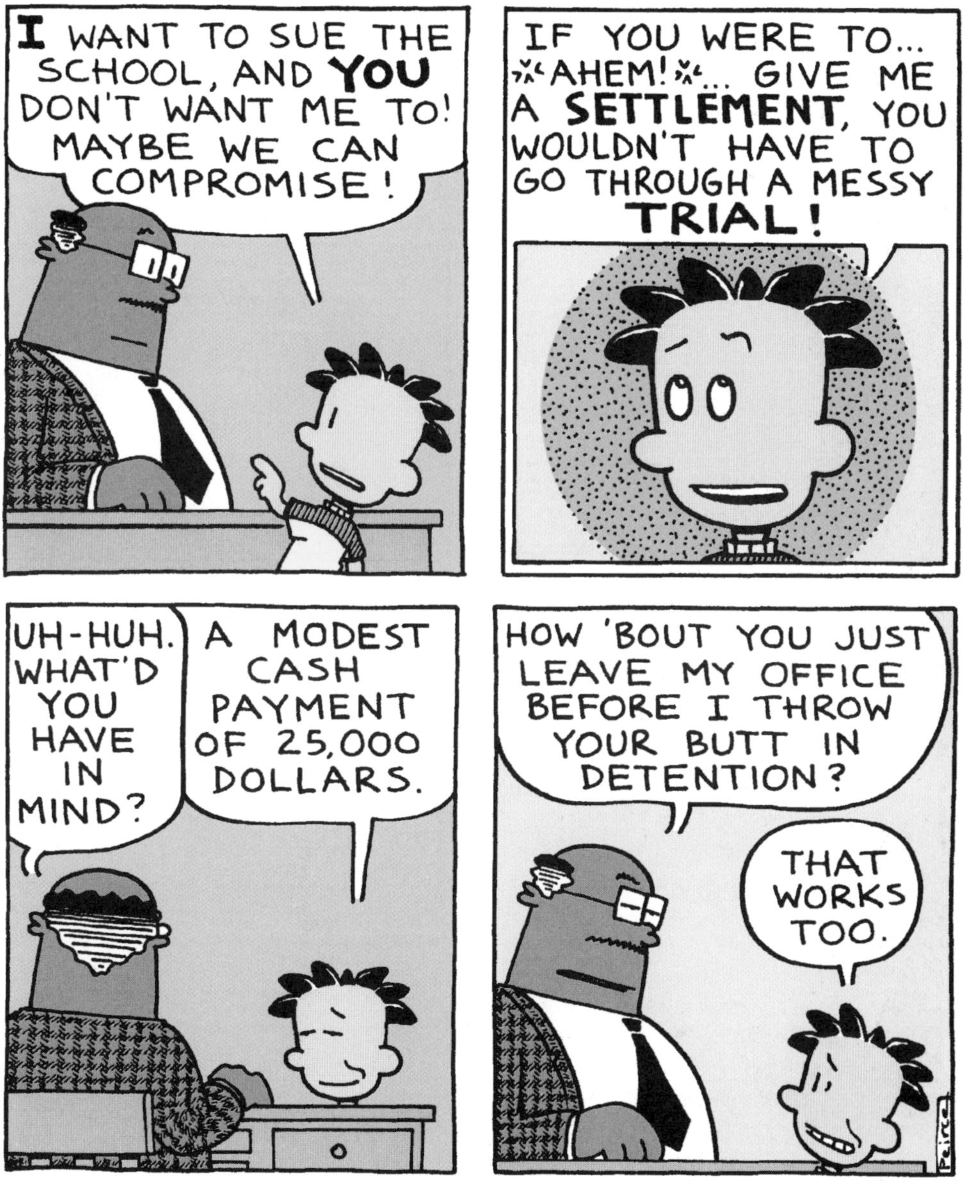
I WANT TO SUE THE SCHOOL, AND YOU DON'T WANT ME TO! MAYBE WE CAN COMPROMISE!
IF YOU WERE TO... AHEM!... GIVE ME A SETTLEMENT, YOU WOULDN'T HAVE TO GO THROUGH A MESSY TRIAL!
UH-HUH. WHAT'D YOU HAVE IN MIND?
A MODEST CASH PAYMENT OF 25,000 DOLLARS.
HOW 'BOUT YOU JUST LEAVE MY OFFICE BEFORE I THROW YOUR BUTT IN DETENTION?
THAT WORKS TOO.
Peirce

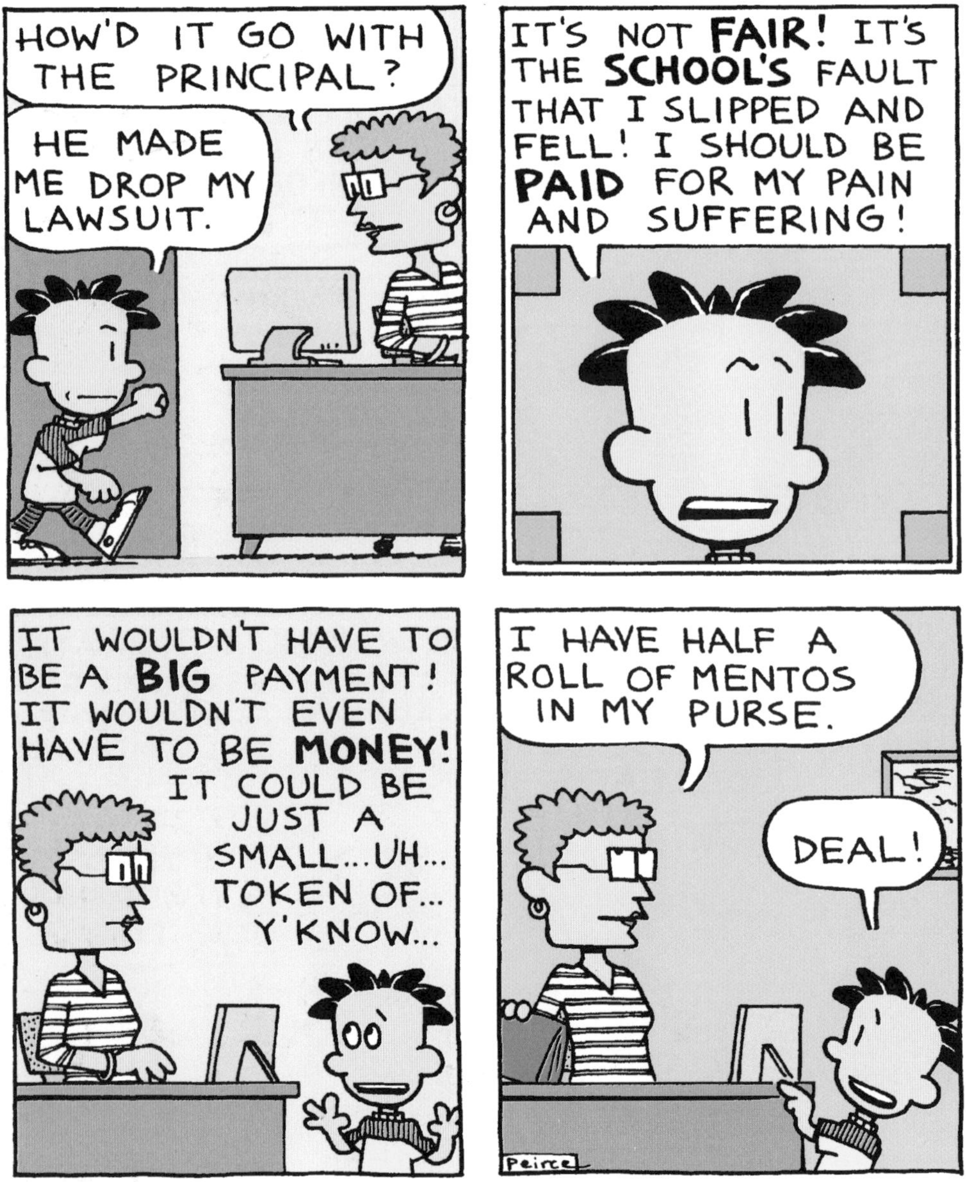
HOW'D IT GO WITH THE PRINCIPAL?
HE MADE ME DROP MY LAWSUIT.
IT'S NOT FAIR! IT'S THE SCHOOL'S FAULT THAT I SLIPPED AND FELL! I SHOULD BE PAID FOR MY PAIN AND SUFFERING!
IT WOULDN'T HAVE TO BE A BIG PAYMENT! IT WOULDN'T EVEN HAVE TO BE MONEY!
IT COULD BE JUST A SMALL...UH... TOKEN OF... Y'KNOW...
I HAVE HALF A ROLL OF MENTOS IN MY PURSE.
DEAL!
Peirce

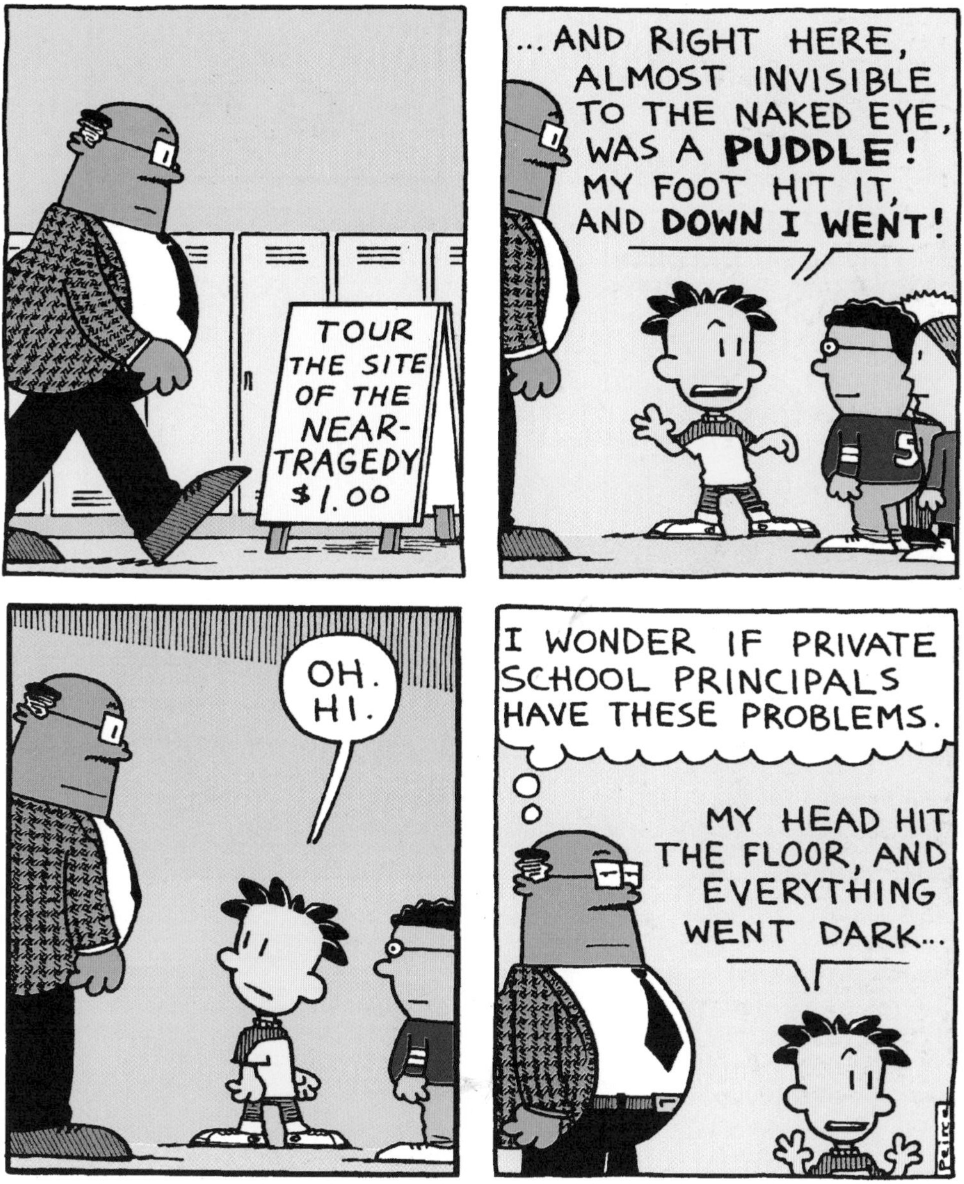
TOUR THE SITE OF THE NEAR-TRAGEDY $1.00
...AND RIGHT HERE, ALMOST INVISIBLE TO THE NAKED EYE, WAS A **PUDDLE**! MY FOOT HIT IT, AND **DOWN I WENT**!
OH. HI.
I WONDER IF PRIVATE SCHOOL PRINCIPALS HAVE THESE PROBLEMS.
MY HEAD HIT THE FLOOR, AND EVERYTHING WENT DARK...
Peirce

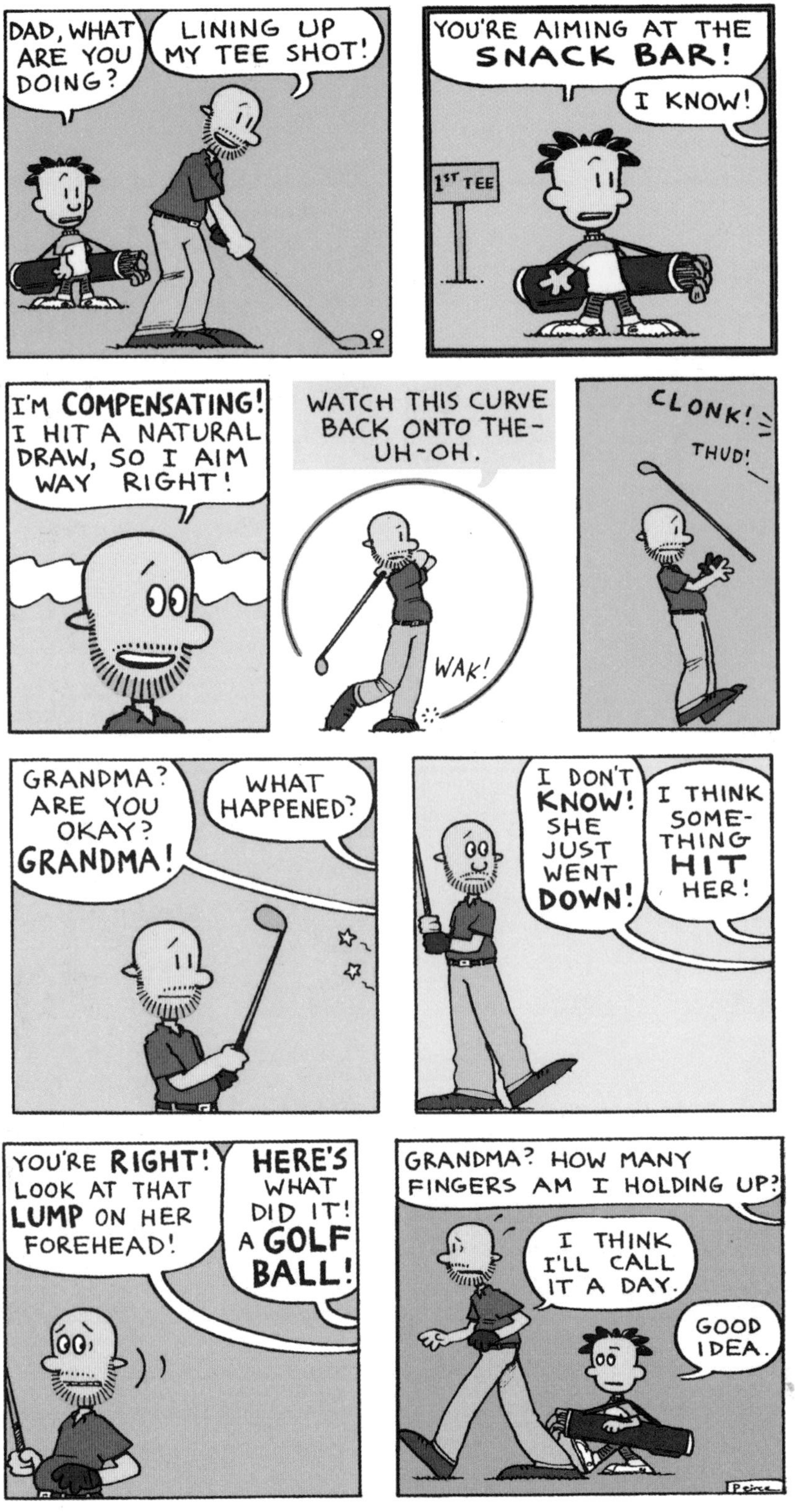
DAD, WHAT ARE YOU DOING?
LINING UP MY TEE SHOT!
YOU'RE AIMING AT THE SNACK BAR!
I KNOW!
1ST TEE
I'M COMPENSATING! I HIT A NATURAL DRAW, SO I AIM WAY RIGHT!
WATCH THIS CURVE BACK ONTO THE- UH-OH.
WAK!
CLONK!
THUD!
GRANDMA? ARE YOU OKAY? GRANDMA!
WHAT HAPPENED?
I DON'T KNOW! SHE JUST WENT DOWN!
I THINK SOMETHING HIT HER!
YOU'RE RIGHT! LOOK AT THAT LUMP ON HER FOREHEAD!
HERE'S WHAT DID IT! A GOLF BALL!
GRANDMA? HOW MANY FINGERS AM I HOLDING UP?
I THINK I'LL CALL IT A DAY.
GOOD IDEA.
Peirce

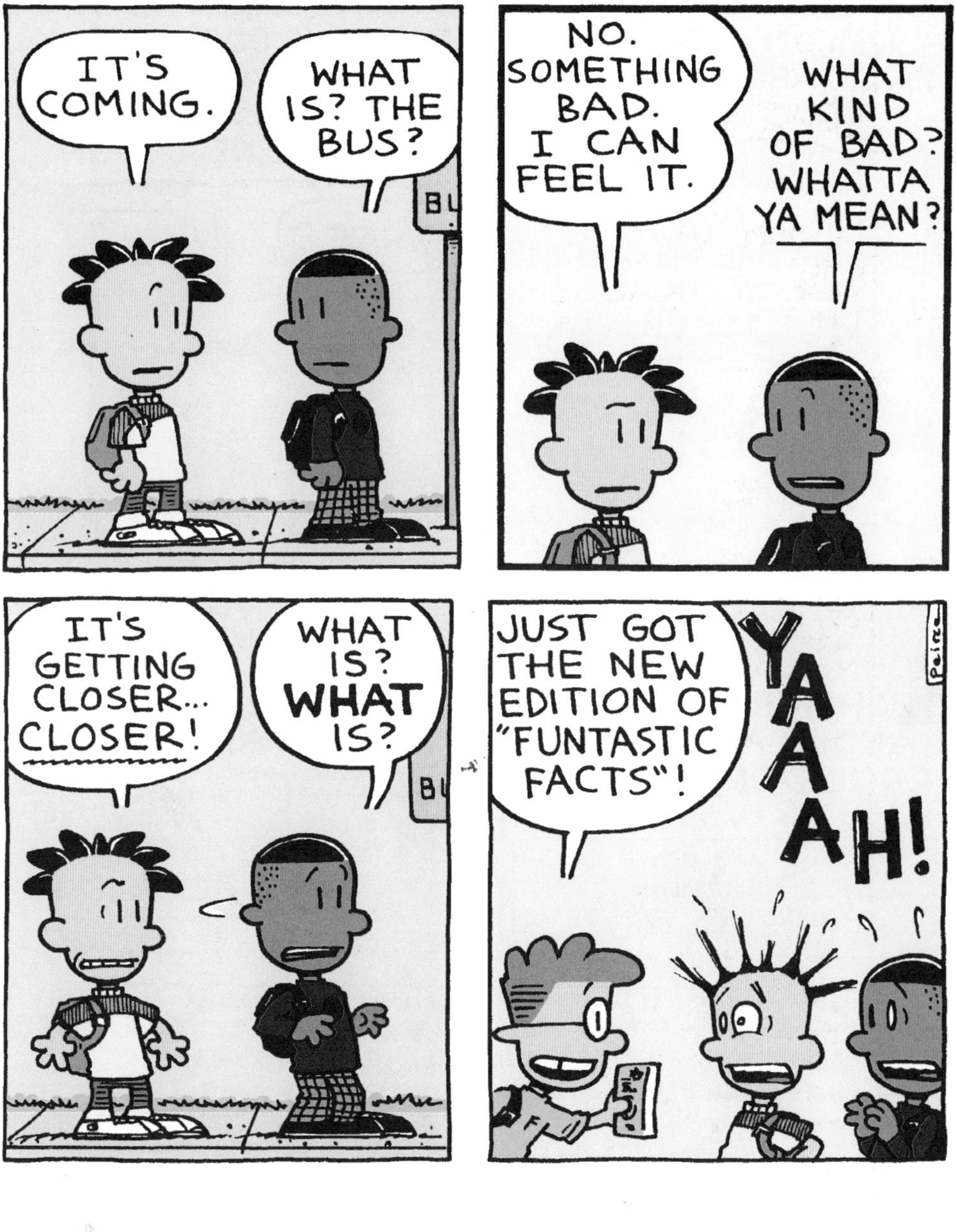
IT'S COMING.
WHAT IS? THE BUS?
NO. SOMETHING BAD. I CAN FEEL IT.
WHAT KIND OF BAD? WHATTA YA MEAN?
IT'S GETTING CLOSER... CLOSER!
WHAT IS? WHAT IS?
JUST GOT THE NEW EDITION OF "FUNTASTIC FACTS"!
YAAAAH!
Peirce

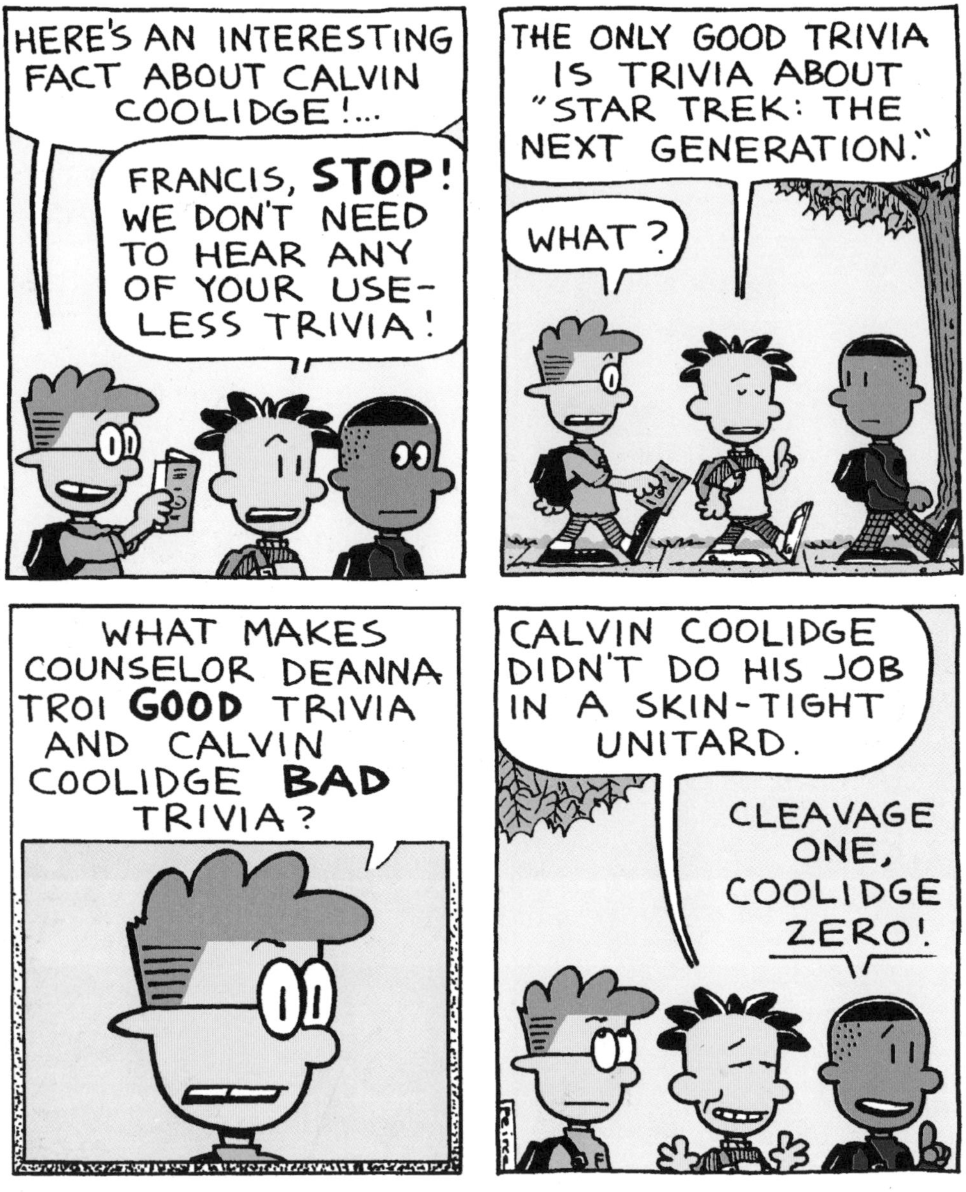
HERE'S AN INTERESTING FACT ABOUT CALVIN COOLIDGE!...
FRANCIS, **STOP**! WE DON'T NEED TO HEAR ANY OF YOUR USELESS TRIVIA!
THE ONLY GOOD TRIVIA IS TRIVIA ABOUT "STAR TREK: THE NEXT GENERATION."
WHAT?
WHAT MAKES COUNSELOR DEANNA TROI **GOOD** TRIVIA AND CALVIN COOLIDGE **BAD** TRIVIA?
CALVIN COOLIDGE DIDN'T DO HIS JOB IN A SKIN-TIGHT UNITARD.
CLEAVAGE ONE, COOLIDGE ZERO!

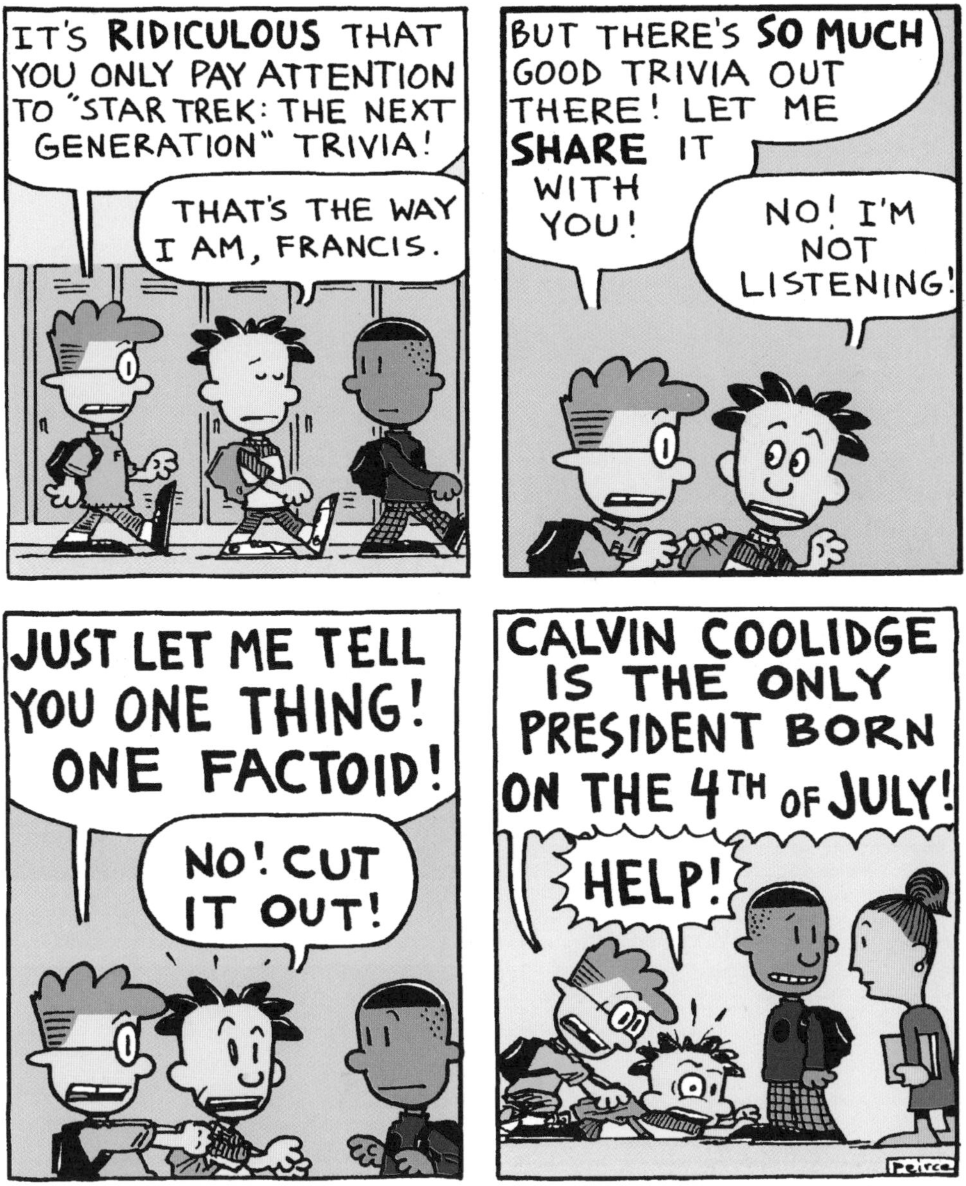
IT'S RIDICULOUS THAT YOU ONLY PAY ATTENTION TO "STAR TREK: THE NEXT GENERATION" TRIVIA!
THAT'S THE WAY I AM, FRANCIS.
BUT THERE'S SO MUCH GOOD TRIVIA OUT THERE! LET ME SHARE IT WITH YOU!
NO! I'M NOT LISTENING!
JUST LET ME TELL YOU ONE THING! ONE FACTOID!
NO! CUT IT OUT!
CALVIN COOLIDGE IS THE ONLY PRESIDENT BORN ON THE 4TH OF JULY!
HELP!
Peirce

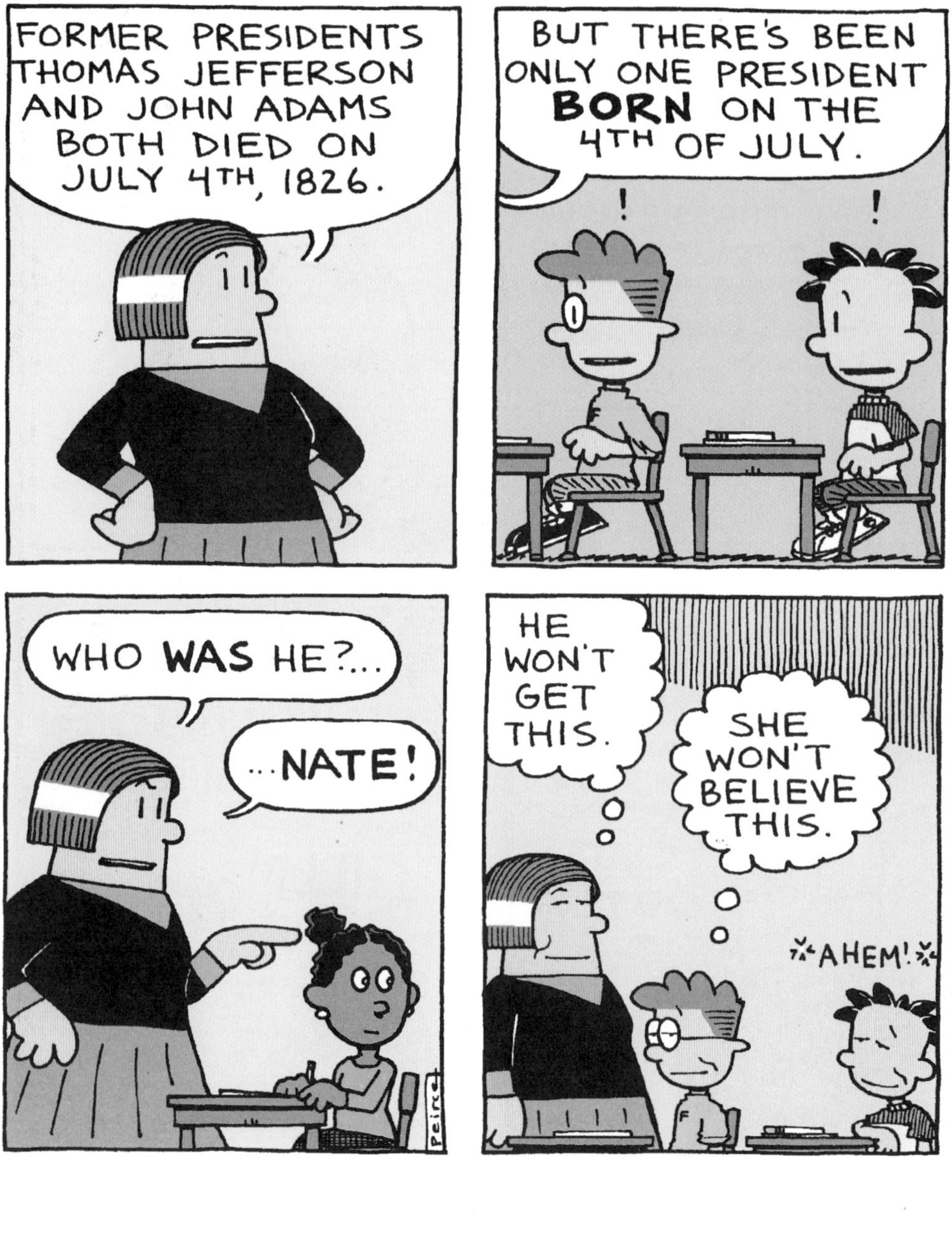
FORMER PRESIDENTS THOMAS JEFFERSON AND JOHN ADAMS BOTH DIED ON JULY 4TH, 1826.
BUT THERE'S BEEN ONLY ONE PRESIDENT **BORN** ON THE 4TH OF JULY.
!
!
WHO **WAS** HE?...
...**NATE!**
HE WON'T GET THIS.
SHE WON'T BELIEVE THIS.
AHEM!

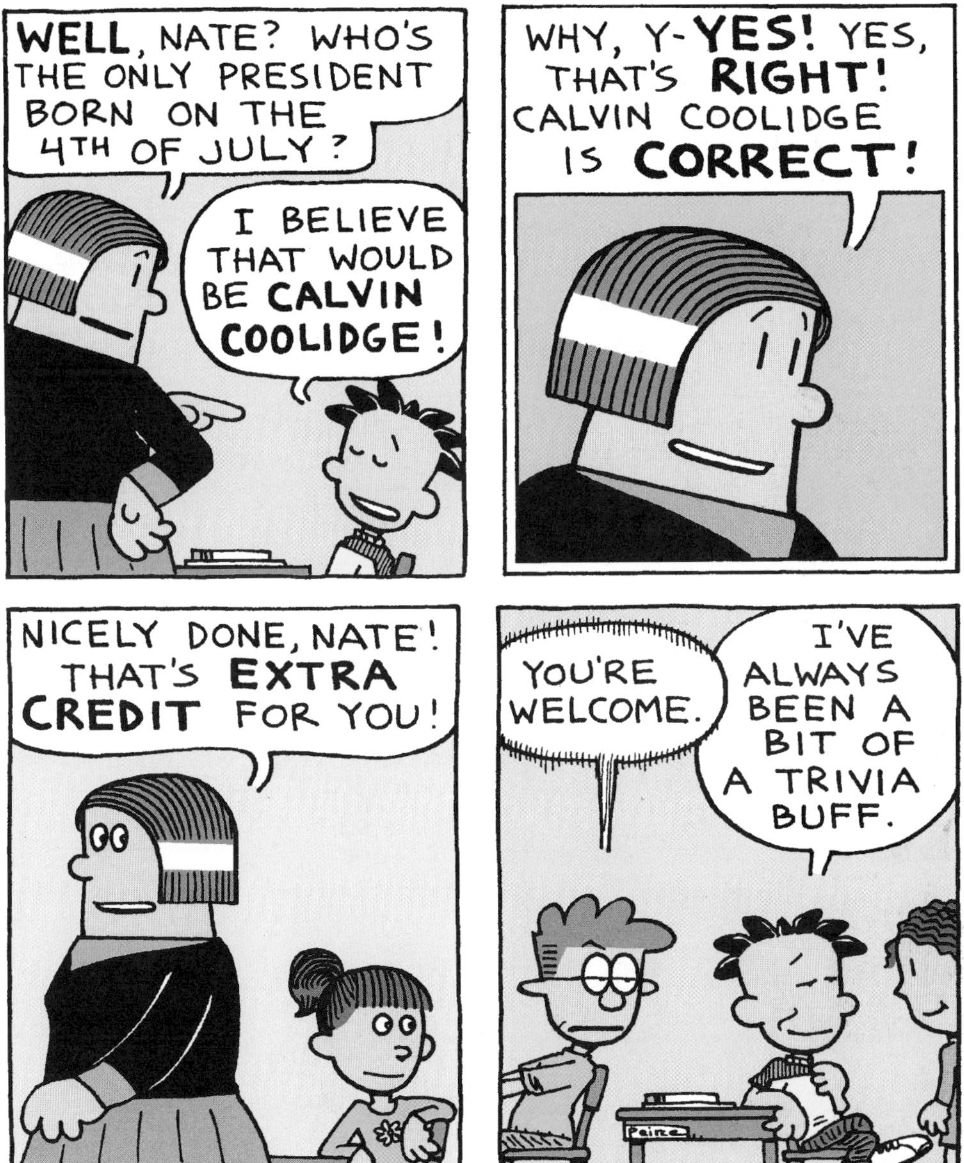
WELL, NATE? WHO'S THE ONLY PRESIDENT BORN ON THE 4TH OF JULY?
I BELIEVE THAT WOULD BE CALVIN COOLIDGE!
WHY, Y-YES! YES, THAT'S RIGHT! CALVIN COOLIDGE IS CORRECT!
NICELY DONE, NATE! THAT'S EXTRA CREDIT FOR YOU!
YOU'RE WELCOME.
I'VE ALWAYS BEEN A BIT OF A TRIVIA BUFF.

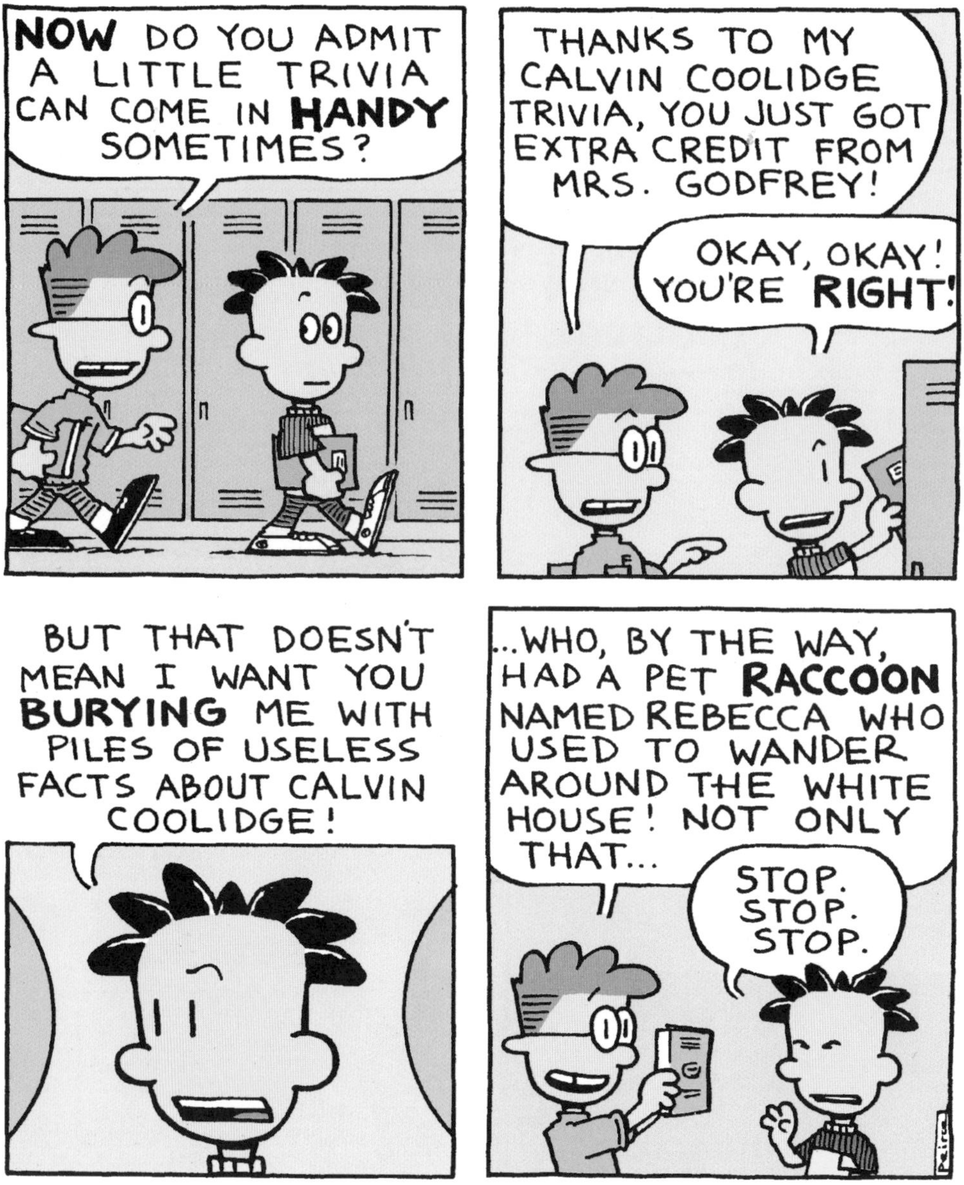
NOW DO YOU ADMIT A LITTLE TRIVIA CAN COME IN HANDY SOMETIMES?
THANKS TO MY CALVIN COOLIDGE TRIVIA, YOU JUST GOT EXTRA CREDIT FROM MRS. GODFREY!
OKAY, OKAY! YOU'RE RIGHT!
BUT THAT DOESN'T MEAN I WANT YOU BURYING ME WITH PILES OF USELESS FACTS ABOUT CALVIN COOLIDGE!
...WHO, BY THE WAY, HAD A PET RACCOON NAMED REBECCA WHO USED TO WANDER AROUND THE WHITE HOUSE! NOT ONLY THAT...
STOP. STOP. STOP.
Peirce

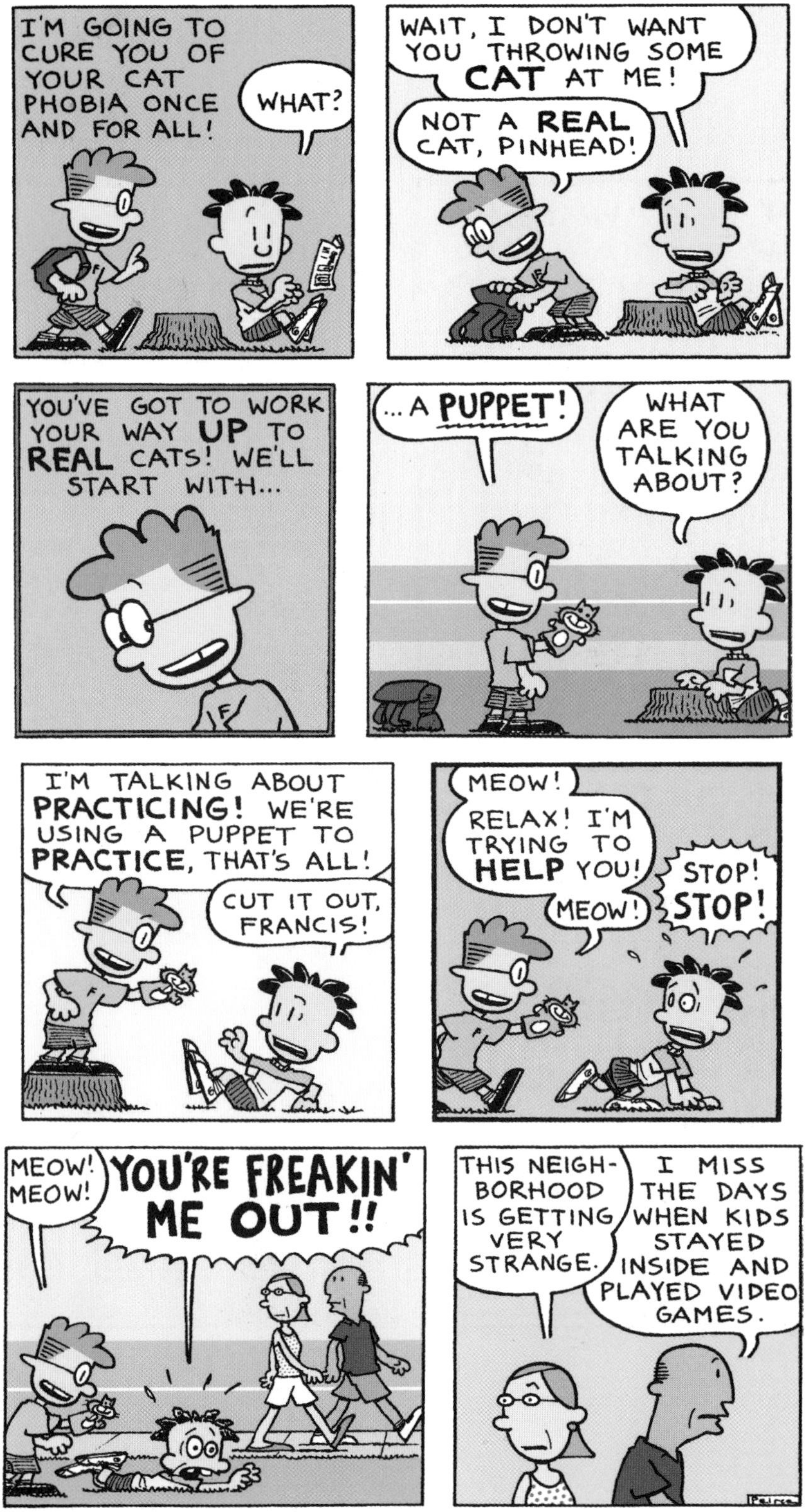
I'M GOING TO CURE YOU OF YOUR CAT PHOBIA ONCE AND FOR ALL!
WHAT?
WAIT, I DON'T WANT YOU THROWING SOME **CAT** AT ME!
NOT A **REAL** CAT, PINHEAD!
YOU'VE GOT TO WORK YOUR WAY **UP** TO **REAL** CATS! WE'LL START WITH...
... A PUPPET!
WHAT ARE YOU TALKING ABOUT?
I'M TALKING ABOUT **PRACTICING!** WE'RE USING A PUPPET TO **PRACTICE**, THAT'S ALL!
CUT IT OUT, FRANCIS!
MEOW!
RELAX! I'M TRYING TO **HELP** YOU!
MEOW!
STOP! **STOP!**
MEOW! MEOW!
YOU'RE FREAKIN' ME OUT!!
THIS NEIGHBORHOOD IS GETTING VERY STRANGE.
I MISS THE DAYS WHEN KIDS STAYED INSIDE AND PLAYED VIDEO GAMES.
Peirce

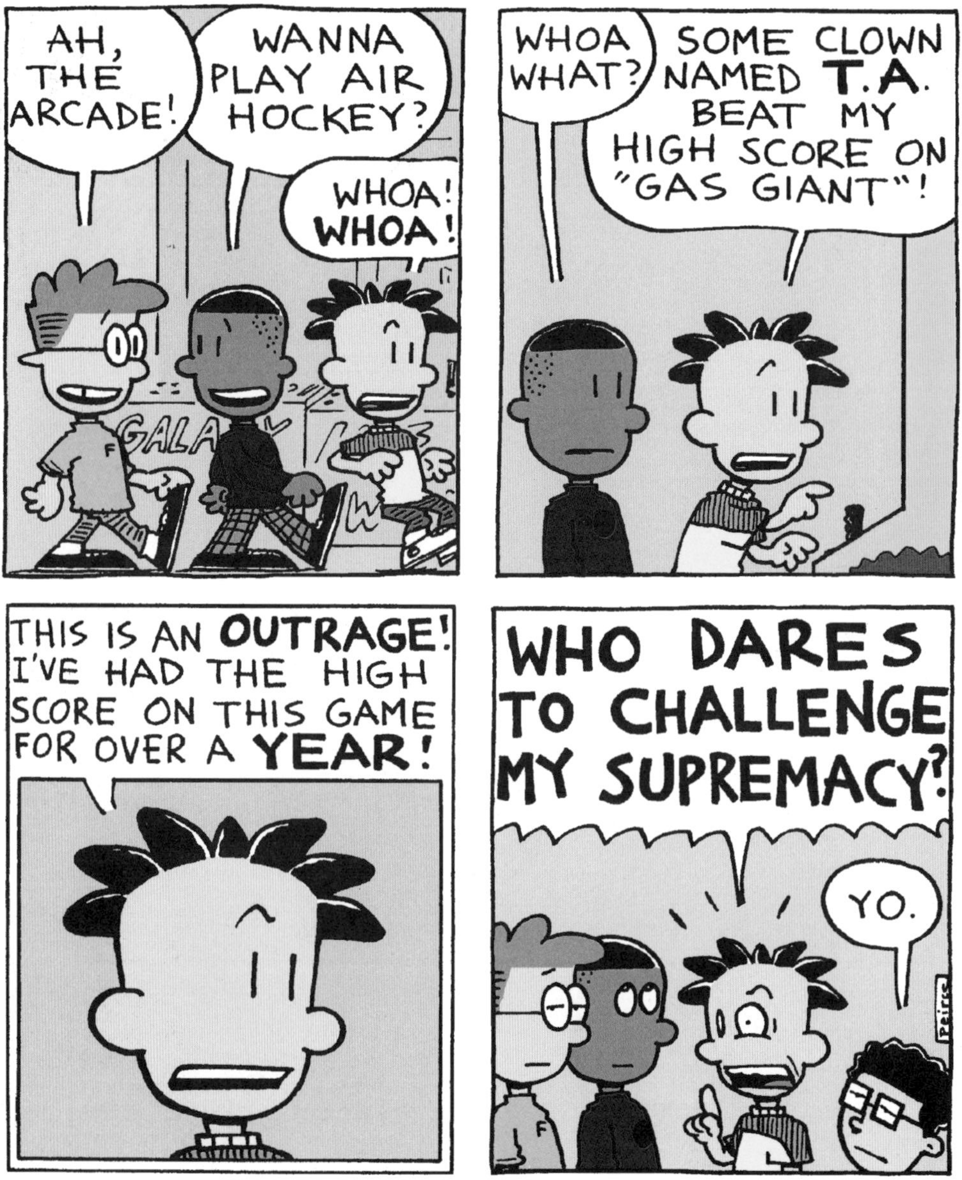
AH, THE ARCADE!
WANNA PLAY AIR HOCKEY?
WHOA! **WHOA**!
GALA
WHOA WHAT?
SOME CLOWN NAMED **T.A.** BEAT MY HIGH SCORE ON "GAS GIANT"!
THIS IS AN **OUTRAGE**! I'VE HAD THE HIGH SCORE ON THIS GAME FOR OVER A **YEAR**!
WHO DARES TO CHALLENGE MY SUPREMACY?
YO.
Peirce

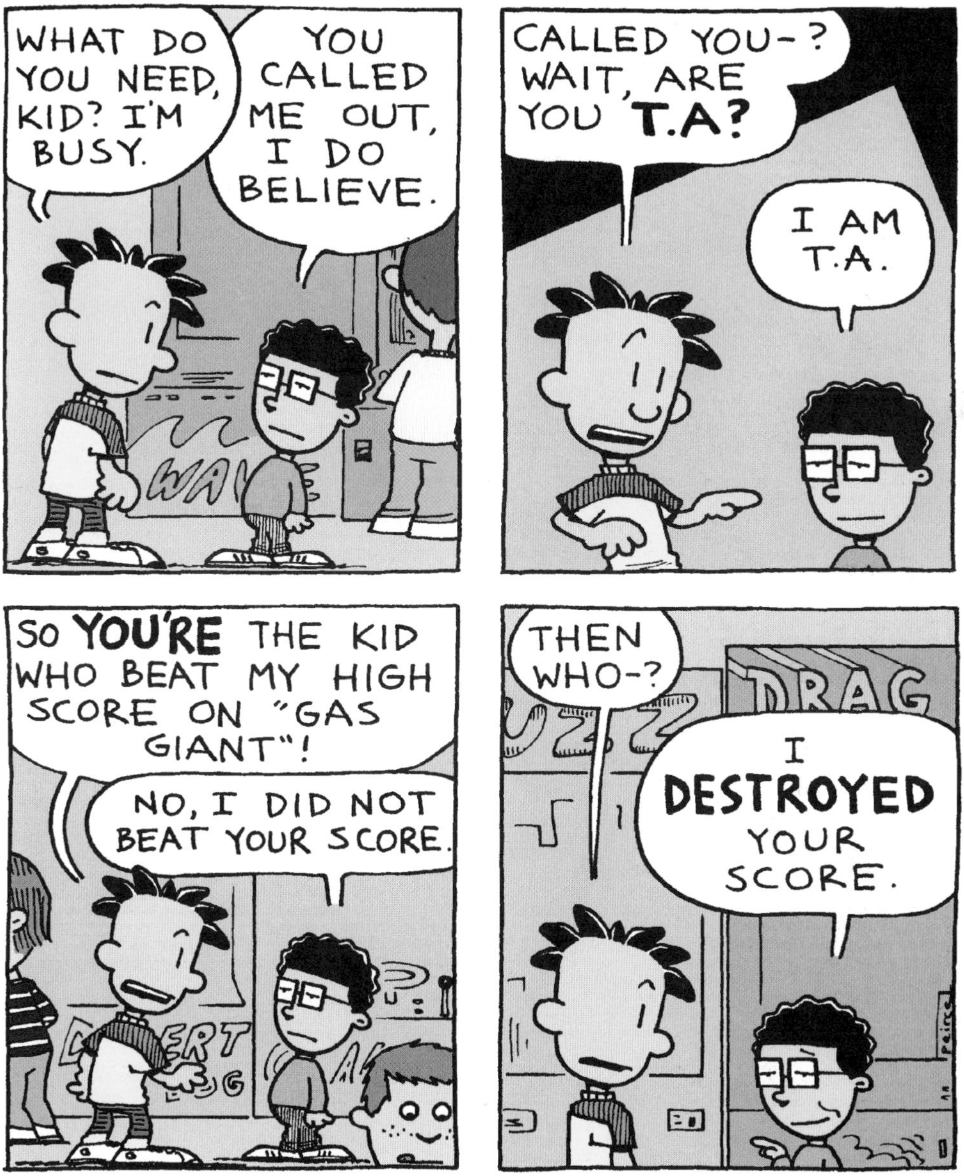
WHAT DO YOU NEED, KID? I'M BUSY.
YOU CALLED ME OUT, I DO BELIEVE.
CALLED YOU-? WAIT, ARE YOU **T.A?**
I AM T.A.
SO **YOU'RE** THE KID WHO BEAT MY HIGH SCORE ON "GAS GIANT"!
NO, I DID NOT BEAT YOUR SCORE.
THEN WHO-?
DRAG
I **DESTROYED** YOUR SCORE.

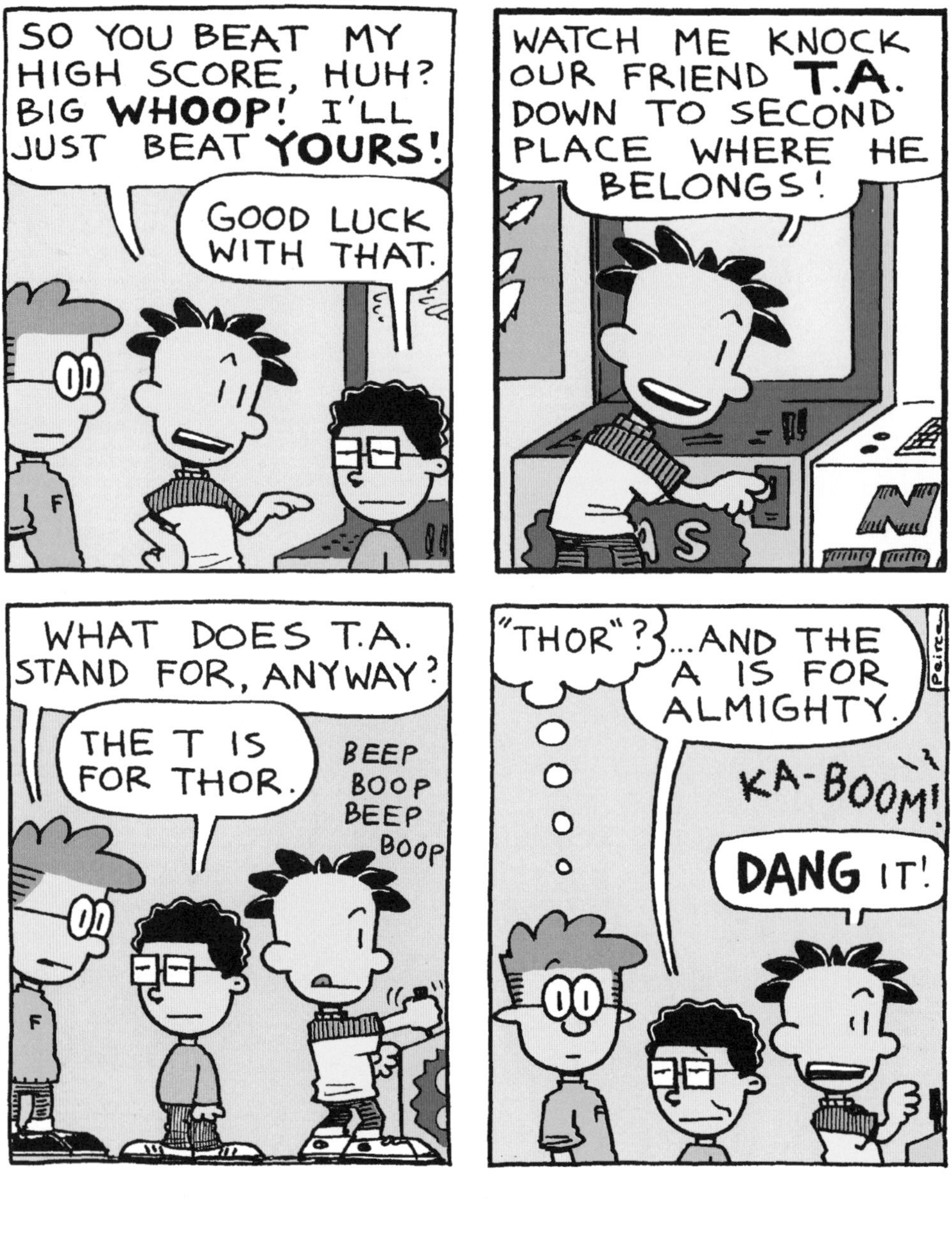
SO YOU BEAT MY HIGH SCORE, HUH? BIG WHOOP! I'LL JUST BEAT YOURS!
GOOD LUCK WITH THAT.
WATCH ME KNOCK OUR FRIEND T.A. DOWN TO SECOND PLACE WHERE HE BELONGS!
WHAT DOES T.A. STAND FOR, ANYWAY?
THE T IS FOR THOR.
BEEP BOOP BEEP BOOP
"THOR"?
...AND THE A IS FOR ALMIGHTY.
KA-BOOM!
DANG IT!
Peirce

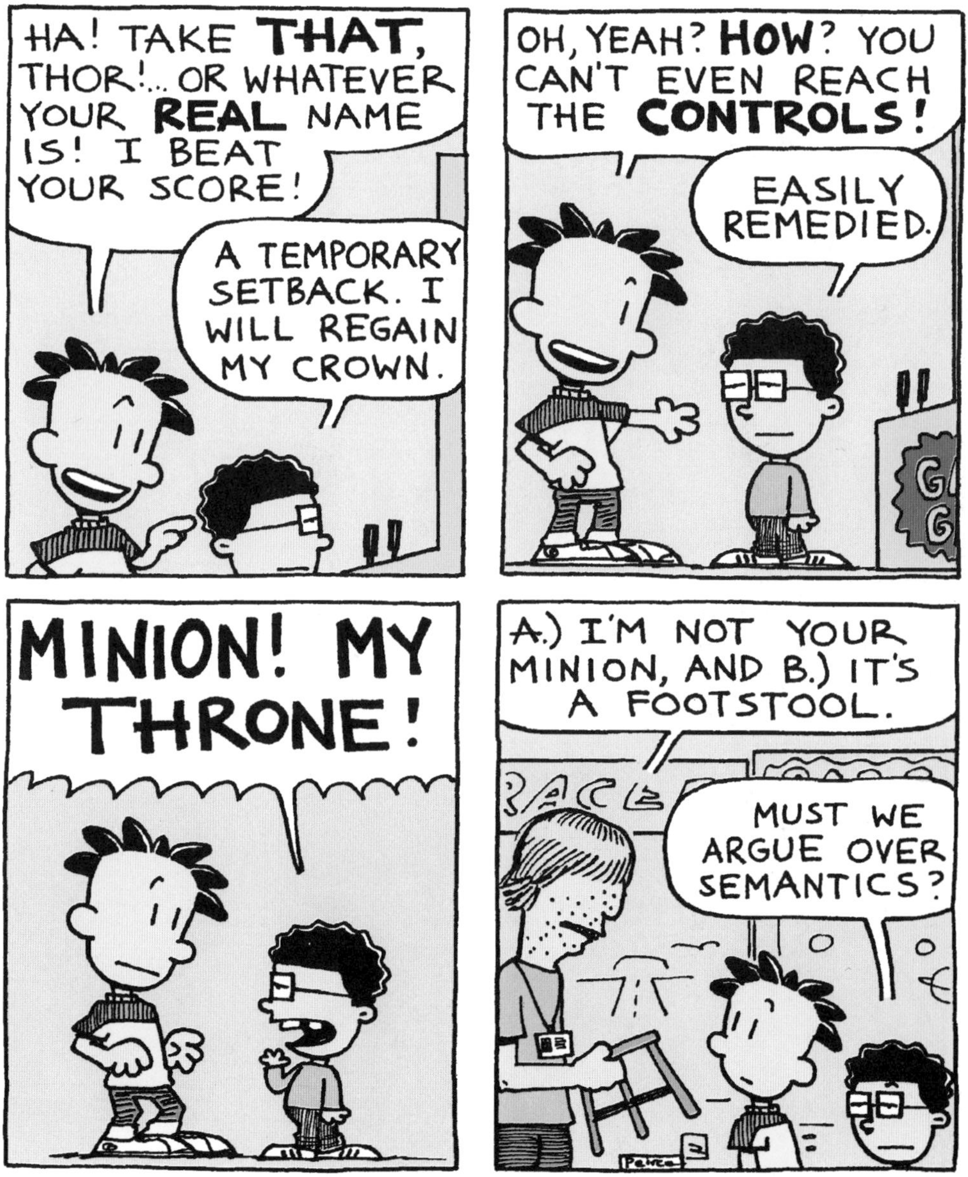
HA! TAKE THAT, THOR!... OR WHATEVER YOUR REAL NAME IS! I BEAT YOUR SCORE!
A TEMPORARY SETBACK. I WILL REGAIN MY CROWN.
OH, YEAH? HOW? YOU CAN'T EVEN REACH THE CONTROLS!
EASILY REMEDIED.
MINION! MY THRONE!
A.) I'M NOT YOUR MINION, AND B.) IT'S A FOOTSTOOL.
MUST WE ARGUE OVER SEMANTICS?

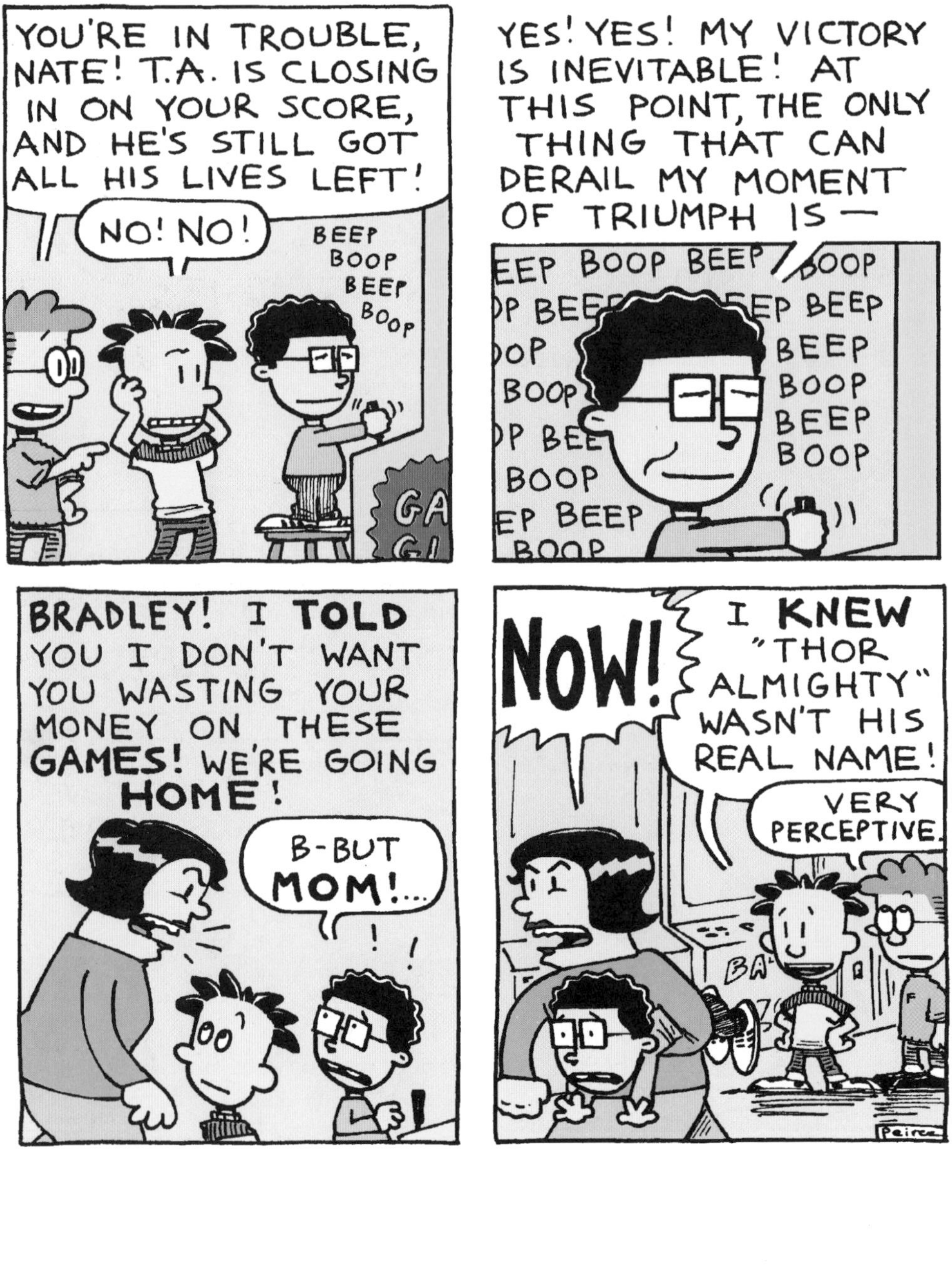

YOU'RE IN TROUBLE, NATE! T.A. IS CLOSING IN ON YOUR SCORE, AND HE'S STILL GOT ALL HIS LIVES LEFT!
NO! NO!
BEEP BOOP BEEP BOOP
YES! YES! MY VICTORY IS INEVITABLE! AT THIS POINT, THE ONLY THING THAT CAN DERAIL MY MOMENT OF TRIUMPH IS—
BRADLEY! I TOLD YOU I DON'T WANT YOU WASTING YOUR MONEY ON THESE GAMES! WE'RE GOING HOME!
B-BUT MOM!...
NOW!
I KNEW "THOR ALMIGHTY" WASN'T HIS REAL NAME!
VERY PERCEPTIVE.
Peirce

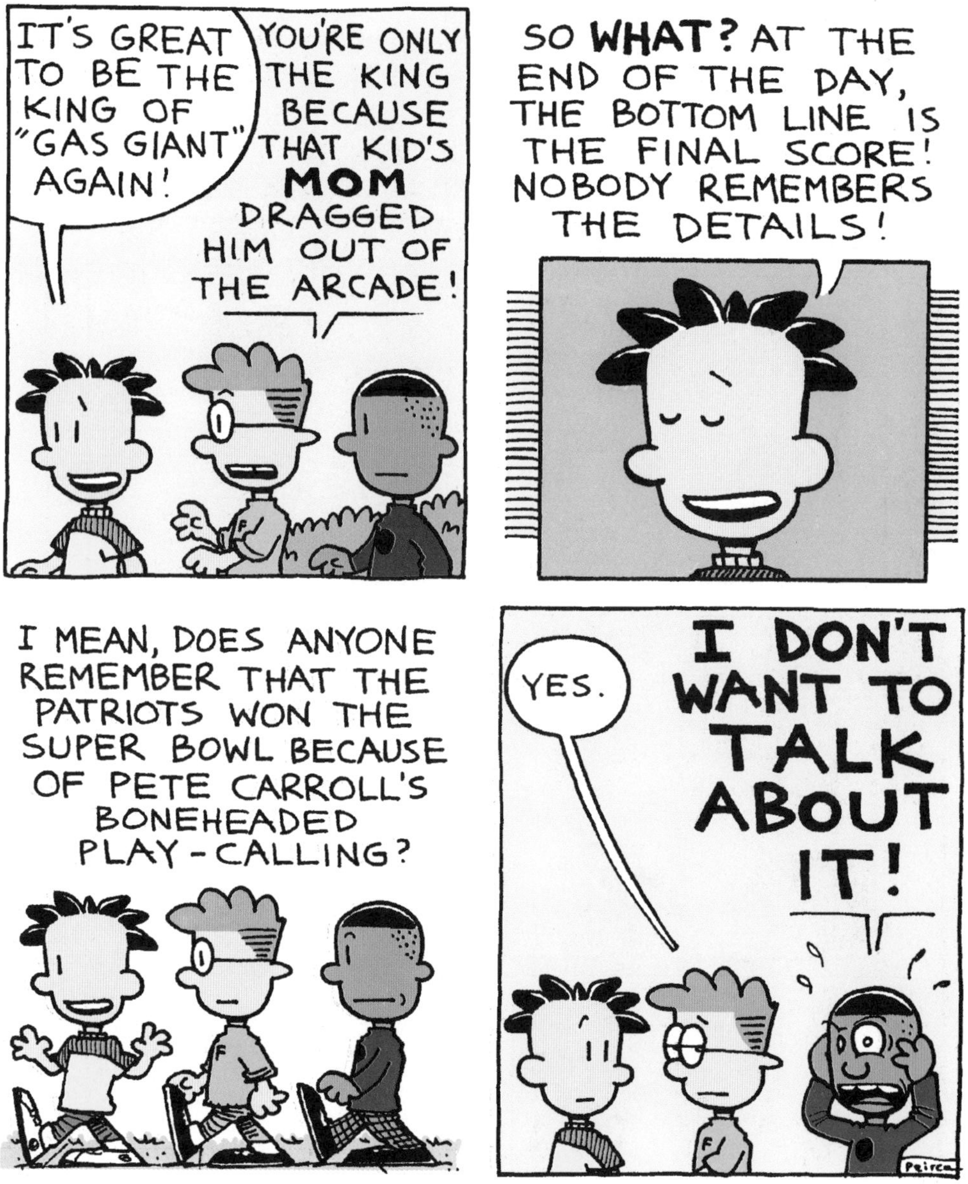
IT'S GREAT TO BE THE KING OF "GAS GIANT" AGAIN!
YOU'RE ONLY THE KING BECAUSE THAT KID'S **MOM** DRAGGED HIM OUT OF THE ARCADE!
SO **WHAT?** AT THE END OF THE DAY, THE BOTTOM LINE IS THE FINAL SCORE! NOBODY REMEMBERS THE DETAILS!
I MEAN, DOES ANYONE REMEMBER THAT THE PATRIOTS WON THE SUPER BOWL BECAUSE OF PETE CARROLL'S BONEHEADED PLAY-CALLING?
YES.
I DON'T WANT TO TALK ABOUT IT!
Peirce

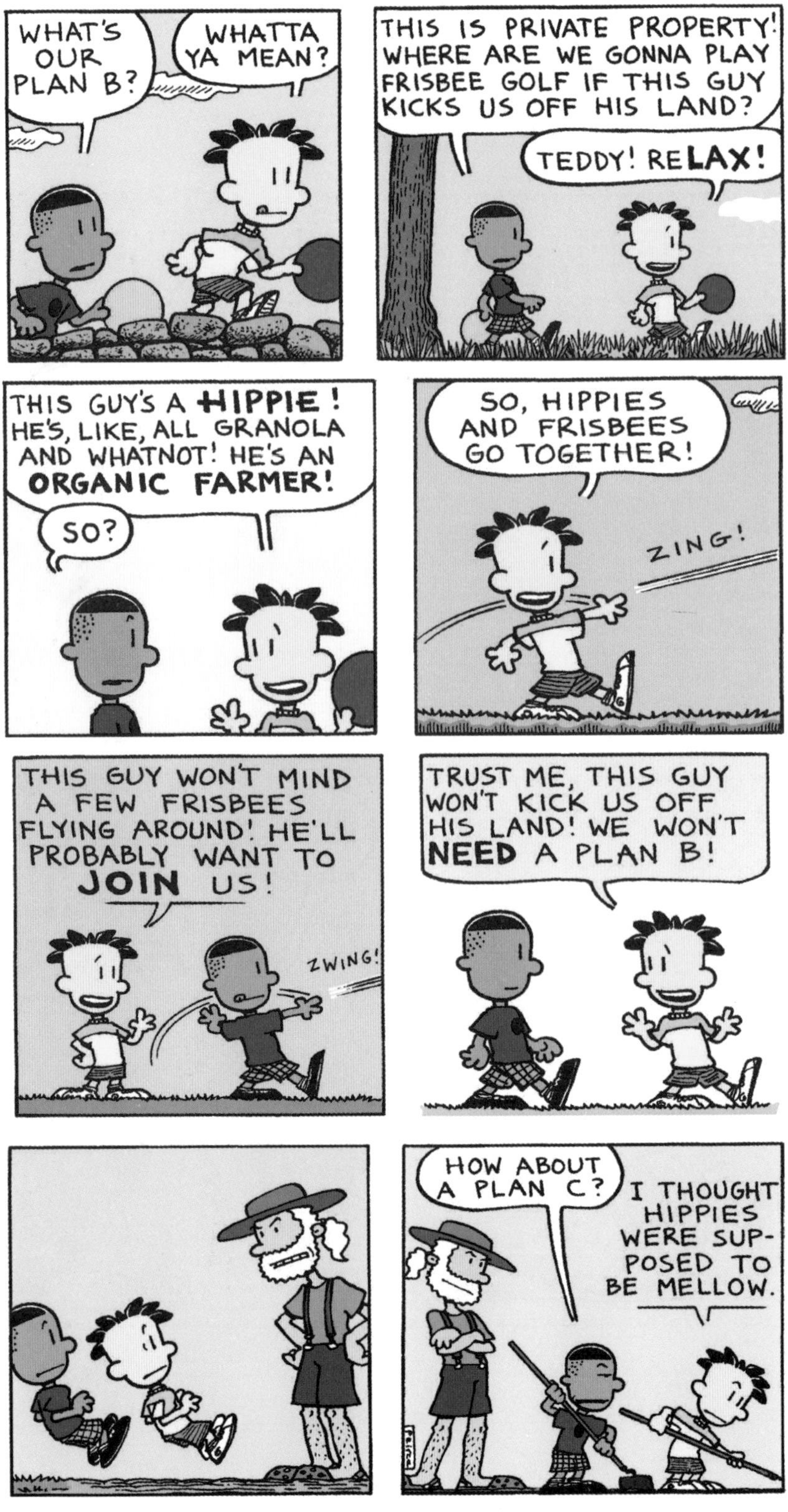
WHAT'S OUR PLAN B?
WHATTA YA MEAN?
THIS IS PRIVATE PROPERTY! WHERE ARE WE GONNA PLAY FRISBEE GOLF IF THIS GUY KICKS US OFF HIS LAND?
TEDDY! RELAX!
THIS GUY'S A HIPPIE! HE'S, LIKE, ALL GRANOLA AND WHATNOT! HE'S AN ORGANIC FARMER!
SO?
SO, HIPPIES AND FRISBEES GO TOGETHER!
ZING!
THIS GUY WON'T MIND A FEW FRISBEES FLYING AROUND! HE'LL PROBABLY WANT TO JOIN US!
ZWING!
TRUST ME, THIS GUY WON'T KICK US OFF HIS LAND! WE WON'T NEED A PLAN B!
HOW ABOUT A PLAN C?
I THOUGHT HIPPIES WERE SUPPOSED TO BE MELLOW.

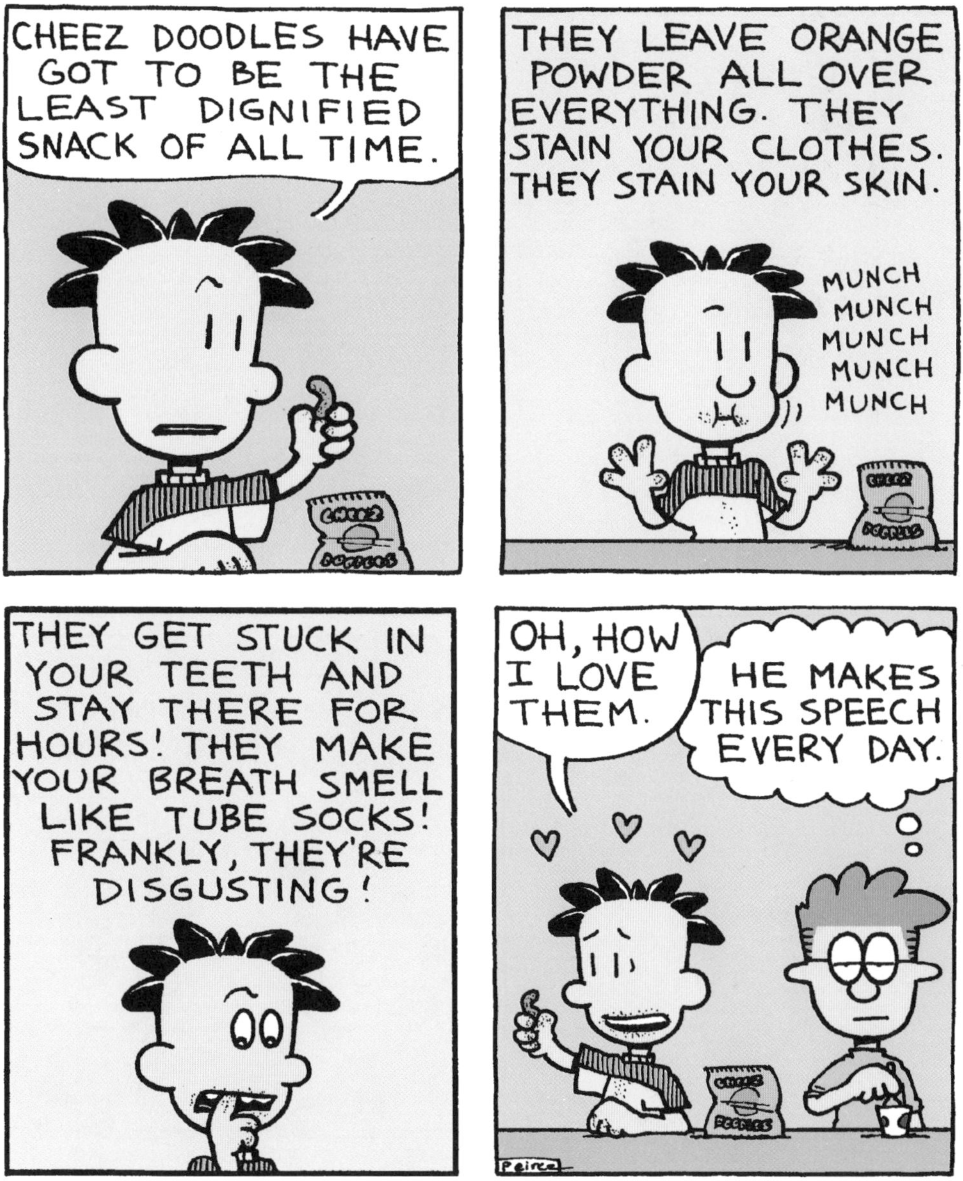
CHEEZ DOODLES HAVE GOT TO BE THE LEAST DIGNIFIED SNACK OF ALL TIME.
THEY LEAVE ORANGE POWDER ALL OVER EVERYTHING. THEY STAIN YOUR CLOTHES. THEY STAIN YOUR SKIN.
MUNCH MUNCH MUNCH MUNCH MUNCH
THEY GET STUCK IN YOUR TEETH AND STAY THERE FOR HOURS! THEY MAKE YOUR BREATH SMELL LIKE TUBE SOCKS! FRANKLY, THEY'RE DISGUSTING!
OH, HOW I LOVE THEM.
HE MAKES THIS SPEECH EVERY DAY.
Peirce

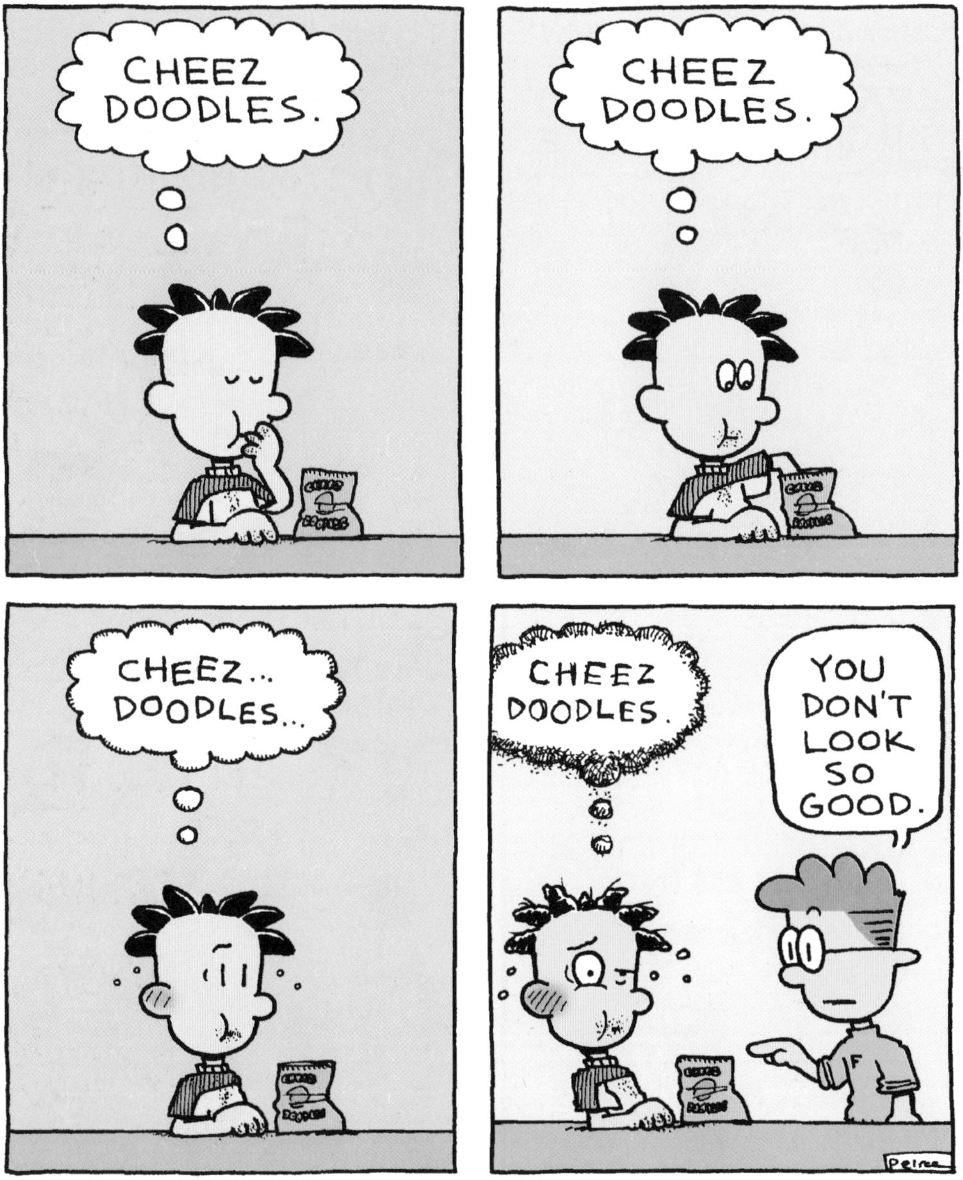
CHEEZ DOODLES.
CHEEZ DOODLES.
CHEEZ... DOODLES...
CHEEZ DOODLES.
YOU DON'T LOOK SO GOOD.
Peirce

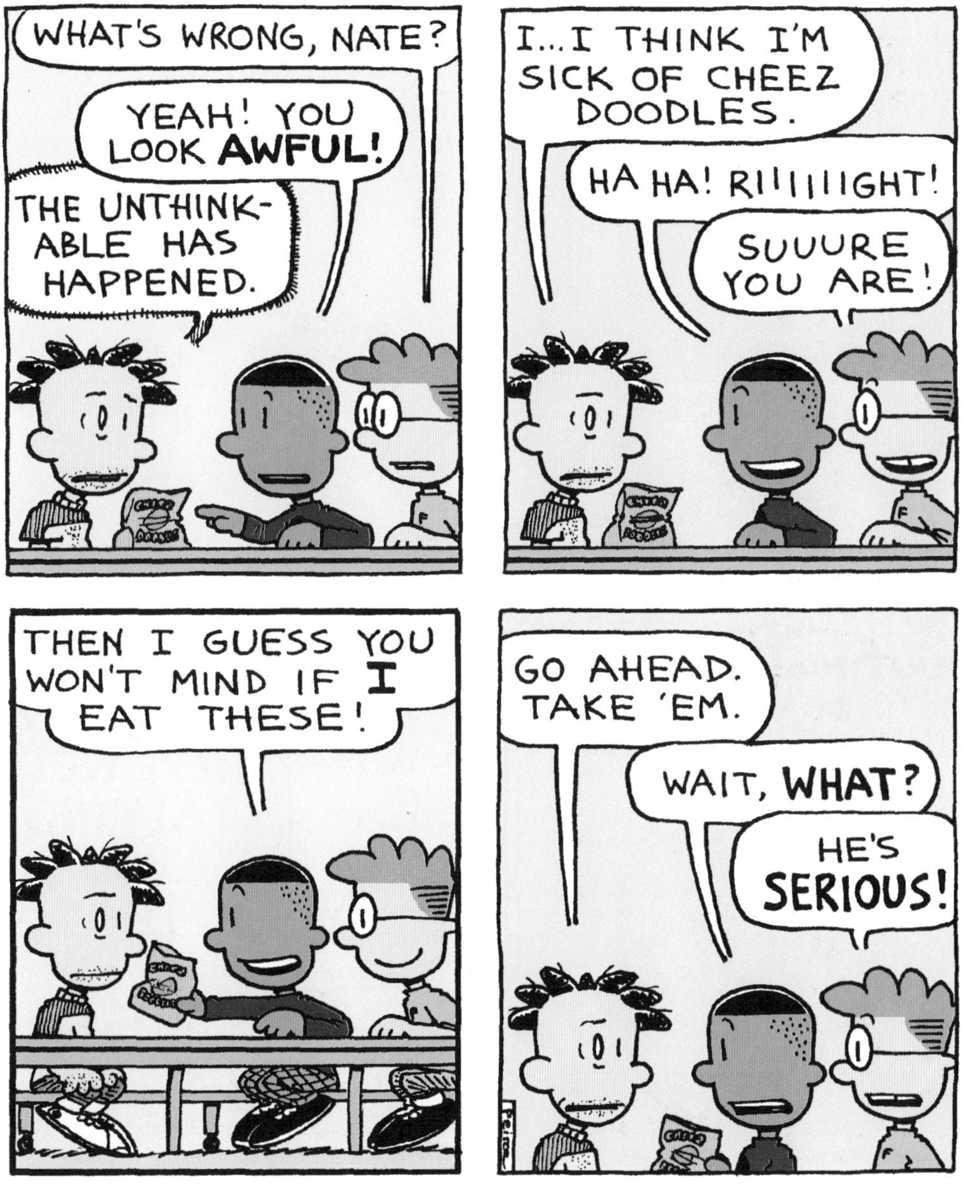

WHAT'S WRONG, NATE?
YEAH! YOU LOOK **AWFUL!**
THE UNTHINK-ABLE HAS HAPPENED.
I...I THINK I'M SICK OF CHEEZ DOODLES.
HA HA! RIIIIIIGHT!
SUUURE YOU ARE!
THEN I GUESS YOU WON'T MIND IF **I** EAT THESE!
GO AHEAD. TAKE 'EM.
WAIT, **WHAT?**
HE'S **SERIOUS!**

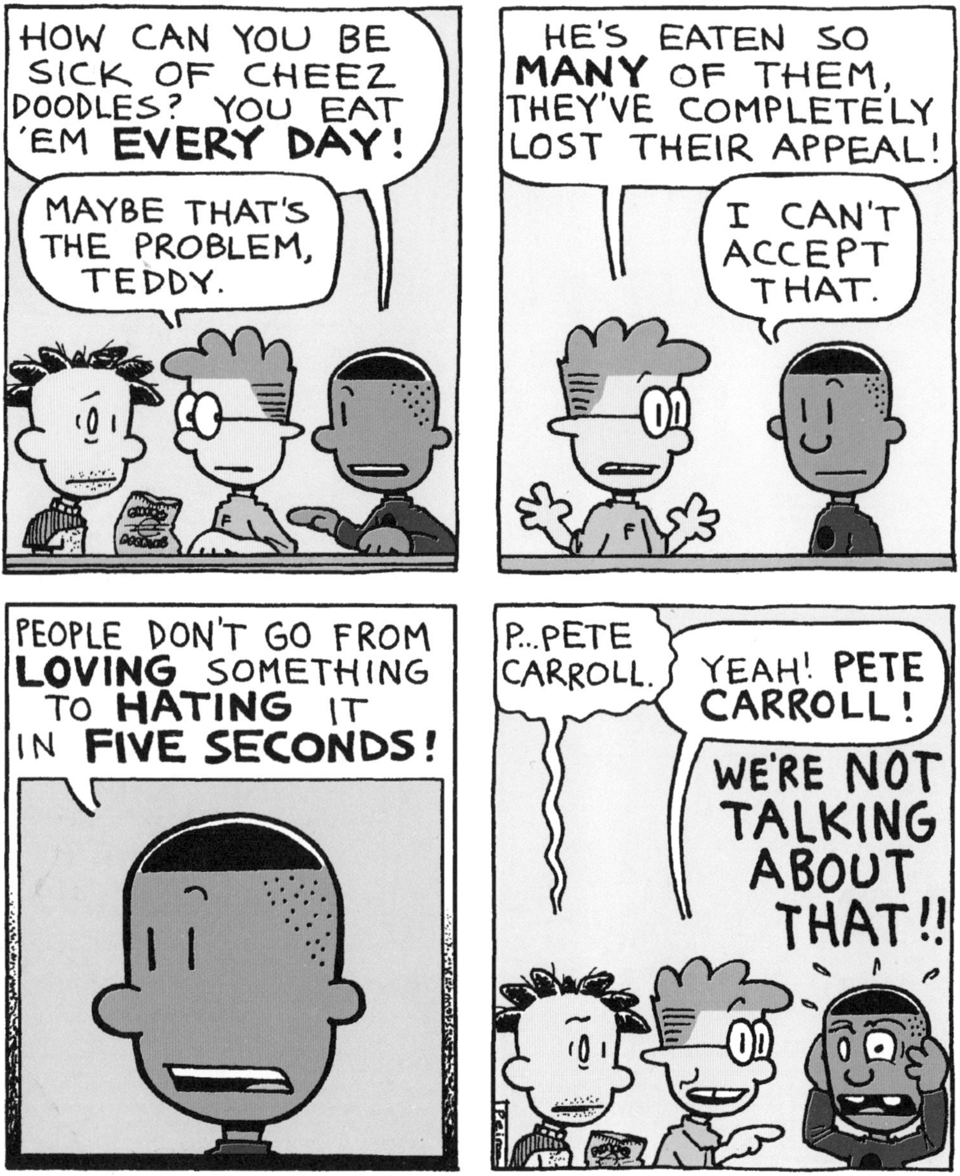

HOW CAN YOU BE SICK OF CHEEZ DOODLES? YOU EAT 'EM EVERY DAY!
MAYBE THAT'S THE PROBLEM, TEDDY.
HE'S EATEN SO MANY OF THEM, THEY'VE COMPLETELY LOST THEIR APPEAL!
I CAN'T ACCEPT THAT.
PEOPLE DON'T GO FROM LOVING SOMETHING TO HATING IT IN FIVE SECONDS!
P...PETE CARROLL.
YEAH! PETE CARROLL!
WE'RE NOT TALKING ABOUT THAT!!

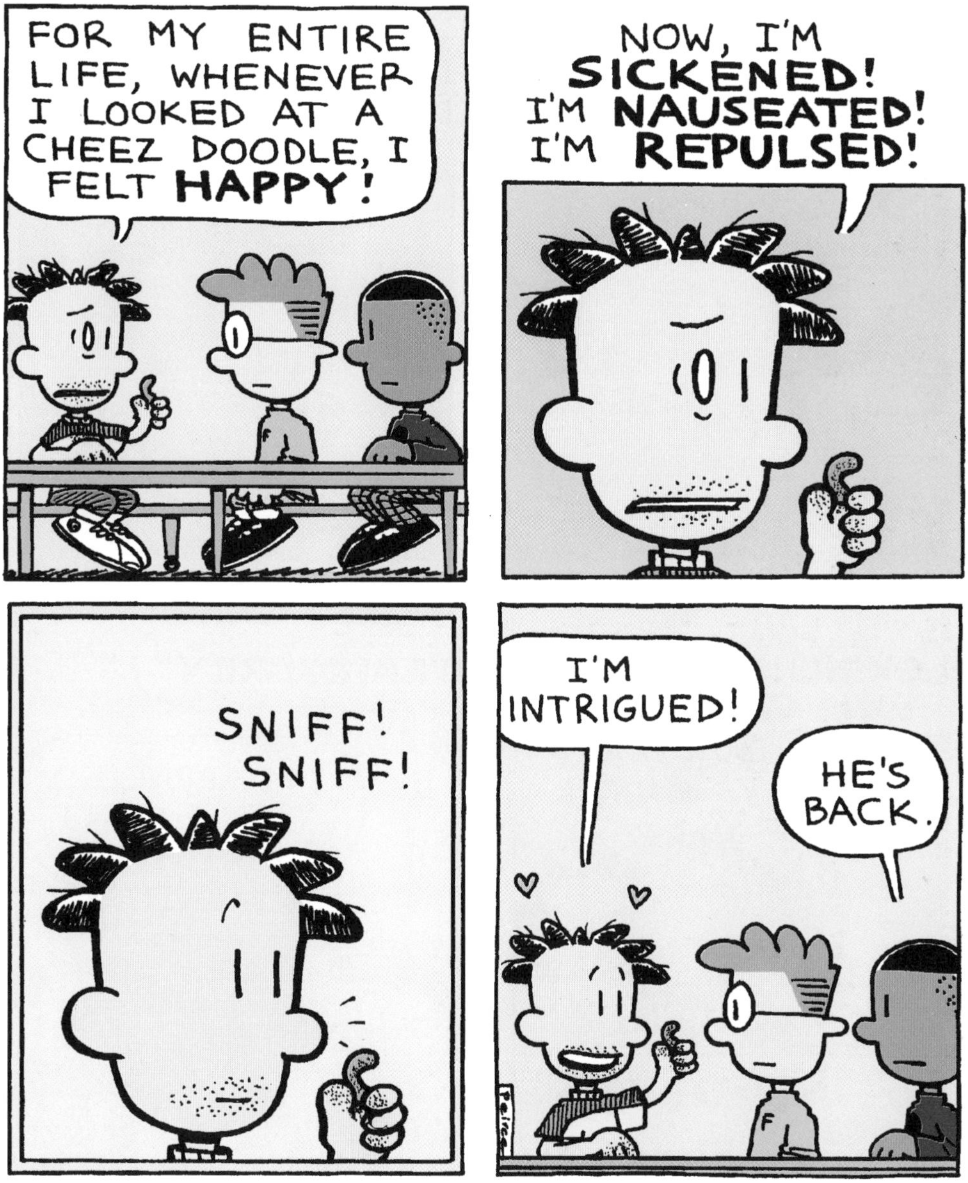
FOR MY ENTIRE LIFE, WHENEVER I LOOKED AT A CHEEZ DOODLE, I FELT **HAPPY**!
NOW, I'M **SICKENED**! I'M **NAUSEATED**! I'M **REPULSED**!
SNIFF! SNIFF!
I'M INTRIGUED!
HE'S BACK.

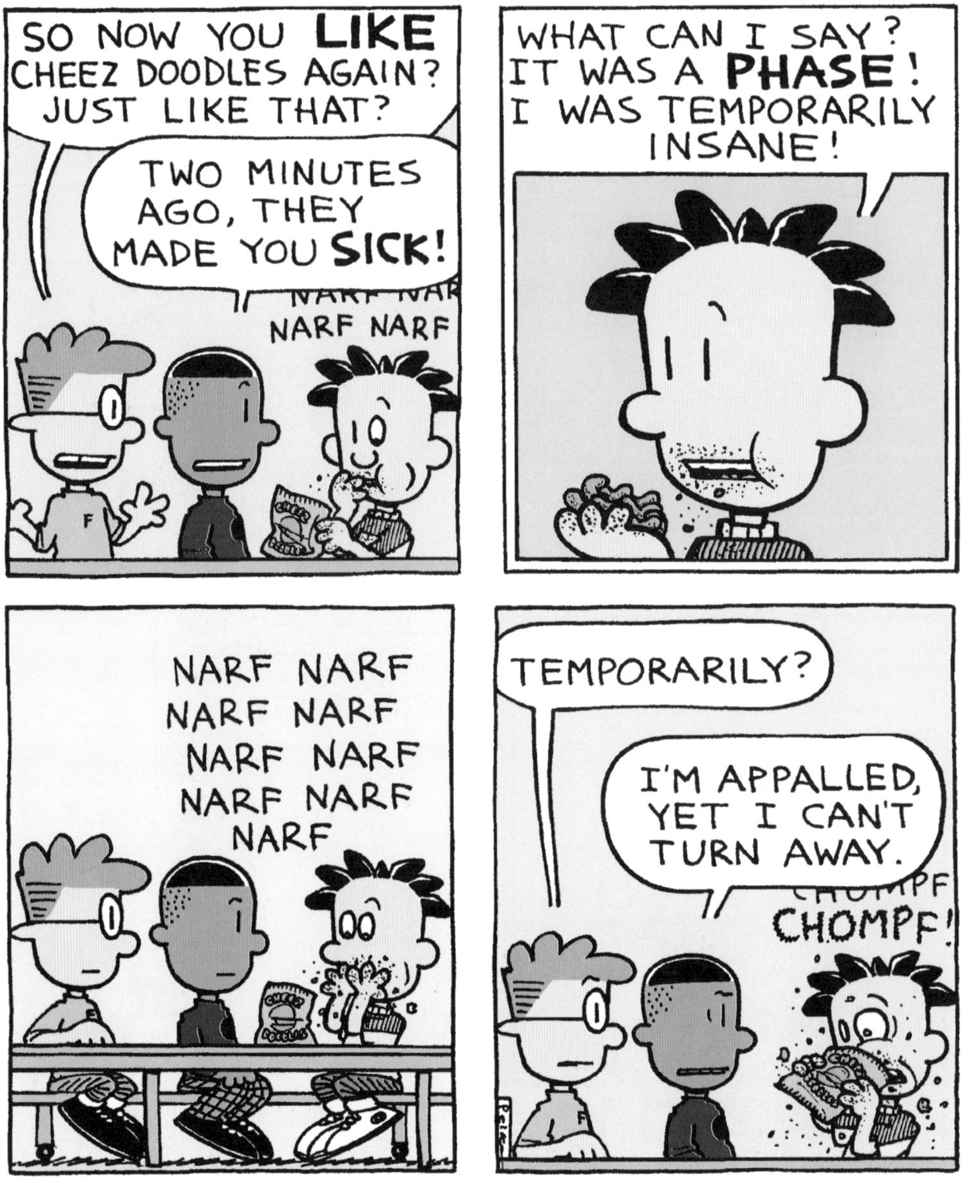

SO NOW YOU **LIKE** CHEEZ DOODLES AGAIN? JUST LIKE THAT?
TWO MINUTES AGO, THEY MADE YOU **SICK**!
NARF NARF
WHAT CAN I SAY? IT WAS A **PHASE**! I WAS TEMPORARILY INSANE!
NARF NARF NARF NARF NARF NARF NARF NARF NARF
TEMPORARILY?
I'M APPALLED, YET I CAN'T TURN AWAY.
CHOMPF!

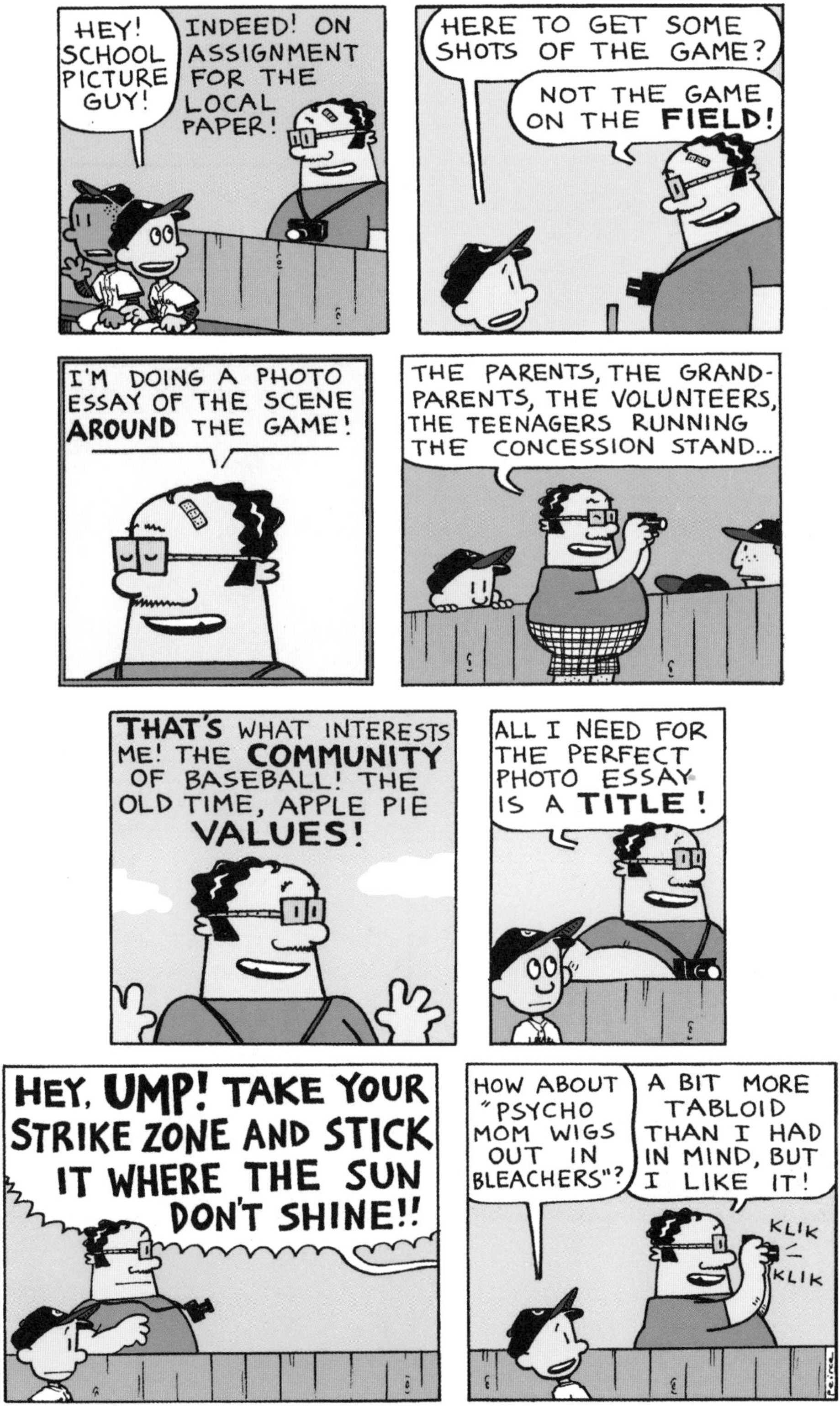
HEY! SCHOOL PICTURE GUY!
INDEED! ON ASSIGNMENT FOR THE LOCAL PAPER!
HERE TO GET SOME SHOTS OF THE GAME?
NOT THE GAME ON THE FIELD!
I'M DOING A PHOTO ESSAY OF THE SCENE AROUND THE GAME!
THE PARENTS, THE GRAND-PARENTS, THE VOLUNTEERS, THE TEENAGERS RUNNING THE CONCESSION STAND...
THAT'S WHAT INTERESTS ME! THE COMMUNITY OF BASEBALL! THE OLD TIME, APPLE PIE VALUES!
ALL I NEED FOR THE PERFECT PHOTO ESSAY IS A TITLE!
HEY, UMP! TAKE YOUR STRIKE ZONE AND STICK IT WHERE THE SUN DON'T SHINE!!
HOW ABOUT "PSYCHO MOM WIGS OUT IN BLEACHERS"?
A BIT MORE TABLOID THAN I HAD IN MIND, BUT I LIKE IT!
KLIK
KLIK

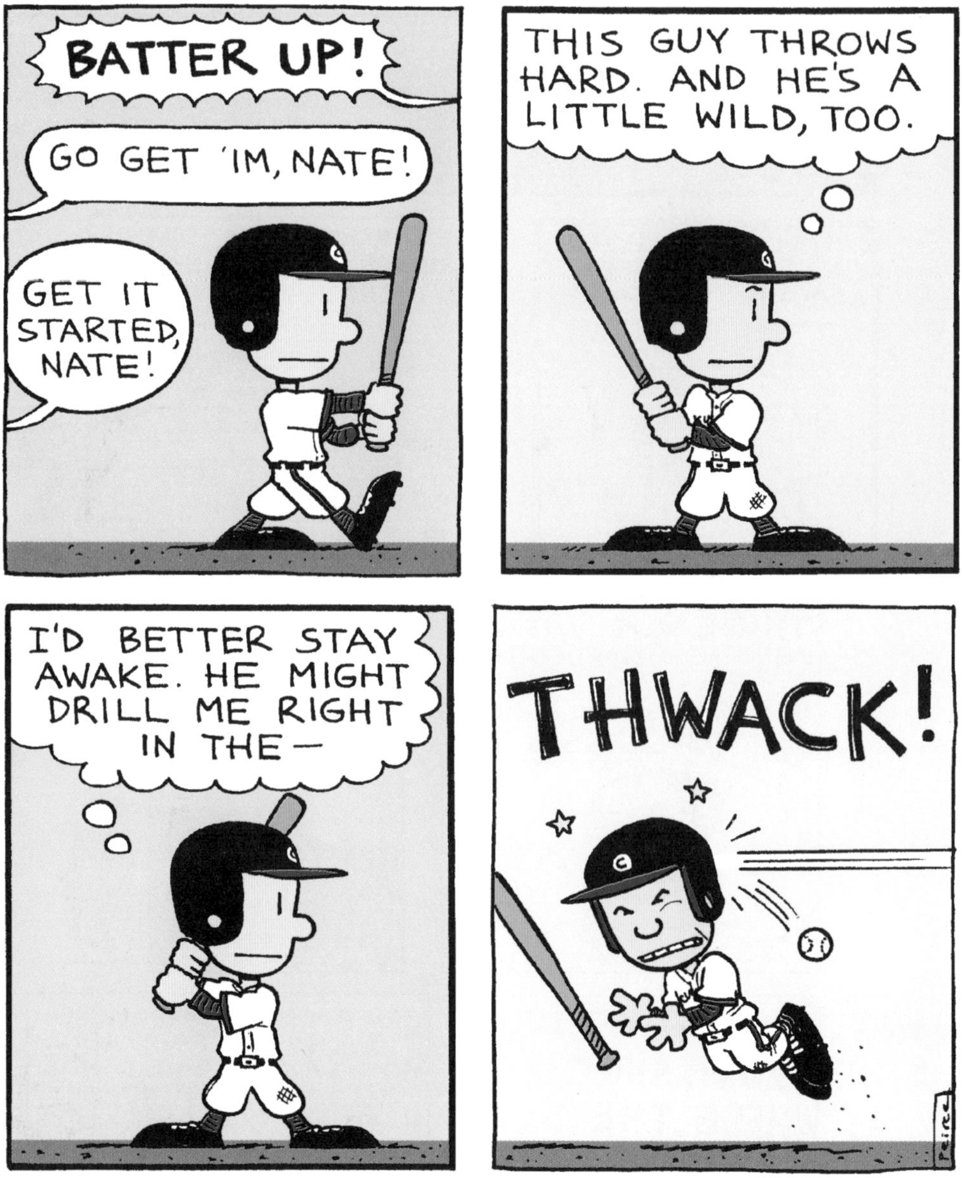
BATTER UP!
GO GET 'IM, NATE!
GET IT STARTED, NATE!
THIS GUY THROWS HARD. AND HE'S A LITTLE WILD, TOO.
I'D BETTER STAY AWAKE. HE MIGHT DRILL ME RIGHT IN THE—
THWACK!

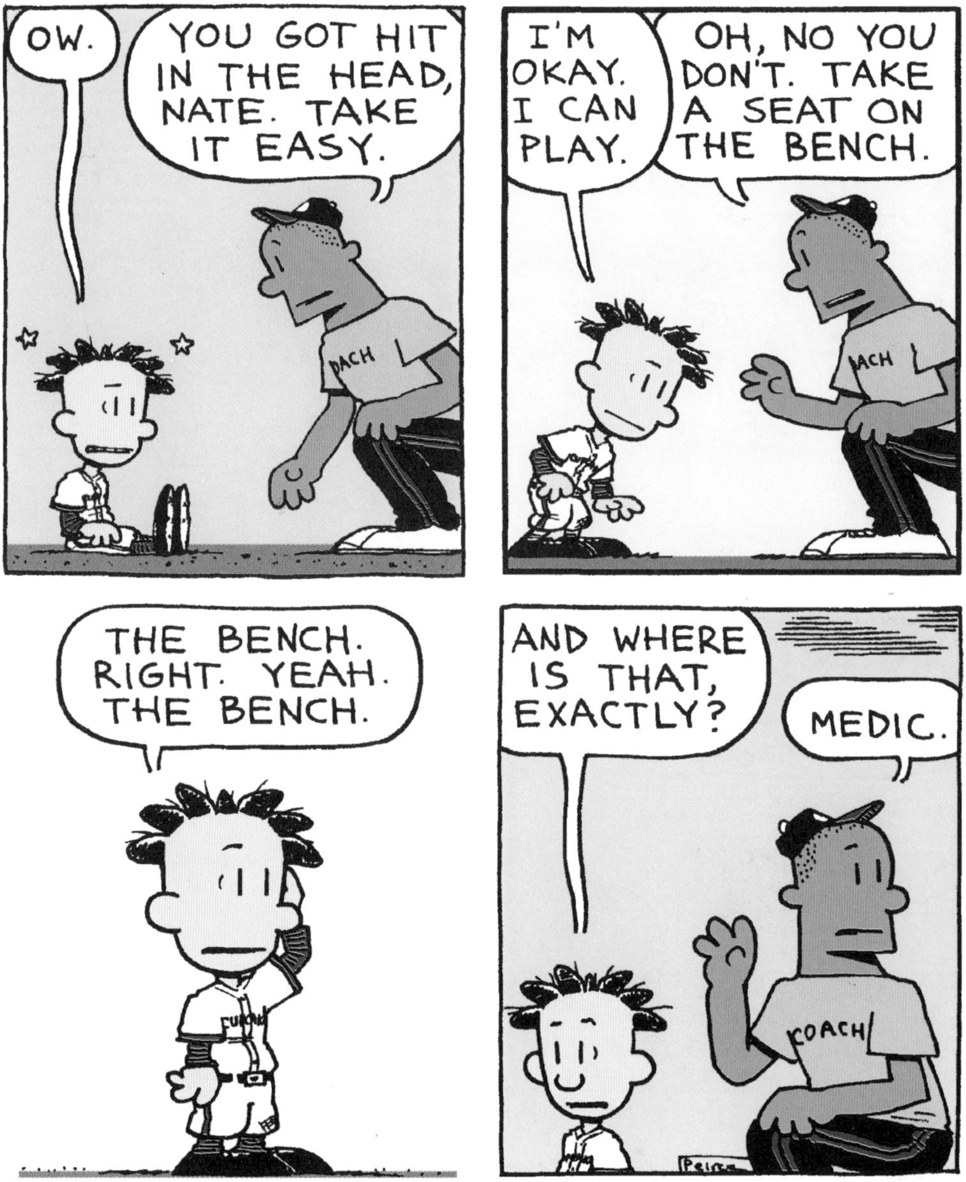
OW.
YOU GOT HIT IN THE HEAD, NATE. TAKE IT EASY.
I'M OKAY. I CAN PLAY.
OH, NO YOU DON'T. TAKE A SEAT ON THE BENCH.
THE BENCH. RIGHT. YEAH. THE BENCH.
AND WHERE IS THAT, EXACTLY?
MEDIC.

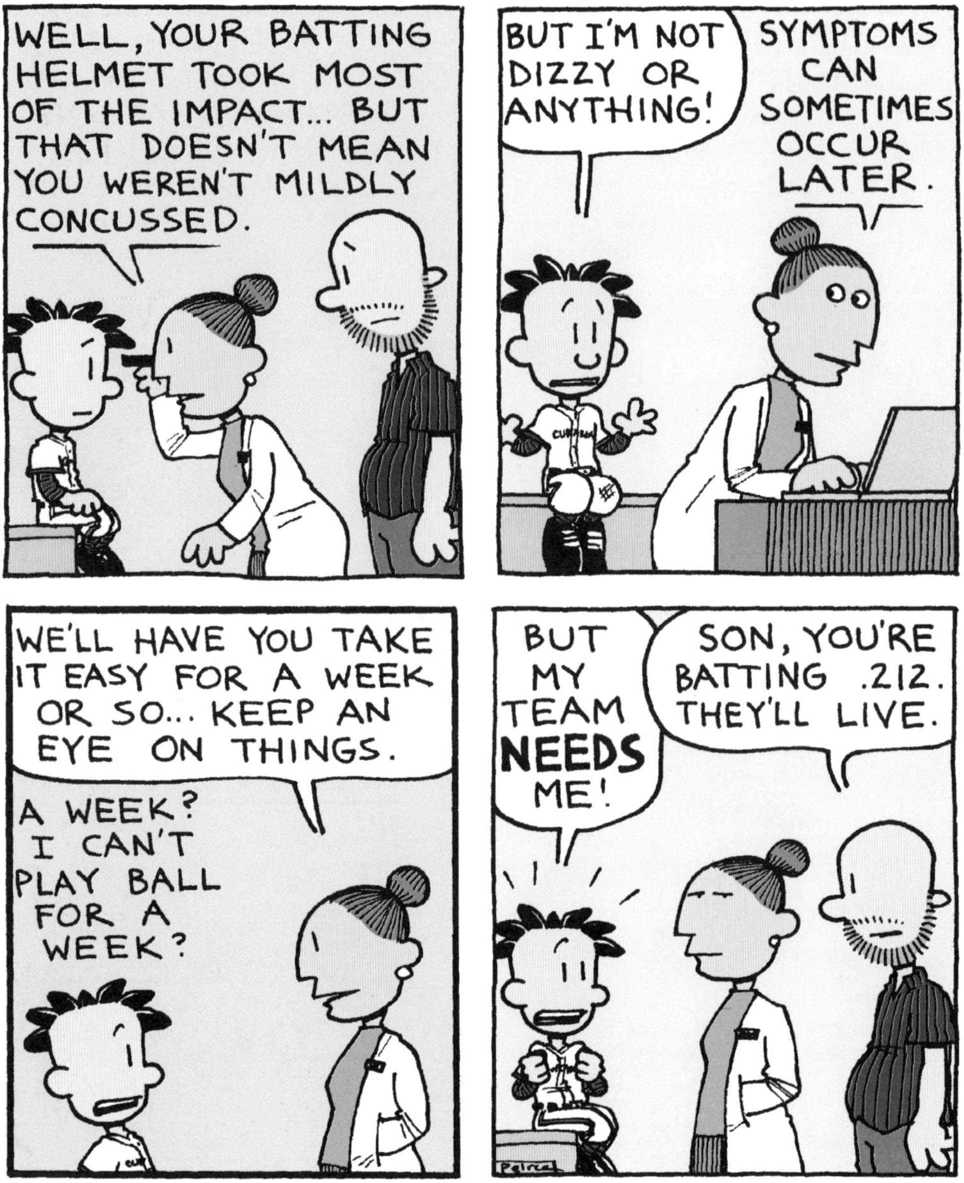
WELL, YOUR BATTING HELMET TOOK MOST OF THE IMPACT... BUT THAT DOESN'T MEAN YOU WEREN'T MILDLY CONCUSSED.
BUT I'M NOT DIZZY OR ANYTHING!
SYMPTOMS CAN SOMETIMES OCCUR LATER.
WE'LL HAVE YOU TAKE IT EASY FOR A WEEK OR SO... KEEP AN EYE ON THINGS.
A WEEK? I CAN'T PLAY BALL FOR A WEEK?
BUT MY TEAM **NEEDS** ME!
SON, YOU'RE BATTING .212. THEY'LL LIVE.
Peirce

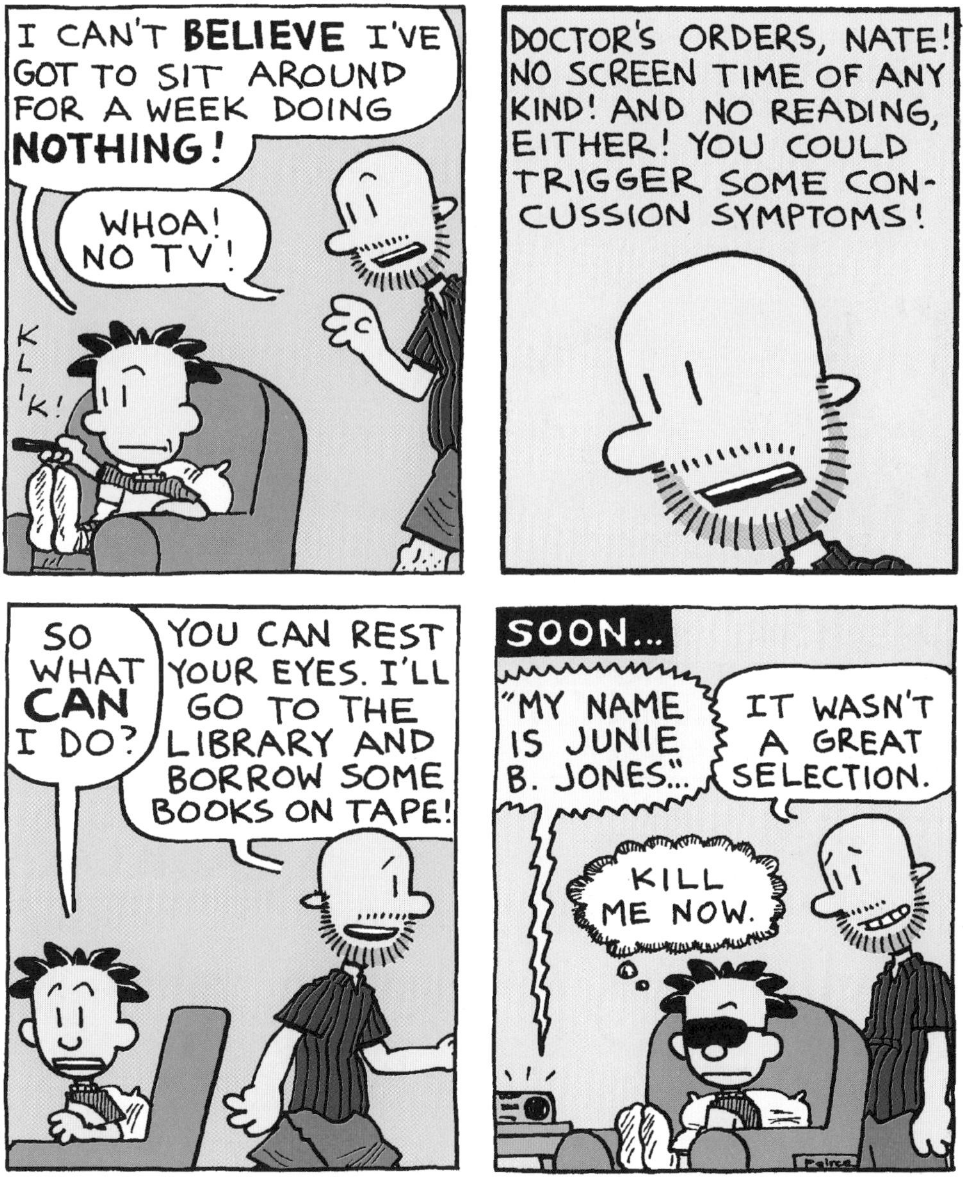
I CAN'T **BELIEVE** I'VE GOT TO SIT AROUND FOR A WEEK DOING **NOTHING**!
WHOA! NO TV!
KLIK!
DOCTOR'S ORDERS, NATE! NO SCREEN TIME OF ANY KIND! AND NO READING, EITHER! YOU COULD TRIGGER SOME CONCUSSION SYMPTOMS!
SO WHAT **CAN** I DO?
YOU CAN REST YOUR EYES. I'LL GO TO THE LIBRARY AND BORROW SOME BOOKS ON TAPE!
SOON...
"MY NAME IS JUNIE B. JONES."...
IT WASN'T A GREAT SELECTION.
KILL ME NOW.

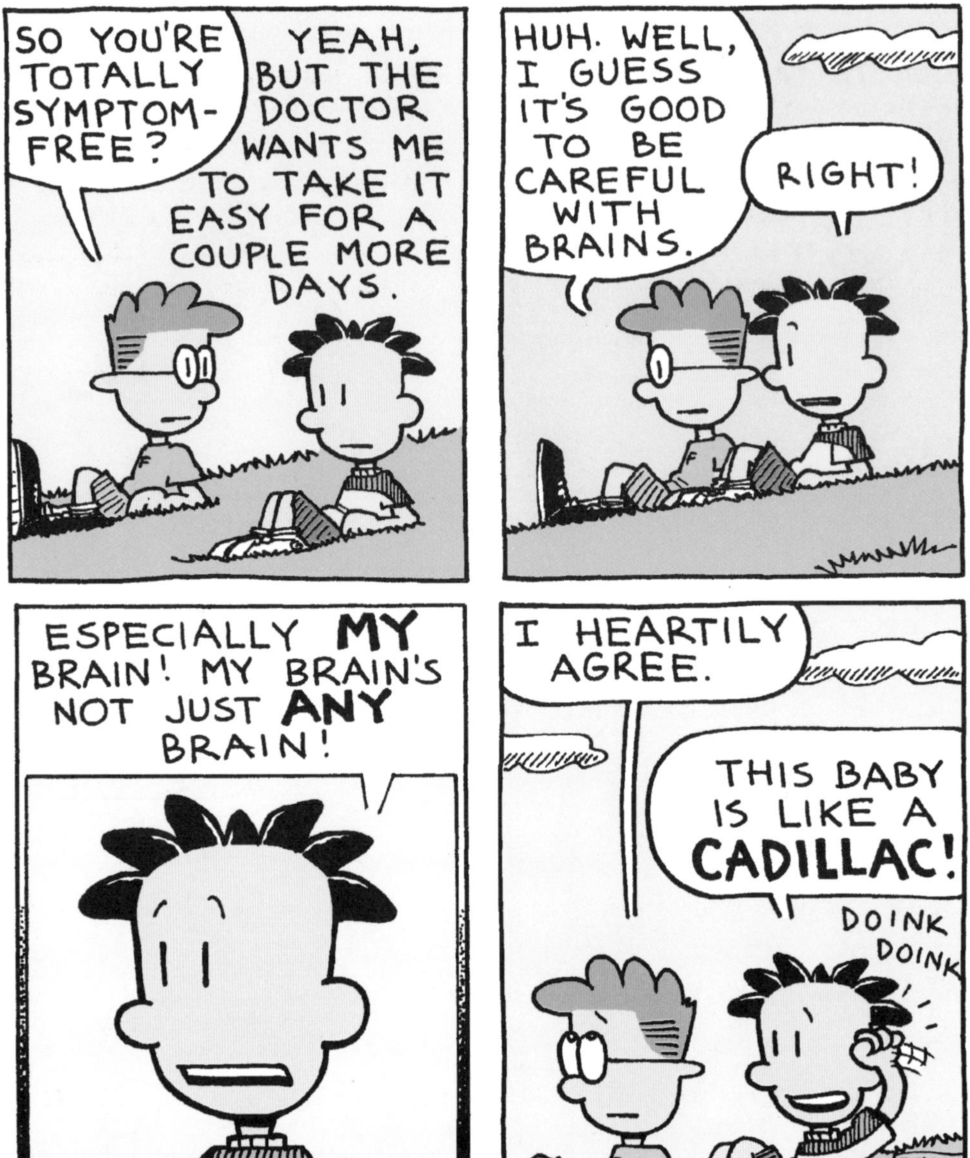
SO YOU'RE TOTALLY SYMPTOM-FREE?
YEAH, BUT THE DOCTOR WANTS ME TO TAKE IT EASY FOR A COUPLE MORE DAYS.
HUH. WELL, I GUESS IT'S GOOD TO BE CAREFUL WITH BRAINS.
RIGHT!
ESPECIALLY MY BRAIN! MY BRAIN'S NOT JUST ANY BRAIN!
I HEARTILY AGREE.
THIS BABY IS LIKE A CADILLAC!
DOINK
DOINK

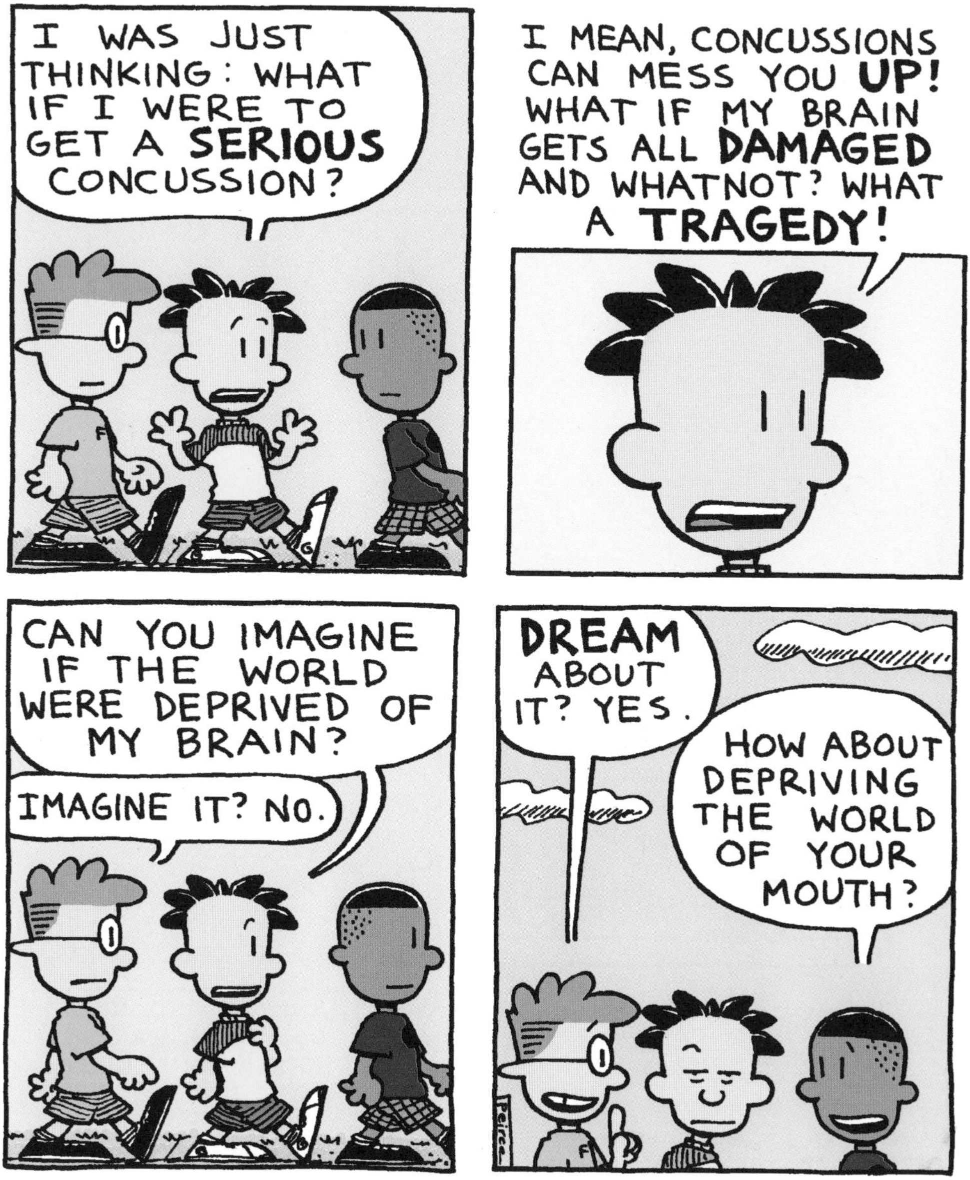
I WAS JUST THINKING: WHAT IF I WERE TO GET A **SERIOUS** CONCUSSION?
I MEAN, CONCUSSIONS CAN MESS YOU **UP**! WHAT IF MY BRAIN GETS ALL **DAMAGED** AND WHATNOT? WHAT A **TRAGEDY**!
CAN YOU IMAGINE IF THE WORLD WERE DEPRIVED OF MY BRAIN?
IMAGINE IT? NO.
DREAM ABOUT IT? YES.
HOW ABOUT DEPRIVING THE WORLD OF YOUR MOUTH?
Peirce

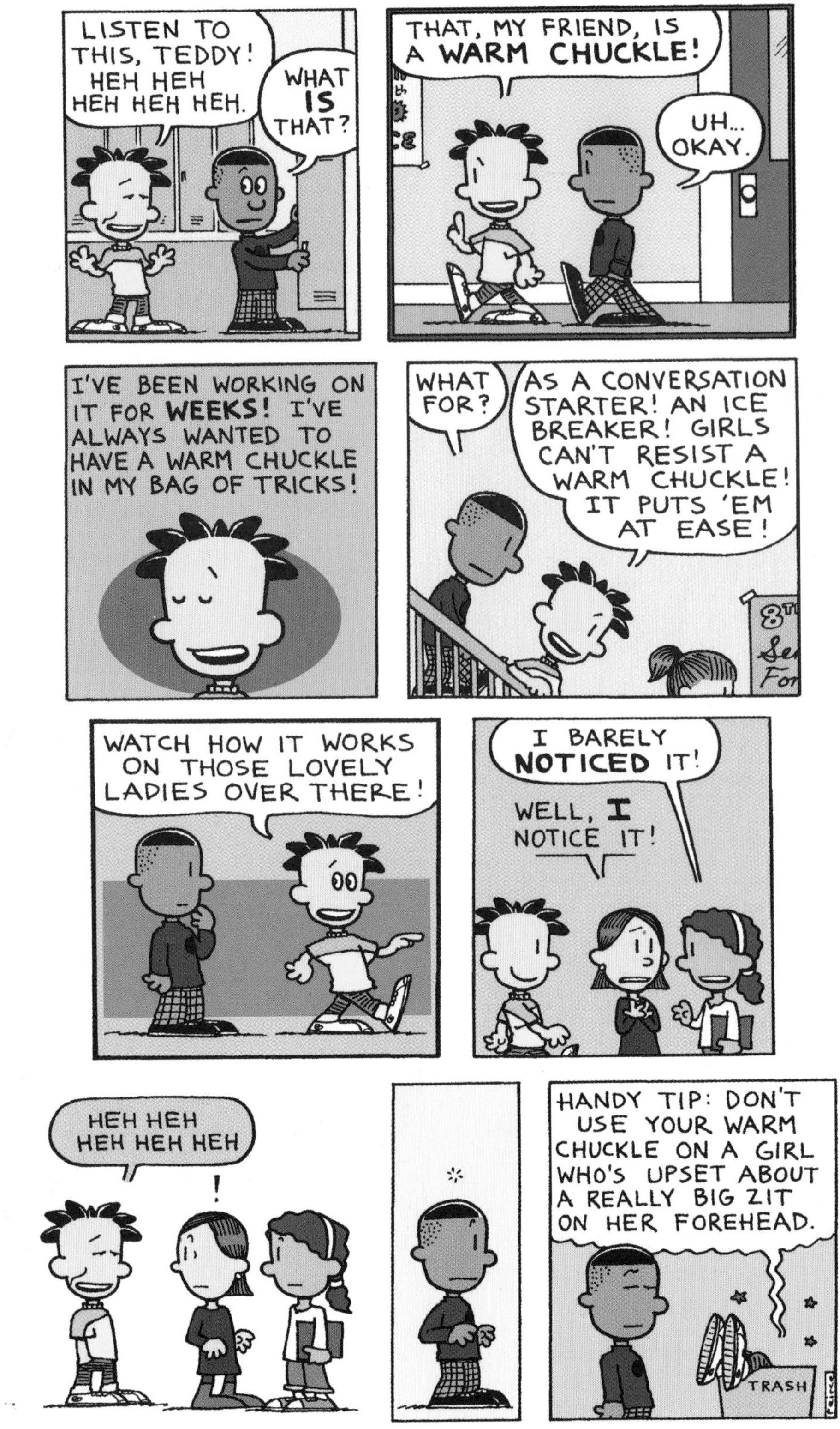
LISTEN TO THIS, TEDDY! HEH HEH HEH HEH HEH.
WHAT IS THAT?
THAT, MY FRIEND, IS A WARM CHUCKLE!
UH... OKAY.
I'VE BEEN WORKING ON IT FOR WEEKS! I'VE ALWAYS WANTED TO HAVE A WARM CHUCKLE IN MY BAG OF TRICKS!
WHAT FOR?
AS A CONVERSATION STARTER! AN ICE BREAKER! GIRLS CAN'T RESIST A WARM CHUCKLE! IT PUTS 'EM AT EASE!
WATCH HOW IT WORKS ON THOSE LOVELY LADIES OVER THERE!
I BARELY NOTICED IT!
WELL, I NOTICE IT!
HEH HEH HEH HEH HEH
!
HANDY TIP: DON'T USE YOUR WARM CHUCKLE ON A GIRL WHO'S UPSET ABOUT A REALLY BIG ZIT ON HER FOREHEAD.
TRASH

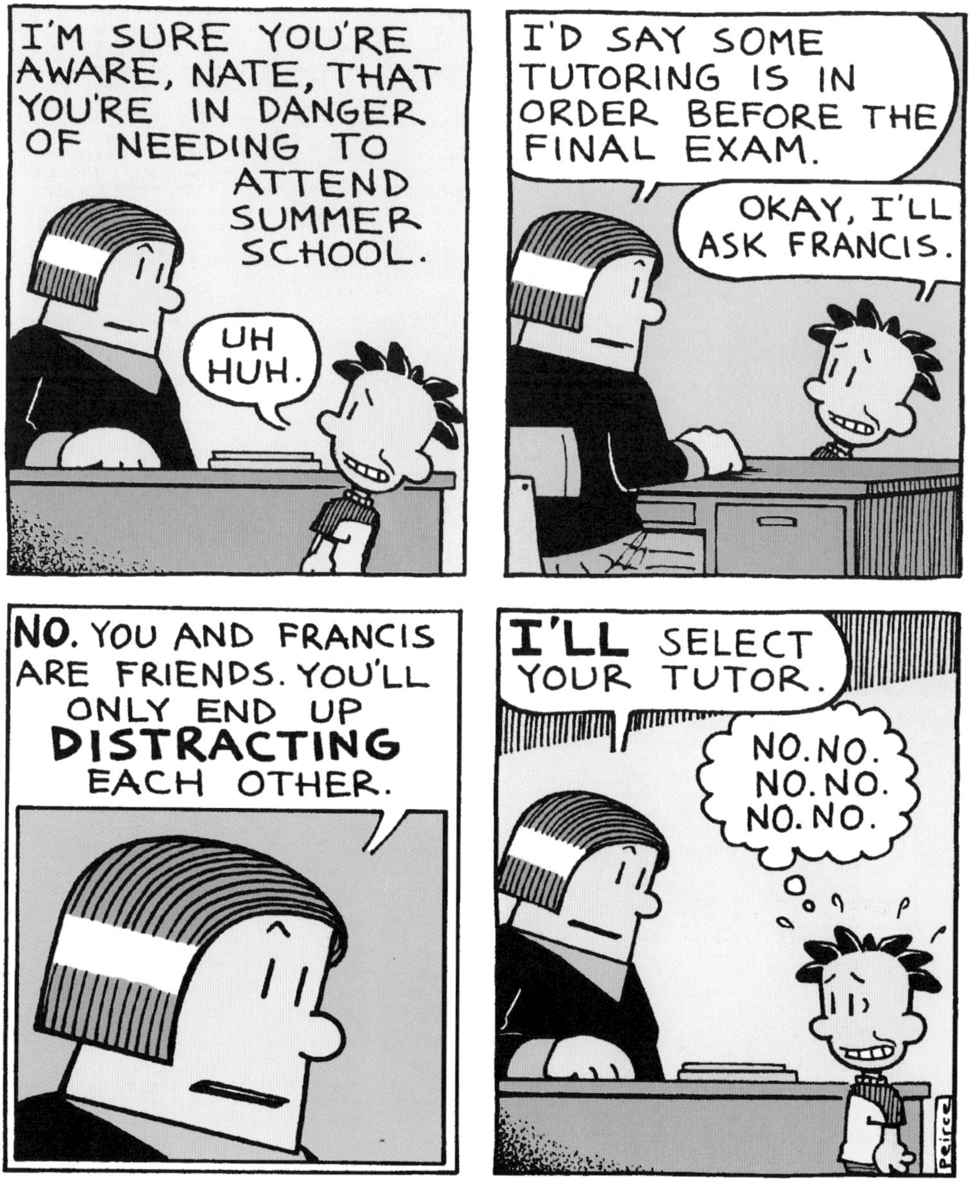
I'M SURE YOU'RE AWARE, NATE, THAT YOU'RE IN DANGER OF NEEDING TO ATTEND SUMMER SCHOOL.
UH HUH.
I'D SAY SOME TUTORING IS IN ORDER BEFORE THE FINAL EXAM.
OKAY, I'LL ASK FRANCIS.
NO. YOU AND FRANCIS ARE FRIENDS. YOU'LL ONLY END UP DISTRACTING EACH OTHER.
I'LL SELECT YOUR TUTOR.
NO. NO. NO. NO. NO. NO.
Peirce

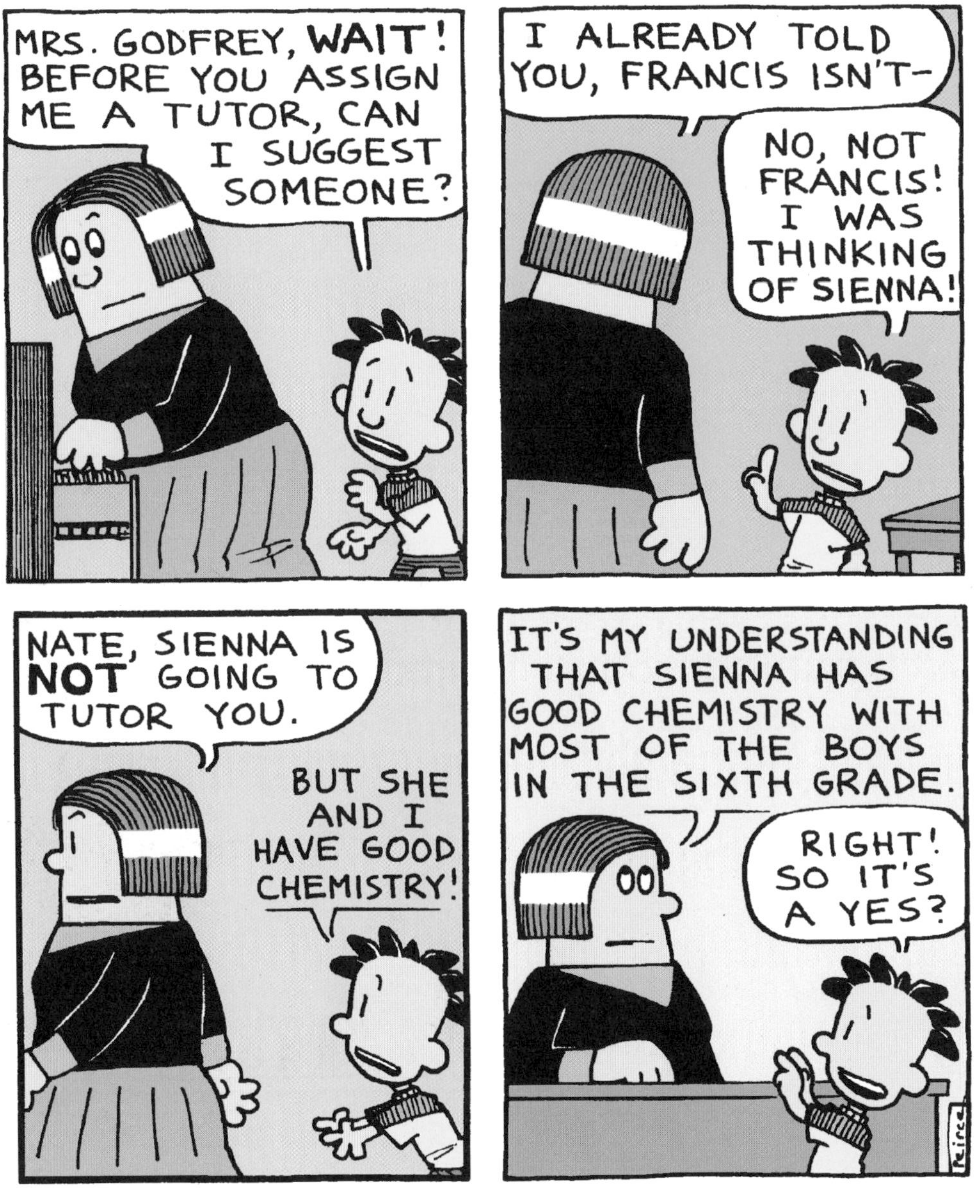
MRS. GODFREY, WAIT! BEFORE YOU ASSIGN ME A TUTOR, CAN I SUGGEST SOMEONE?
I ALREADY TOLD YOU, FRANCIS ISN'T—
NO, NOT FRANCIS! I WAS THINKING OF SIENNA!
NATE, SIENNA IS NOT GOING TO TUTOR YOU.
BUT SHE AND I HAVE GOOD CHEMISTRY!
IT'S MY UNDERSTANDING THAT SIENNA HAS GOOD CHEMISTRY WITH MOST OF THE BOYS IN THE SIXTH GRADE.
RIGHT! SO IT'S A YES?
Peirce

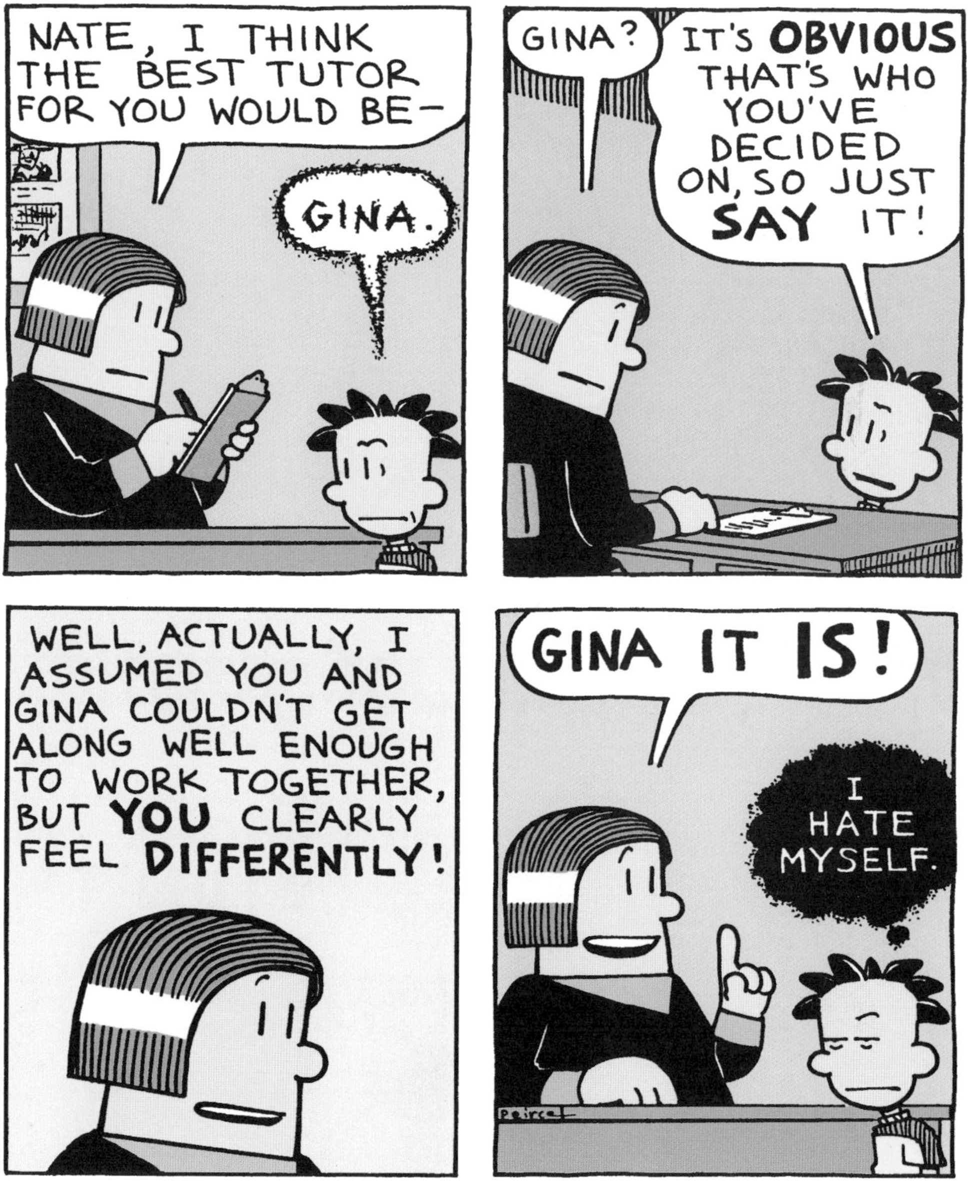
NATE, I THINK THE BEST TUTOR FOR YOU WOULD BE—
GINA.
GINA?
IT'S OBVIOUS THAT'S WHO YOU'VE DECIDED ON, SO JUST SAY IT!
WELL, ACTUALLY, I ASSUMED YOU AND GINA COULDN'T GET ALONG WELL ENOUGH TO WORK TOGETHER, BUT YOU CLEARLY FEEL DIFFERENTLY!
GINA IT IS!
I HATE MYSELF.
Peirce

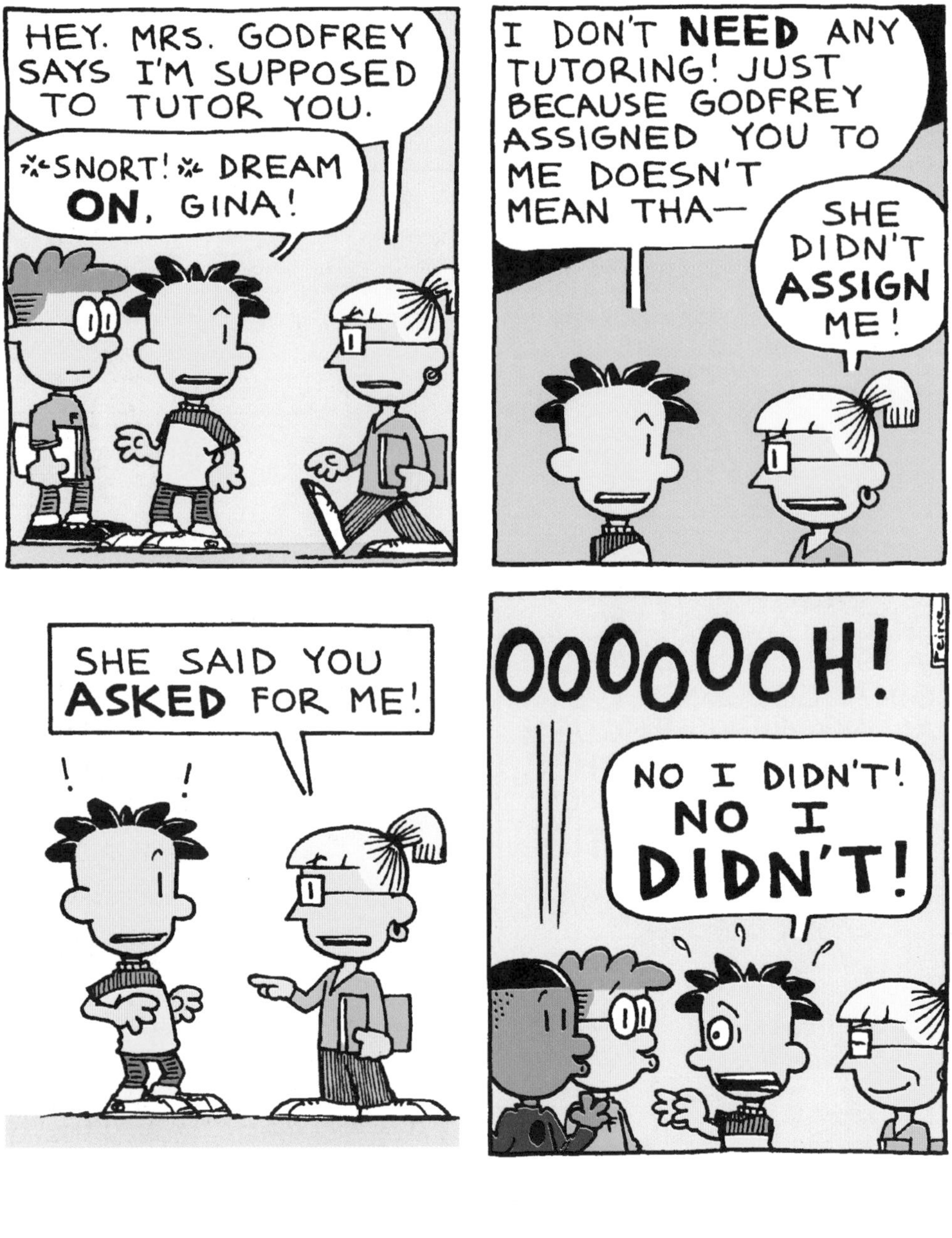
HEY. MRS. GODFREY SAYS I'M SUPPOSED TO TUTOR YOU.
SNORT! DREAM ON, GINA!
I DON'T NEED ANY TUTORING! JUST BECAUSE GODFREY ASSIGNED YOU TO ME DOESN'T MEAN THA—
SHE DIDN'T ASSIGN ME!
SHE SAID YOU ASKED FOR ME!
! !
OOOOOOH!
NO I DIDN'T! NO I DIDN'T!
Peirce

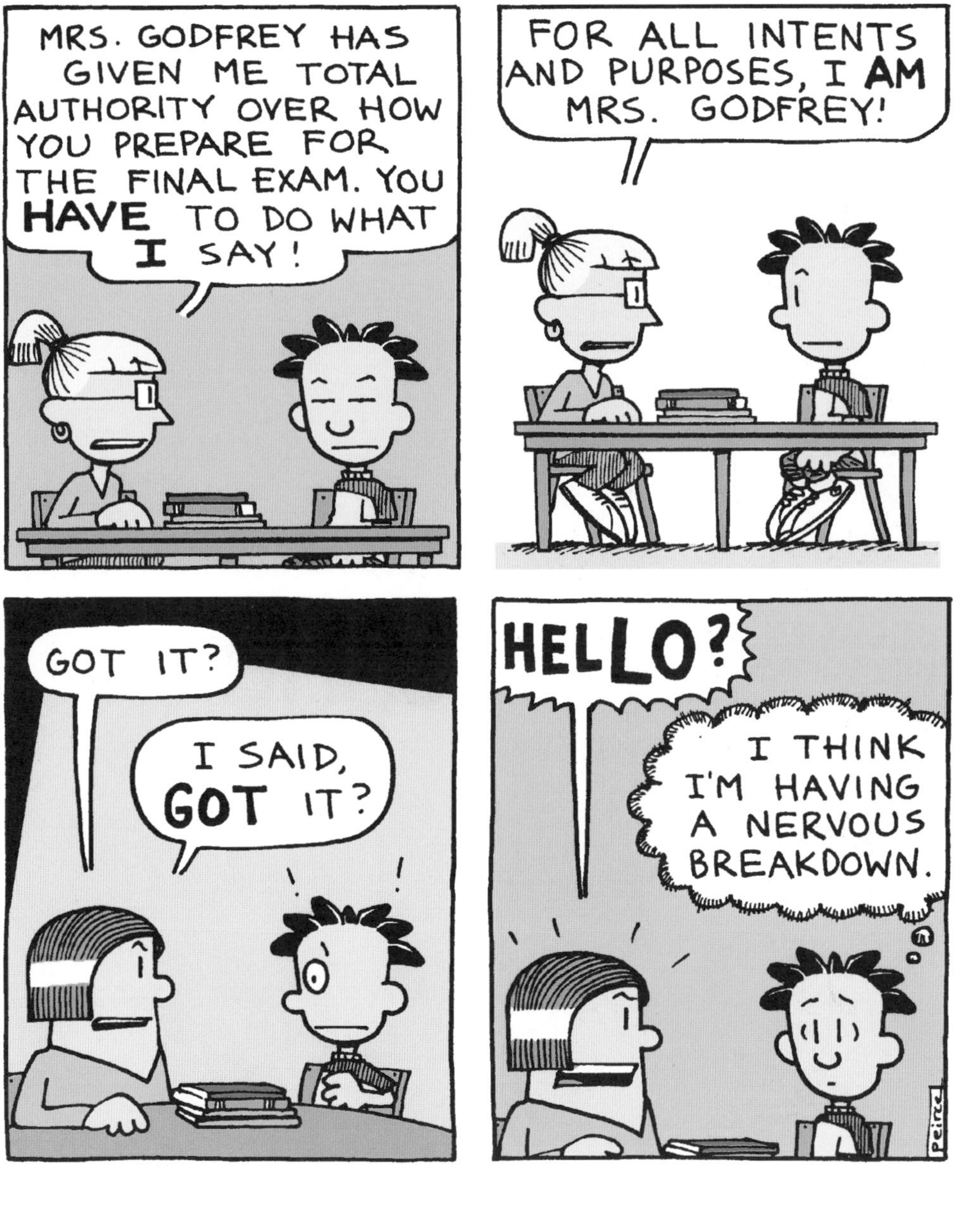
MRS. GODFREY HAS GIVEN ME TOTAL AUTHORITY OVER HOW YOU PREPARE FOR THE FINAL EXAM. YOU HAVE TO DO WHAT I SAY!
FOR ALL INTENTS AND PURPOSES, I AM MRS. GODFREY!
GOT IT?
I SAID, GOT IT?
HELLO?
I THINK I'M HAVING A NERVOUS BREAKDOWN.
peirce

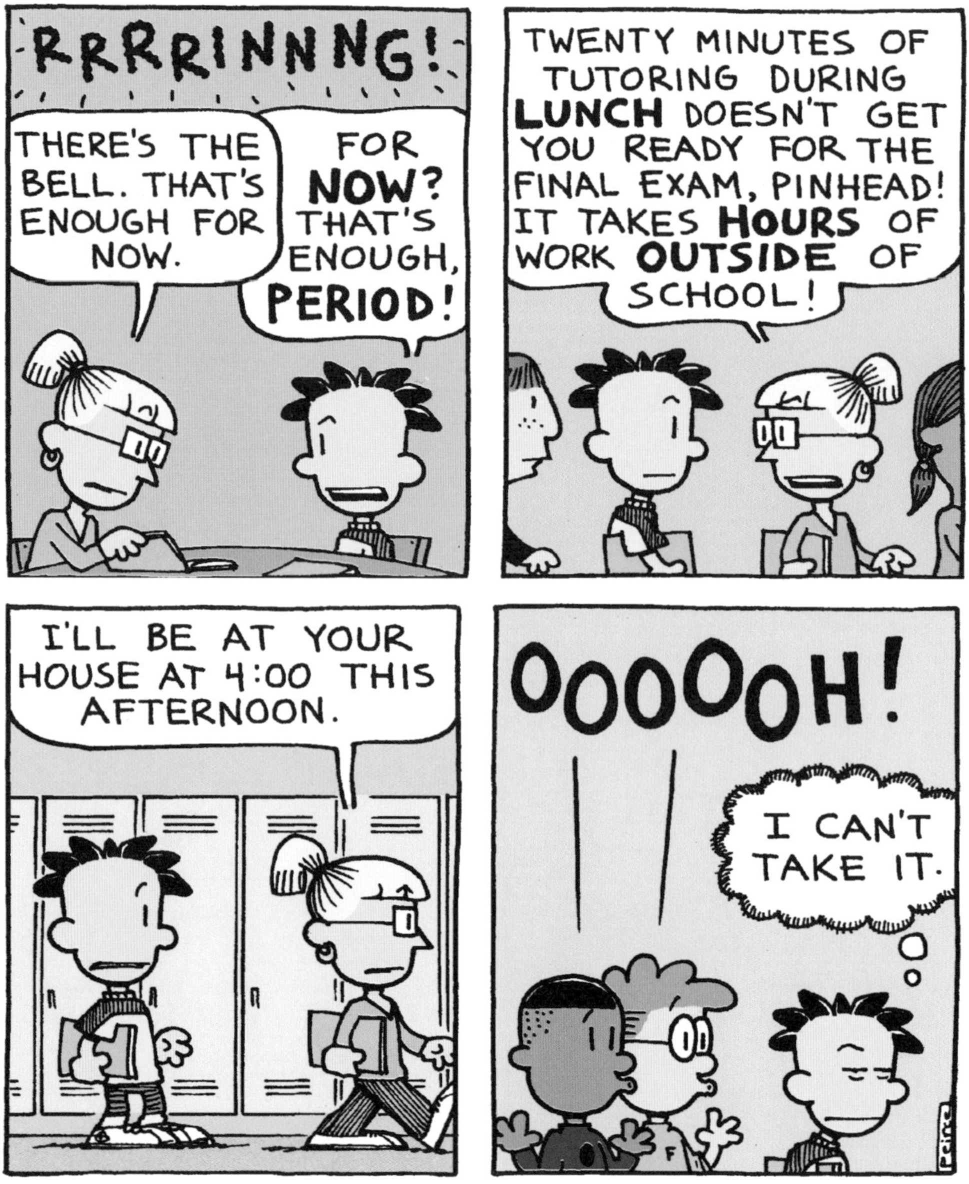
RRRRINNNG!
THERE'S THE BELL. THAT'S ENOUGH FOR NOW.
FOR NOW? THAT'S ENOUGH, PERIOD!
TWENTY MINUTES OF TUTORING DURING LUNCH DOESN'T GET YOU READY FOR THE FINAL EXAM, PINHEAD! IT TAKES HOURS OF WORK OUTSIDE OF SCHOOL!
I'LL BE AT YOUR HOUSE AT 4:00 THIS AFTERNOON.
OOOOOH!
I CAN'T TAKE IT.
Peirce

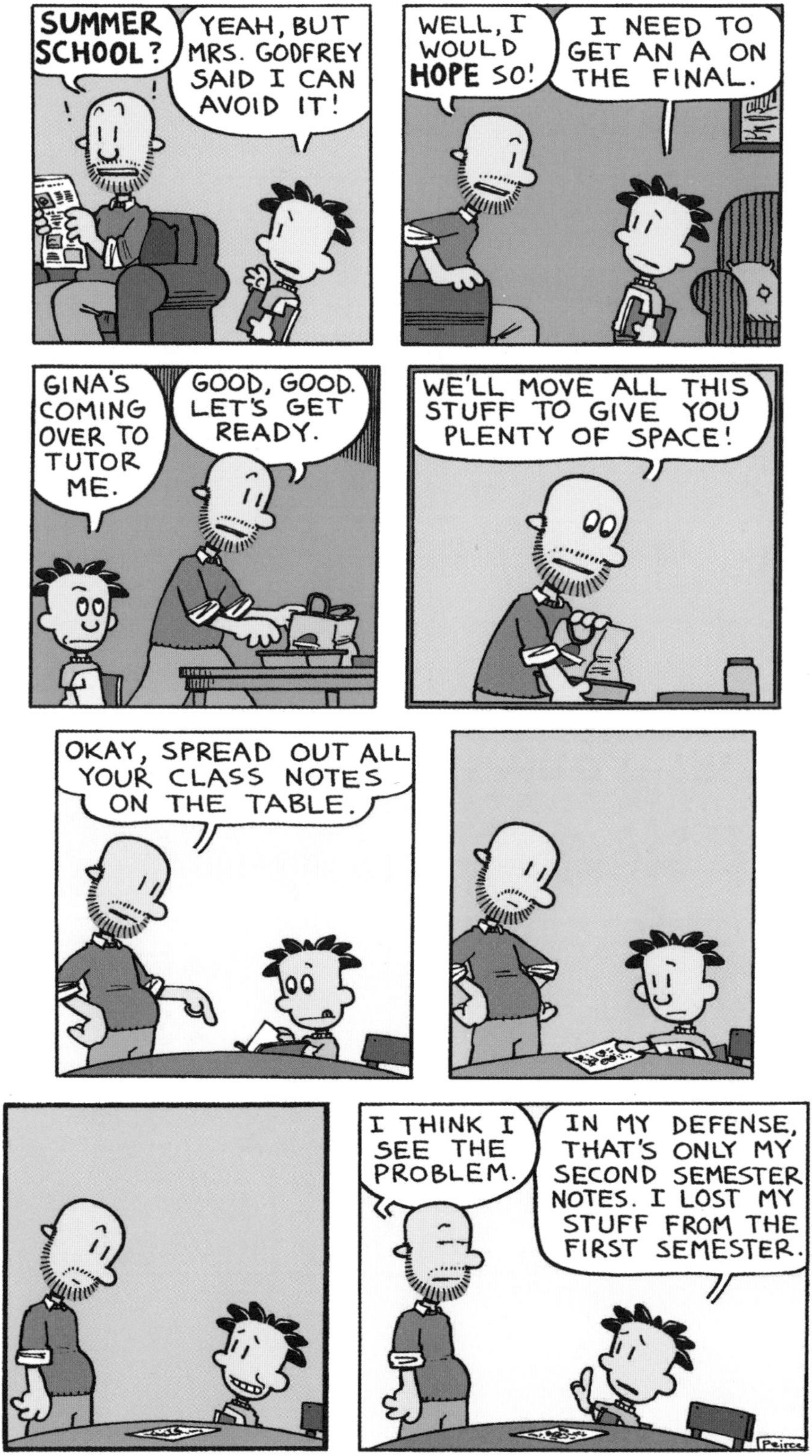
SUMMER SCHOOL?
YEAH, BUT MRS. GODFREY SAID I CAN AVOID IT!
WELL, I WOULD HOPE SO!
I NEED TO GET AN A ON THE FINAL.
GINA'S COMING OVER TO TUTOR ME.
GOOD, GOOD. LET'S GET READY.
WE'LL MOVE ALL THIS STUFF TO GIVE YOU PLENTY OF SPACE!
OKAY, SPREAD OUT ALL YOUR CLASS NOTES ON THE TABLE.
I THINK I SEE THE PROBLEM.
IN MY DEFENSE, THAT'S ONLY MY SECOND SEMESTER NOTES. I LOST MY STUFF FROM THE FIRST SEMESTER.
Peirce

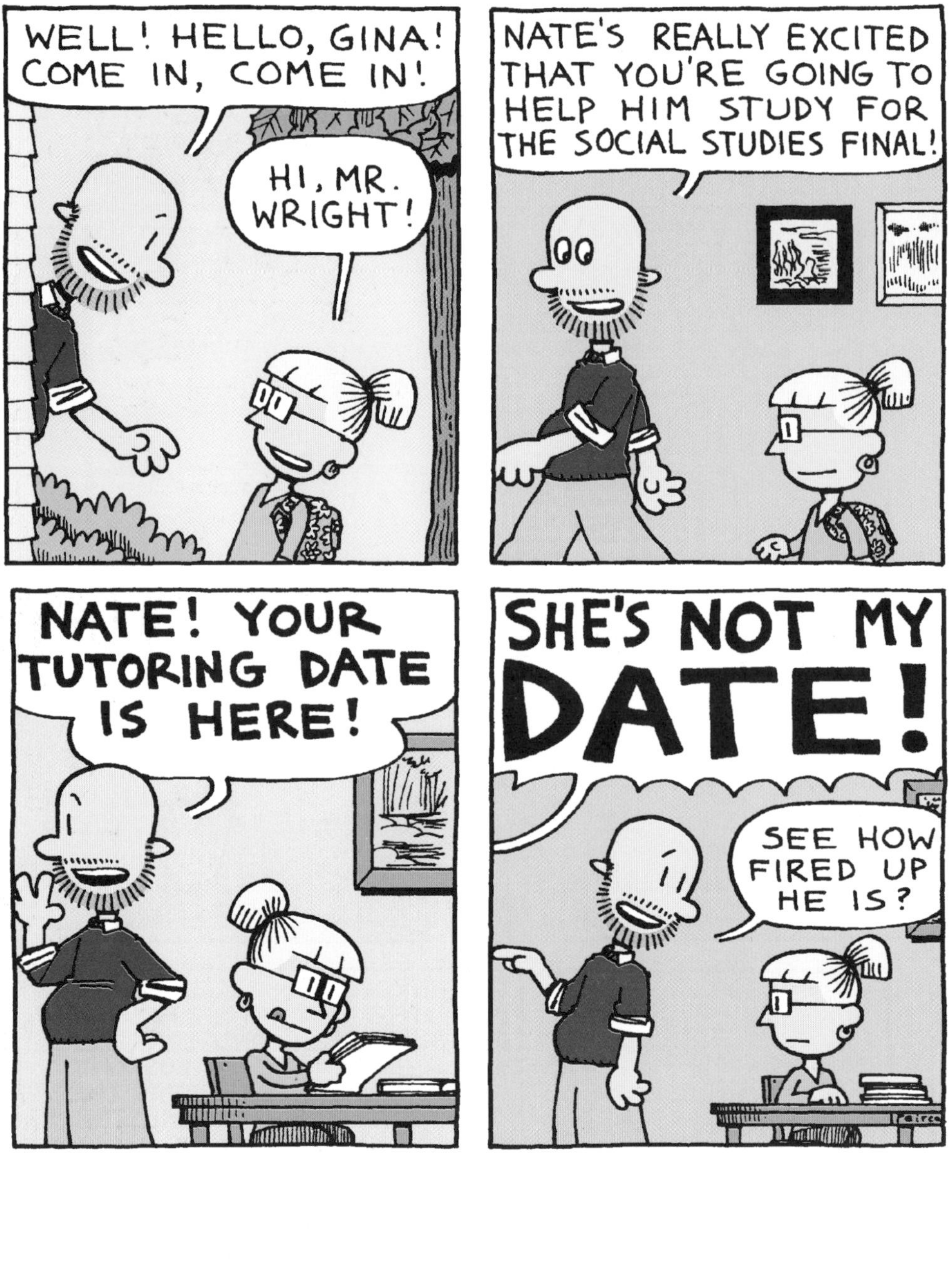
WELL! HELLO, GINA! COME IN, COME IN!
HI, MR. WRIGHT!
NATE'S REALLY EXCITED THAT YOU'RE GOING TO HELP HIM STUDY FOR THE SOCIAL STUDIES FINAL!
NATE! YOUR TUTORING DATE IS HERE!
SHE'S NOT MY DATE!
SEE HOW FIRED UP HE IS?

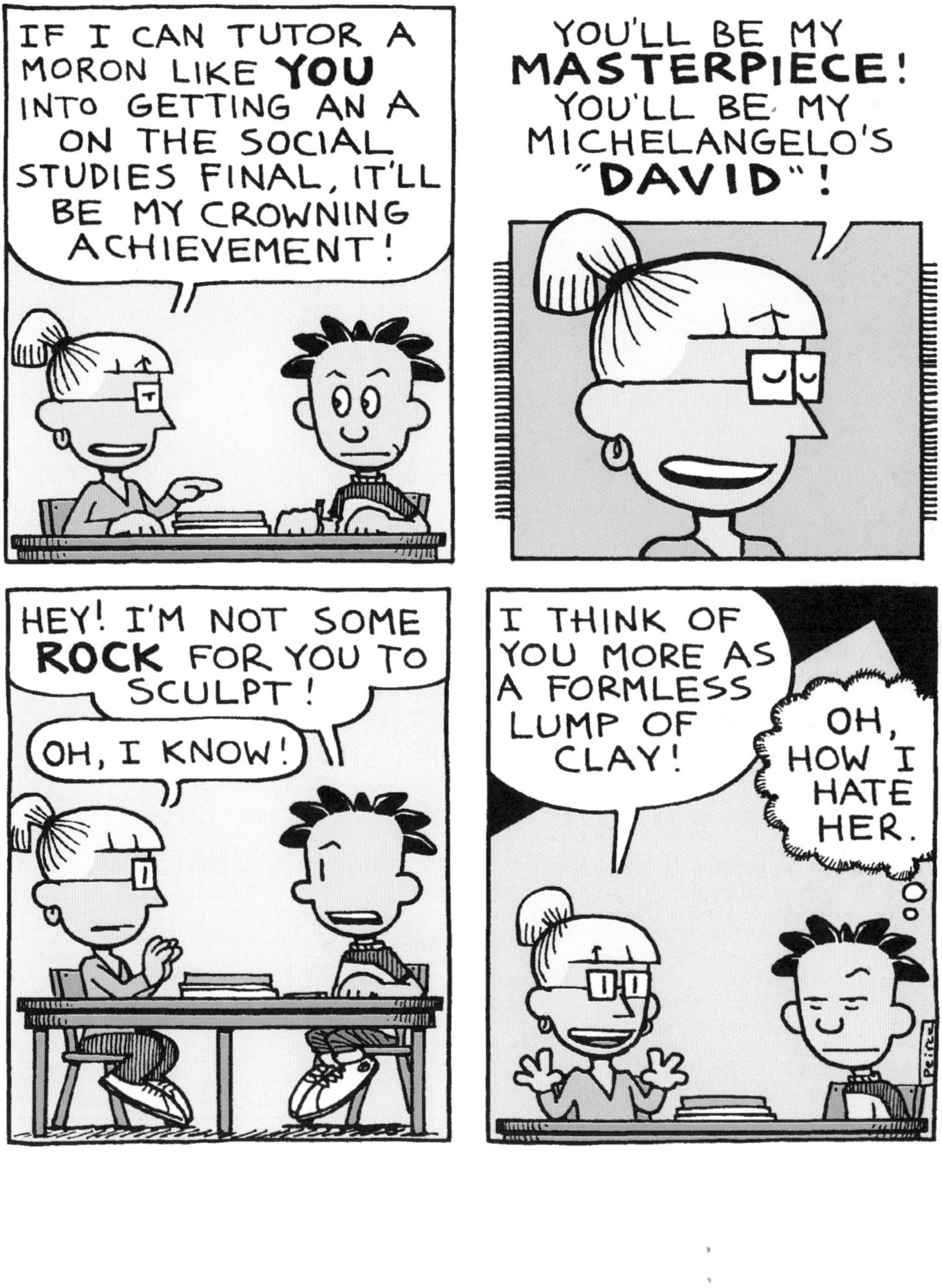
IF I CAN TUTOR A MORON LIKE YOU INTO GETTING AN A ON THE SOCIAL STUDIES FINAL, IT'LL BE MY CROWNING ACHIEVEMENT!
YOU'LL BE MY MASTERPIECE! YOU'LL BE MY MICHELANGELO'S "DAVID"!
HEY! I'M NOT SOME ROCK FOR YOU TO SCULPT!
OH, I KNOW!
I THINK OF YOU MORE AS A FORMLESS LUMP OF CLAY!
OH, HOW I HATE HER.
Peirce

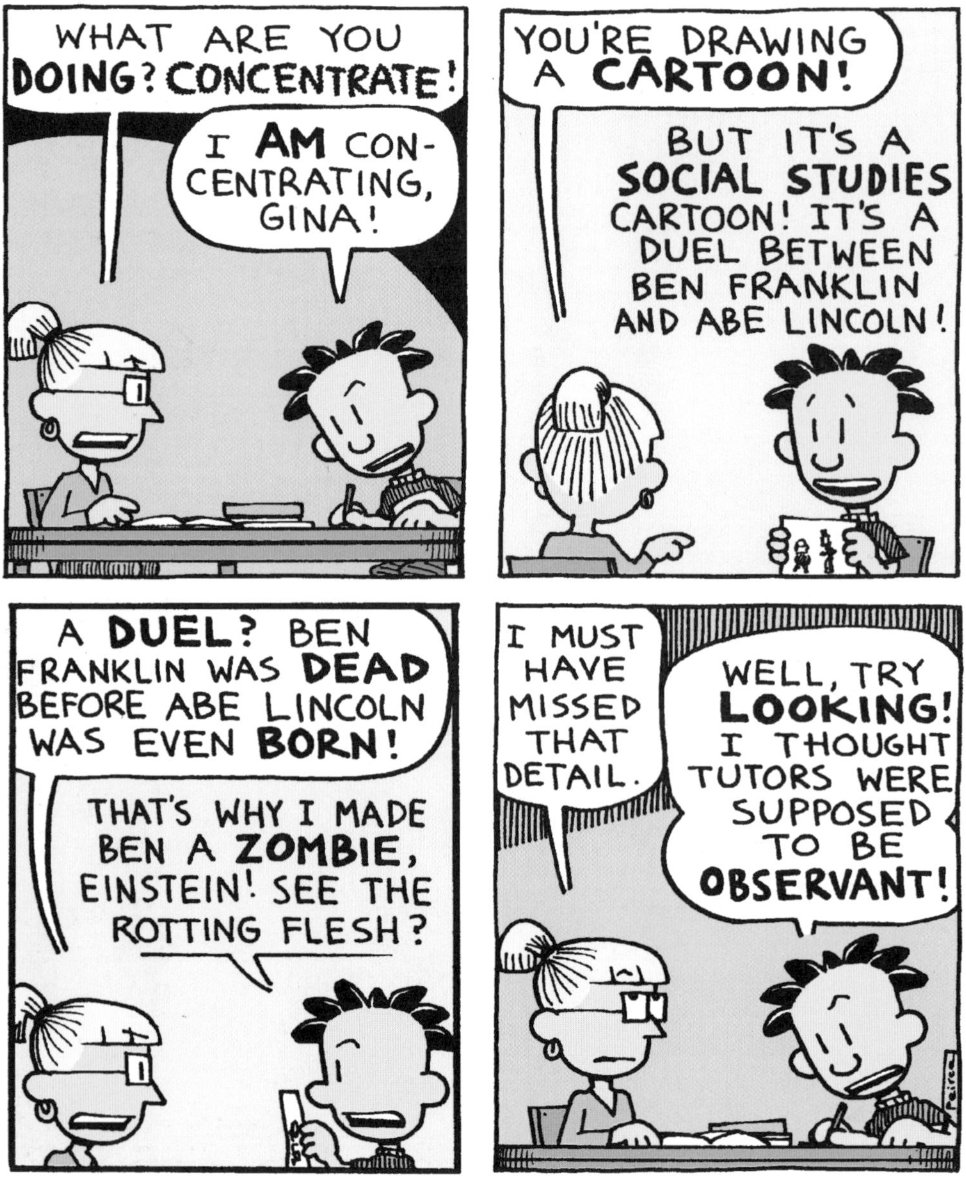
WHAT ARE YOU DOING? CONCENTRATE!
I AM CONCENTRATING, GINA!
YOU'RE DRAWING A CARTOON!
BUT IT'S A SOCIAL STUDIES CARTOON! IT'S A DUEL BETWEEN BEN FRANKLIN AND ABE LINCOLN!
A DUEL? BEN FRANKLIN WAS DEAD BEFORE ABE LINCOLN WAS EVEN BORN!
THAT'S WHY I MADE BEN A ZOMBIE, EINSTEIN! SEE THE ROTTING FLESH?
I MUST HAVE MISSED THAT DETAIL.
WELL, TRY LOOKING! I THOUGHT TUTORS WERE SUPPOSED TO BE OBSERVANT!
Peirce

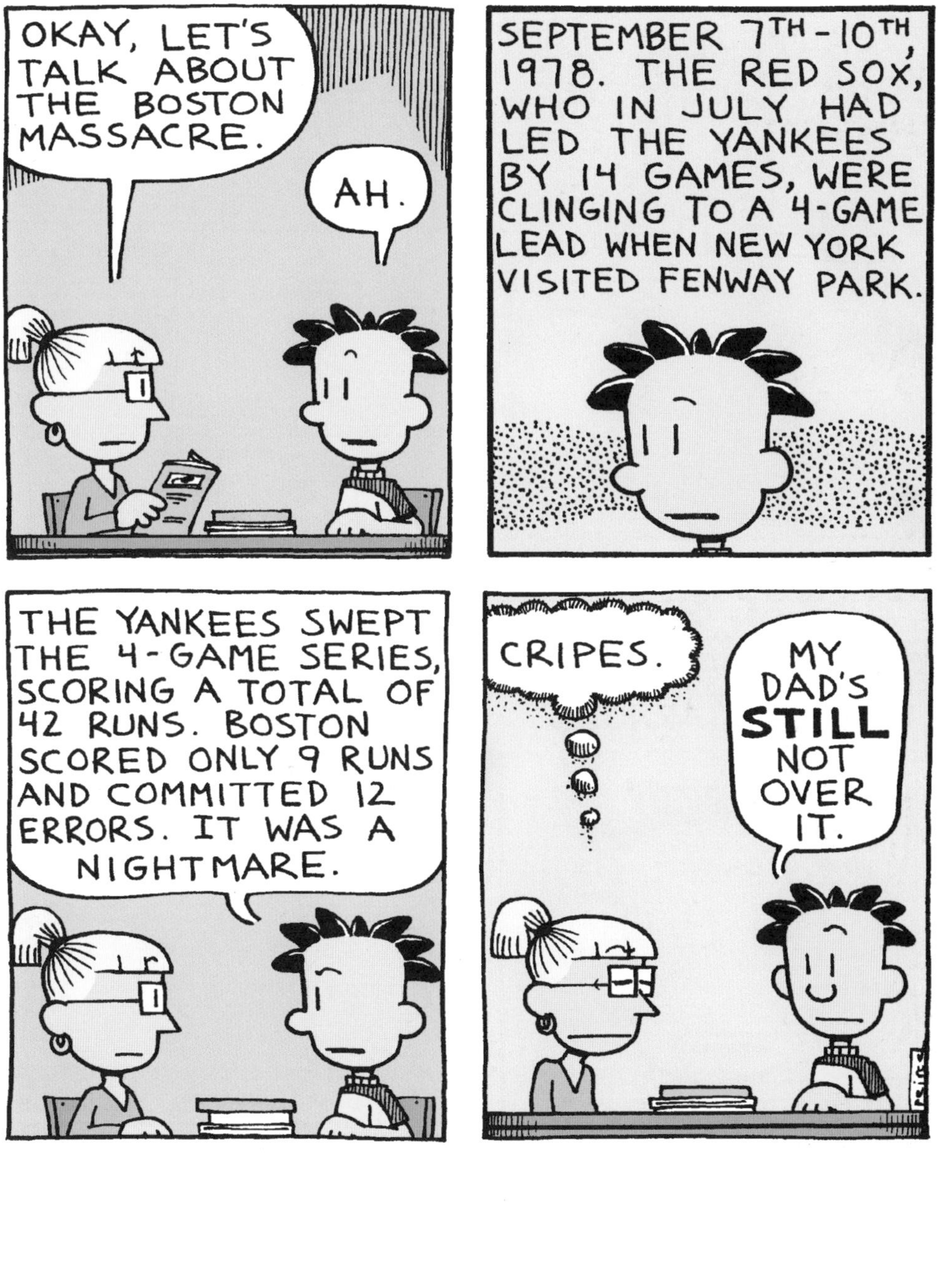
OKAY, LET'S TALK ABOUT THE BOSTON MASSACRE.
AH.
SEPTEMBER 7TH-10TH, 1978. THE RED SOX, WHO IN JULY HAD LED THE YANKEES BY 14 GAMES, WERE CLINGING TO A 4-GAME LEAD WHEN NEW YORK VISITED FENWAY PARK.
THE YANKEES SWEPT THE 4-GAME SERIES, SCORING A TOTAL OF 42 RUNS. BOSTON SCORED ONLY 9 RUNS AND COMMITTED 12 ERRORS. IT WAS A NIGHTMARE.
CRIPES.
MY DAD'S **STILL** NOT OVER IT.
PEIRCE

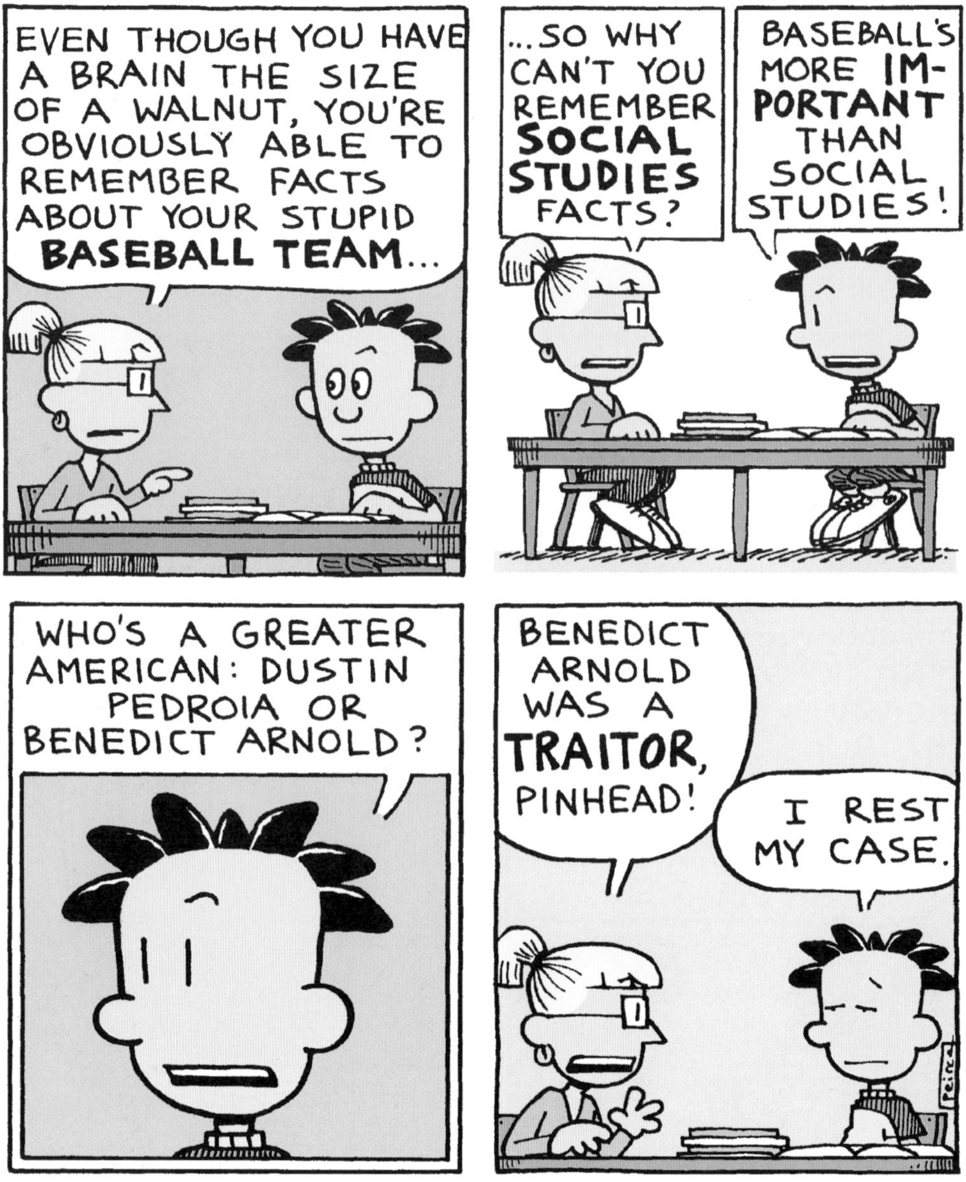
EVEN THOUGH YOU HAVE A BRAIN THE SIZE OF A WALNUT, YOU'RE OBVIOUSLY ABLE TO REMEMBER FACTS ABOUT YOUR STUPID **BASEBALL TEAM**...
...SO WHY CAN'T YOU REMEMBER **SOCIAL STUDIES** FACTS?
BASEBALL'S MORE **IMPORTANT** THAN SOCIAL STUDIES!
WHO'S A GREATER AMERICAN: DUSTIN PEDROIA OR BENEDICT ARNOLD?
BENEDICT ARNOLD WAS A **TRAITOR**, PINHEAD!
I REST MY CASE.
PEIRCE

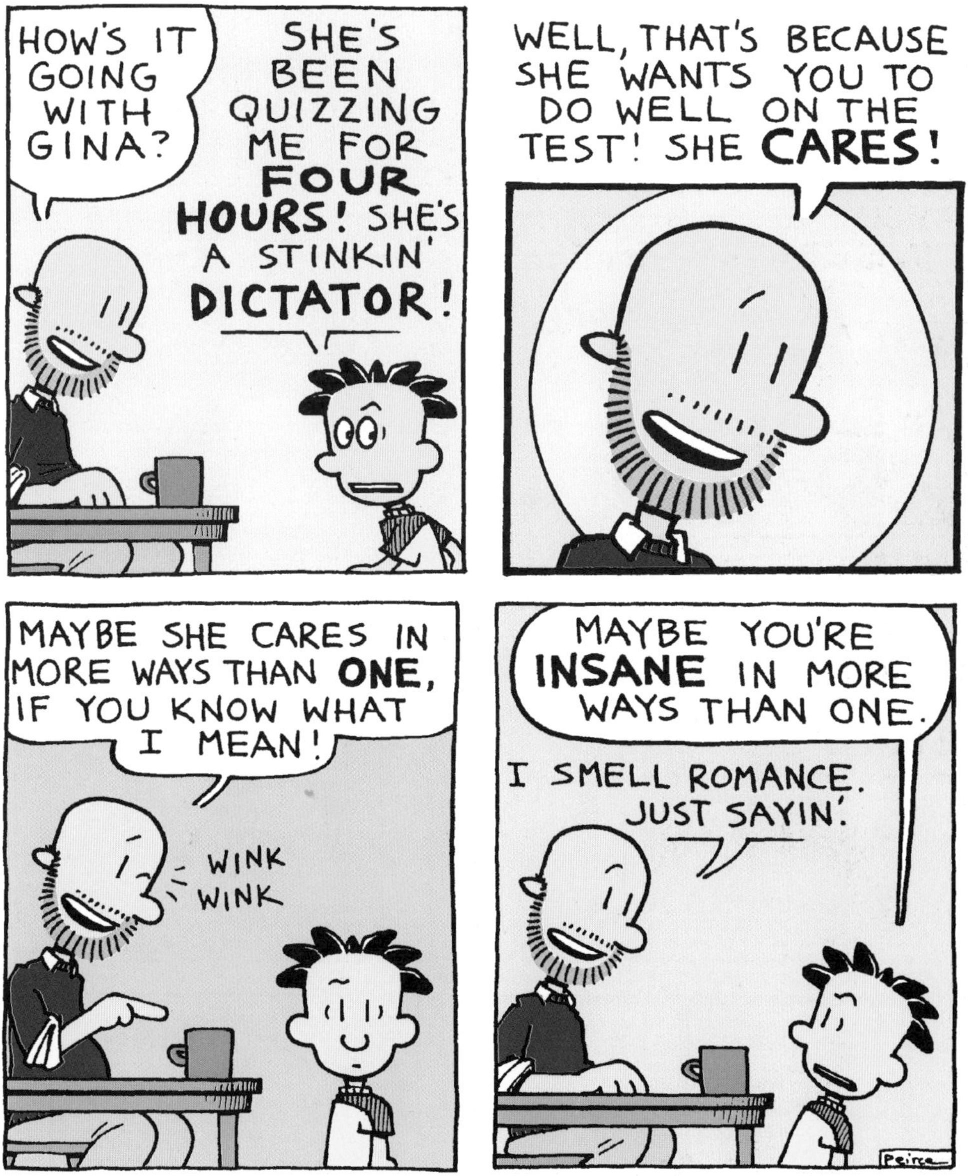
HOW'S IT GOING WITH GINA?
SHE'S BEEN QUIZZING ME FOR **FOUR HOURS!** SHE'S A STINKIN' **DICTATOR!**
WELL, THAT'S BECAUSE SHE WANTS YOU TO DO WELL ON THE TEST! SHE **CARES!**
MAYBE SHE CARES IN MORE WAYS THAN **ONE**, IF YOU KNOW WHAT I MEAN!
WINK WINK
MAYBE YOU'RE **INSANE** IN MORE WAYS THAN ONE.
I SMELL ROMANCE. JUST SAYIN'.
Peirce

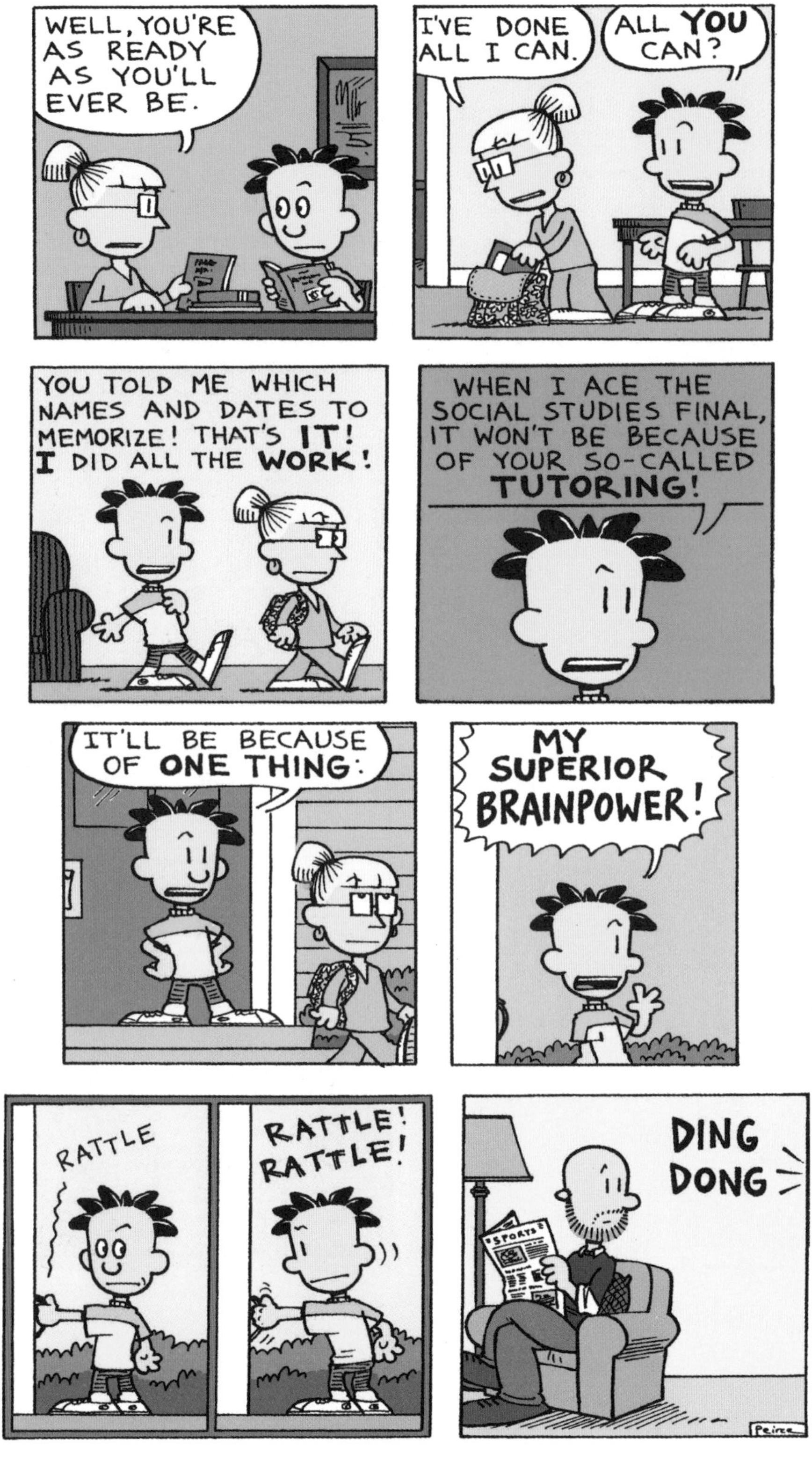
WELL, YOU'RE AS READY AS YOU'LL EVER BE.
I'VE DONE ALL I CAN.
ALL YOU CAN?
YOU TOLD ME WHICH NAMES AND DATES TO MEMORIZE! THAT'S IT! I DID ALL THE WORK!
WHEN I ACE THE SOCIAL STUDIES FINAL, IT WON'T BE BECAUSE OF YOUR SO-CALLED TUTORING!
IT'LL BE BECAUSE OF ONE THING:
MY SUPERIOR BRAINPOWER!
RATTLE
RATTLE! RATTLE!
DING DONG
SPORTS
Peirce

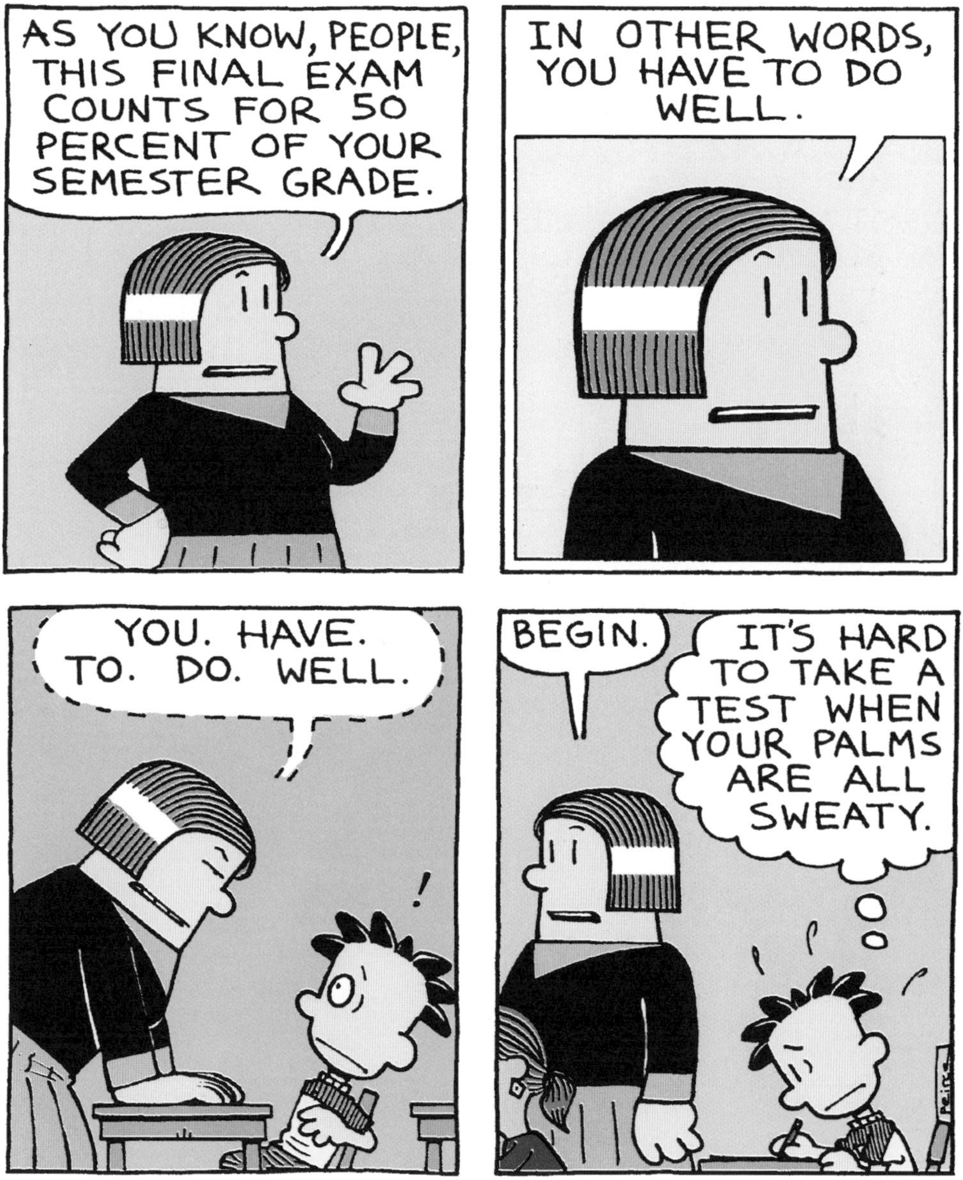
AS YOU KNOW, PEOPLE, THIS FINAL EXAM COUNTS FOR 50 PERCENT OF YOUR SEMESTER GRADE.
IN OTHER WORDS, YOU HAVE TO DO WELL.
YOU. HAVE. TO. DO. WELL.
!
BEGIN.
IT'S HARD TO TAKE A TEST WHEN YOUR PALMS ARE ALL SWEATY.

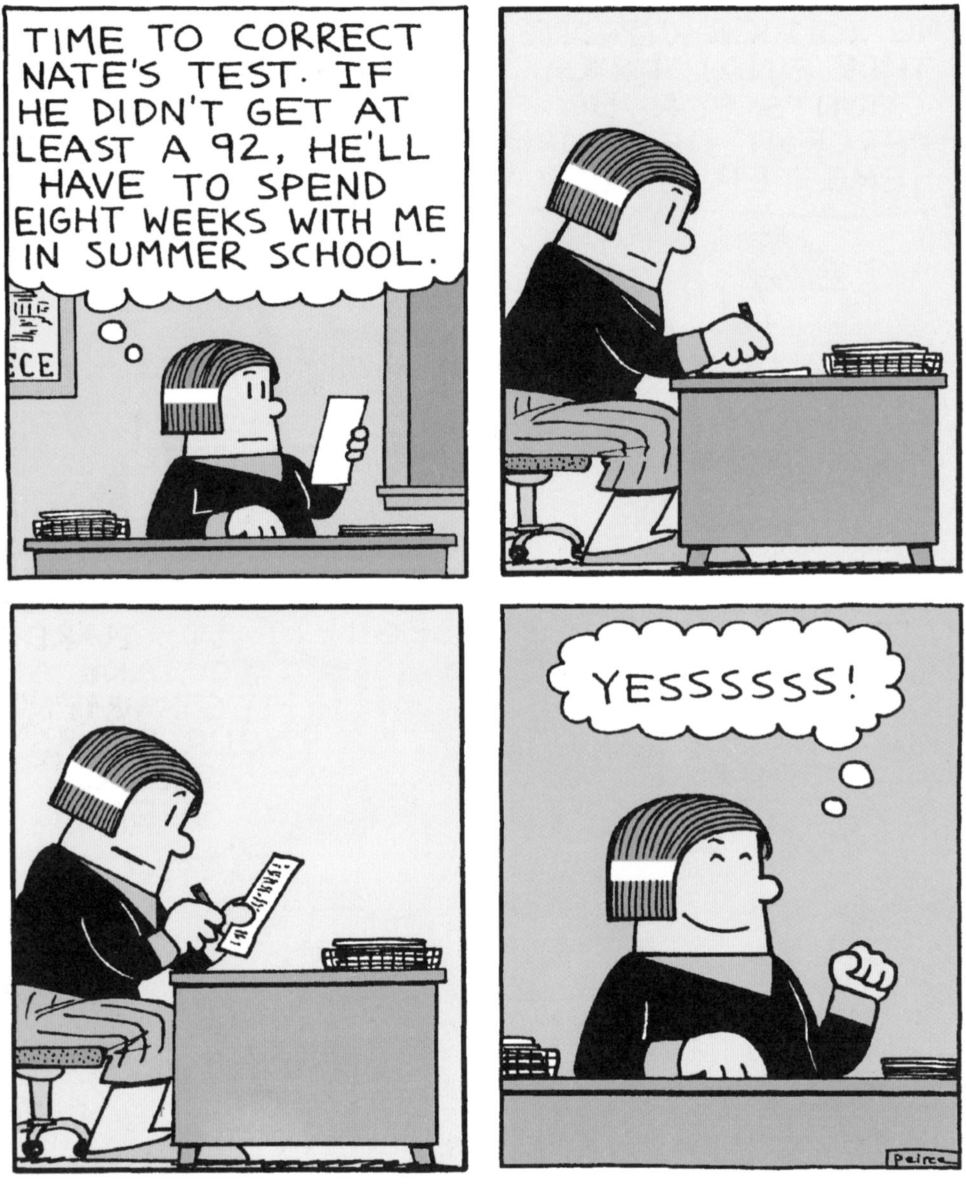
TIME TO CORRECT NATE'S TEST. IF HE DIDN'T GET AT LEAST A 92, HE'LL HAVE TO SPEND EIGHT WEEKS WITH ME IN SUMMER SCHOOL.
YESSSSSS!
Peirce

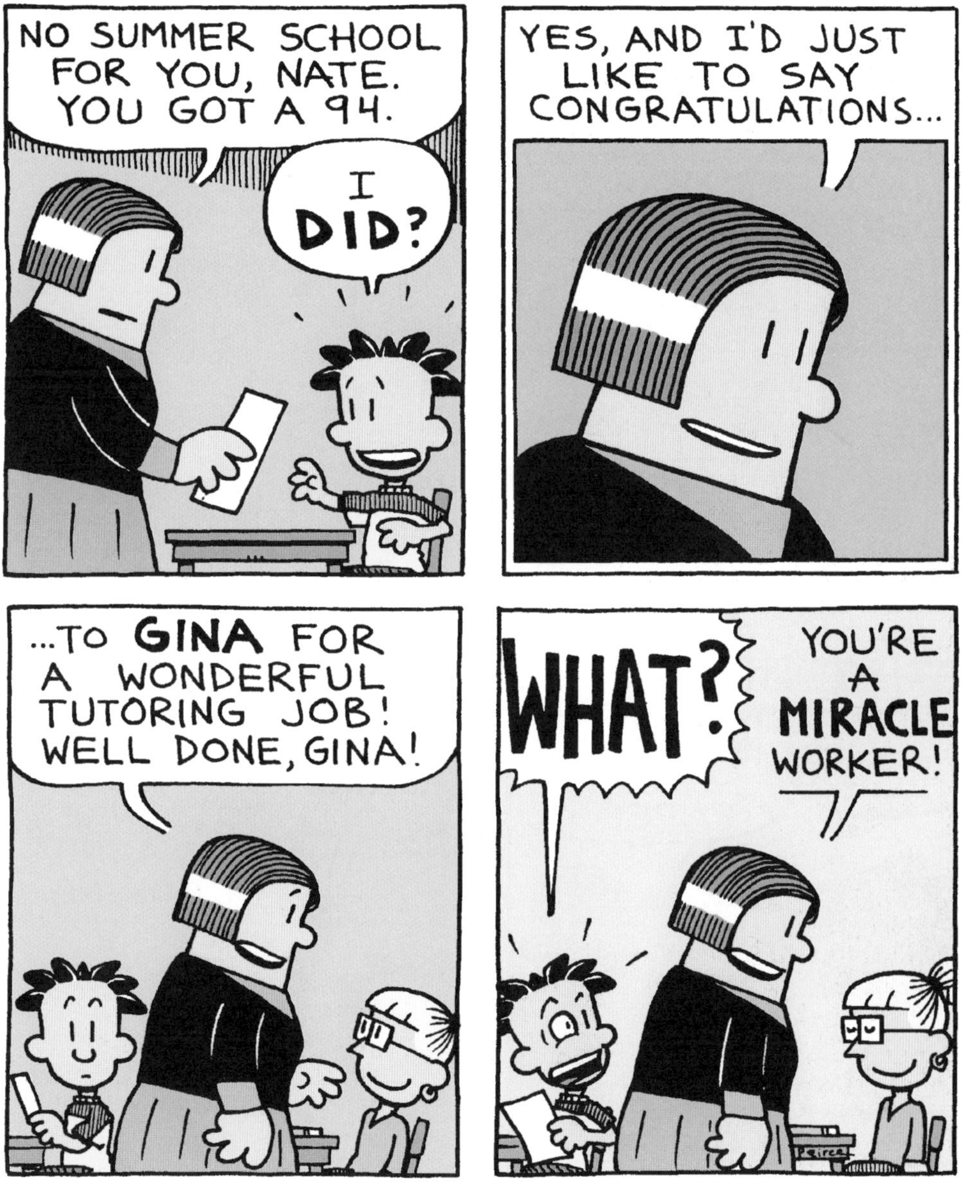
NO SUMMER SCHOOL FOR YOU, NATE. YOU GOT A 94.
I DID?
YES, AND I'D JUST LIKE TO SAY CONGRATULATIONS...
...TO GINA FOR A WONDERFUL TUTORING JOB! WELL DONE, GINA!
WHAT?
YOU'RE A MIRACLE WORKER!

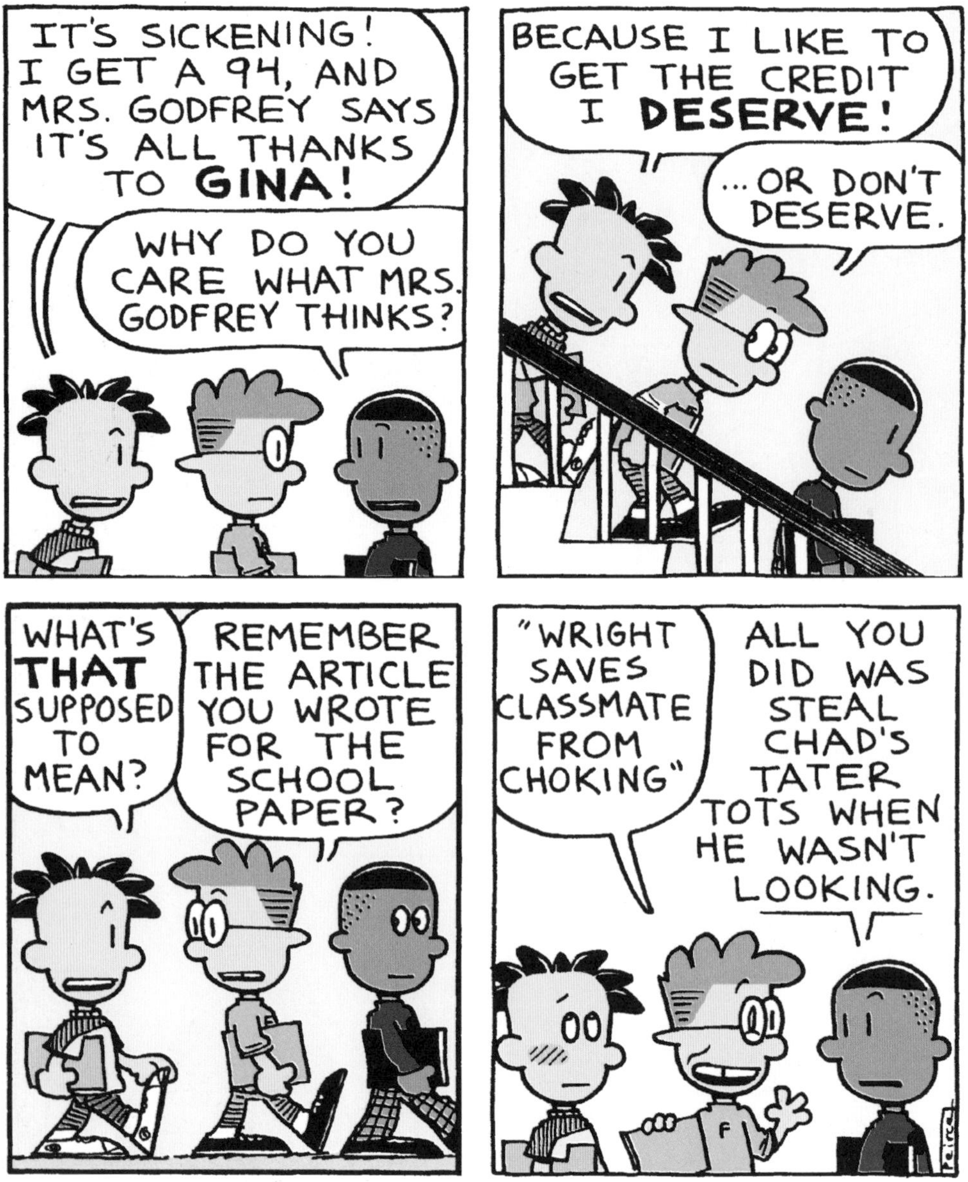
IT'S SICKENING! I GET A 94, AND MRS. GODFREY SAYS IT'S ALL THANKS TO GINA!
WHY DO YOU CARE WHAT MRS. GODFREY THINKS?
BECAUSE I LIKE TO GET THE CREDIT I DESERVE!
...OR DON'T DESERVE.
WHAT'S THAT SUPPOSED TO MEAN?
REMEMBER THE ARTICLE YOU WROTE FOR THE SCHOOL PAPER?
"WRIGHT SAVES CLASSMATE FROM CHOKING"
ALL YOU DID WAS STEAL CHAD'S TATER TOTS WHEN HE WASN'T LOOKING.
Peirce

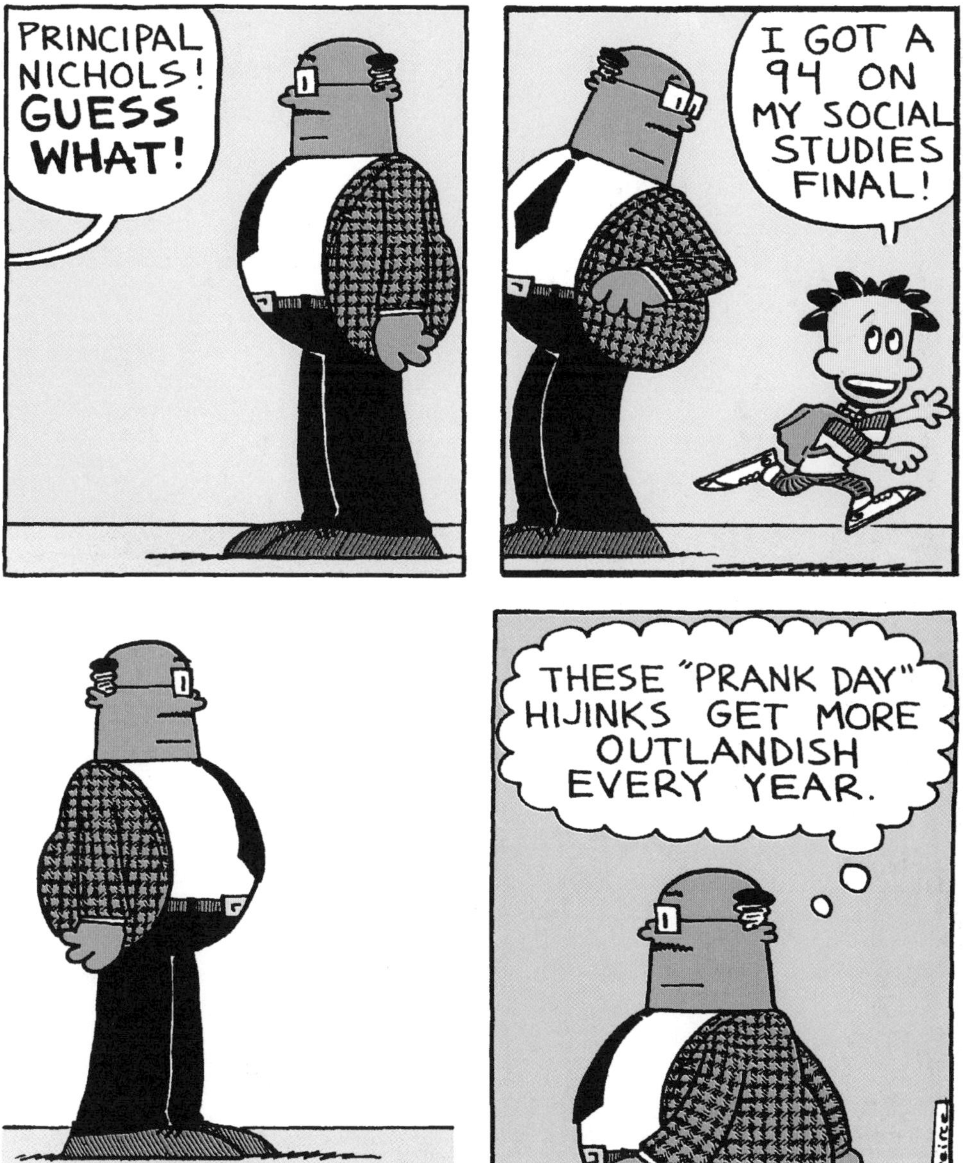
PRINCIPAL NICHOLS! GUESS WHAT!
I GOT A 94 ON MY SOCIAL STUDIES FINAL!
THESE "PRANK DAY" HIJINKS GET MORE OUTLANDISH EVERY YEAR.

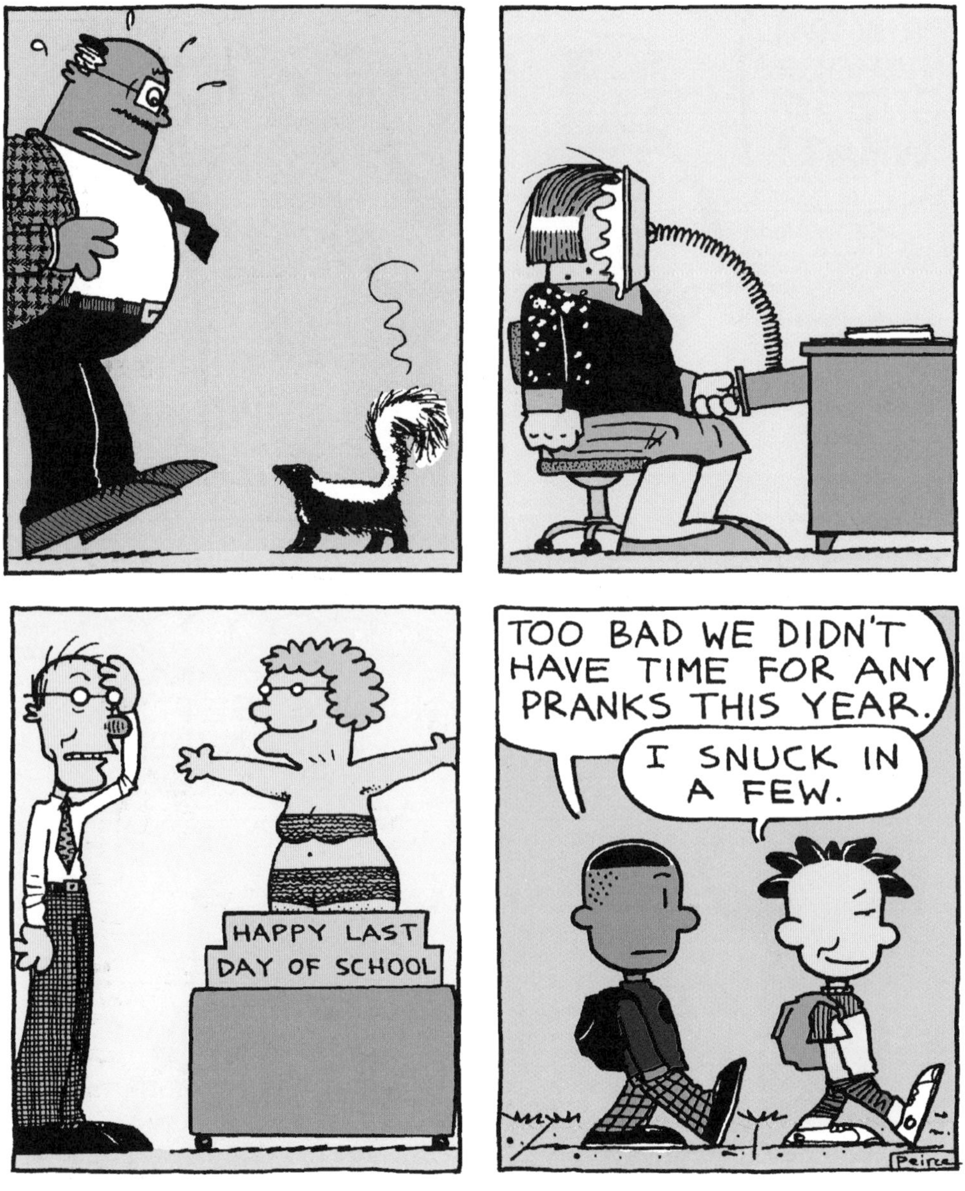
HAPPY LAST DAY OF SCHOOL
TOO BAD WE DIDN'T HAVE TIME FOR ANY PRANKS THIS YEAR.
I SNUCK IN A FEW.
Peirce

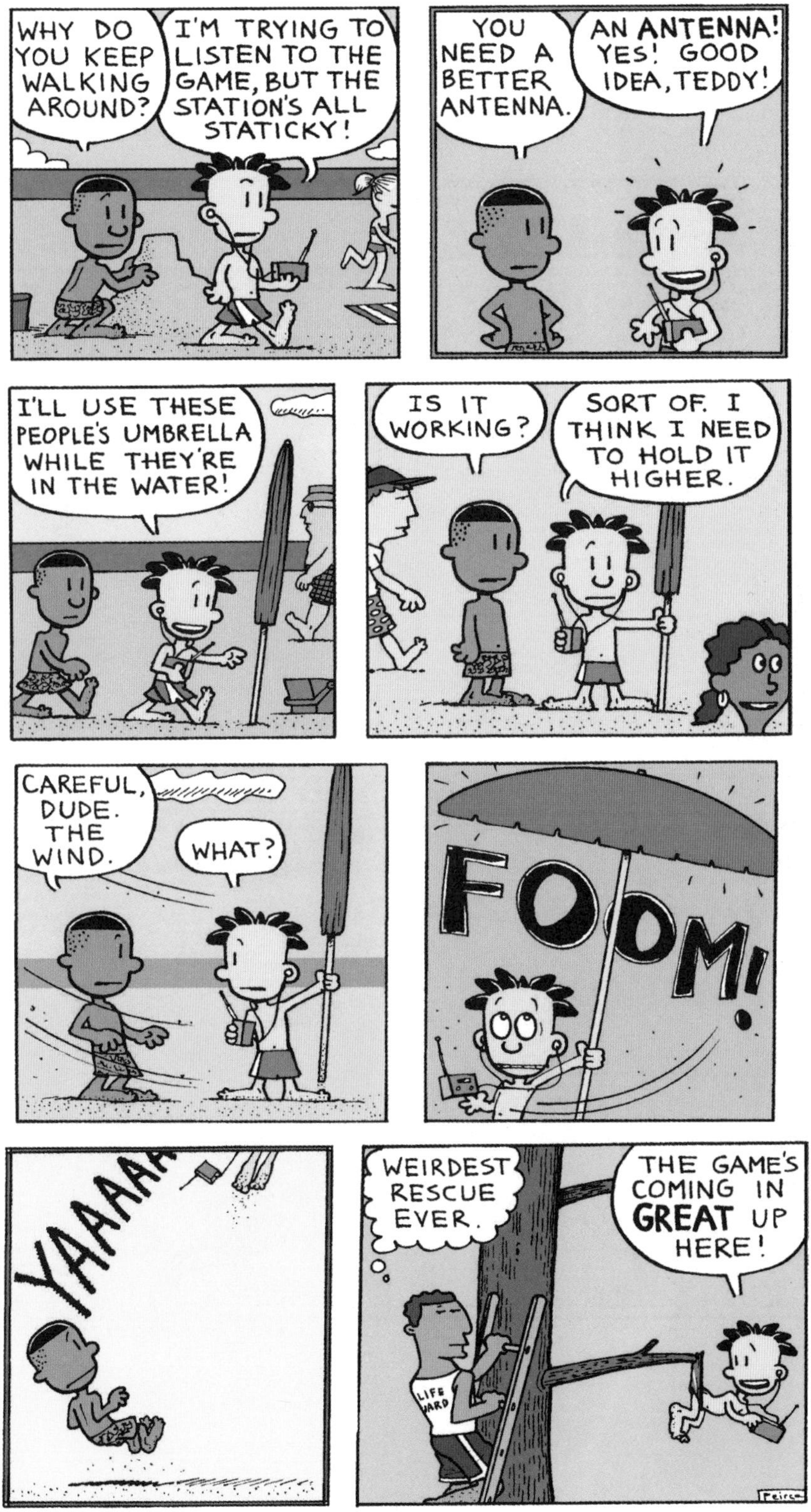
WHY DO YOU KEEP WALKING AROUND?
I'M TRYING TO LISTEN TO THE GAME, BUT THE STATION'S ALL STATICKY!
YOU NEED A BETTER ANTENNA.
AN **ANTENNA**! YES! GOOD IDEA, TEDDY!
I'LL USE THESE PEOPLE'S UMBRELLA WHILE THEY'RE IN THE WATER!
IS IT WORKING?
SORT OF. I THINK I NEED TO HOLD IT HIGHER.
CAREFUL, DUDE. THE WIND.
WHAT?
FOOM!
YAAAA
WEIRDEST RESCUE EVER.
THE GAME'S COMING IN **GREAT** UP HERE!
LIFE GUARD
Peirce

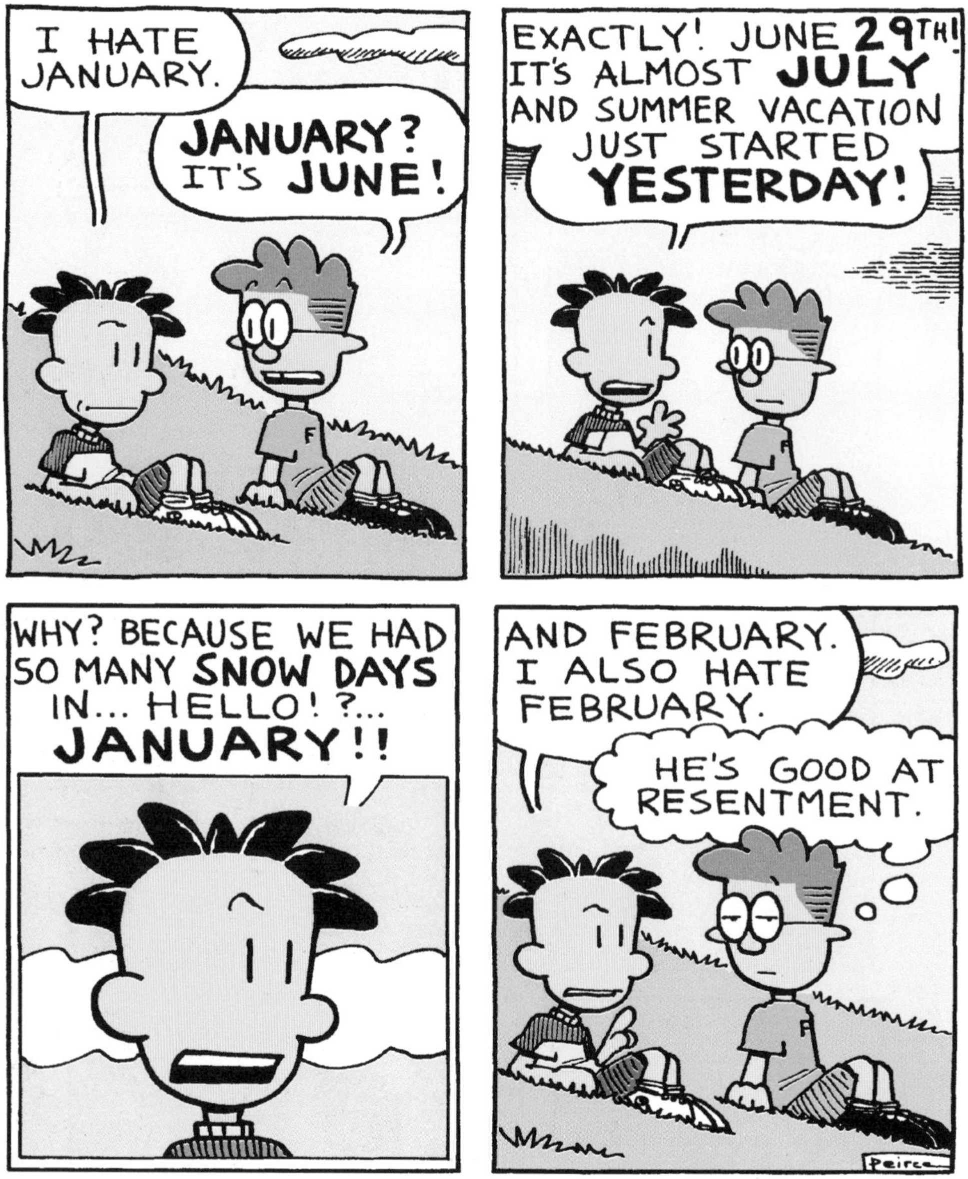
I HATE JANUARY.
JANUARY? IT'S JUNE!
EXACTLY! JUNE 29TH! IT'S ALMOST JULY AND SUMMER VACATION JUST STARTED YESTERDAY!
WHY? BECAUSE WE HAD SO MANY SNOW DAYS IN... HELLO! ?... JANUARY!!
AND FEBRUARY. I ALSO HATE FEBRUARY.
HE'S GOOD AT RESENTMENT.
Peirce

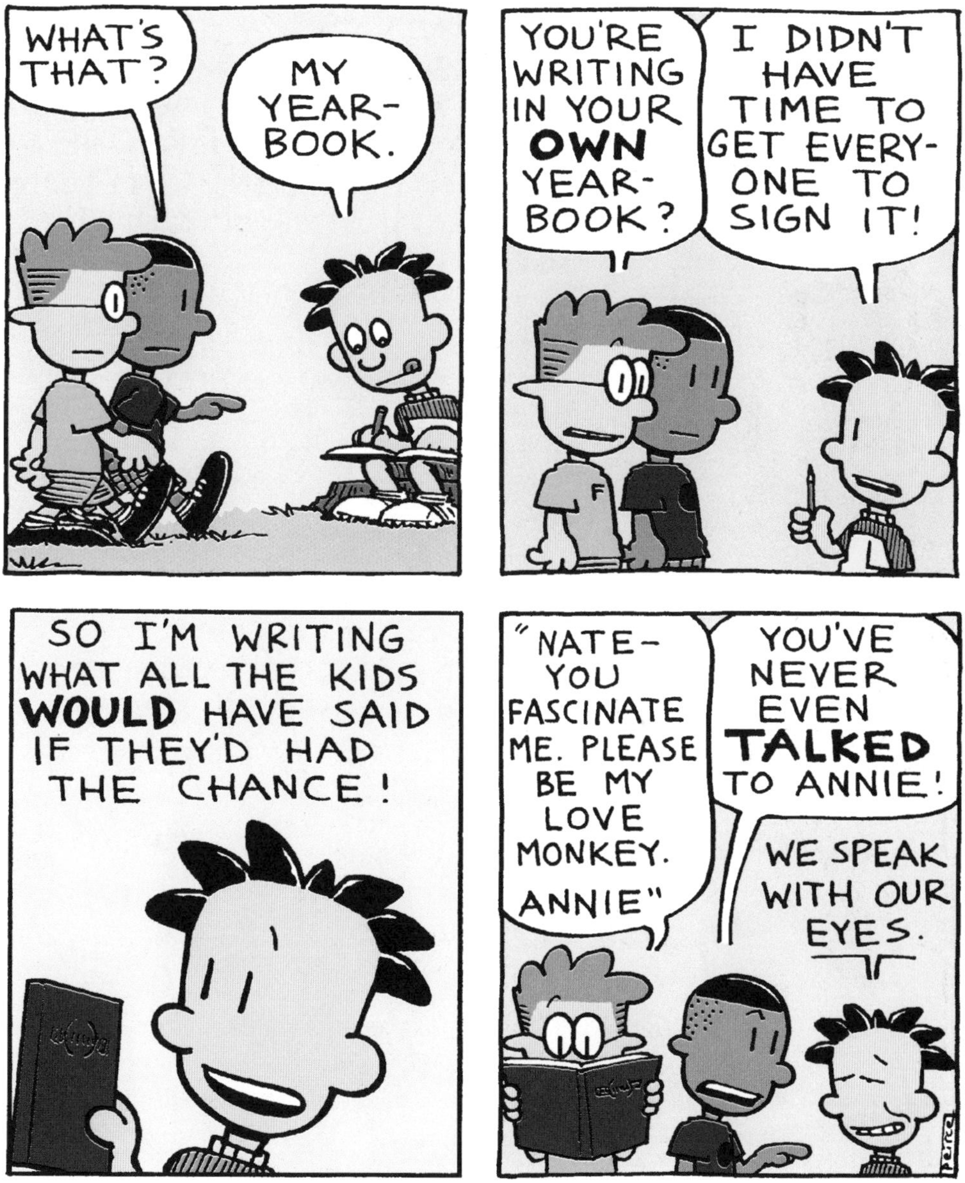
WHAT'S THAT?
MY YEAR-BOOK.
YOU'RE WRITING IN YOUR OWN YEAR-BOOK?
I DIDN'T HAVE TIME TO GET EVERY-ONE TO SIGN IT!
SO I'M WRITING WHAT ALL THE KIDS WOULD HAVE SAID IF THEY'D HAD THE CHANCE!
"NATE- YOU FASCINATE ME. PLEASE BE MY LOVE MONKEY. ANNIE"
YOU'VE NEVER EVEN TALKED TO ANNIE!
WE SPEAK WITH OUR EYES.

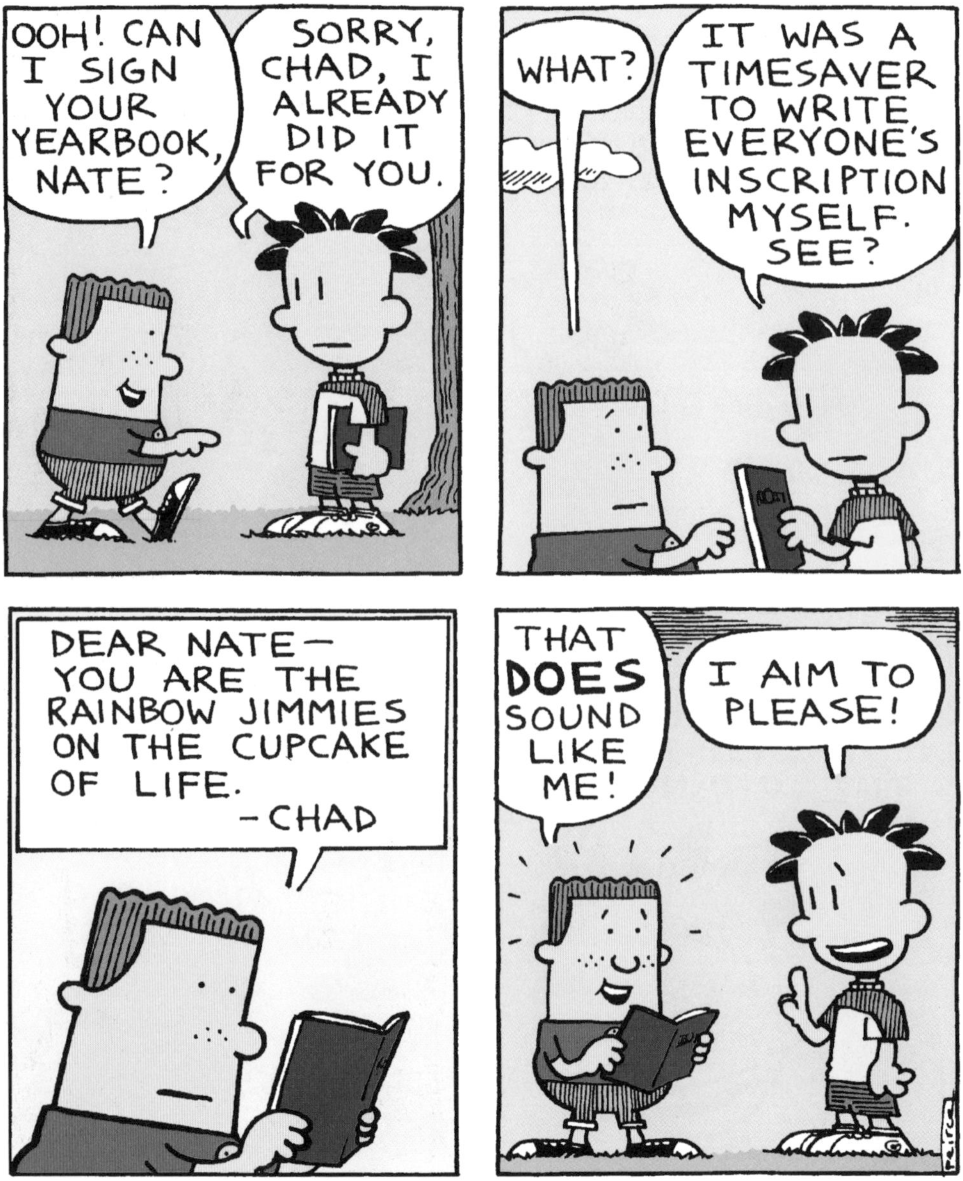
OOH! CAN I SIGN YOUR YEARBOOK, NATE?
SORRY, CHAD, I ALREADY DID IT FOR YOU.
WHAT?
IT WAS A TIMESAVER TO WRITE EVERYONE'S INSCRIPTION MYSELF. SEE?
DEAR NATE— YOU ARE THE RAINBOW JIMMIES ON THE CUPCAKE OF LIFE. —CHAD
THAT **DOES** SOUND LIKE ME!
I AIM TO PLEASE!

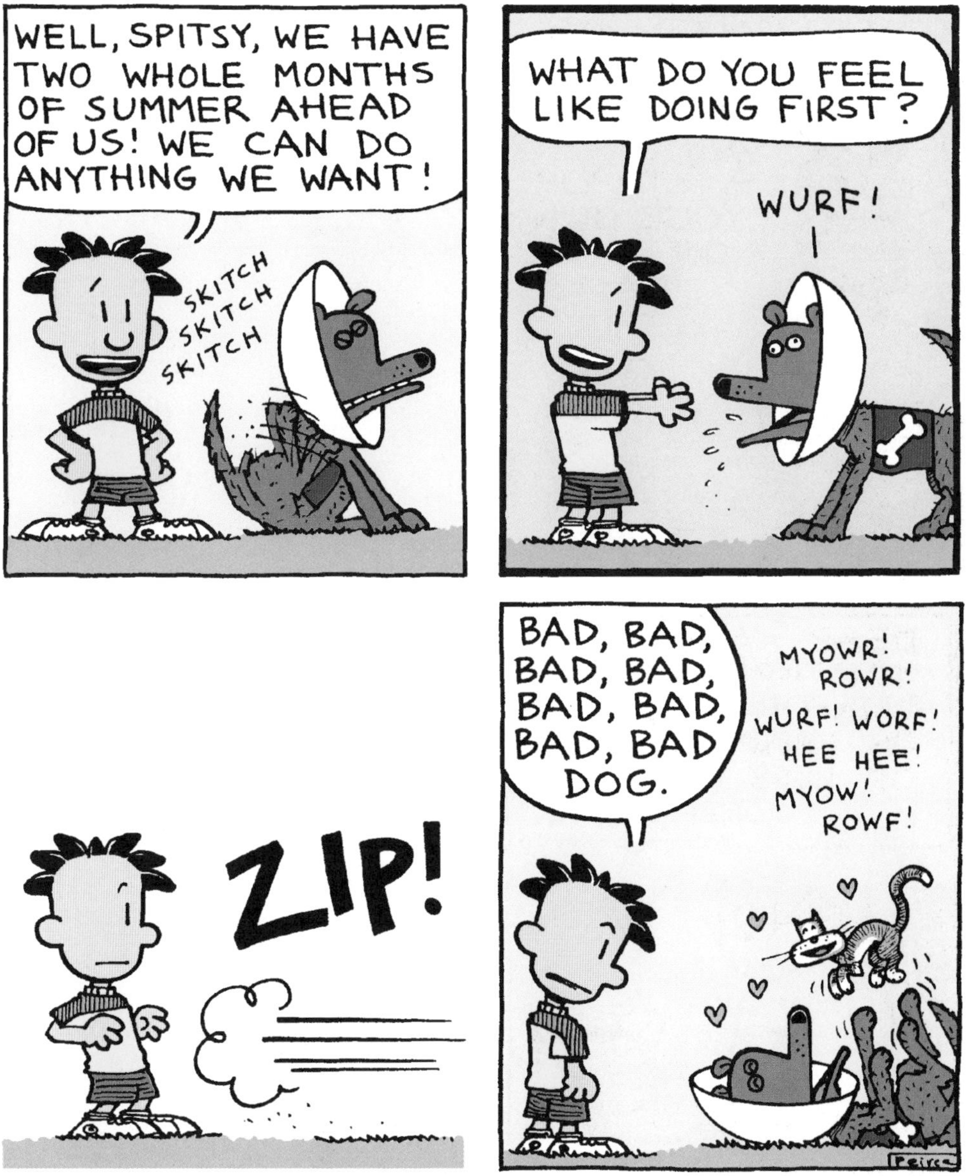
WELL, SPITSY, WE HAVE TWO WHOLE MONTHS OF SUMMER AHEAD OF US! WE CAN DO ANYTHING WE WANT!
SKITCH SKITCH SKITCH
WHAT DO YOU FEEL LIKE DOING FIRST?
WURF!
ZIP!
BAD, BAD, BAD, BAD, BAD, BAD, BAD, BAD DOG.
MYOWR! ROWR!
WURF! WORF!
HEE HEE!
MYOW! ROWF!
Peirce

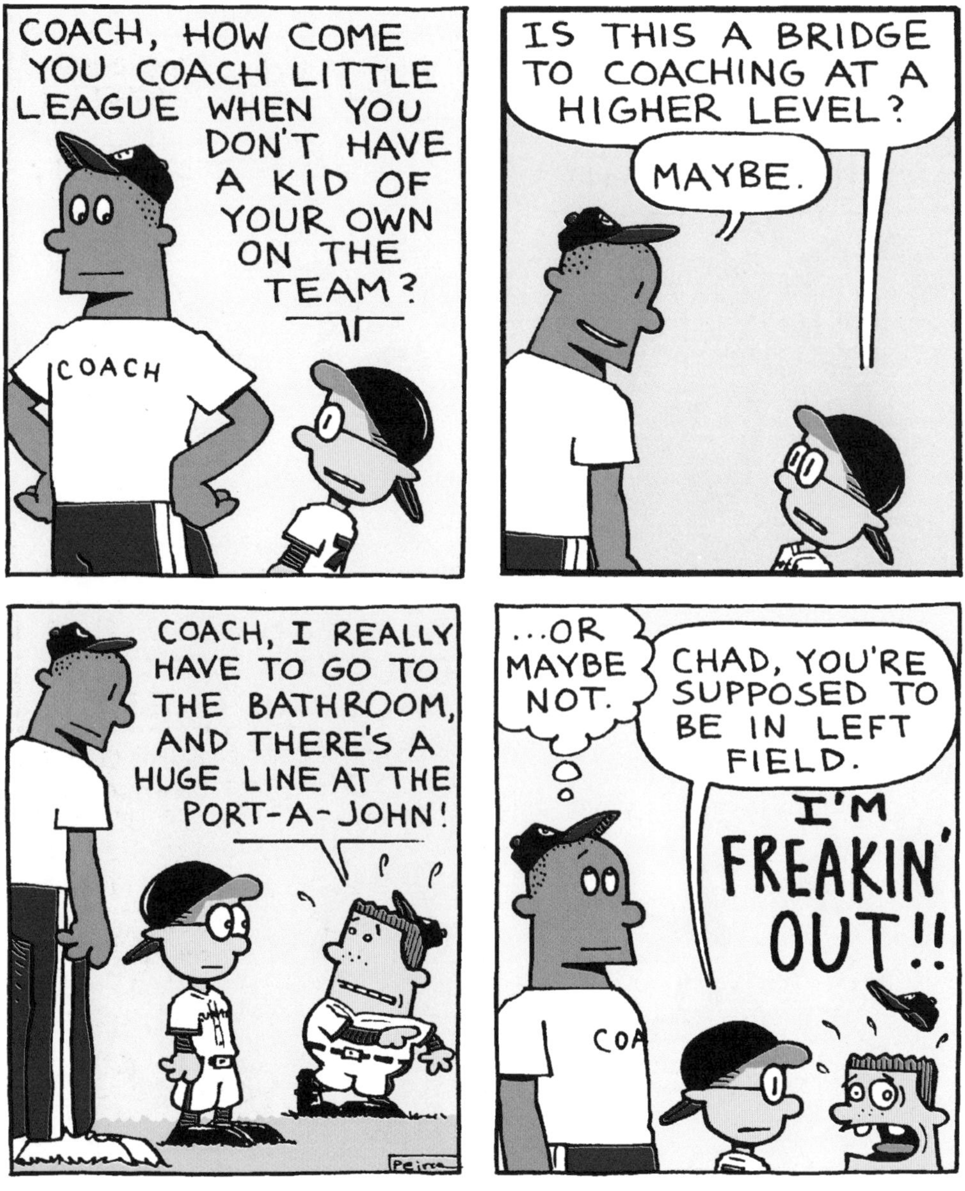
COACH, HOW COME YOU COACH LITTLE LEAGUE WHEN YOU DON'T HAVE A KID OF YOUR OWN ON THE TEAM?
COACH
IS THIS A BRIDGE TO COACHING AT A HIGHER LEVEL?
MAYBE.
COACH, I REALLY HAVE TO GO TO THE BATHROOM, AND THERE'S A HUGE LINE AT THE PORT-A-JOHN!
...OR MAYBE NOT.
CHAD, YOU'RE SUPPOSED TO BE IN LEFT FIELD.
I'M FREAKIN' OUT!!
COA
Peirce

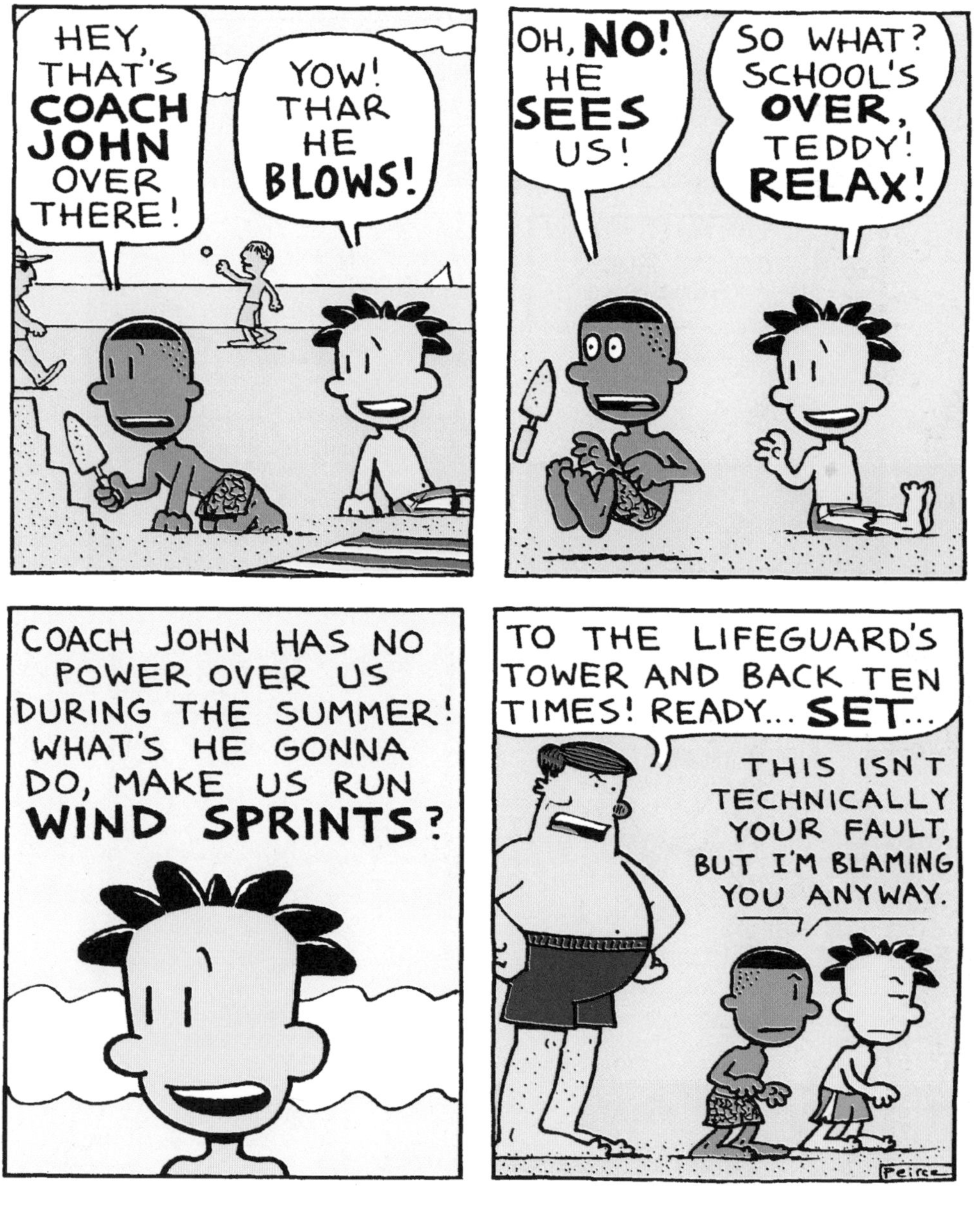
HEY, THAT'S COACH JOHN OVER THERE!
YOW! THAR HE BLOWS!
OH, NO! HE SEES US!
SO WHAT? SCHOOL'S OVER, TEDDY! RELAX!
COACH JOHN HAS NO POWER OVER US DURING THE SUMMER! WHAT'S HE GONNA DO, MAKE US RUN WIND SPRINTS?
TO THE LIFEGUARD'S TOWER AND BACK TEN TIMES! READY... SET...
THIS ISN'T TECHNICALLY YOUR FAULT, BUT I'M BLAMING YOU ANYWAY.
Peirce

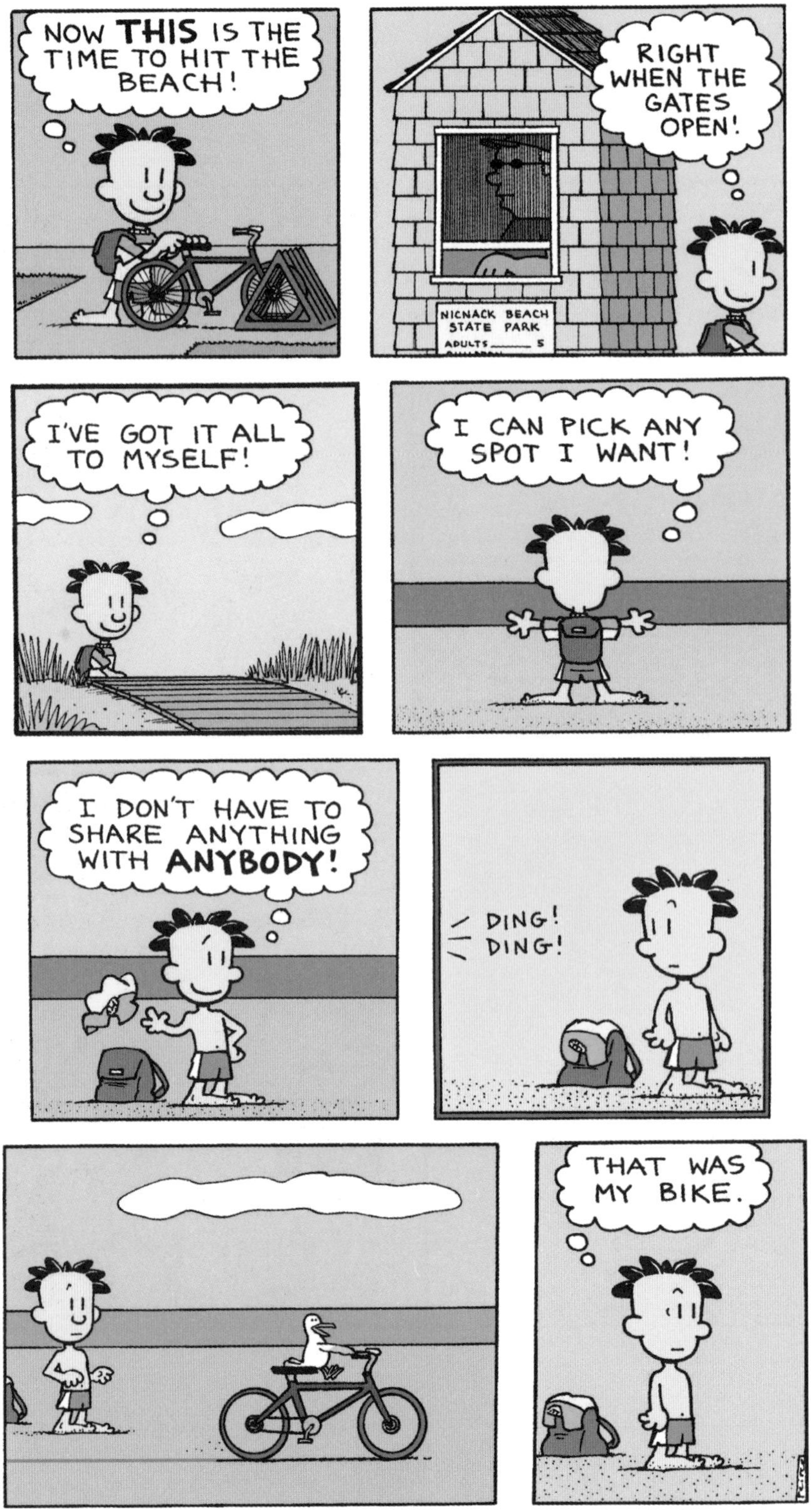
NOW **THIS** IS THE TIME TO HIT THE BEACH!
RIGHT WHEN THE GATES OPEN!
NICNACK BEACH
STATE PARK
I'VE GOT IT ALL TO MYSELF!
I CAN PICK ANY SPOT I WANT!
I DON'T HAVE TO SHARE ANYTHING WITH **ANYBODY!**
DING! DING!
THAT WAS MY BIKE.

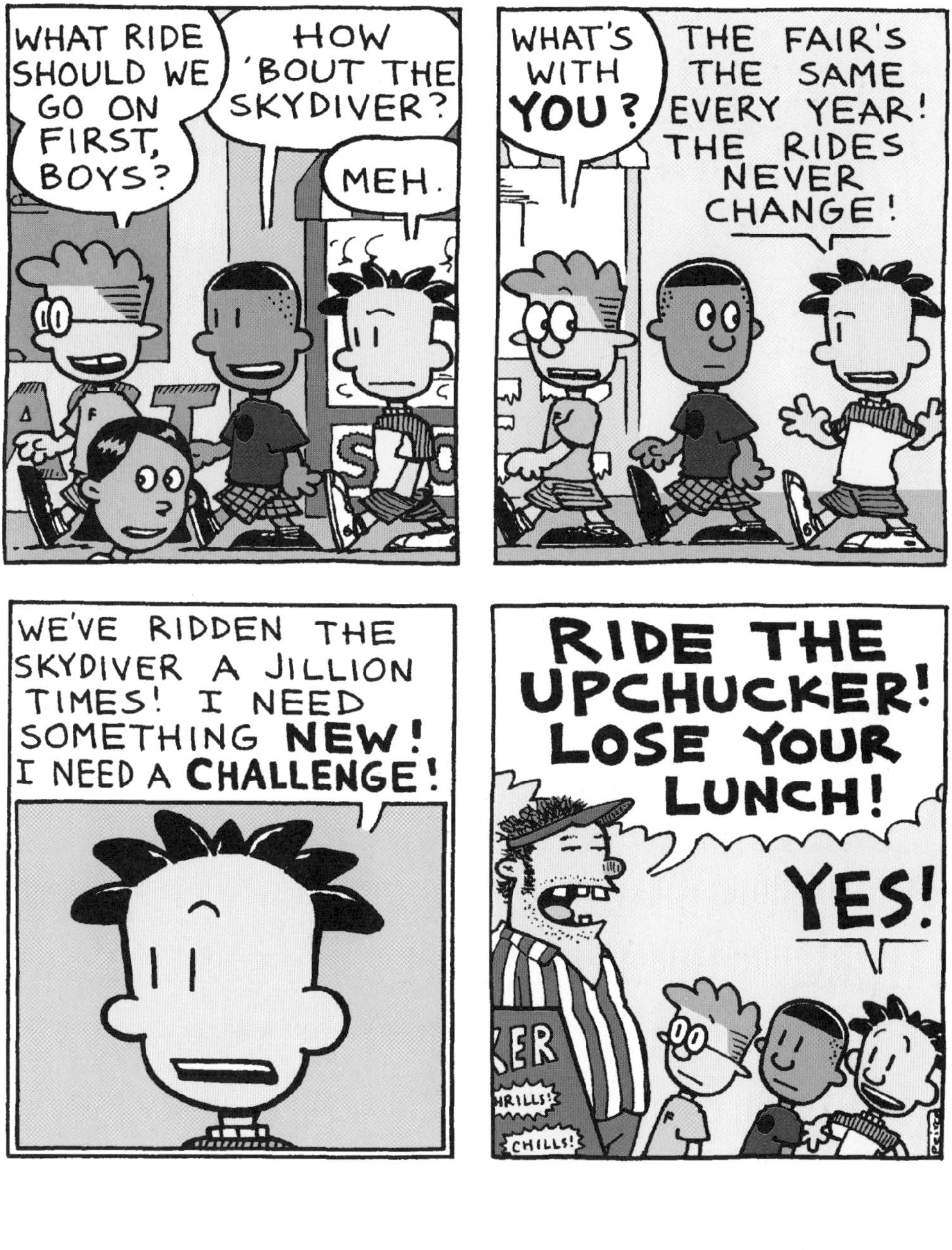
WHAT RIDE SHOULD WE GO ON FIRST, BOYS?
HOW 'BOUT THE SKYDIVER?
MEH.
WHAT'S WITH YOU?
THE FAIR'S THE SAME EVERY YEAR! THE RIDES NEVER CHANGE!
WE'VE RIDDEN THE SKYDIVER A JILLION TIMES! I NEED SOMETHING NEW! I NEED A CHALLENGE!
RIDE THE UPCHUCKER! LOSE YOUR LUNCH!
YES!
CHILLS!

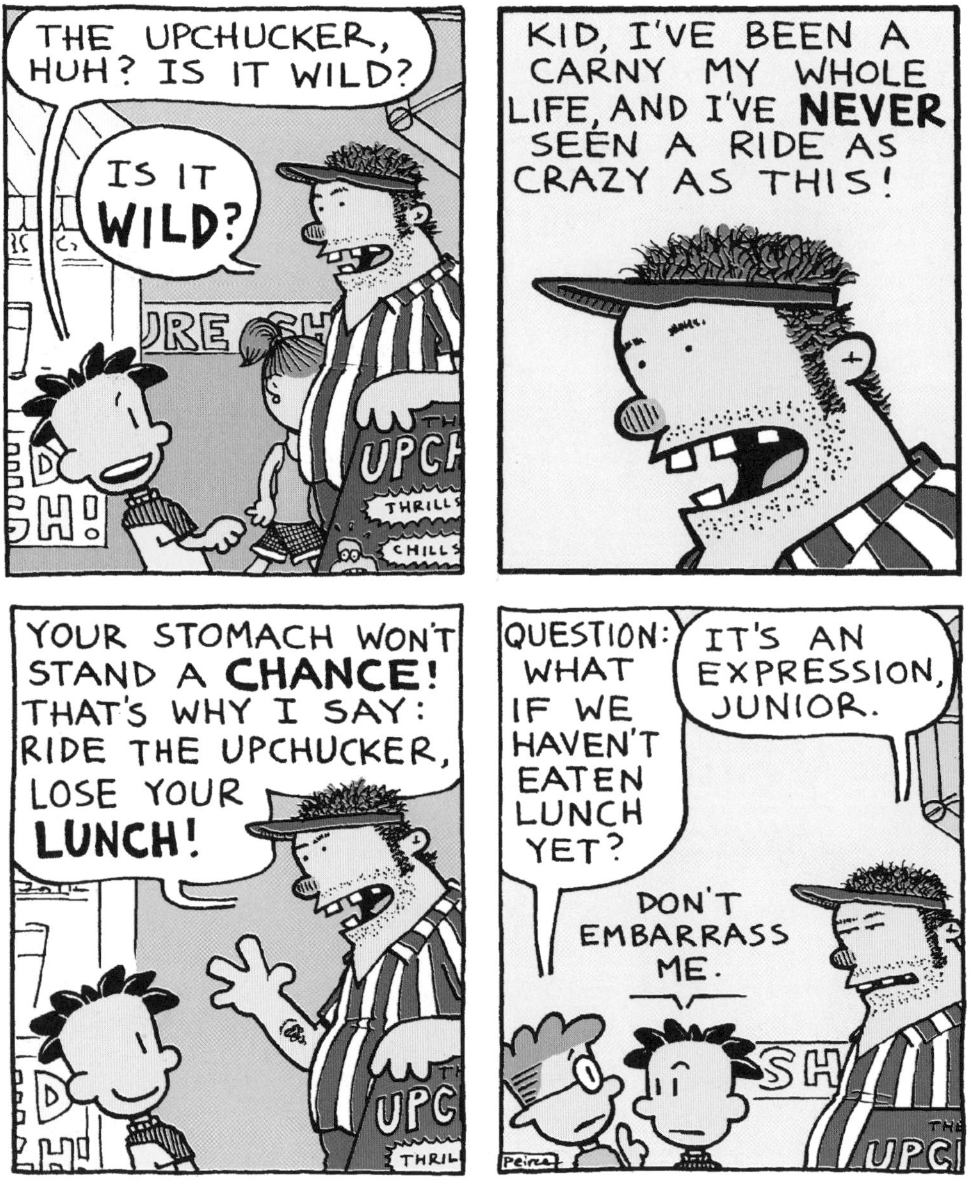
THE UPCHUCKER, HUH? IS IT WILD?
IS IT WILD?
THE UPCHUCKER
THRILLS
CHILLS
KID, I'VE BEEN A CARNY MY WHOLE LIFE, AND I'VE NEVER SEEN A RIDE AS CRAZY AS THIS!
YOUR STOMACH WON'T STAND A CHANCE! THAT'S WHY I SAY: RIDE THE UPCHUCKER, LOSE YOUR LUNCH!
QUESTION: WHAT IF WE HAVEN'T EATEN LUNCH YET?
IT'S AN EXPRESSION, JUNIOR.
DON'T EMBARRASS ME.
Peirce

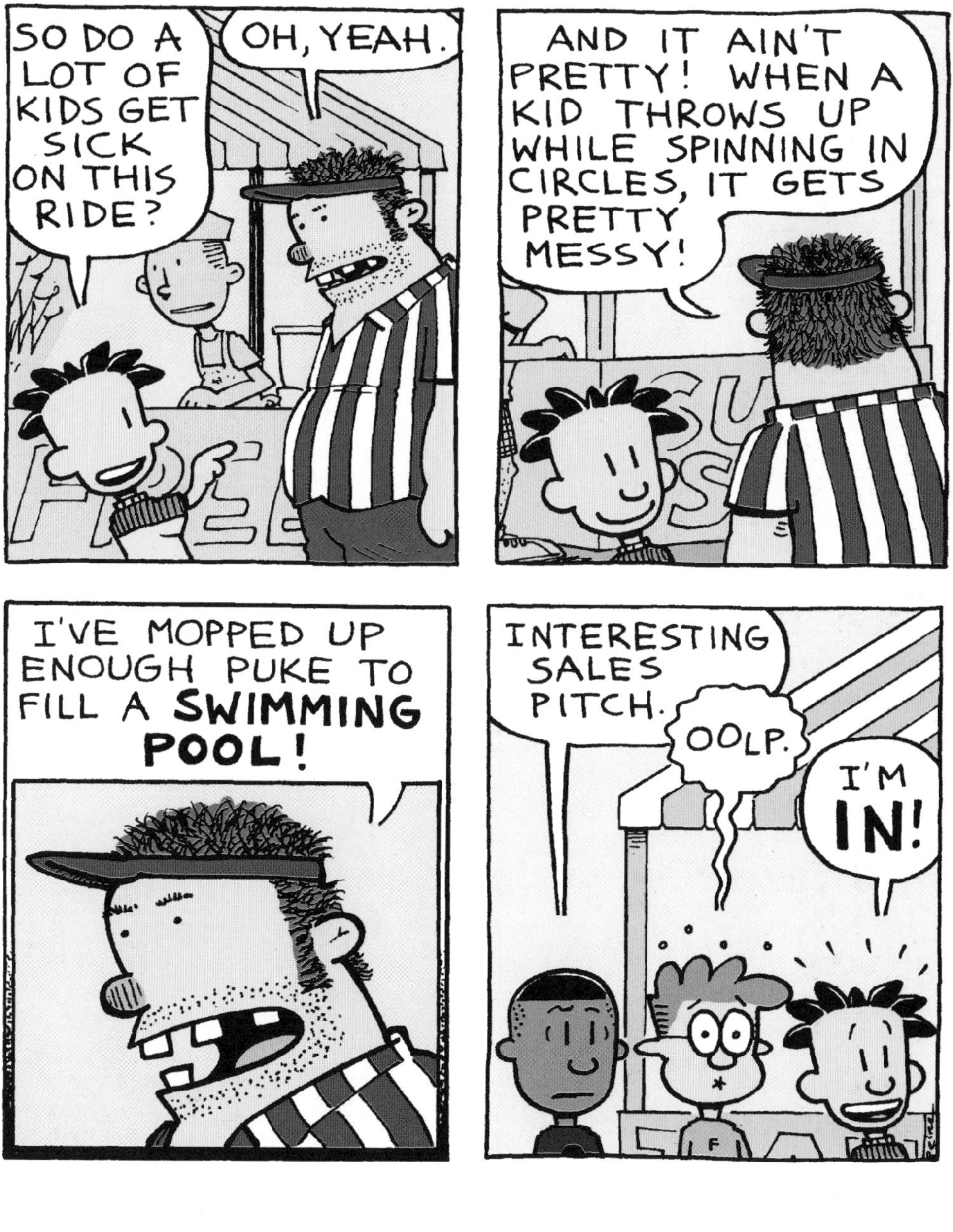
SO DO A LOT OF KIDS GET SICK ON THIS RIDE?
OH, YEAH.
AND IT AIN'T PRETTY! WHEN A KID THROWS UP WHILE SPINNING IN CIRCLES, IT GETS PRETTY MESSY!
I'VE MOPPED UP ENOUGH PUKE TO FILL A **SWIMMING POOL**!
INTERESTING SALES PITCH.
OOLP.
I'M **IN!**

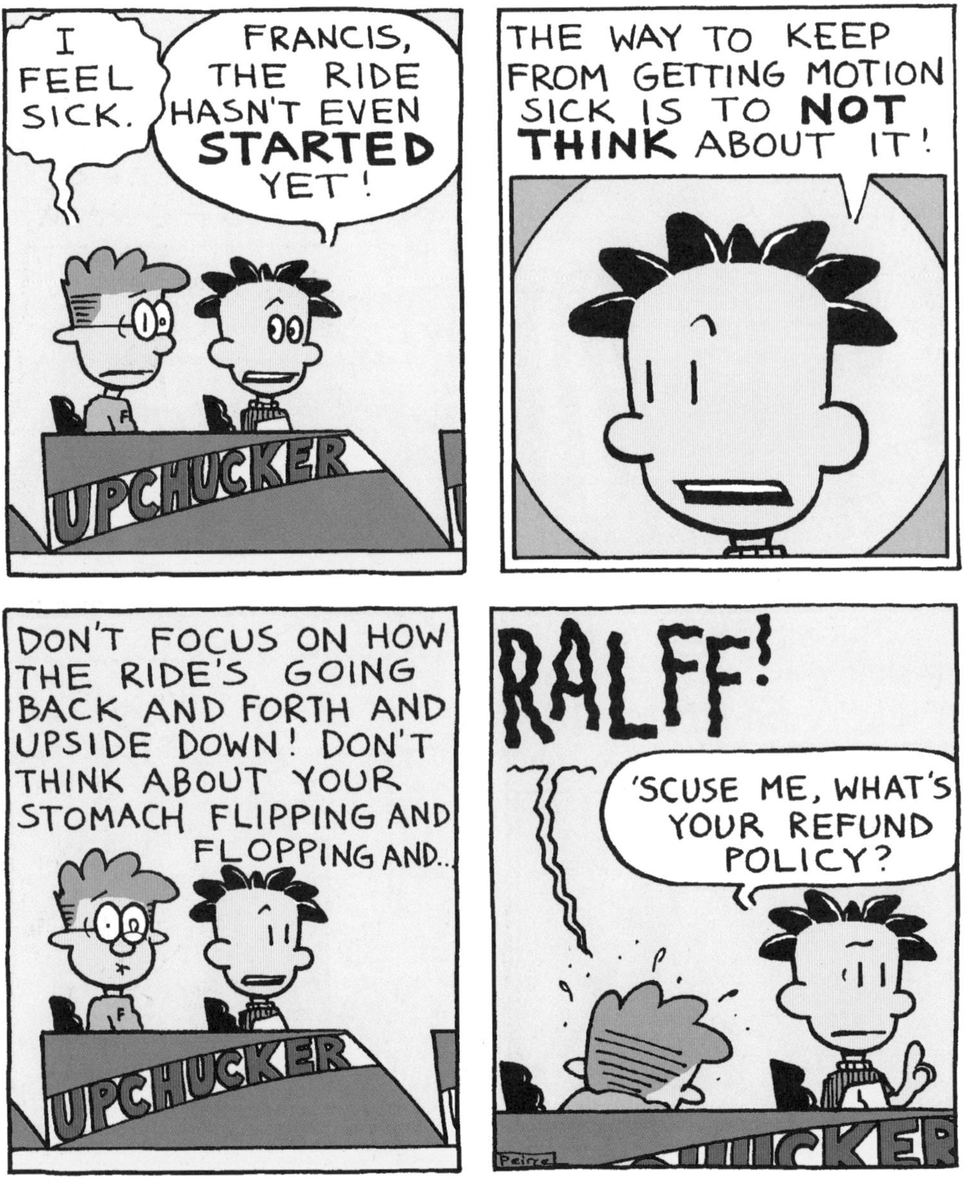
I FEEL SICK.
FRANCIS, THE RIDE HASN'T EVEN STARTED YET!
THE WAY TO KEEP FROM GETTING MOTION SICK IS TO NOT THINK ABOUT IT!
DON'T FOCUS ON HOW THE RIDE'S GOING BACK AND FORTH AND UPSIDE DOWN! DON'T THINK ABOUT YOUR STOMACH FLIPPING AND FLOPPING AND...
RALFF!
'SCUSE ME, WHAT'S YOUR REFUND POLICY?
UPCHUCKER
Peirce

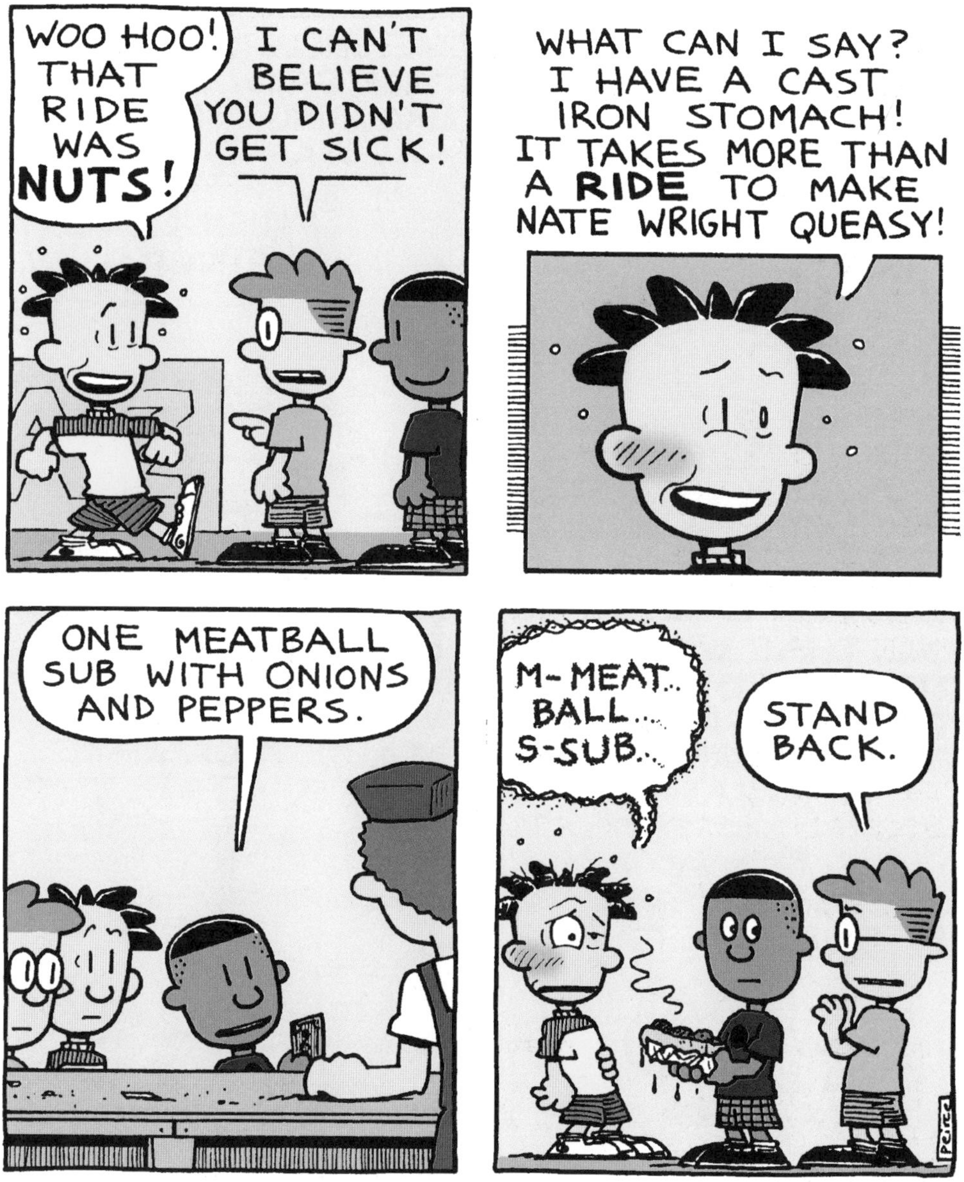
WOO HOO! THAT RIDE WAS **NUTS**!
I CAN'T BELIEVE YOU DIDN'T GET SICK!
WHAT CAN I SAY? I HAVE A CAST IRON STOMACH! IT TAKES MORE THAN A **RIDE** TO MAKE NATE WRIGHT QUEASY!
ONE MEATBALL SUB WITH ONIONS AND PEPPERS.
M-MEAT.. BALL... S-SUB..
STAND BACK.
PEIRCE

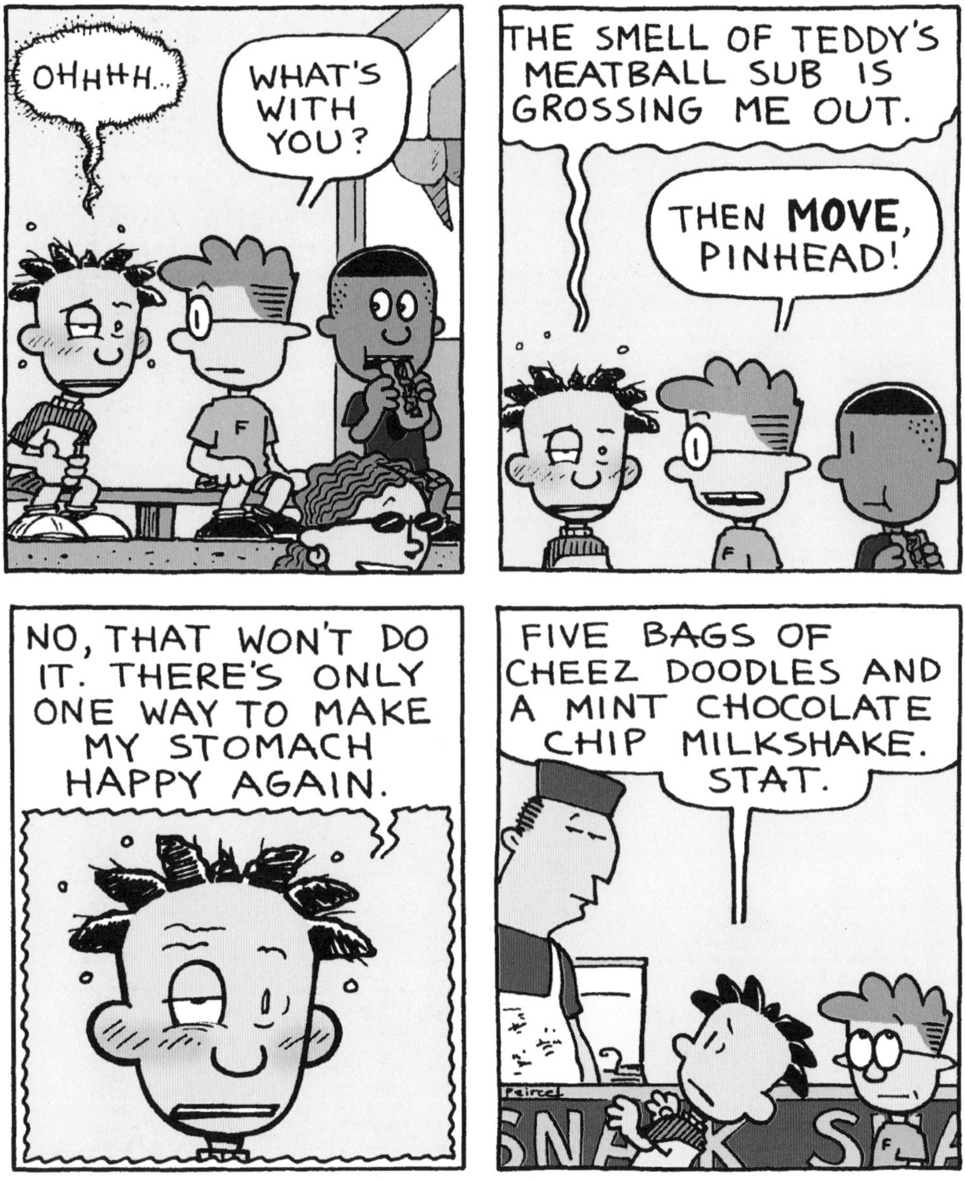
OHHHH...
WHAT'S WITH YOU?
THE SMELL OF TEDDY'S MEATBALL SUB IS GROSSING ME OUT.
THEN **MOVE**, PINHEAD!
NO, THAT WON'T DO IT. THERE'S ONLY ONE WAY TO MAKE MY STOMACH HAPPY AGAIN.
FIVE BAGS OF CHEEZ DOODLES AND A MINT CHOCOLATE CHIP MILKSHAKE. STAT.
Peirce

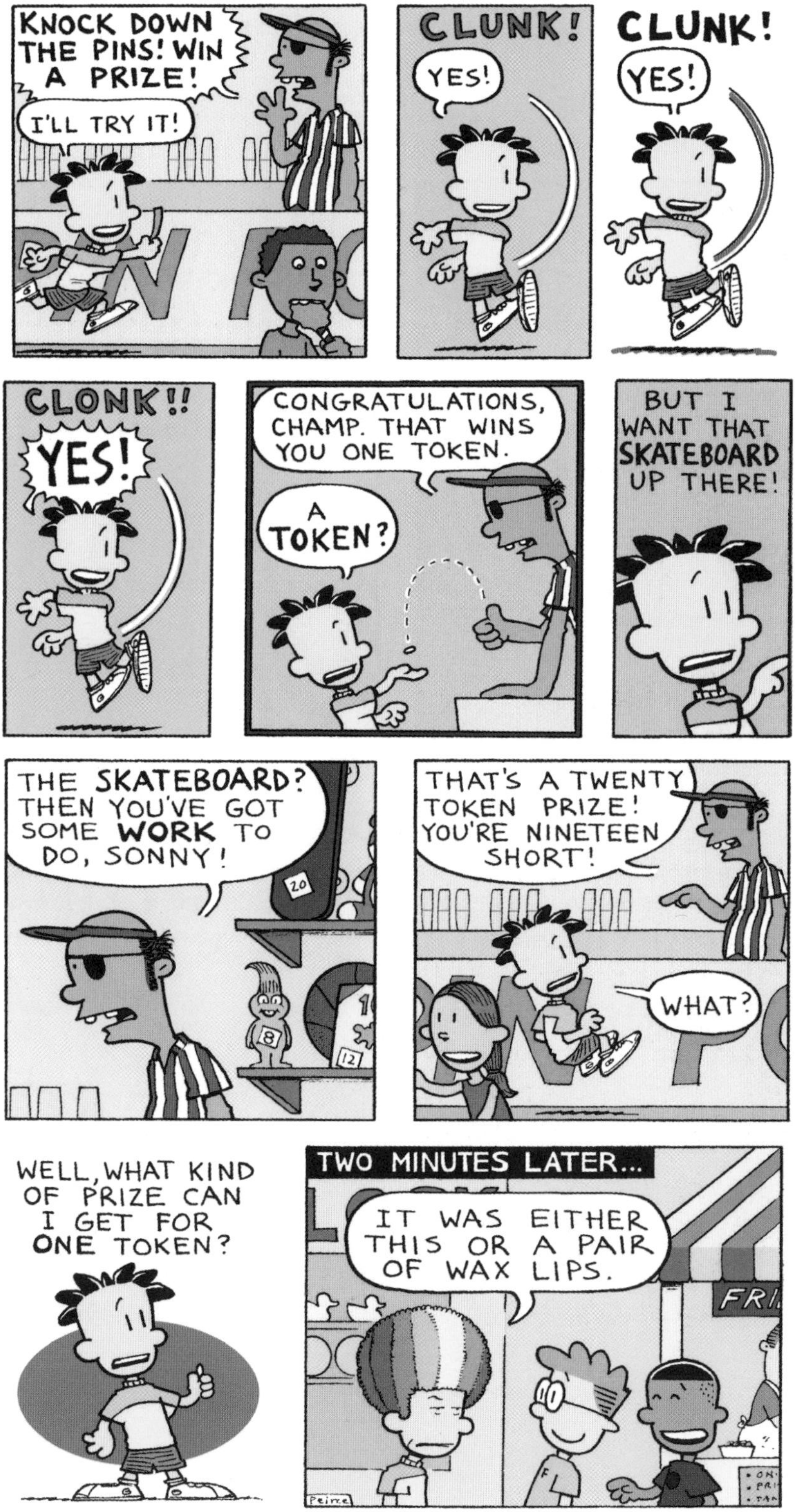
KNOCK DOWN THE PINS! WIN A PRIZE!
I'LL TRY IT!
CLUNK!
YES!
CLUNK!
YES!
CLONK!!
YES!
CONGRATULATIONS, CHAMP. THAT WINS YOU ONE TOKEN.
A TOKEN?
BUT I WANT THAT SKATEBOARD UP THERE!
THE SKATEBOARD? THEN YOU'VE GOT SOME WORK TO DO, SONNY!
20
8
12
THAT'S A TWENTY TOKEN PRIZE! YOU'RE NINETEEN SHORT!
WHAT?
WELL, WHAT KIND OF PRIZE CAN I GET FOR ONE TOKEN?
TWO MINUTES LATER...
IT WAS EITHER THIS OR A PAIR OF WAX LIPS.

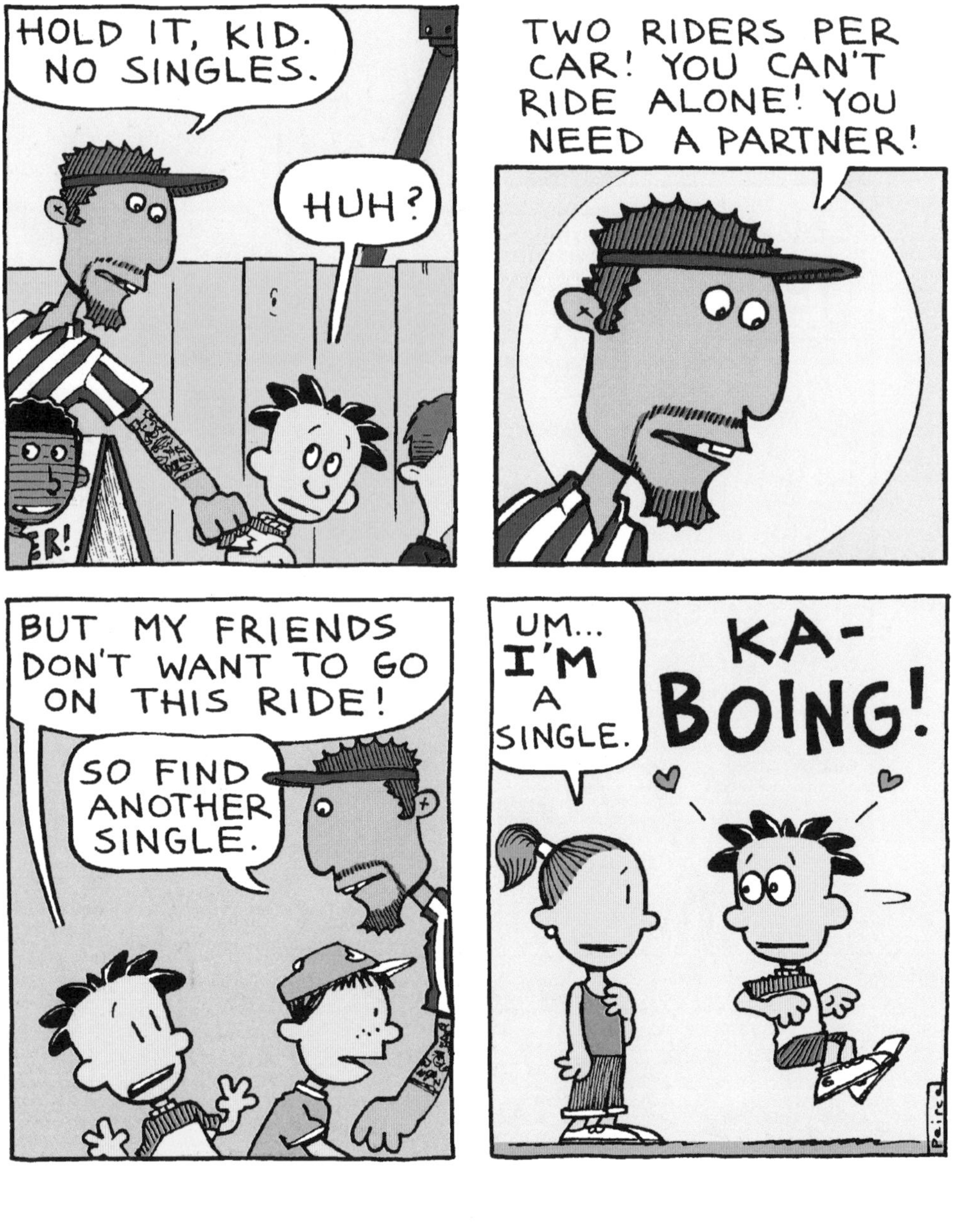
HOLD IT, KID. NO SINGLES.
HUH?
TWO RIDERS PER CAR! YOU CAN'T RIDE ALONE! YOU NEED A PARTNER!
BUT MY FRIENDS DON'T WANT TO GO ON THIS RIDE!
SO FIND ANOTHER SINGLE.
UM... I'M A SINGLE.
KA-BOING!
Peirce

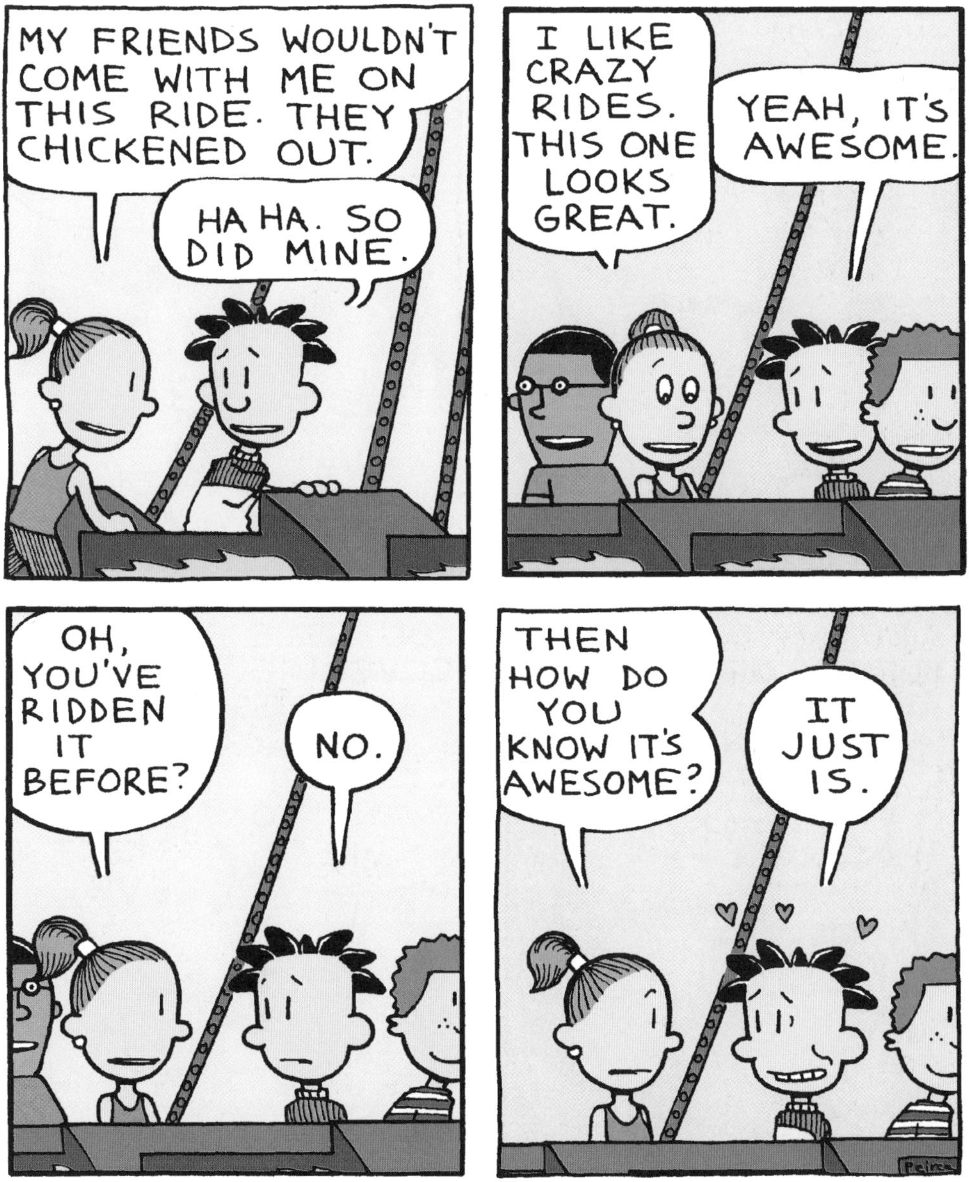
MY FRIENDS WOULDN'T COME WITH ME ON THIS RIDE. THEY CHICKENED OUT.
HA HA. SO DID MINE.
I LIKE CRAZY RIDES. THIS ONE LOOKS GREAT.
YEAH, IT'S AWESOME.
OH, YOU'VE RIDDEN IT BEFORE?
NO.
THEN HOW DO YOU KNOW IT'S AWESOME?
IT JUST IS.

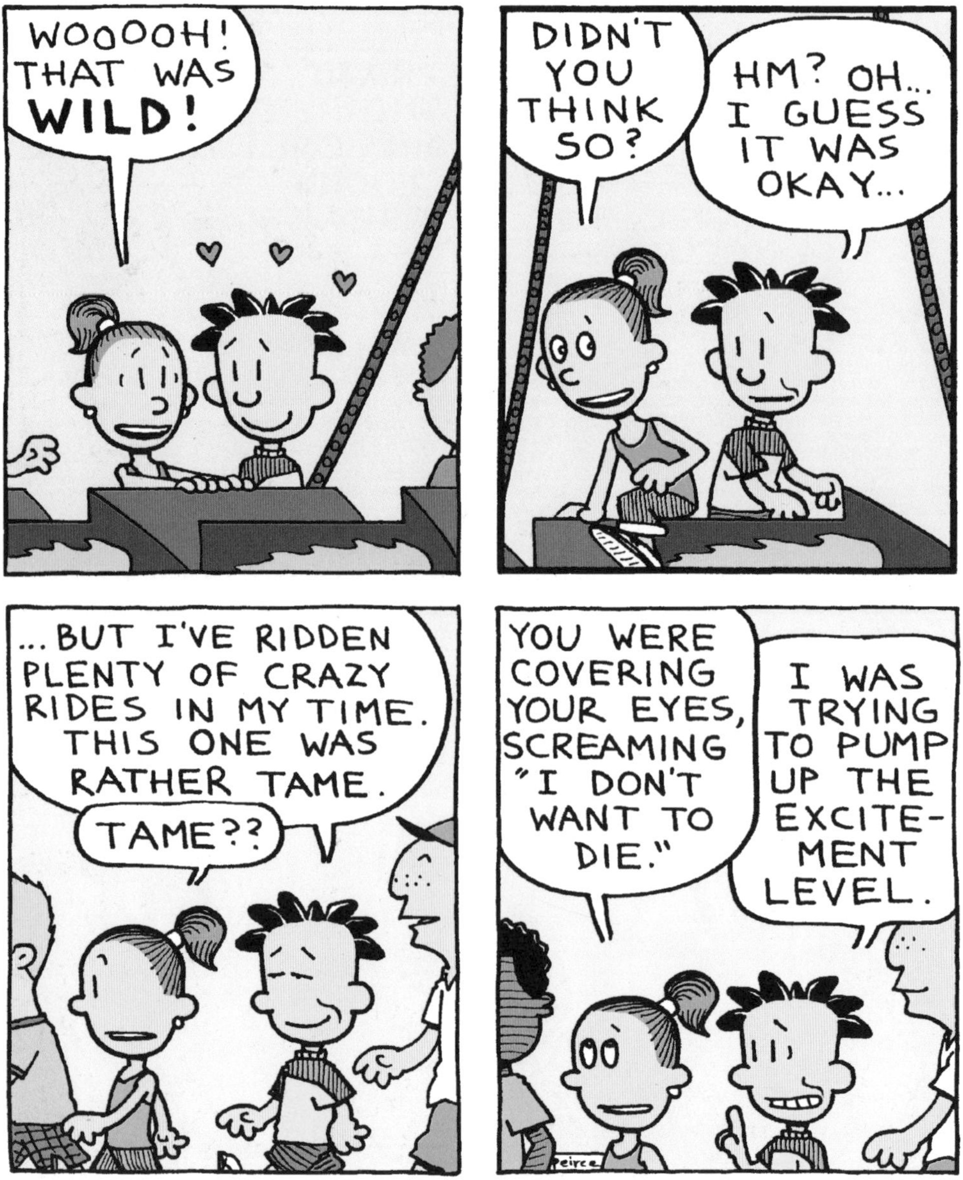
WOOOOH! THAT WAS **WILD!**
DIDN'T YOU THINK SO?
HM? OH... I GUESS IT WAS OKAY...
...BUT I'VE RIDDEN PLENTY OF CRAZY RIDES IN MY TIME. THIS ONE WAS RATHER TAME.
TAME??
YOU WERE COVERING YOUR EYES, SCREAMING "I DON'T WANT TO DIE."
I WAS TRYING TO PUMP UP THE EXCITE-MENT LEVEL.
Peirce

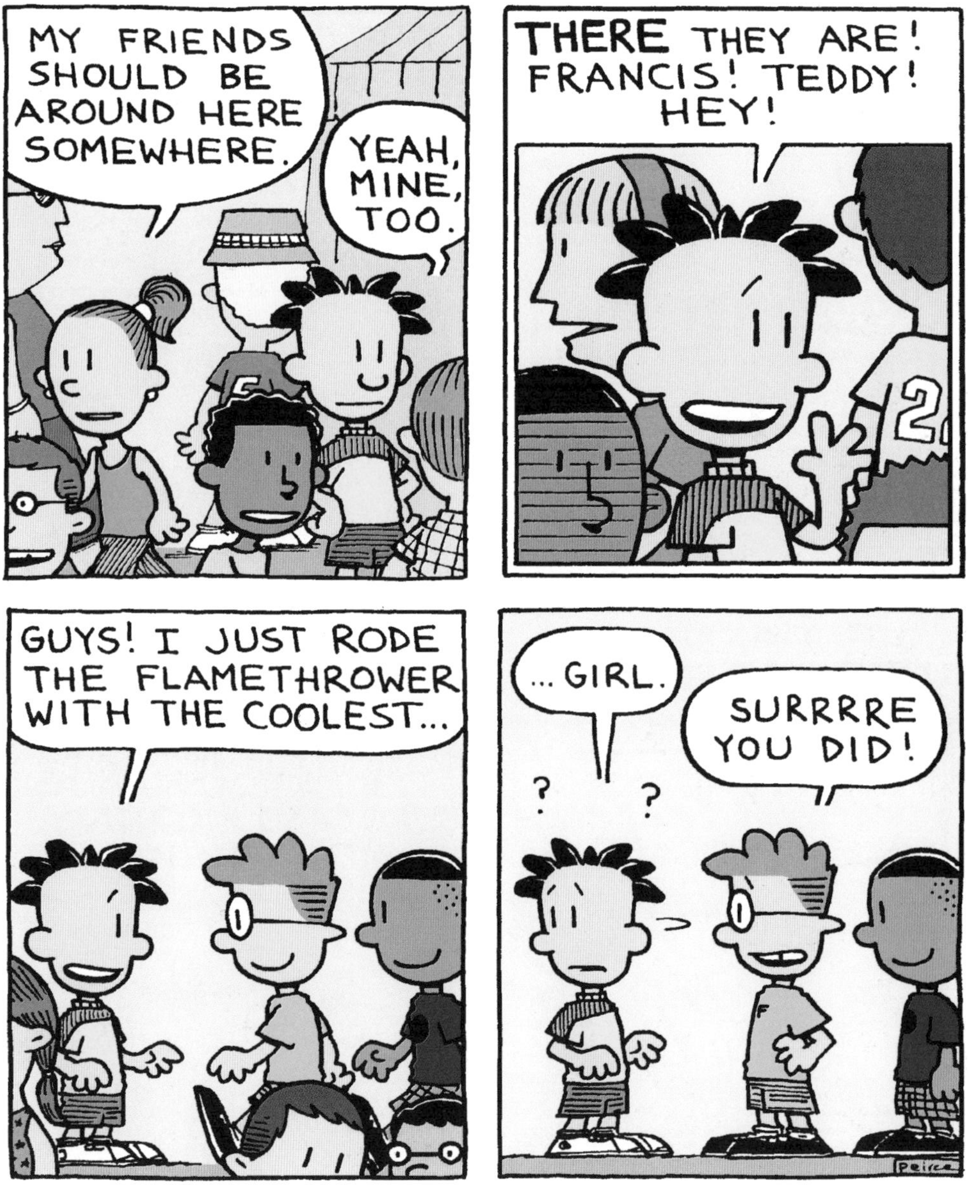
MY FRIENDS SHOULD BE AROUND HERE SOMEWHERE.
YEAH, MINE, TOO.
THERE THEY ARE! FRANCIS! TEDDY! HEY!
GUYS! I JUST RODE THE FLAMETHROWER WITH THE COOLEST...
...GIRL.
? ?
SURRRRE YOU DID!
peirce

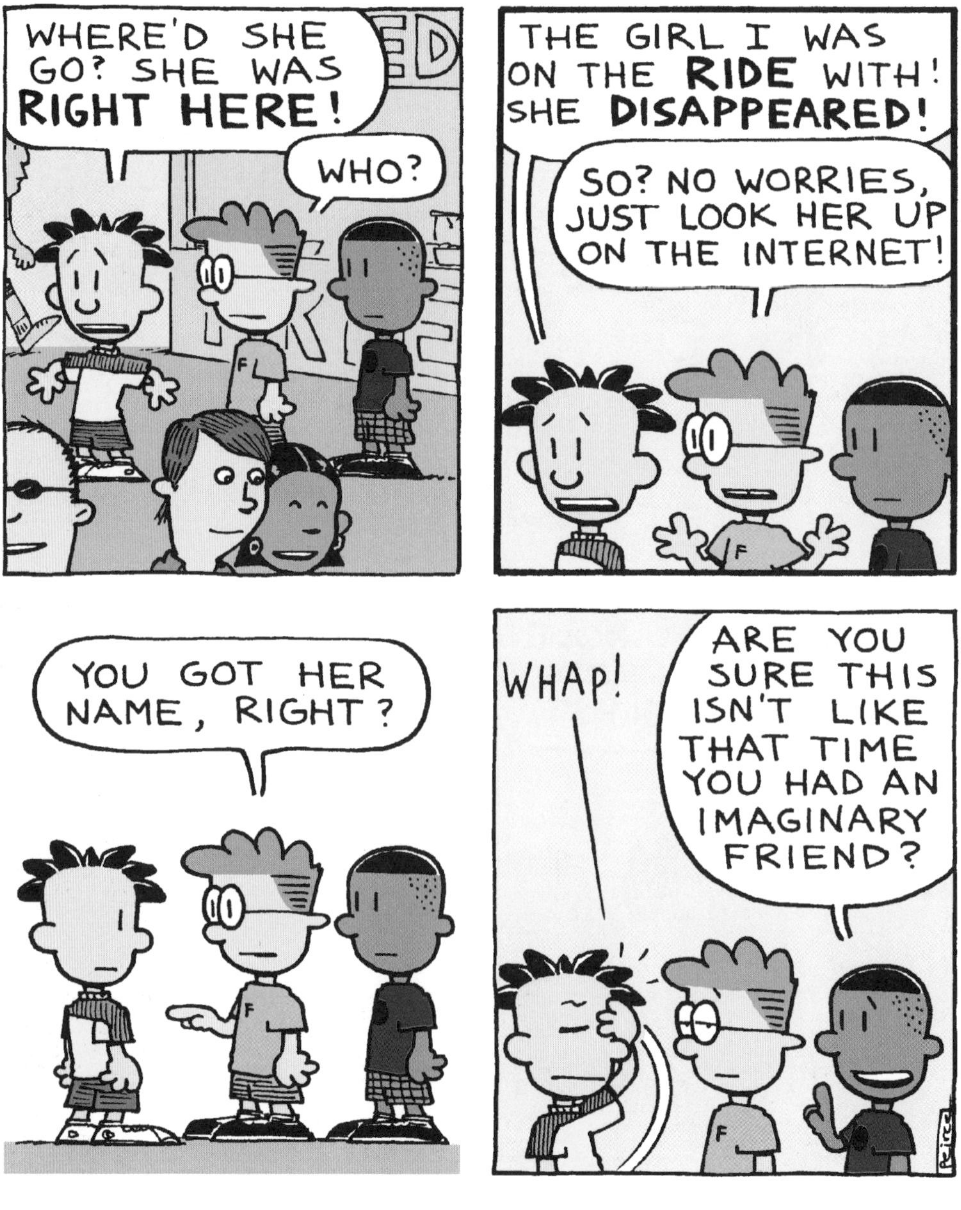
WHERE'D SHE GO? SHE WAS **RIGHT HERE!**
WHO?
THE GIRL I WAS ON THE **RIDE** WITH! SHE **DISAPPEARED!**
SO? NO WORRIES, JUST LOOK HER UP ON THE INTERNET!
YOU GOT HER NAME, RIGHT?
WHAP!
ARE YOU SURE THIS ISN'T LIKE THAT TIME YOU HAD AN IMAGINARY FRIEND?

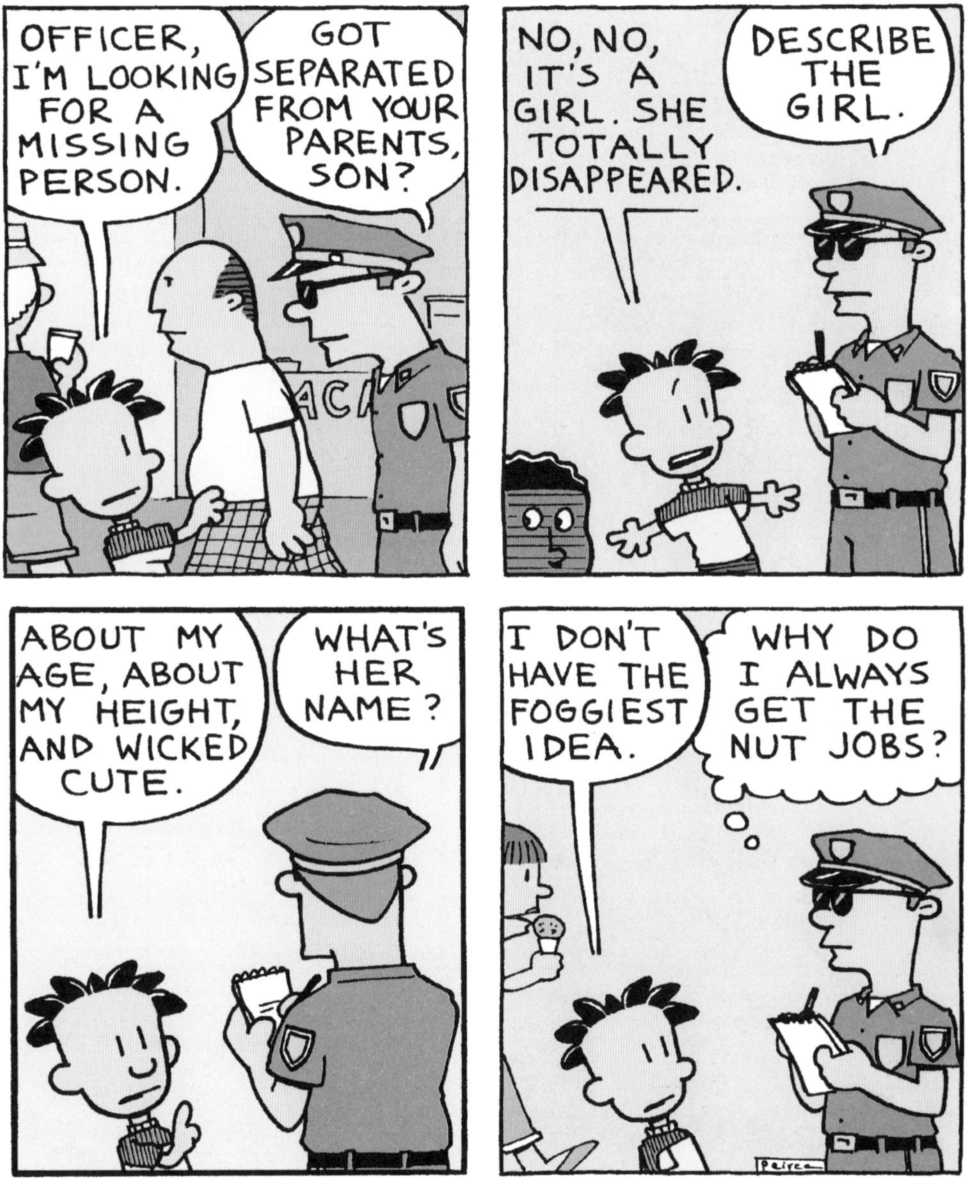
OFFICER, I'M LOOKING FOR A MISSING PERSON.
GOT SEPARATED FROM YOUR PARENTS, SON?
NO, NO, IT'S A GIRL. SHE TOTALLY DISAPPEARED.
DESCRIBE THE GIRL.
ABOUT MY AGE, ABOUT MY HEIGHT, AND WICKED CUTE.
WHAT'S HER NAME?
I DON'T HAVE THE FOGGIEST IDEA.
WHY DO I ALWAYS GET THE NUT JOBS?

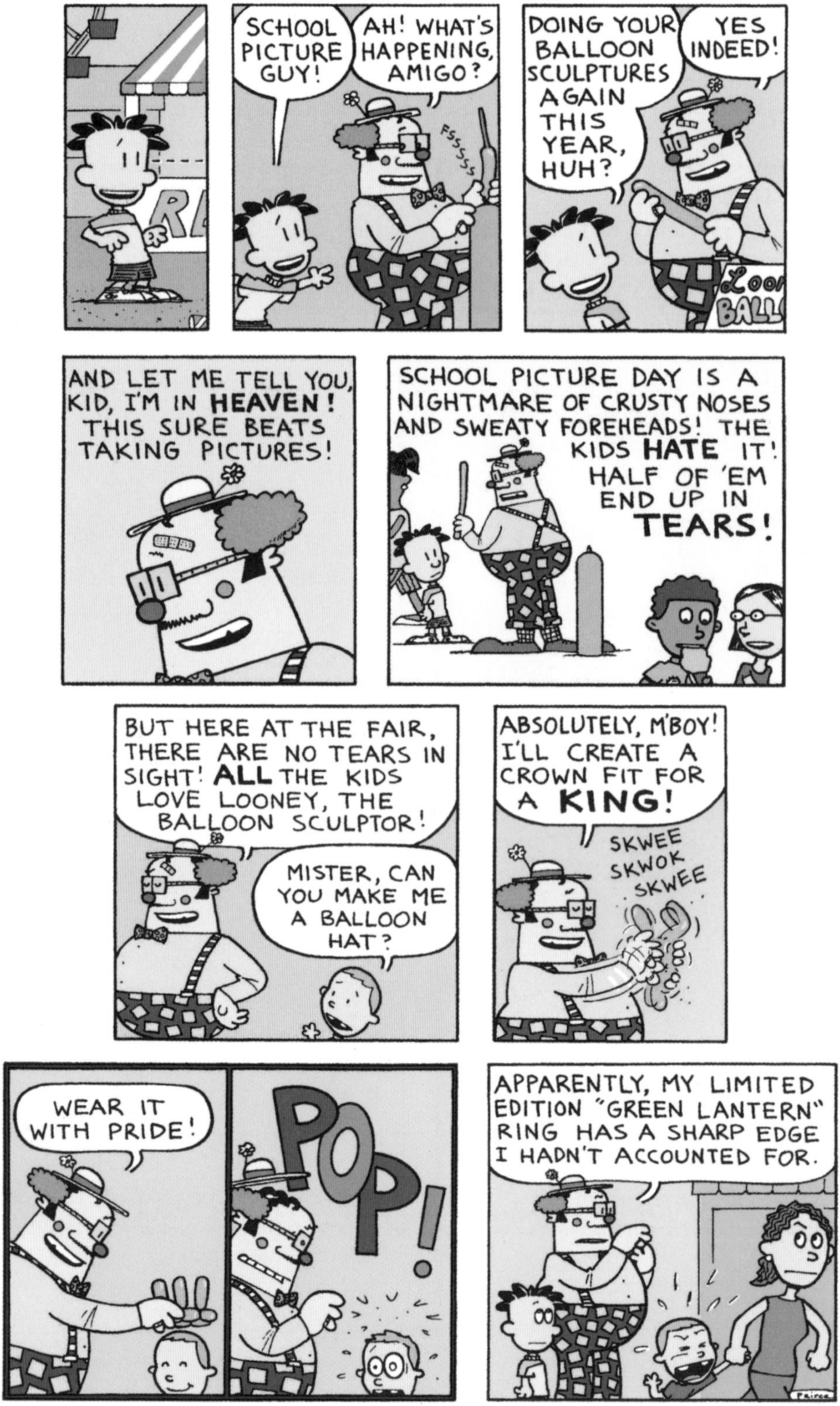
SCHOOL PICTURE GUY!
AH! WHAT'S HAPPENING, AMIGO?
FSSSSS
DOING YOUR BALLOON SCULPTURES AGAIN THIS YEAR, HUH?
YES INDEED!
AND LET ME TELL YOU, KID, I'M IN HEAVEN! THIS SURE BEATS TAKING PICTURES!
SCHOOL PICTURE DAY IS A NIGHTMARE OF CRUSTY NOSES AND SWEATY FOREHEADS! THE KIDS HATE IT! HALF OF 'EM END UP IN TEARS!
BUT HERE AT THE FAIR, THERE ARE NO TEARS IN SIGHT! ALL THE KIDS LOVE LOONEY, THE BALLOON SCULPTOR!
MISTER, CAN YOU MAKE ME A BALLOON HAT?
ABSOLUTELY, M'BOY! I'LL CREATE A CROWN FIT FOR A KING!
SKWEE SKWOK SKWEE
WEAR IT WITH PRIDE!
POP!
APPARENTLY, MY LIMITED EDITION "GREEN LANTERN" RING HAS A SHARP EDGE I HADN'T ACCOUNTED FOR.

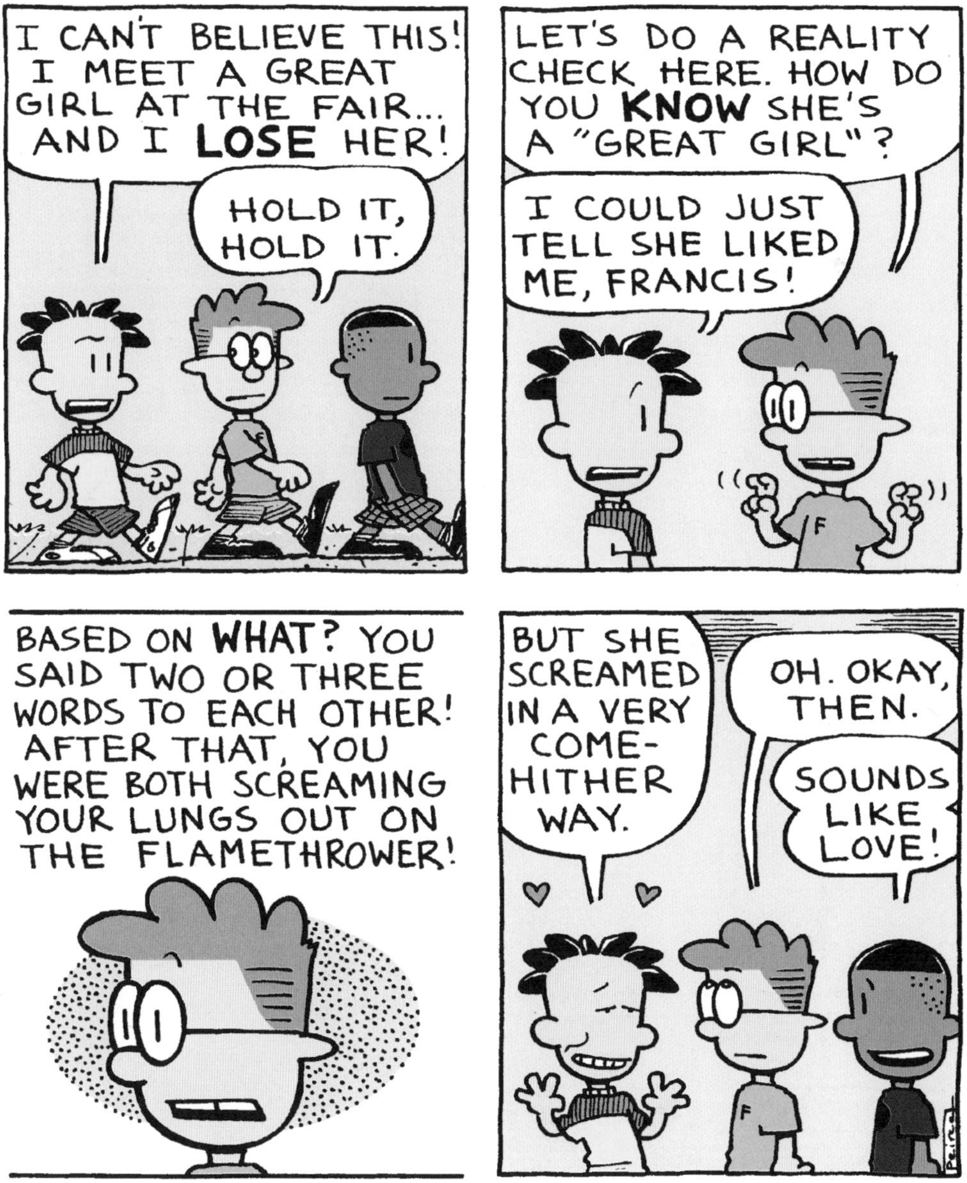
I CAN'T BELIEVE THIS! I MEET A GREAT GIRL AT THE FAIR... AND I **LOSE** HER!
HOLD IT, HOLD IT.
LET'S DO A REALITY CHECK HERE. HOW DO YOU **KNOW** SHE'S A "GREAT GIRL"?
I COULD JUST TELL SHE LIKED ME, FRANCIS!
BASED ON **WHAT**? YOU SAID TWO OR THREE WORDS TO EACH OTHER! AFTER THAT, YOU WERE BOTH SCREAMING YOUR LUNGS OUT ON THE FLAMETHROWER!
BUT SHE SCREAMED IN A VERY COME-HITHER WAY.
OH. OKAY, THEN.
SOUNDS LIKE LOVE!
Peirce

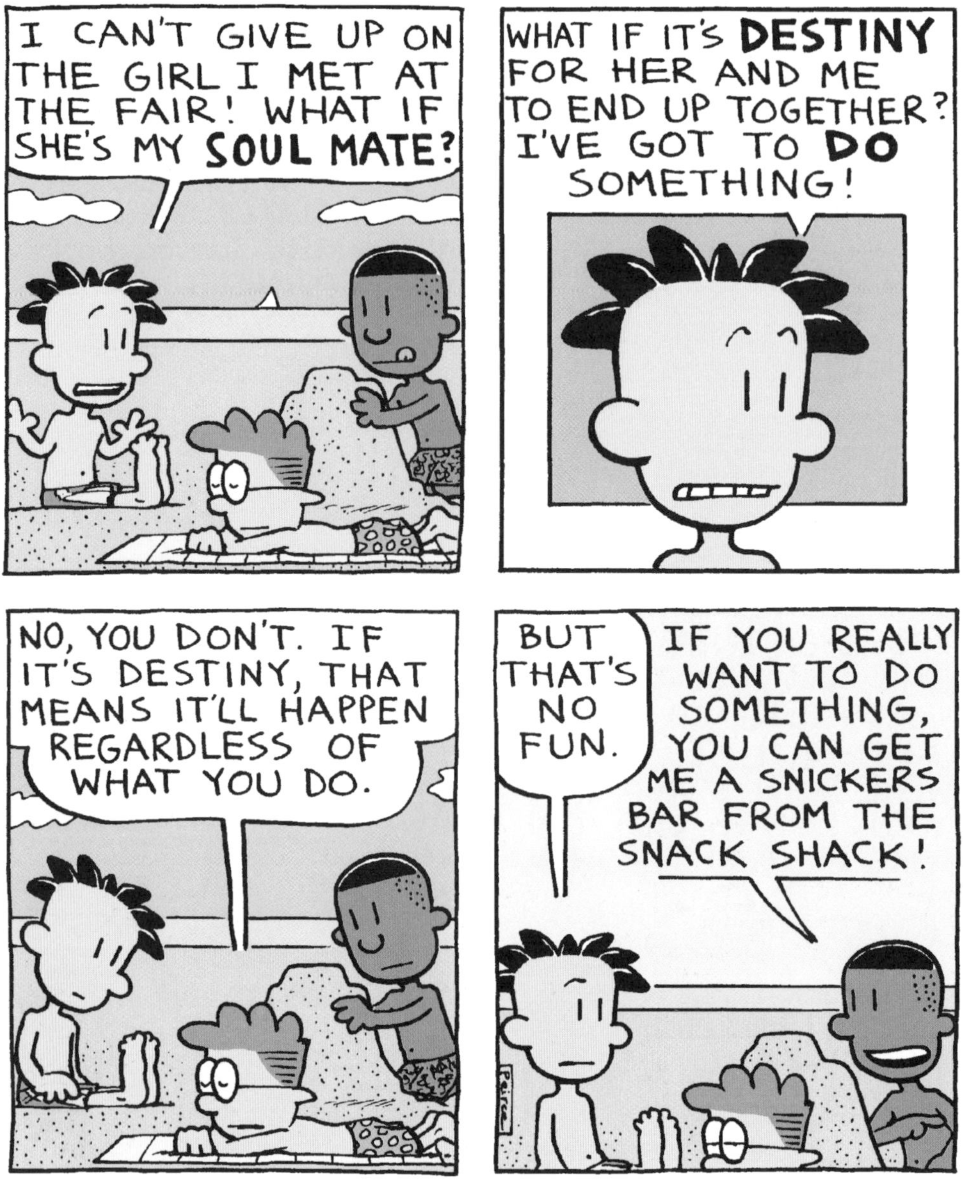
I CAN'T GIVE UP ON THE GIRL I MET AT THE FAIR! WHAT IF SHE'S MY SOUL MATE?
WHAT IF IT'S DESTINY FOR HER AND ME TO END UP TOGETHER? I'VE GOT TO DO SOMETHING!
NO, YOU DON'T. IF IT'S DESTINY, THAT MEANS IT'LL HAPPEN REGARDLESS OF WHAT YOU DO.
BUT THAT'S NO FUN.
IF YOU REALLY WANT TO DO SOMETHING, YOU CAN GET ME A SNICKERS BAR FROM THE SNACK SHACK!
Peirce

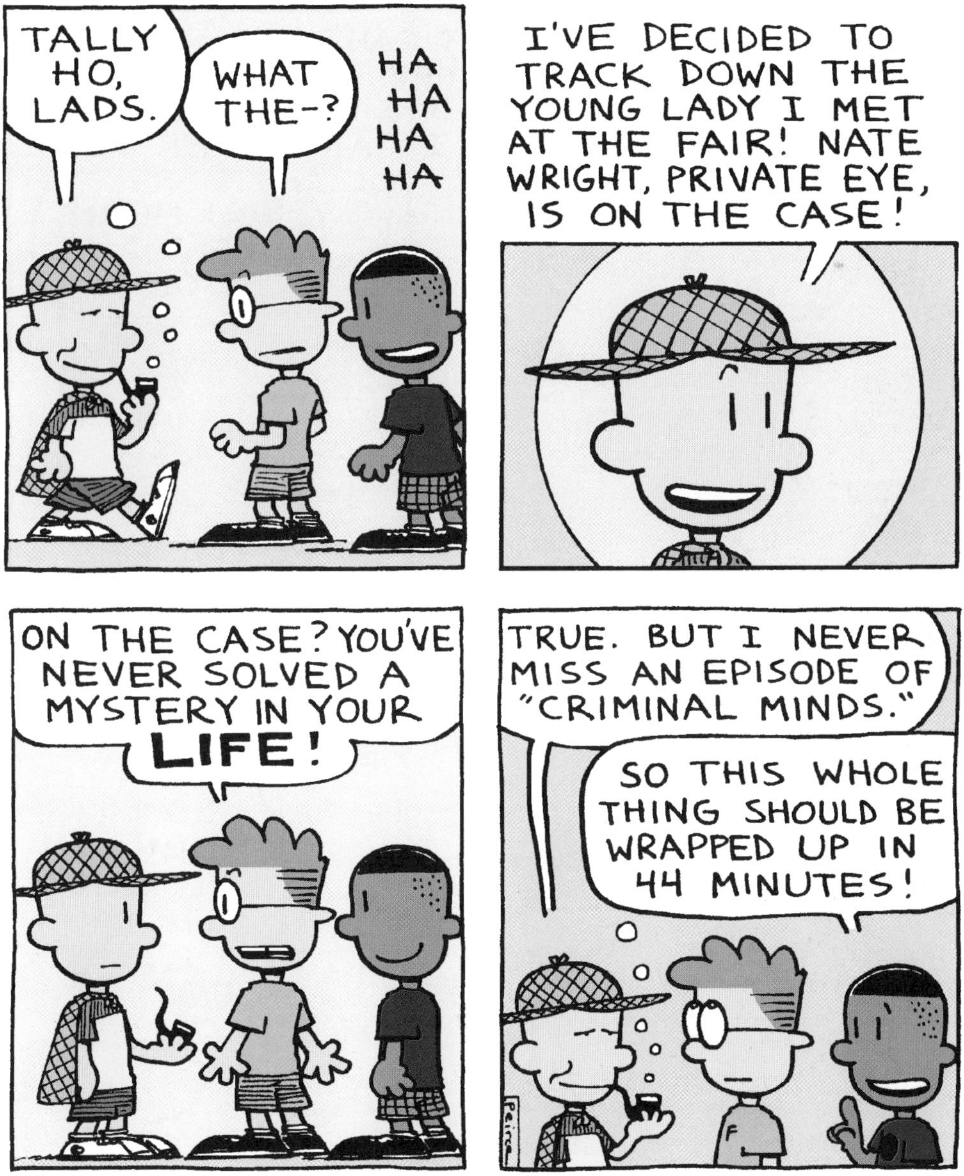
TALLY HO, LADS.
WHAT THE-?
HA HA HA HA
I'VE DECIDED TO TRACK DOWN THE YOUNG LADY I MET AT THE FAIR! NATE WRIGHT, PRIVATE EYE, IS ON THE CASE!
ON THE CASE? YOU'VE NEVER SOLVED A MYSTERY IN YOUR **LIFE**!
TRUE. BUT I NEVER MISS AN EPISODE OF "CRIMINAL MINDS."
SO THIS WHOLE THING SHOULD BE WRAPPED UP IN 44 MINUTES!
Peirce

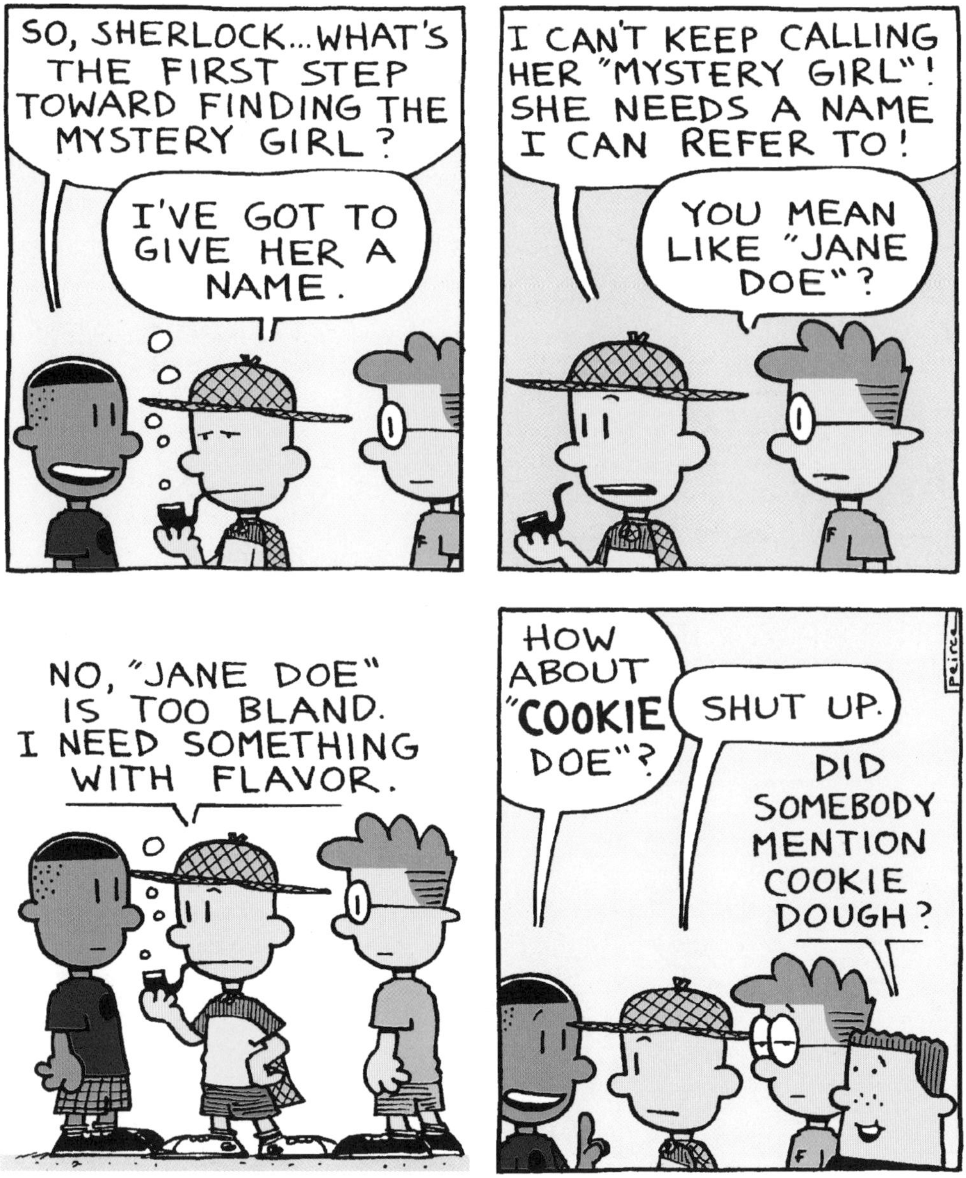
SO, SHERLOCK...WHAT'S THE FIRST STEP TOWARD FINDING THE MYSTERY GIRL?
I'VE GOT TO GIVE HER A NAME.
I CAN'T KEEP CALLING HER "MYSTERY GIRL"! SHE NEEDS A NAME I CAN REFER TO!
YOU MEAN LIKE "JANE DOE"?
NO, "JANE DOE" IS TOO BLAND. I NEED SOMETHING WITH FLAVOR.
HOW ABOUT "COOKIE DOE"?
SHUT UP.
DID SOMEBODY MENTION COOKIE DOUGH?
PEIRCE

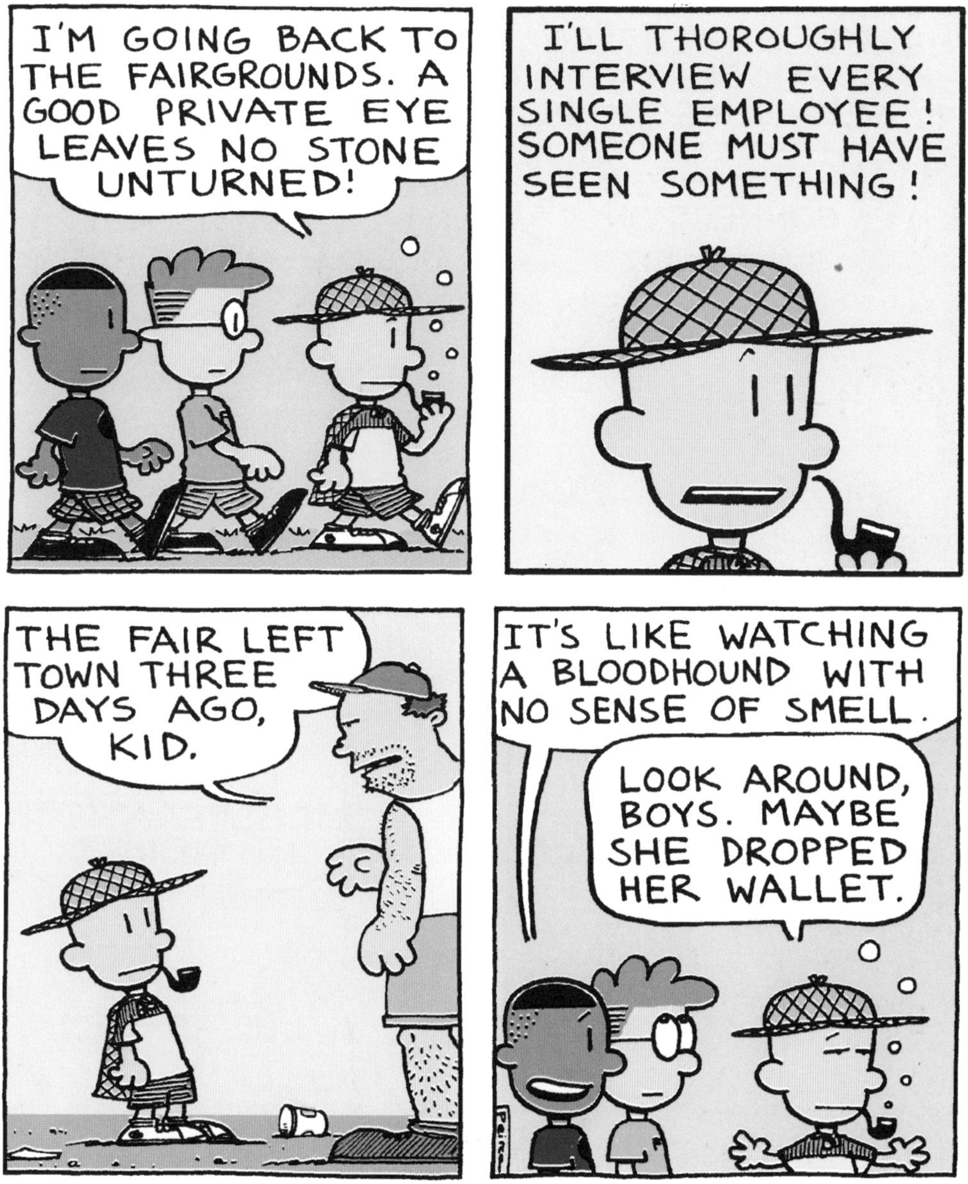
I'M GOING BACK TO THE FAIRGROUNDS. A GOOD PRIVATE EYE LEAVES NO STONE UNTURNED!
I'LL THOROUGHLY INTERVIEW EVERY SINGLE EMPLOYEE! SOMEONE MUST HAVE SEEN SOMETHING!
THE FAIR LEFT TOWN THREE DAYS AGO, KID.
IT'S LIKE WATCHING A BLOODHOUND WITH NO SENSE OF SMELL.
LOOK AROUND, BOYS. MAYBE SHE DROPPED HER WALLET.
Peirce

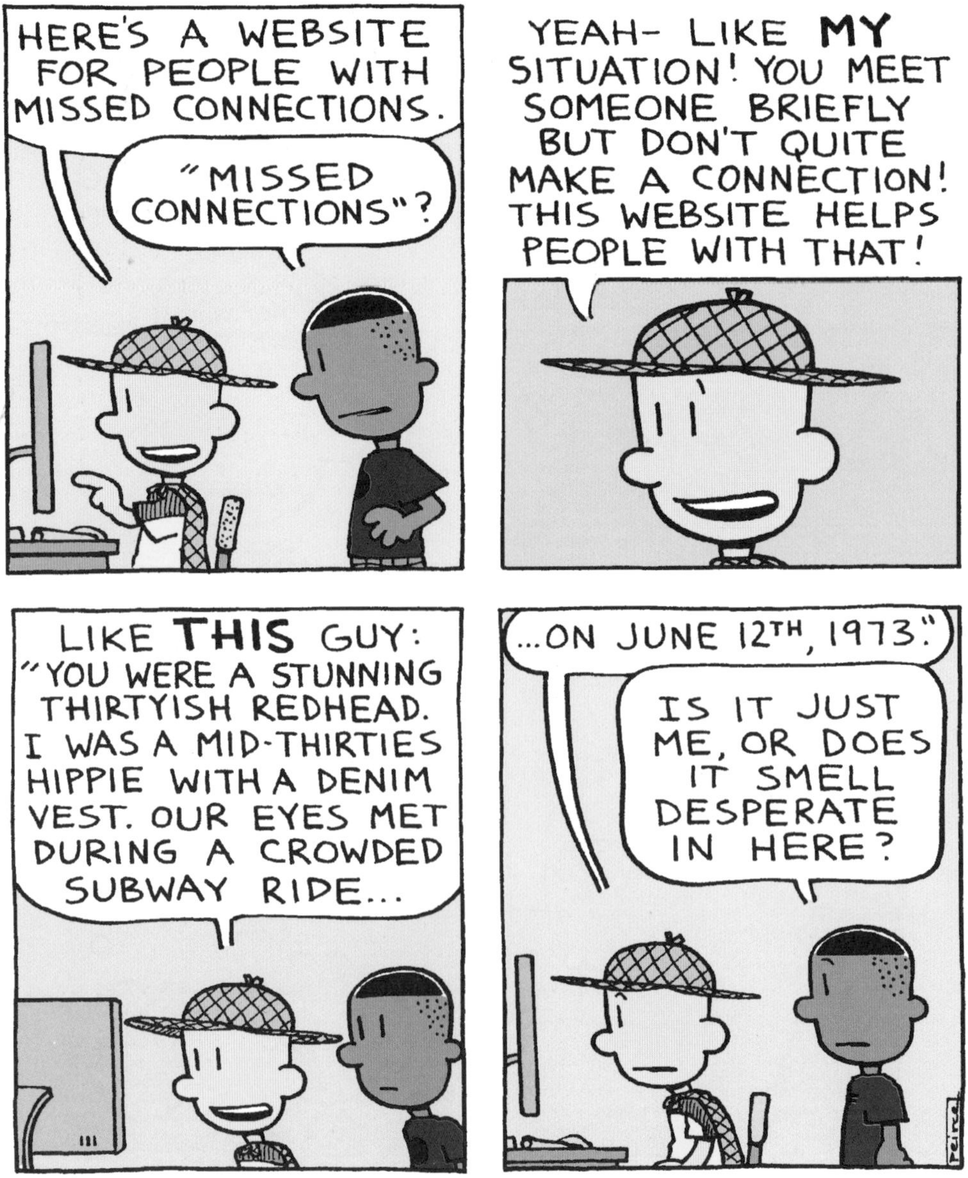
HERE'S A WEBSITE FOR PEOPLE WITH MISSED CONNECTIONS.
"MISSED CONNECTIONS"?
YEAH- LIKE **MY** SITUATION! YOU MEET SOMEONE BRIEFLY BUT DON'T QUITE MAKE A CONNECTION! THIS WEBSITE HELPS PEOPLE WITH THAT!
LIKE **THIS** GUY: "YOU WERE A STUNNING THIRTYISH REDHEAD. I WAS A MID-THIRTIES HIPPIE WITH A DENIM VEST. OUR EYES MET DURING A CROWDED SUBWAY RIDE...
...ON JUNE 12TH, 1973."
IS IT JUST ME, OR DOES IT SMELL DESPERATE IN HERE?
peirce

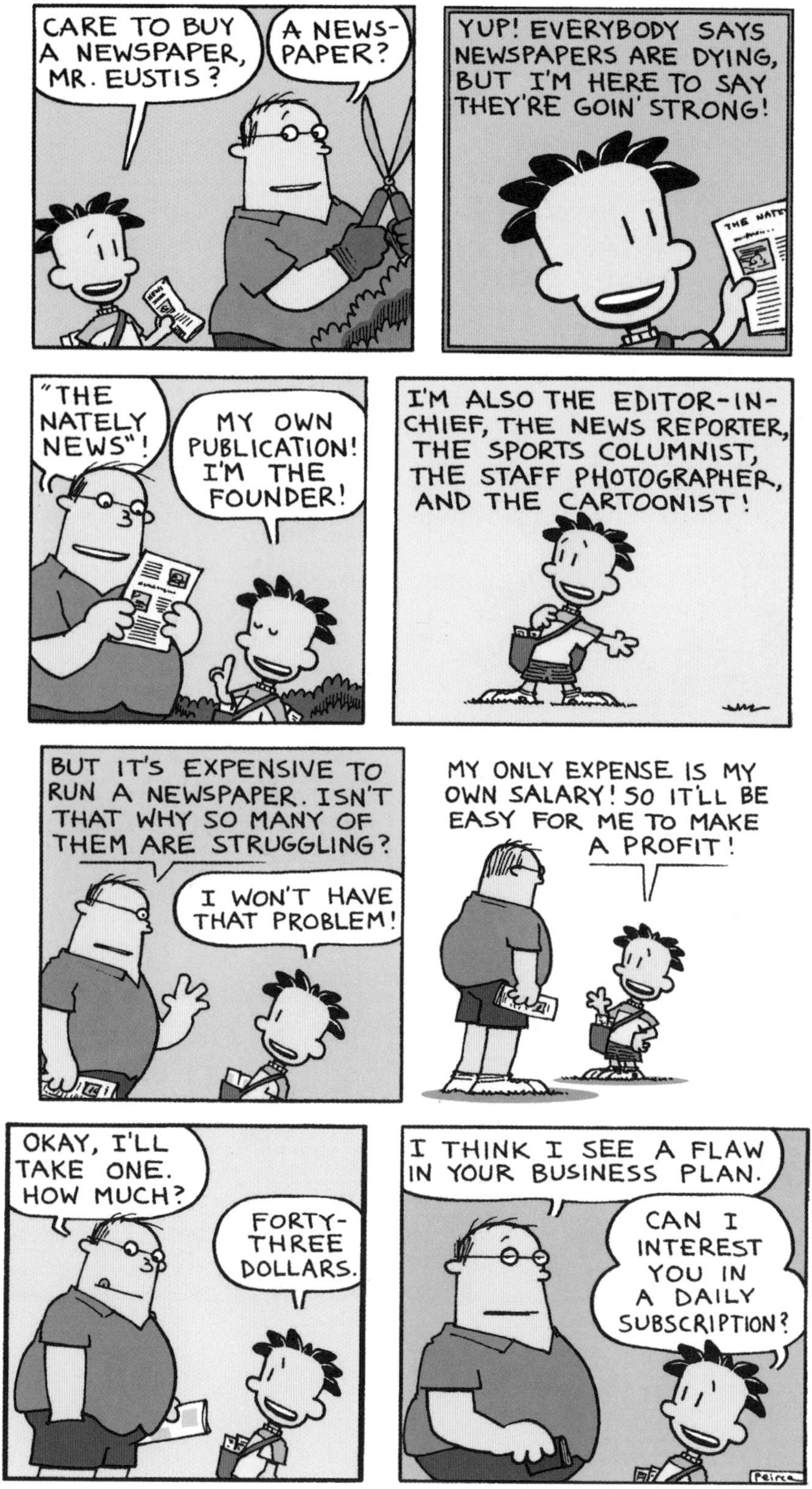
CARE TO BUY A NEWSPAPER, MR. EUSTIS?
A NEWS-PAPER?
YUP! EVERYBODY SAYS NEWSPAPERS ARE DYING, BUT I'M HERE TO SAY THEY'RE GOIN' STRONG!
"THE NATELY NEWS"!
MY OWN PUBLICATION! I'M THE FOUNDER!
I'M ALSO THE EDITOR-IN-CHIEF, THE NEWS REPORTER, THE SPORTS COLUMNIST, THE STAFF PHOTOGRAPHER, AND THE CARTOONIST!
BUT IT'S EXPENSIVE TO RUN A NEWSPAPER. ISN'T THAT WHY SO MANY OF THEM ARE STRUGGLING?
I WON'T HAVE THAT PROBLEM!
MY ONLY EXPENSE IS MY OWN SALARY! SO IT'LL BE EASY FOR ME TO MAKE A PROFIT!
OKAY, I'LL TAKE ONE. HOW MUCH?
FORTY-THREE DOLLARS.
I THINK I SEE A FLAW IN YOUR BUSINESS PLAN.
CAN I INTEREST YOU IN A DAILY SUBSCRIPTION?
Peirce

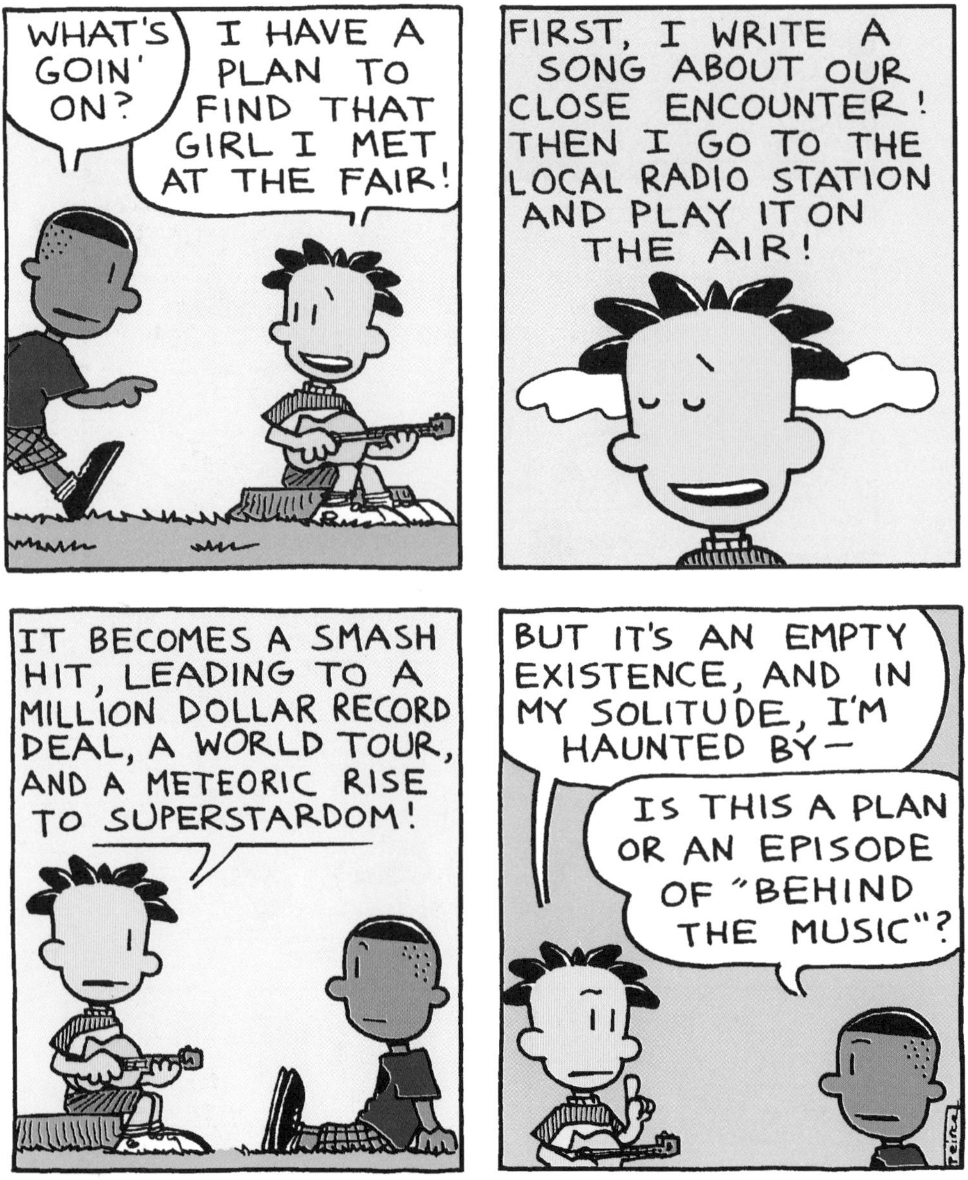
WHAT'S GOIN' ON?
I HAVE A PLAN TO FIND THAT GIRL I MET AT THE FAIR!
FIRST, I WRITE A SONG ABOUT OUR CLOSE ENCOUNTER! THEN I GO TO THE LOCAL RADIO STATION AND PLAY IT ON THE AIR!
IT BECOMES A SMASH HIT, LEADING TO A MILLION DOLLAR RECORD DEAL, A WORLD TOUR, AND A METEORIC RISE TO SUPERSTARDOM!
BUT IT'S AN EMPTY EXISTENCE, AND IN MY SOLITUDE, I'M HAUNTED BY—
IS THIS A PLAN OR AN EPISODE OF "BEHIND THE MUSIC"?

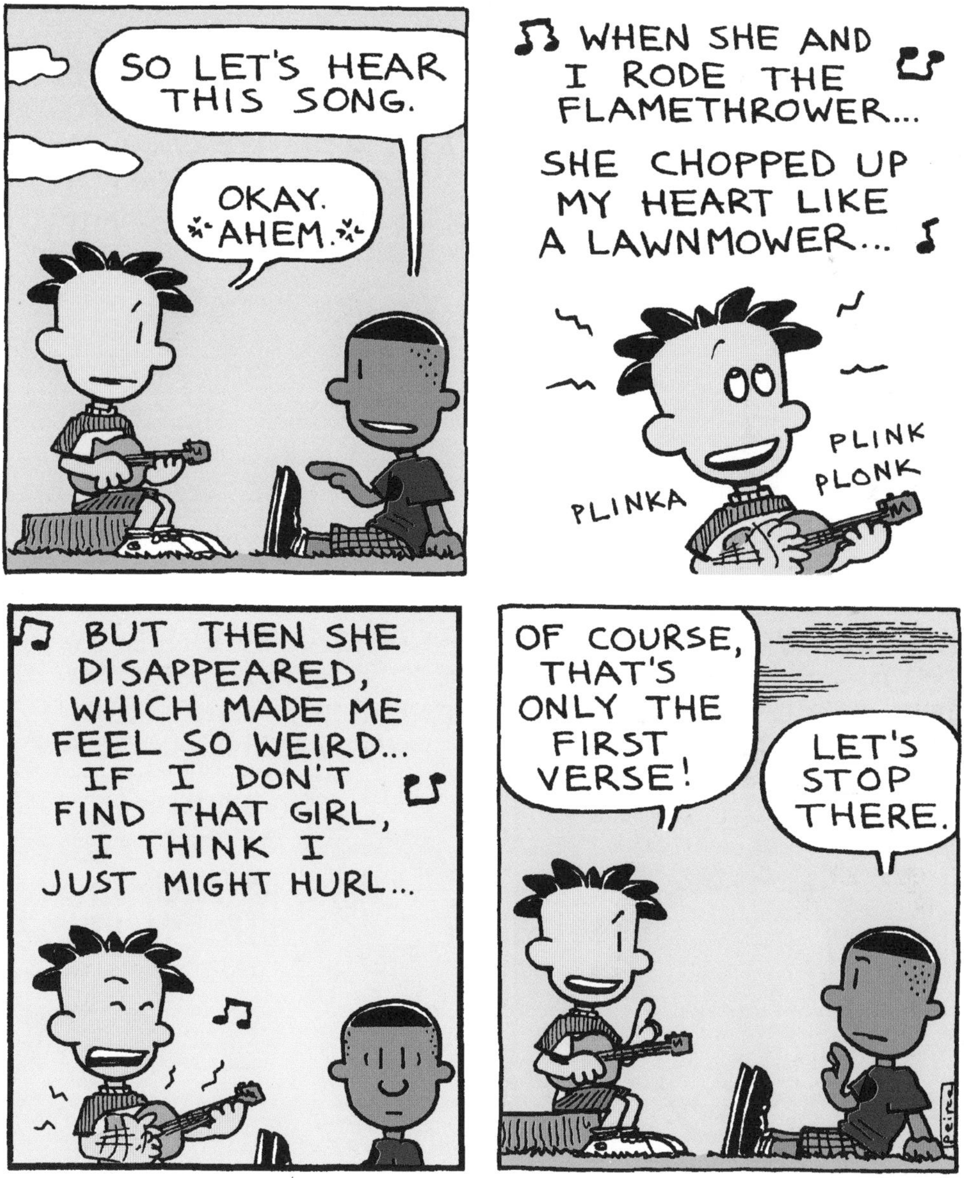
SO LET'S HEAR THIS SONG.
OKAY. AHEM.
WHEN SHE AND I RODE THE FLAMETHROWER...
SHE CHOPPED UP MY HEART LIKE A LAWNMOWER...
PLINK
PLONK
PLINKA
BUT THEN SHE DISAPPEARED, WHICH MADE ME FEEL SO WEIRD... IF I DON'T FIND THAT GIRL, I THINK I JUST MIGHT HURL...
OF COURSE, THAT'S ONLY THE FIRST VERSE!
LET'S STOP THERE.
Peirce

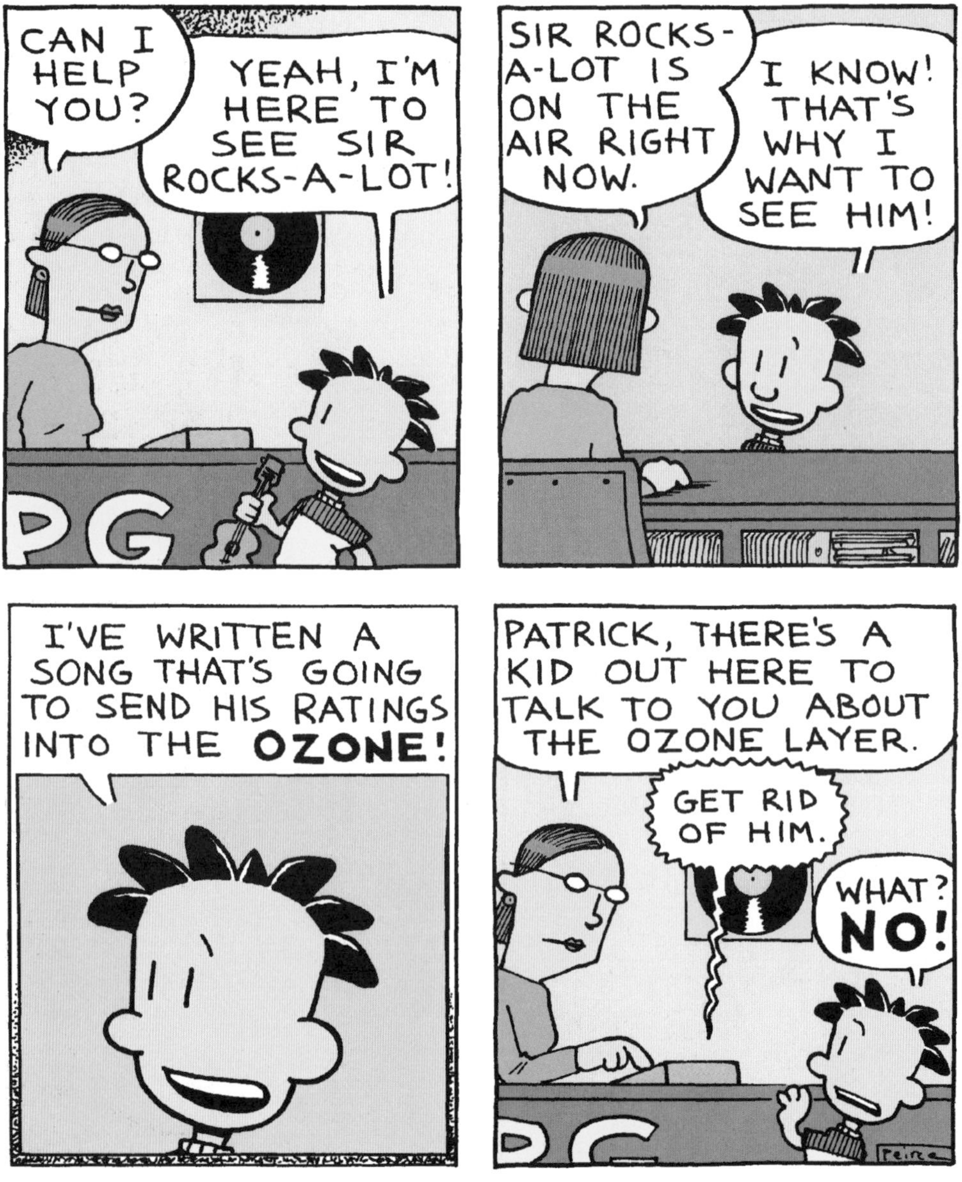
CAN I HELP YOU?
YEAH, I'M HERE TO SEE SIR ROCKS-A-LOT!
PG
SIR ROCKS-A-LOT IS ON THE AIR RIGHT NOW.
I KNOW! THAT'S WHY I WANT TO SEE HIM!
I'VE WRITTEN A SONG THAT'S GOING TO SEND HIS RATINGS INTO THE **OZONE**!
PATRICK, THERE'S A KID OUT HERE TO TALK TO YOU ABOUT THE OZONE LAYER.
GET RID OF HIM.
WHAT? **NO!**
PEIRCE

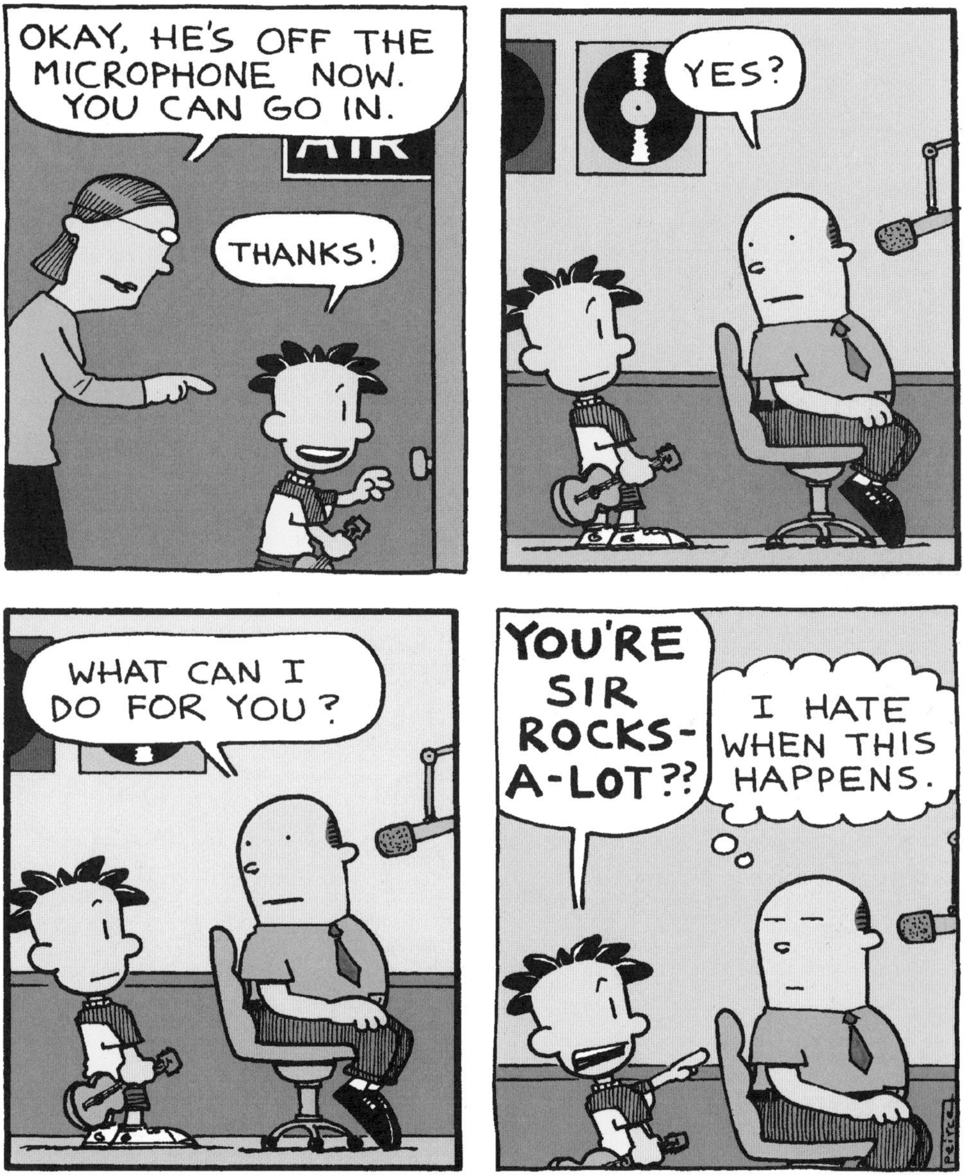
OKAY, HE'S OFF THE MICROPHONE NOW. YOU CAN GO IN.
AIR
THANKS!
YES?
WHAT CAN I DO FOR YOU?
YOU'RE SIR ROCKS-A-LOT??
I HATE WHEN THIS HAPPENS.
peirce

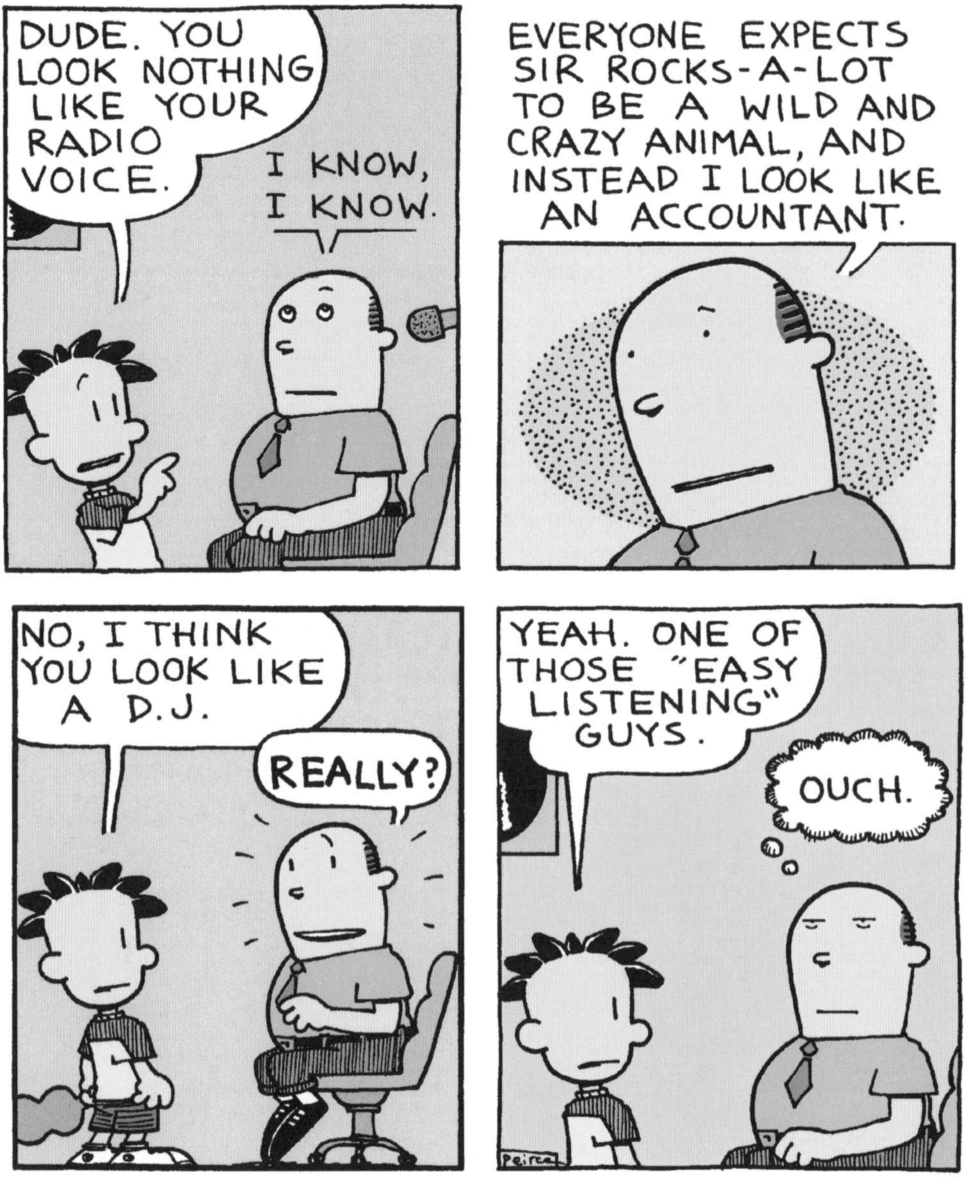
DUDE. YOU LOOK NOTHING LIKE YOUR RADIO VOICE.
I KNOW, I KNOW.
EVERYONE EXPECTS SIR ROCKS-A-LOT TO BE A WILD AND CRAZY ANIMAL, AND INSTEAD I LOOK LIKE AN ACCOUNTANT.
NO, I THINK YOU LOOK LIKE A D.J.
REALLY?
YEAH. ONE OF THOSE "EASY LISTENING" GUYS.
OUCH.
Peirce

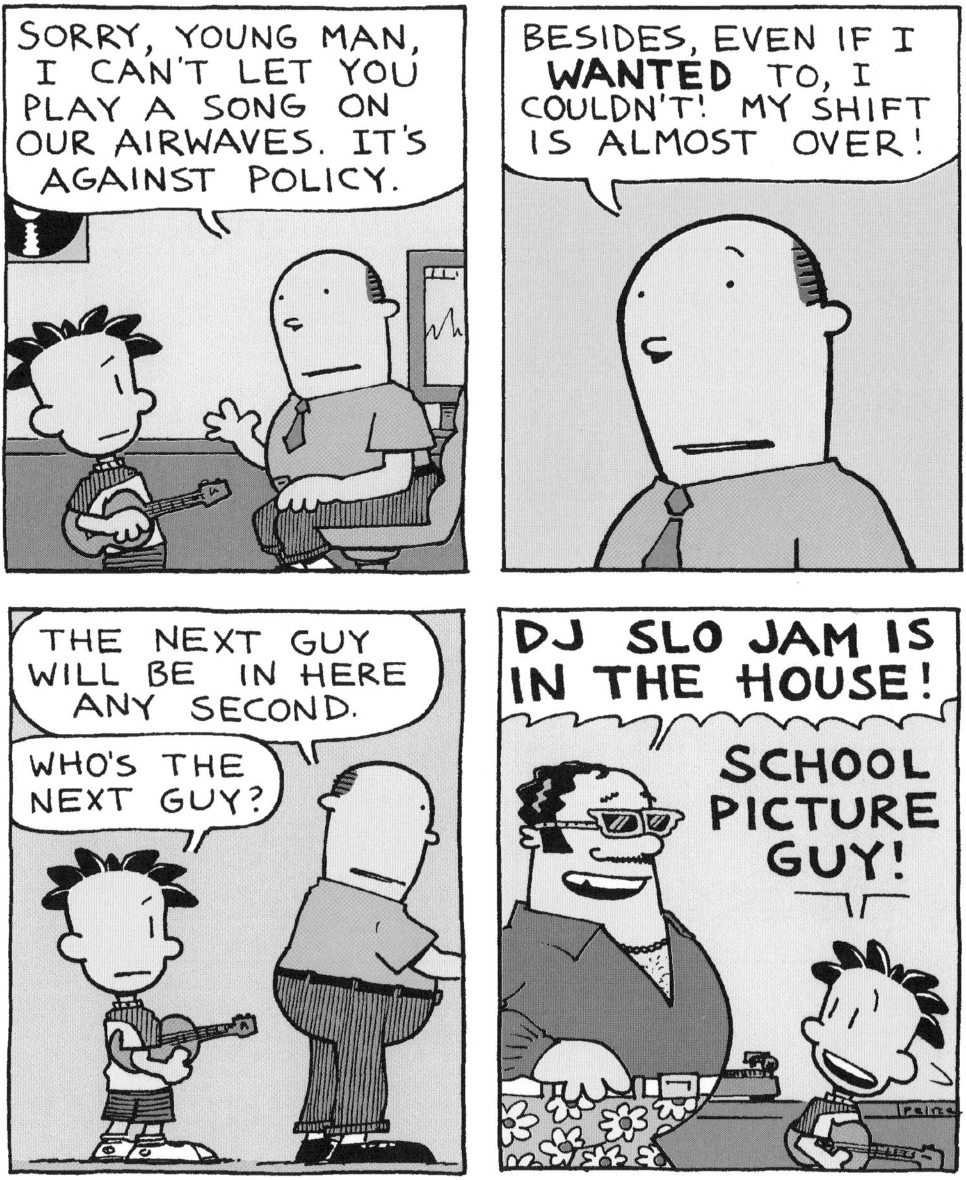
SORRY, YOUNG MAN, I CAN'T LET YOU PLAY A SONG ON OUR AIRWAVES. IT'S AGAINST POLICY.
BESIDES, EVEN IF I **WANTED** TO, I COULDN'T! MY SHIFT IS ALMOST OVER!
THE NEXT GUY WILL BE IN HERE ANY SECOND.
WHO'S THE NEXT GUY?
DJ SLO JAM IS IN THE HOUSE!
SCHOOL PICTURE GUY!

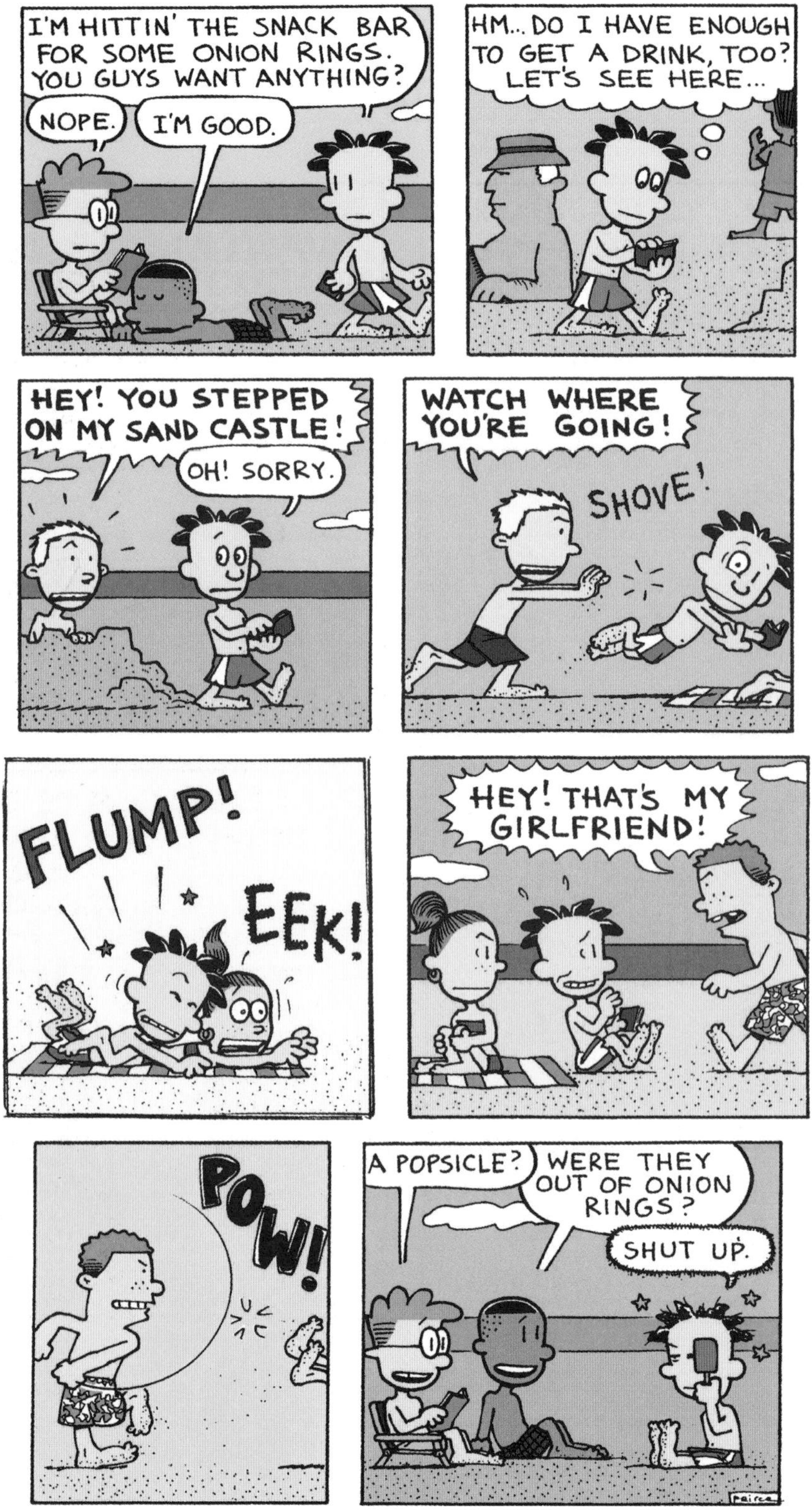
I'M HITTIN' THE SNACK BAR FOR SOME ONION RINGS. YOU GUYS WANT ANYTHING?
NOPE.
I'M GOOD.
HM... DO I HAVE ENOUGH TO GET A DRINK, TOO? LET'S SEE HERE...
HEY! YOU STEPPED ON MY SAND CASTLE!
OH! SORRY.
WATCH WHERE YOU'RE GOING!
SHOVE!
FLUMP!
EEK!
HEY! THAT'S MY GIRLFRIEND!
POW!
A POPSICLE?
WERE THEY OUT OF ONION RINGS?
SHUT UP.

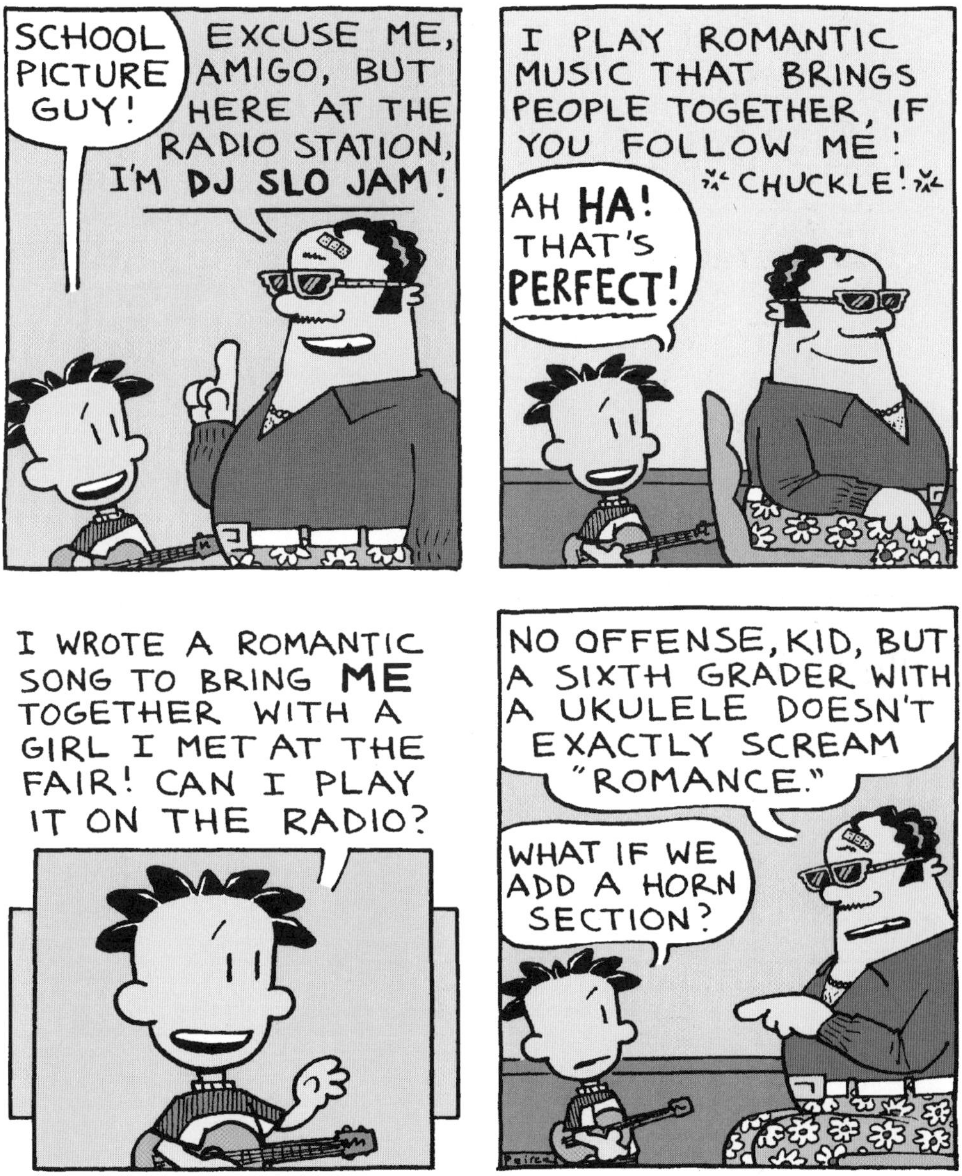
SCHOOL PICTURE GUY!
EXCUSE ME, AMIGO, BUT HERE AT THE RADIO STATION, I'M **DJ SLO JAM**!
I PLAY ROMANTIC MUSIC THAT BRINGS PEOPLE TOGETHER, IF YOU FOLLOW ME!
CHUCKLE!
AH **HA**! THAT'S **PERFECT**!
I WROTE A ROMANTIC SONG TO BRING **ME** TOGETHER WITH A GIRL I MET AT THE FAIR! CAN I PLAY IT ON THE RADIO?
NO OFFENSE, KID, BUT A SIXTH GRADER WITH A UKULELE DOESN'T EXACTLY SCREAM "ROMANCE."
WHAT IF WE ADD A HORN SECTION?

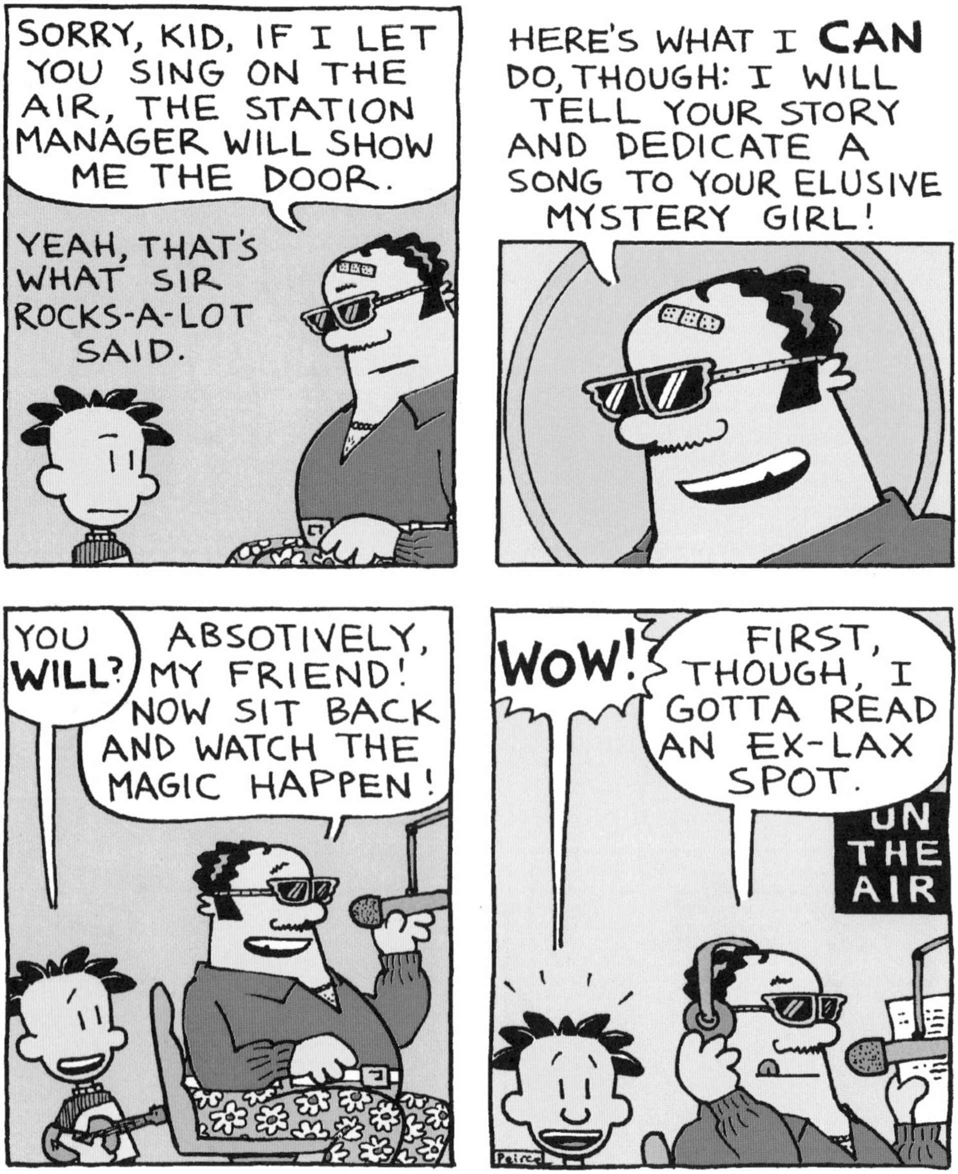
SORRY, KID, IF I LET YOU SING ON THE AIR, THE STATION MANAGER WILL SHOW ME THE DOOR.
YEAH, THAT'S WHAT SIR ROCKS-A-LOT SAID.
HERE'S WHAT I **CAN** DO, THOUGH: I WILL TELL YOUR STORY AND DEDICATE A SONG TO YOUR ELUSIVE MYSTERY GIRL!
YOU **WILL?**
ABSOTIVELY, MY FRIEND! NOW SIT BACK AND WATCH THE MAGIC HAPPEN!
WOW!
FIRST, THOUGH, I GOTTA READ AN EX-LAX SPOT.
ON THE AIR
Peirce

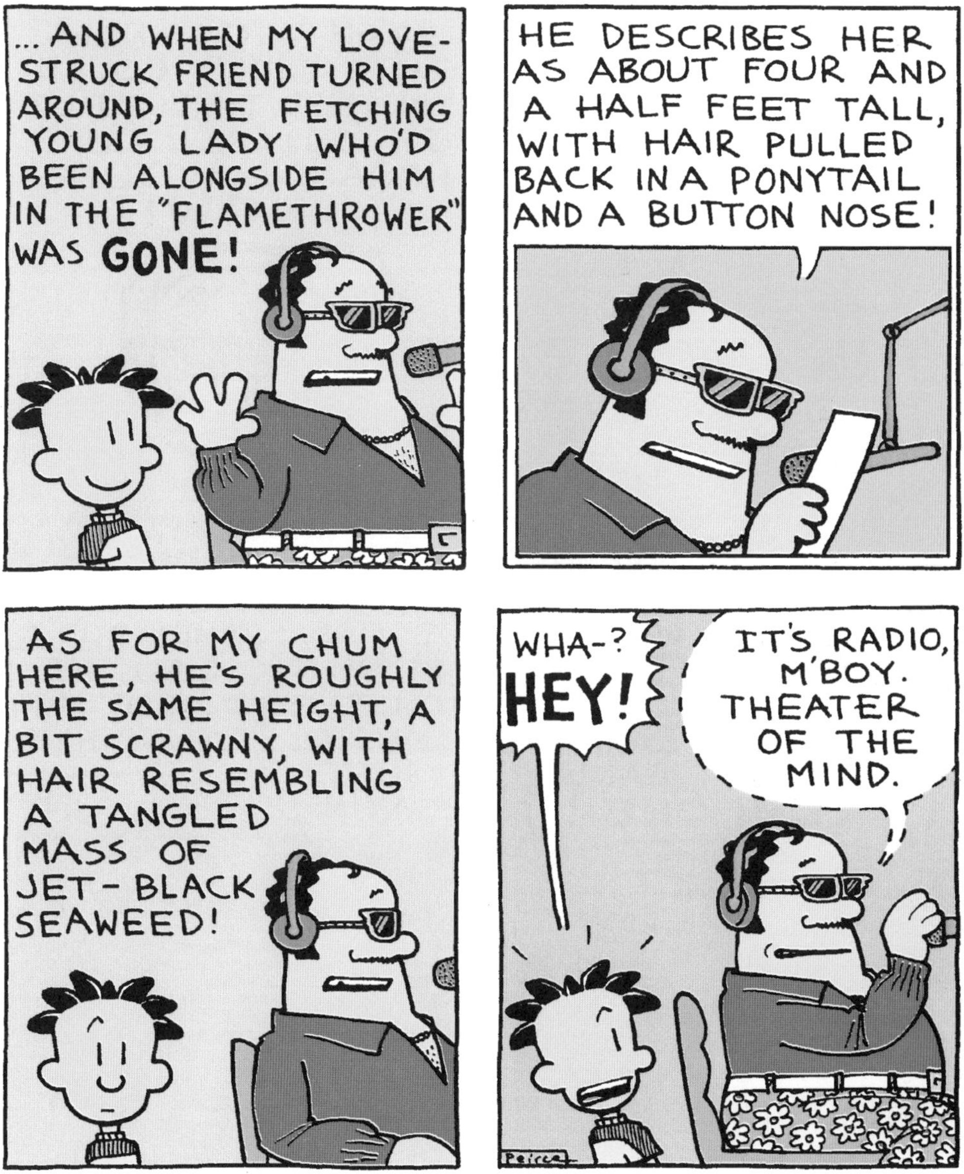
...AND WHEN MY LOVE-STRUCK FRIEND TURNED AROUND, THE FETCHING YOUNG LADY WHO'D BEEN ALONGSIDE HIM IN THE "FLAMETHROWER" WAS **GONE**!
HE DESCRIBES HER AS ABOUT FOUR AND A HALF FEET TALL, WITH HAIR PULLED BACK IN A PONYTAIL AND A BUTTON NOSE!
AS FOR MY CHUM HERE, HE'S ROUGHLY THE SAME HEIGHT, A BIT SCRAWNY, WITH HAIR RESEMBLING A TANGLED MASS OF JET-BLACK SEAWEED!
WHA-? **HEY!**
IT'S RADIO, M'BOY. THEATER OF THE MIND.
Peirce

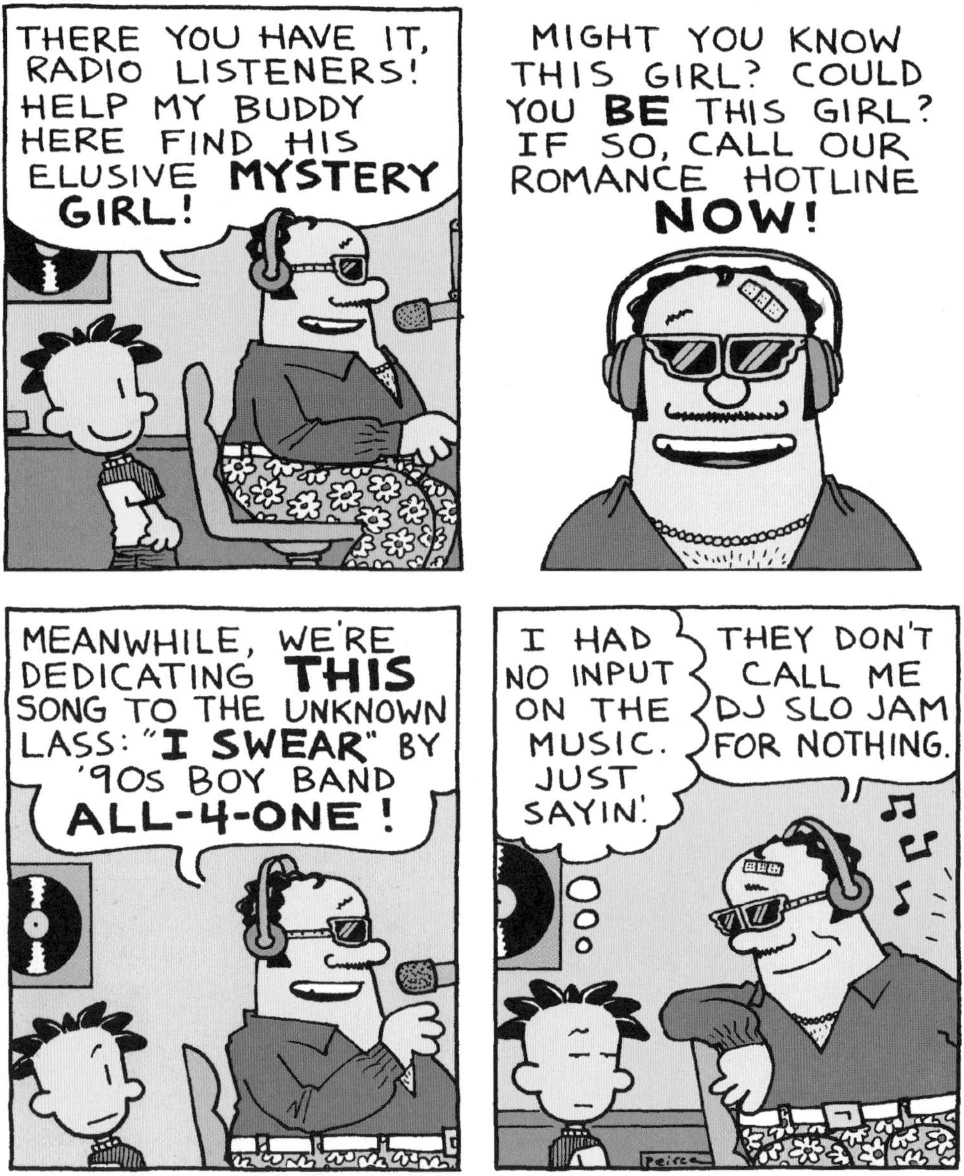
THERE YOU HAVE IT, RADIO LISTENERS! HELP MY BUDDY HERE FIND HIS ELUSIVE **MYSTERY GIRL**!
MIGHT YOU KNOW THIS GIRL? COULD YOU **BE** THIS GIRL? IF SO, CALL OUR ROMANCE HOTLINE **NOW!**
MEANWHILE, WE'RE DEDICATING **THIS** SONG TO THE UNKNOWN LASS: "**I SWEAR**" BY '90s BOY BAND **ALL-4-ONE**!
I HAD NO INPUT ON THE MUSIC. JUST SAYIN'.
THEY DON'T CALL ME DJ SLO JAM FOR NOTHING.
Peirce

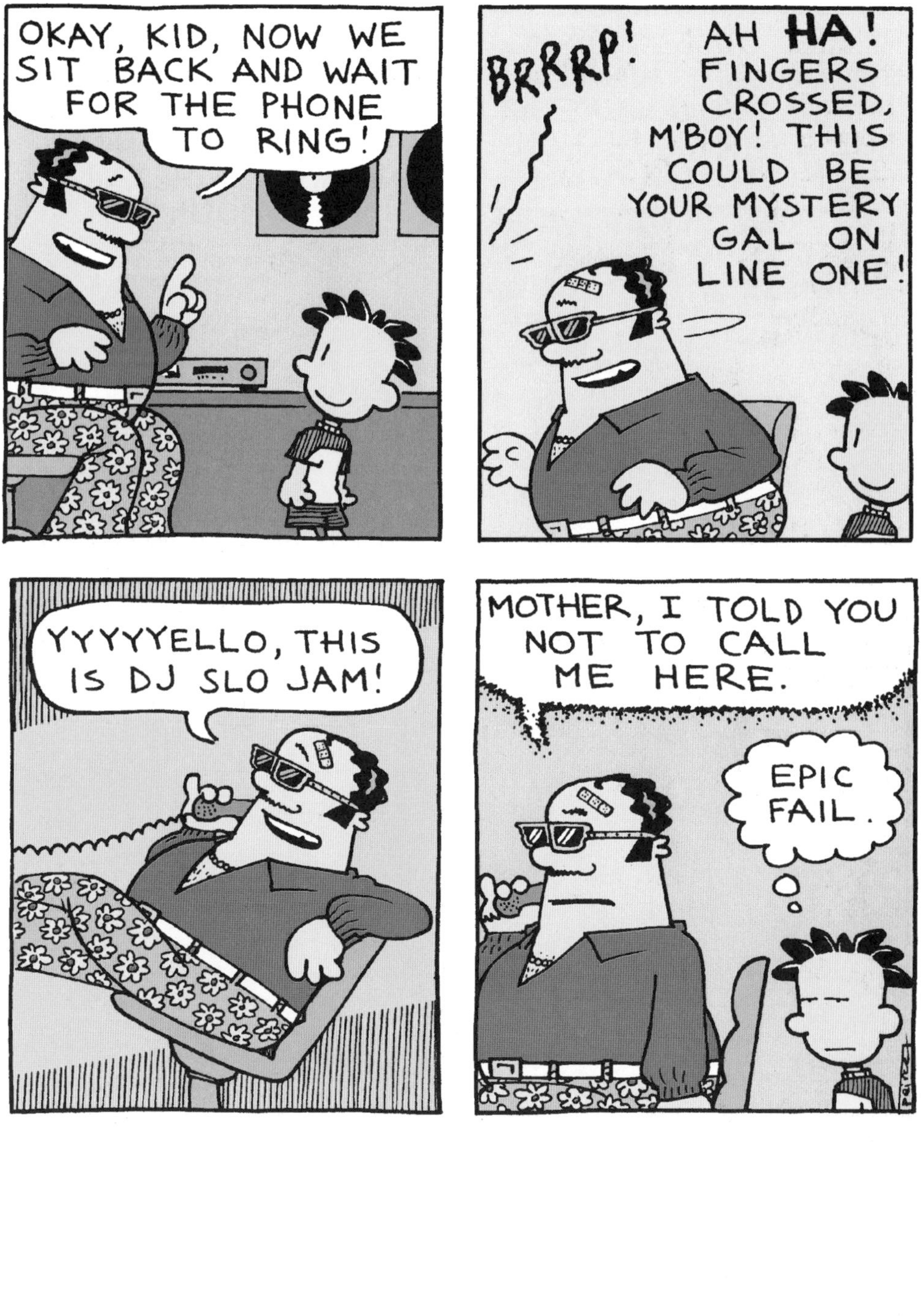
OKAY, KID, NOW WE SIT BACK AND WAIT FOR THE PHONE TO RING!
BRRRP!
AH HA! FINGERS CROSSED, M'BOY! THIS COULD BE YOUR MYSTERY GAL ON LINE ONE!
YYYYYELLO, THIS IS DJ SLO JAM!
MOTHER, I TOLD YOU NOT TO CALL ME HERE.
EPIC FAIL.

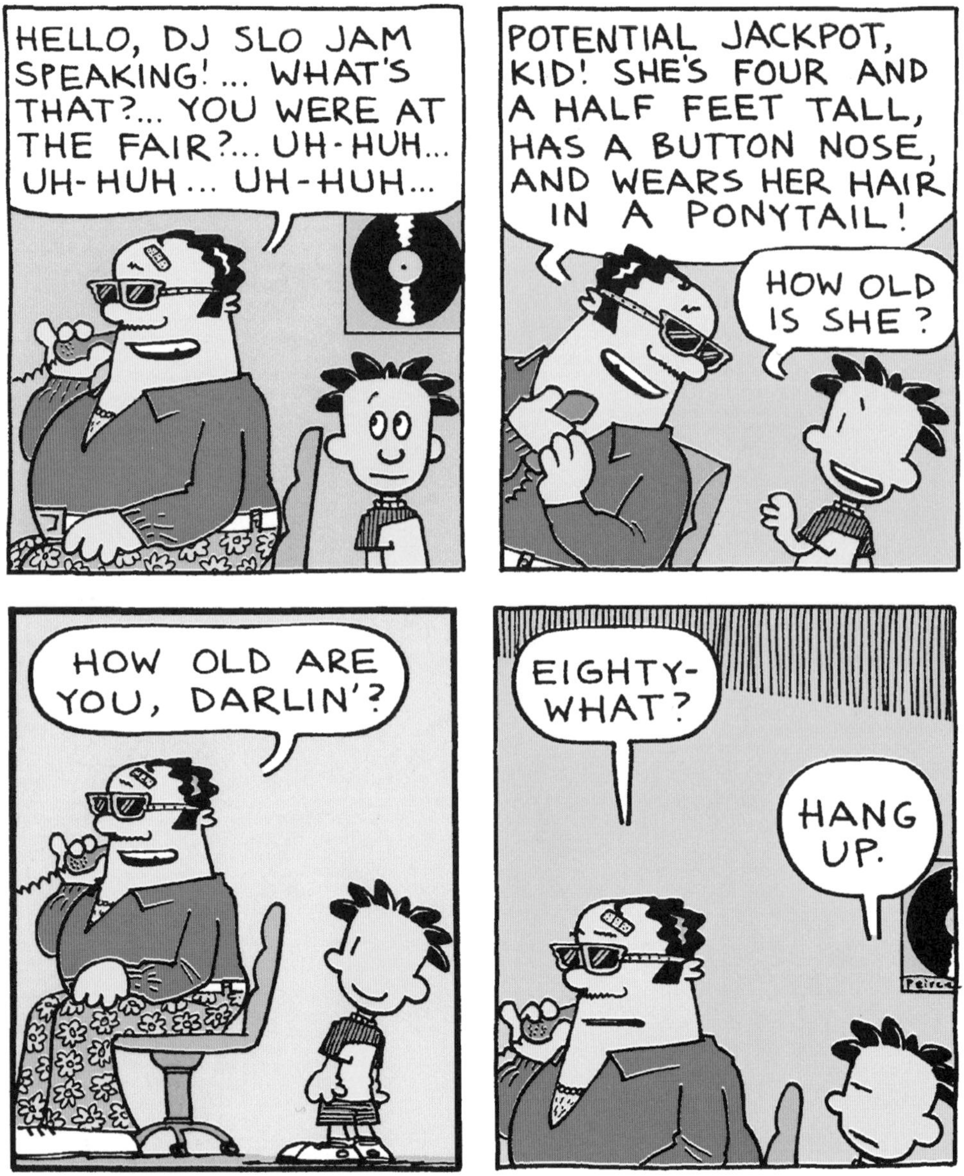
HELLO, DJ SLO JAM SPEAKING! ... WHAT'S THAT?... YOU WERE AT THE FAIR?... UH-HUH... UH-HUH ... UH-HUH...
POTENTIAL JACKPOT, KID! SHE'S FOUR AND A HALF FEET TALL, HAS A BUTTON NOSE, AND WEARS HER HAIR IN A PONYTAIL!
HOW OLD IS SHE?
HOW OLD ARE YOU, DARLIN'?
EIGHTY-WHAT?
HANG UP.
Peirce

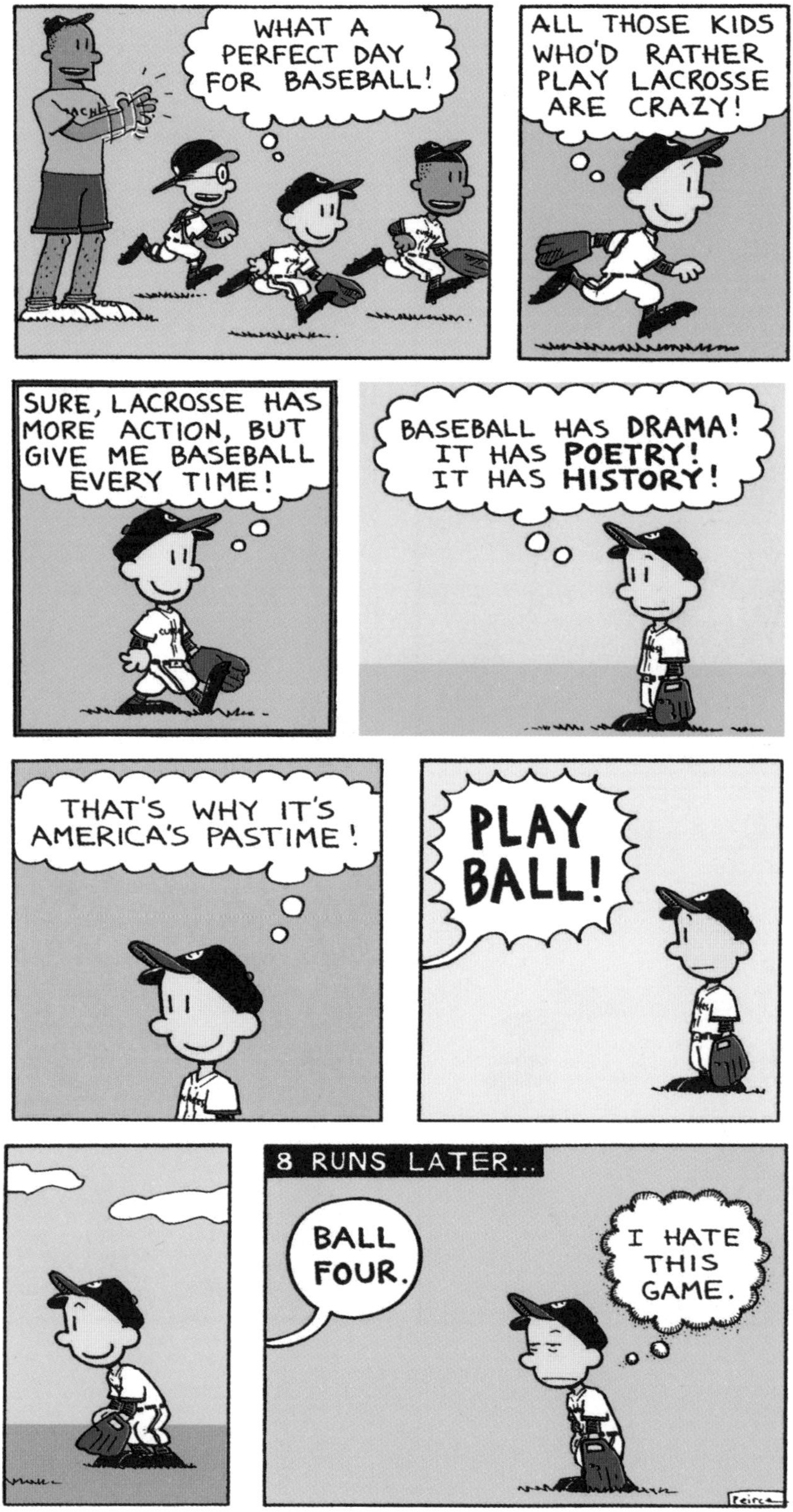
WHAT A PERFECT DAY FOR BASEBALL!
ALL THOSE KIDS WHO'D RATHER PLAY LACROSSE ARE CRAZY!
SURE, LACROSSE HAS MORE ACTION, BUT GIVE ME BASEBALL EVERY TIME!
BASEBALL HAS DRAMA! IT HAS POETRY! IT HAS HISTORY!
THAT'S WHY IT'S AMERICA'S PASTIME!
PLAY BALL!
8 RUNS LATER...
BALL FOUR.
I HATE THIS GAME.

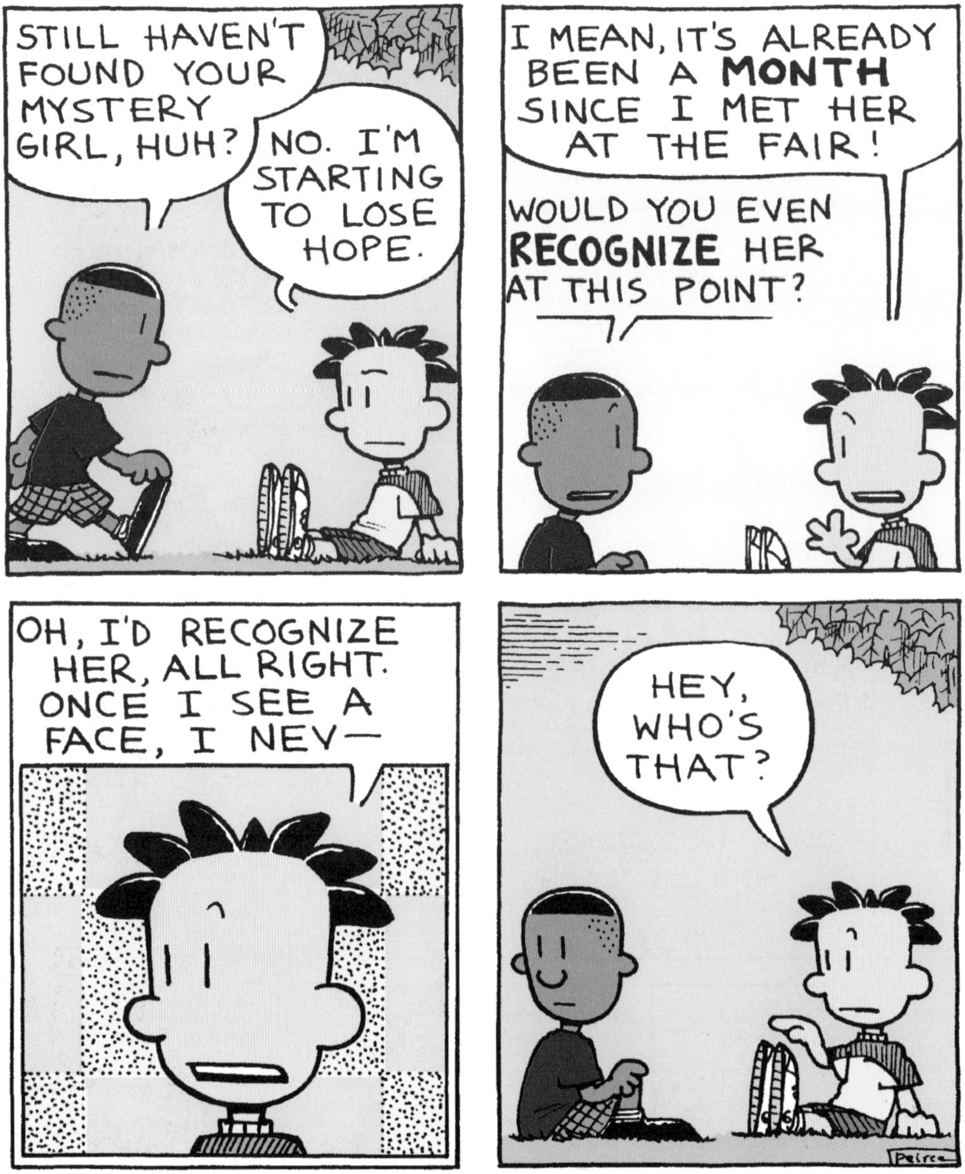
STILL HAVEN'T FOUND YOUR MYSTERY GIRL, HUH?
NO. I'M STARTING TO LOSE HOPE.
I MEAN, IT'S ALREADY BEEN A **MONTH** SINCE I MET HER AT THE FAIR!
WOULD YOU EVEN **RECOGNIZE** HER AT THIS POINT?
OH, I'D RECOGNIZE HER, ALL RIGHT. ONCE I SEE A FACE, I NEV—
HEY, WHO'S THAT?
Peirce

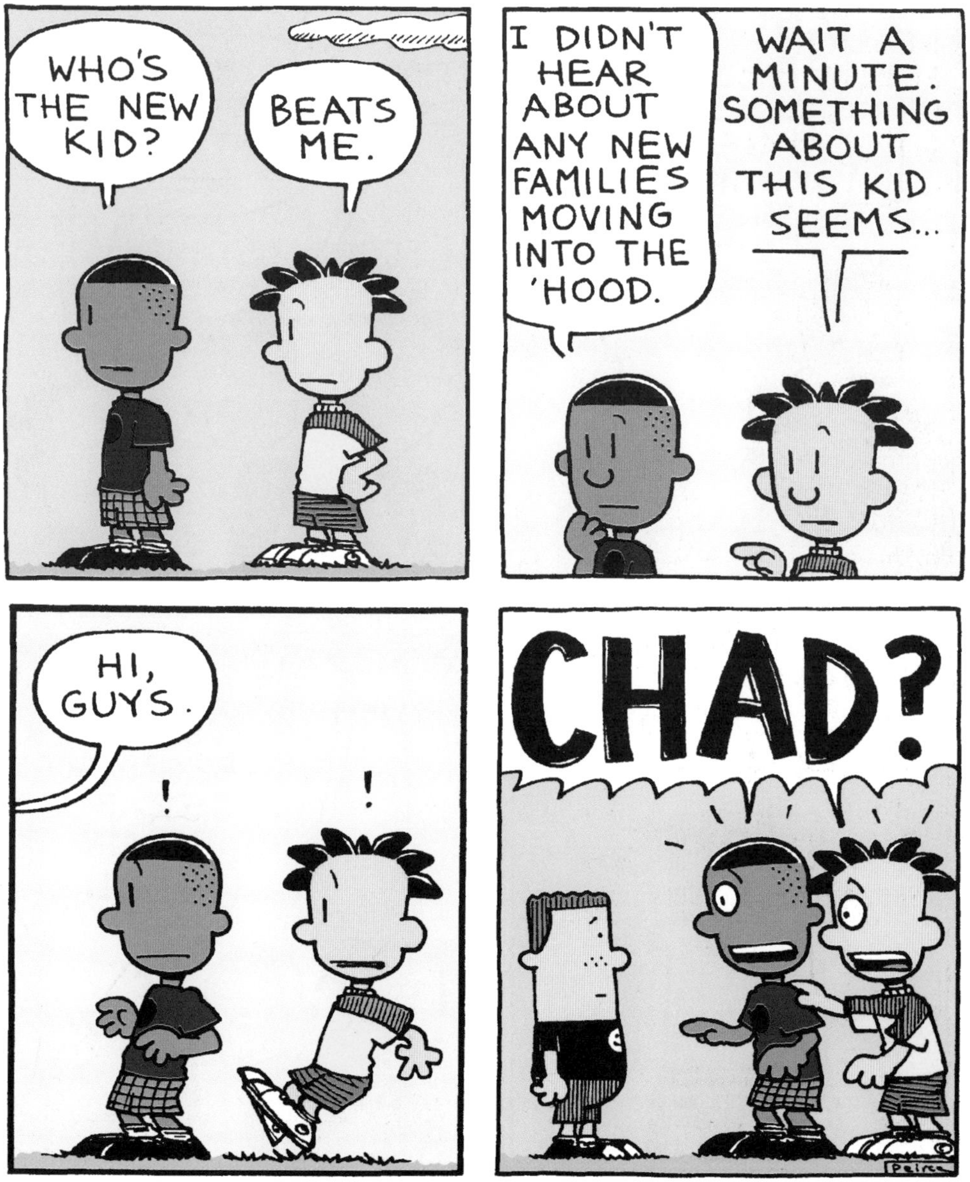
WHO'S THE NEW KID?
BEATS ME.
I DIDN'T HEAR ABOUT ANY NEW FAMILIES MOVING INTO THE 'HOOD.
WAIT A MINUTE. SOMETHING ABOUT THIS KID SEEMS...
HI, GUYS.
!
!
CHAD?

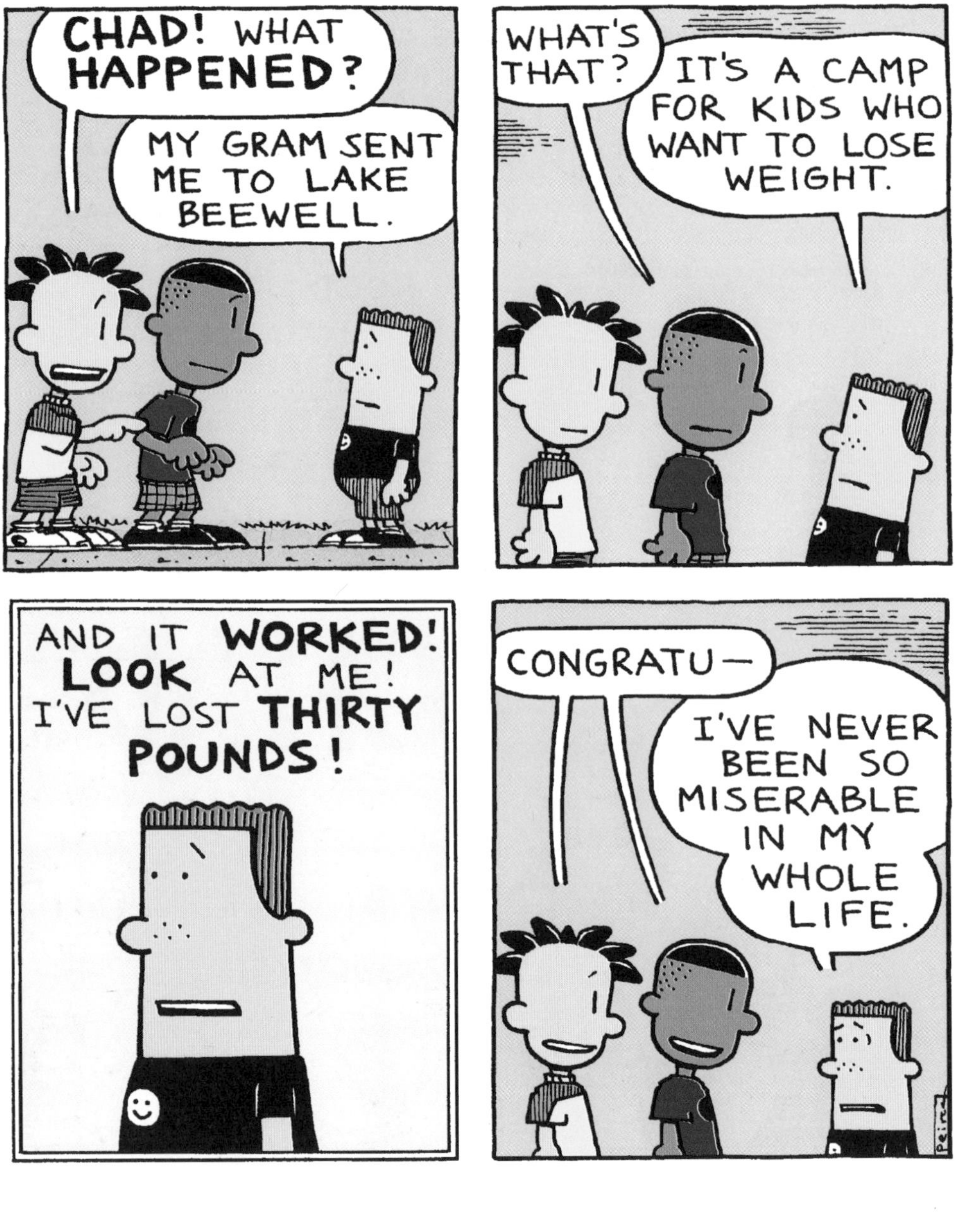
CHAD! WHAT HAPPENED?
MY GRAM SENT ME TO LAKE BEEWELL.
WHAT'S THAT?
IT'S A CAMP FOR KIDS WHO WANT TO LOSE WEIGHT.
AND IT WORKED! LOOK AT ME! I'VE LOST THIRTY POUNDS!
CONGRATU—
I'VE NEVER BEEN SO MISERABLE IN MY WHOLE LIFE.

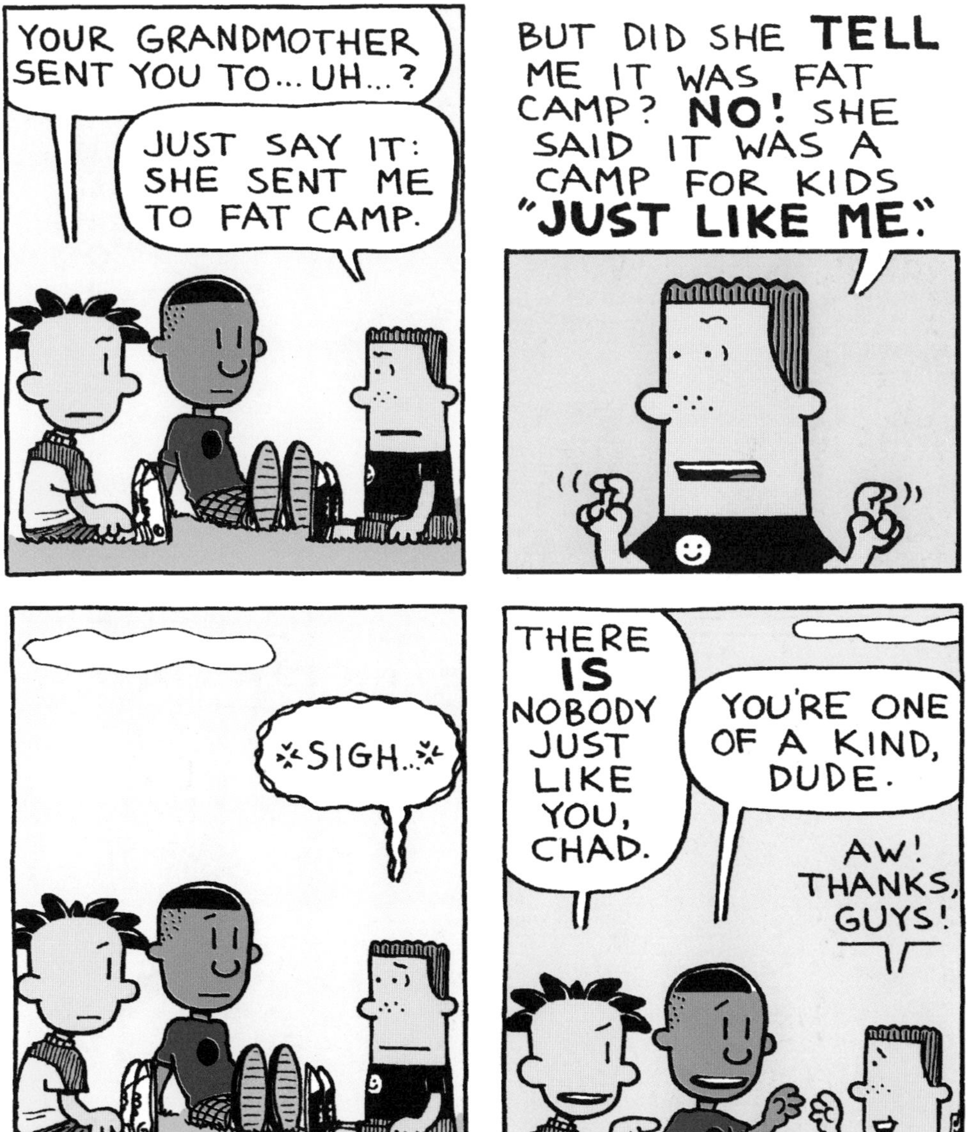

YOUR GRANDMOTHER SENT YOU TO... UH...?
JUST SAY IT: SHE SENT ME TO FAT CAMP.
BUT DID SHE TELL ME IT WAS FAT CAMP? NO! SHE SAID IT WAS A CAMP FOR KIDS "JUST LIKE ME."
SIGH..
THERE IS NOBODY JUST LIKE YOU, CHAD.
YOU'RE ONE OF A KIND, DUDE.
AW! THANKS, GUYS!

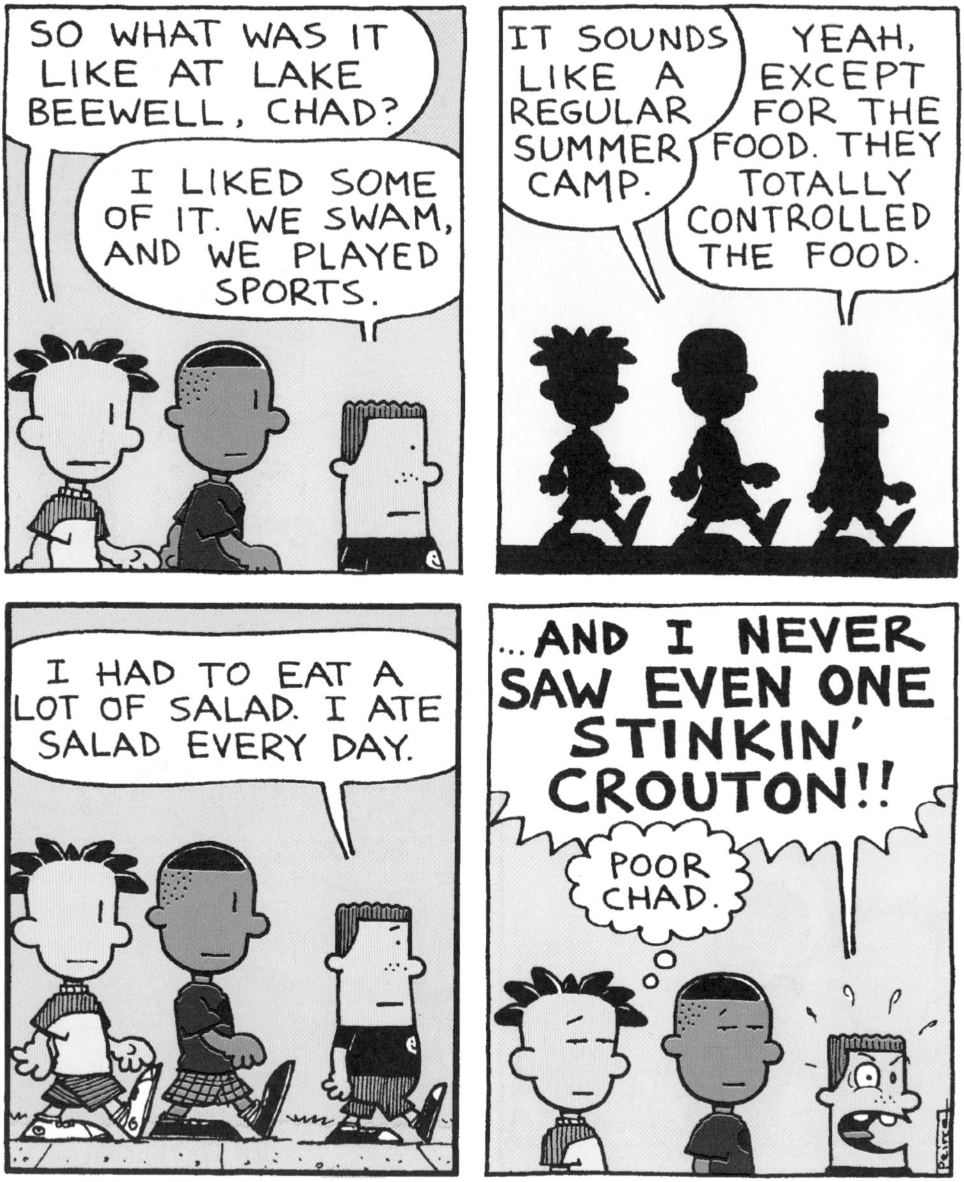
SO WHAT WAS IT LIKE AT LAKE BEEWELL, CHAD?
I LIKED SOME OF IT. WE SWAM, AND WE PLAYED SPORTS.
IT SOUNDS LIKE A REGULAR SUMMER CAMP.
YEAH, EXCEPT FOR THE FOOD. THEY TOTALLY CONTROLLED THE FOOD.
I HAD TO EAT A LOT OF SALAD. I ATE SALAD EVERY DAY.
...AND I NEVER SAW EVEN ONE STINKIN' CROUTON!!
POOR CHAD.
Peirce

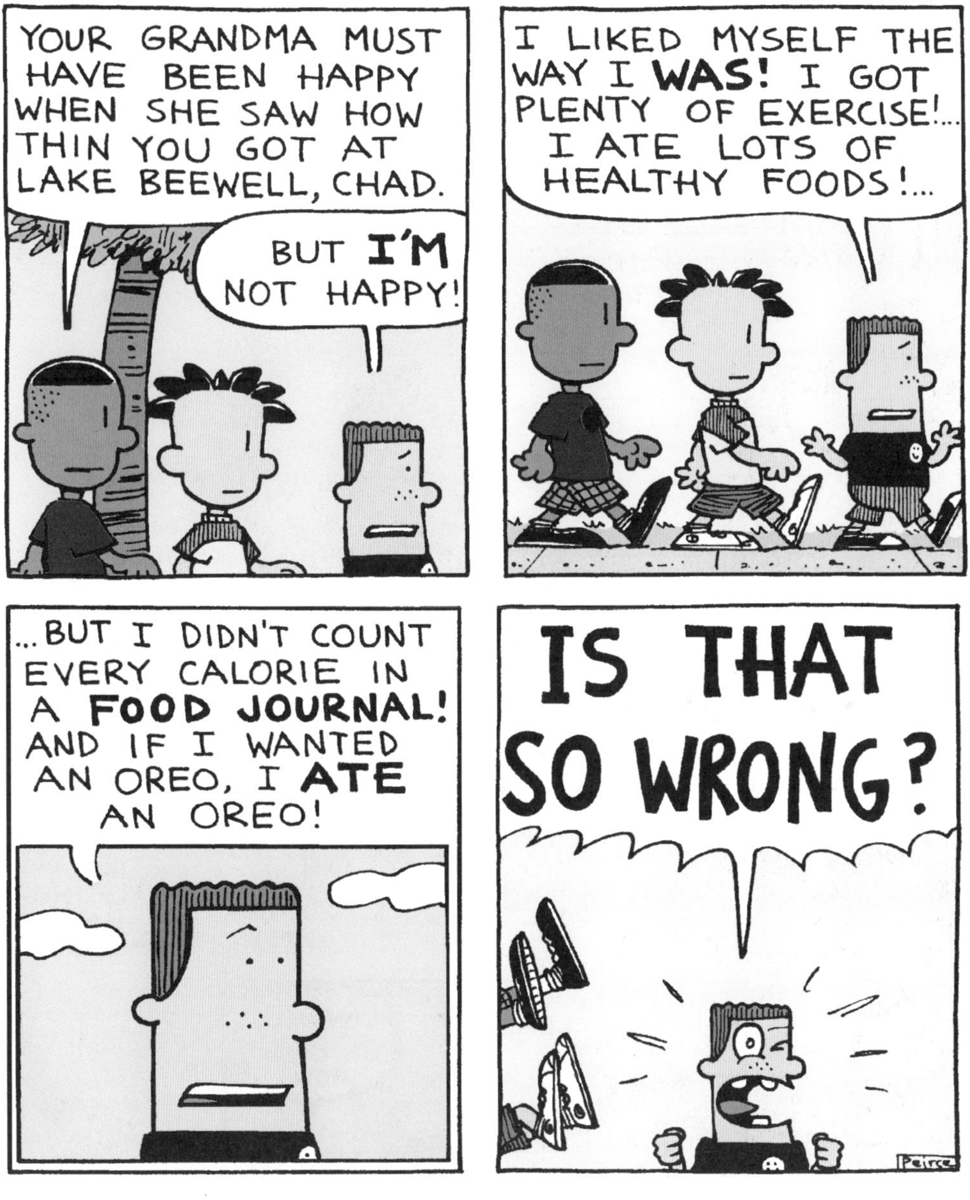
YOUR GRANDMA MUST HAVE BEEN HAPPY WHEN SHE SAW HOW THIN YOU GOT AT LAKE BEEWELL, CHAD.
BUT I'M NOT HAPPY!
I LIKED MYSELF THE WAY I WAS! I GOT PLENTY OF EXERCISE!... I ATE LOTS OF HEALTHY FOODS!...
...BUT I DIDN'T COUNT EVERY CALORIE IN A FOOD JOURNAL! AND IF I WANTED AN OREO, I ATE AN OREO!
IS THAT SO WRONG?
Peirce

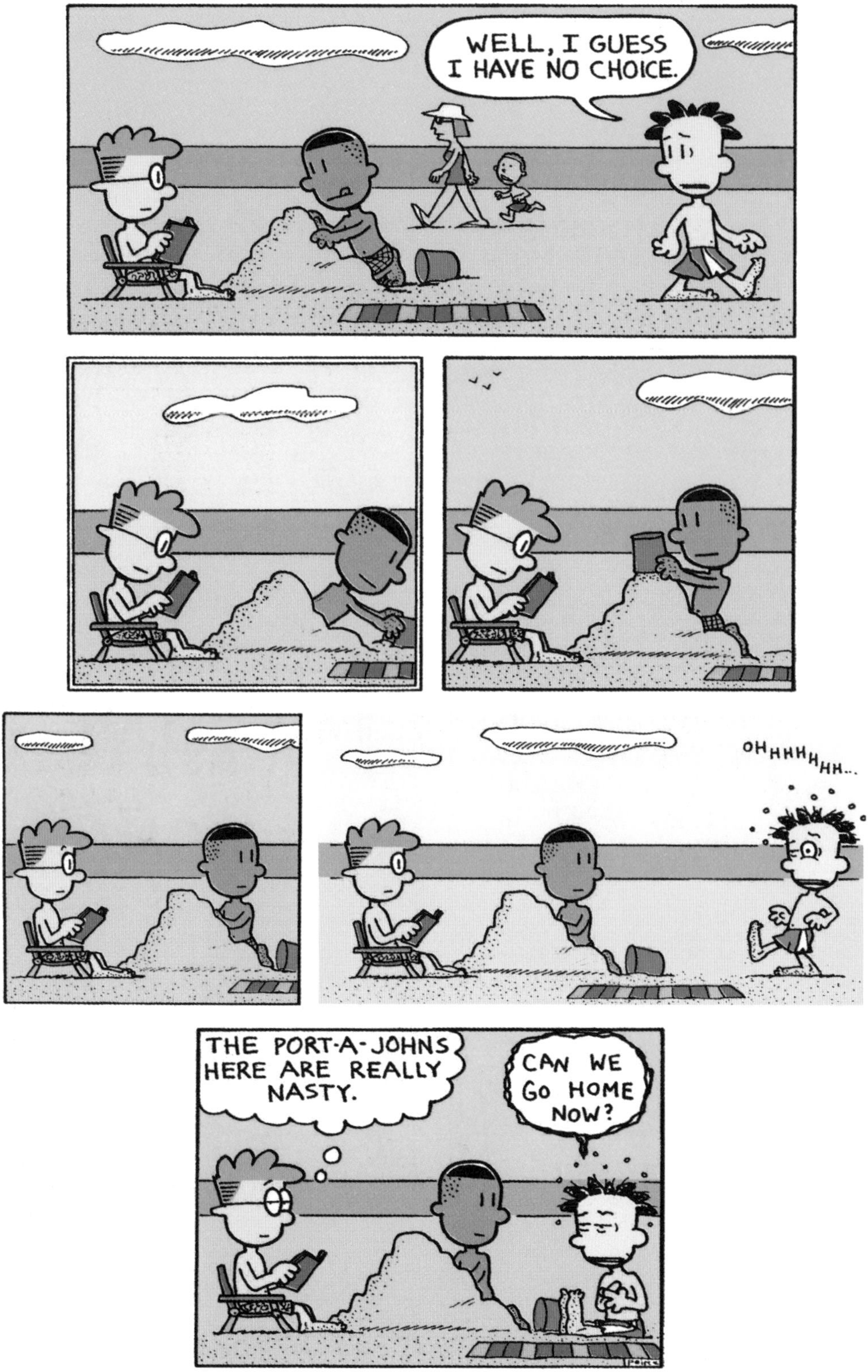
WELL, I GUESS I HAVE NO CHOICE.
OHHHHHHH...
THE PORT-A-JOHNS HERE ARE REALLY NASTY.
CAN WE GO HOME NOW?

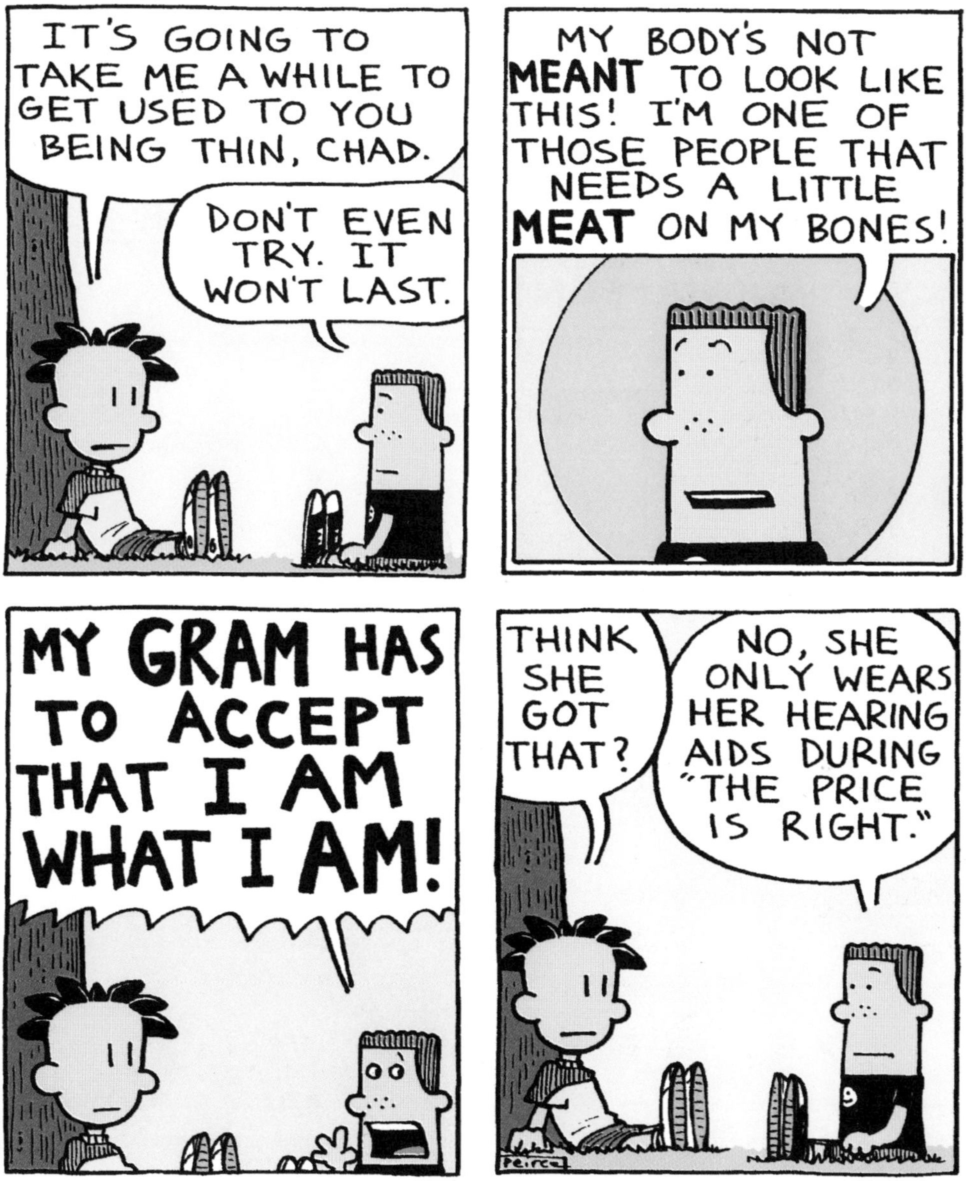
IT'S GOING TO TAKE ME A WHILE TO GET USED TO YOU BEING THIN, CHAD.
DON'T EVEN TRY. IT WON'T LAST.
MY BODY'S NOT MEANT TO LOOK LIKE THIS! I'M ONE OF THOSE PEOPLE THAT NEEDS A LITTLE MEAT ON MY BONES!
MY GRAM HAS TO ACCEPT THAT I AM WHAT I AM!
THINK SHE GOT THAT?
NO, SHE ONLY WEARS HER HEARING AIDS DURING "THE PRICE IS RIGHT."
PEIRCE

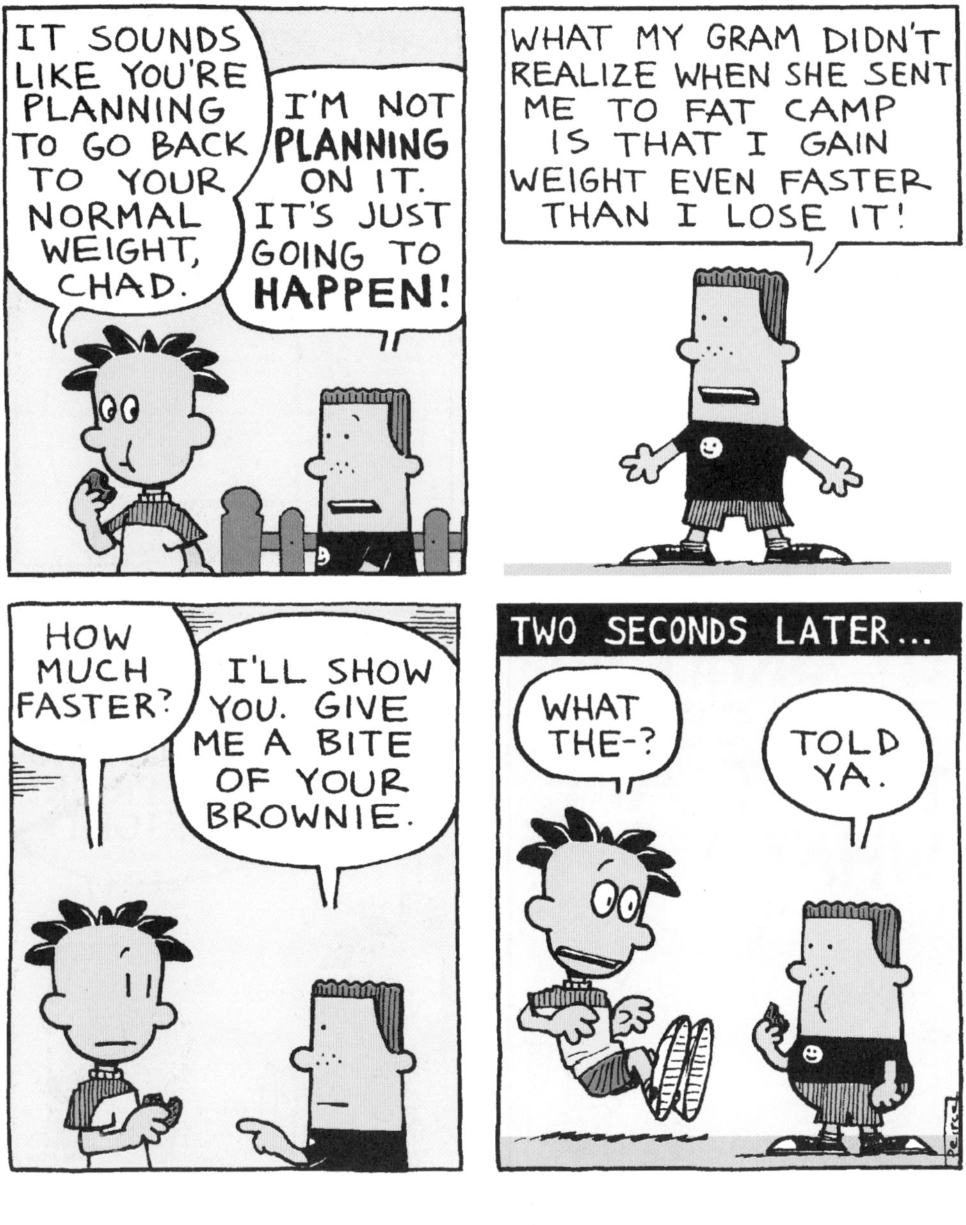
IT SOUNDS LIKE YOU'RE PLANNING TO GO BACK TO YOUR NORMAL WEIGHT, CHAD.
I'M NOT **PLANNING** ON IT. IT'S JUST GOING TO **HAPPEN!**
WHAT MY GRAM DIDN'T REALIZE WHEN SHE SENT ME TO FAT CAMP IS THAT I GAIN WEIGHT EVEN FASTER THAN I LOSE IT!
HOW MUCH FASTER?
I'LL SHOW YOU. GIVE ME A BITE OF YOUR BROWNIE.
TWO SECONDS LATER...
WHAT THE-?
TOLD YA.
Peirce

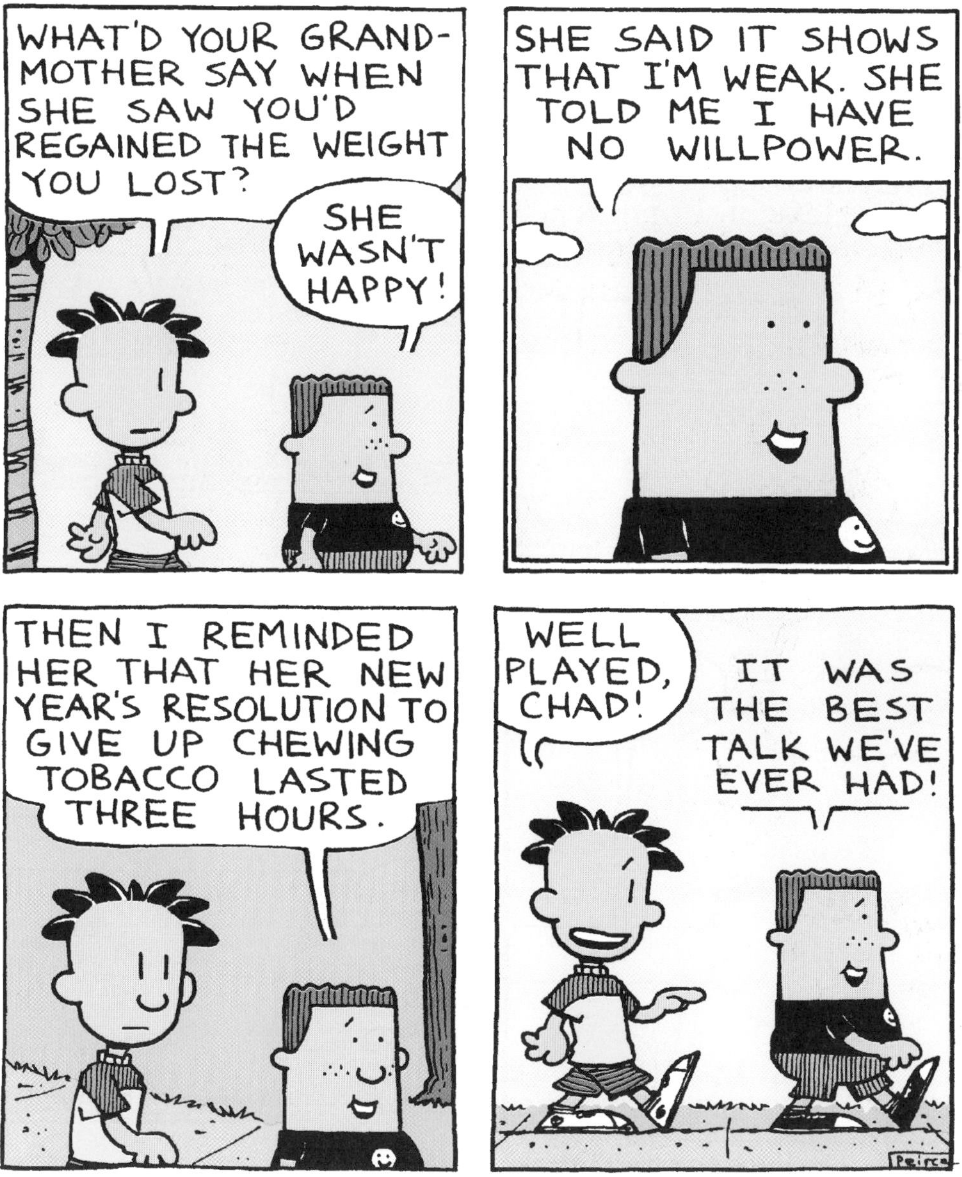
WHAT'D YOUR GRAND-MOTHER SAY WHEN SHE SAW YOU'D REGAINED THE WEIGHT YOU LOST?
SHE WASN'T HAPPY!
SHE SAID IT SHOWS THAT I'M WEAK. SHE TOLD ME I HAVE NO WILLPOWER.
THEN I REMINDED HER THAT HER NEW YEAR'S RESOLUTION TO GIVE UP CHEWING TOBACCO LASTED THREE HOURS.
WELL PLAYED, CHAD!
IT WAS THE BEST TALK WE'VE EVER HAD!
Peirce

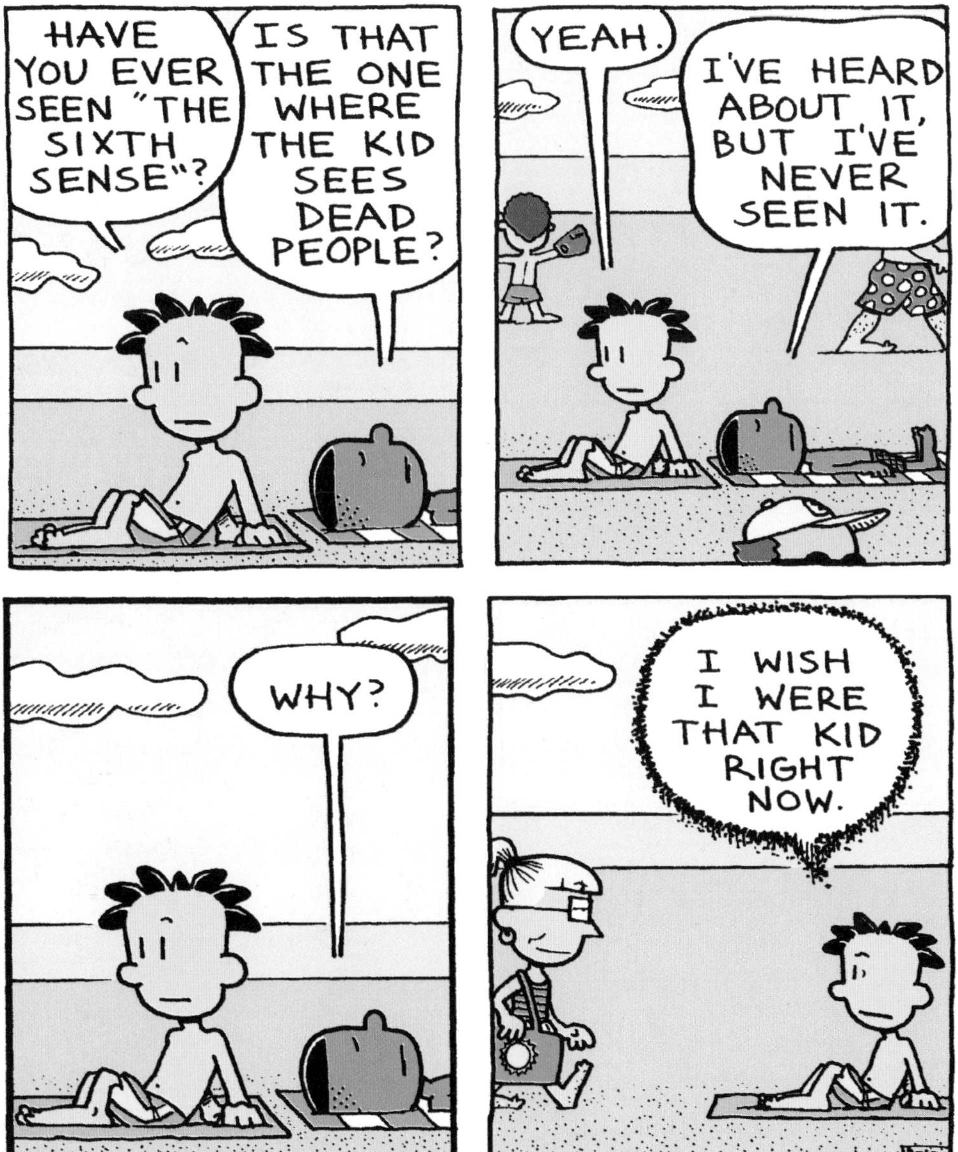
HAVE YOU EVER SEEN "THE SIXTH SENSE"?
IS THAT THE ONE WHERE THE KID SEES DEAD PEOPLE?
YEAH.
I'VE HEARD ABOUT IT, BUT I'VE NEVER SEEN IT.
WHY?
I WISH I WERE THAT KID RIGHT NOW.

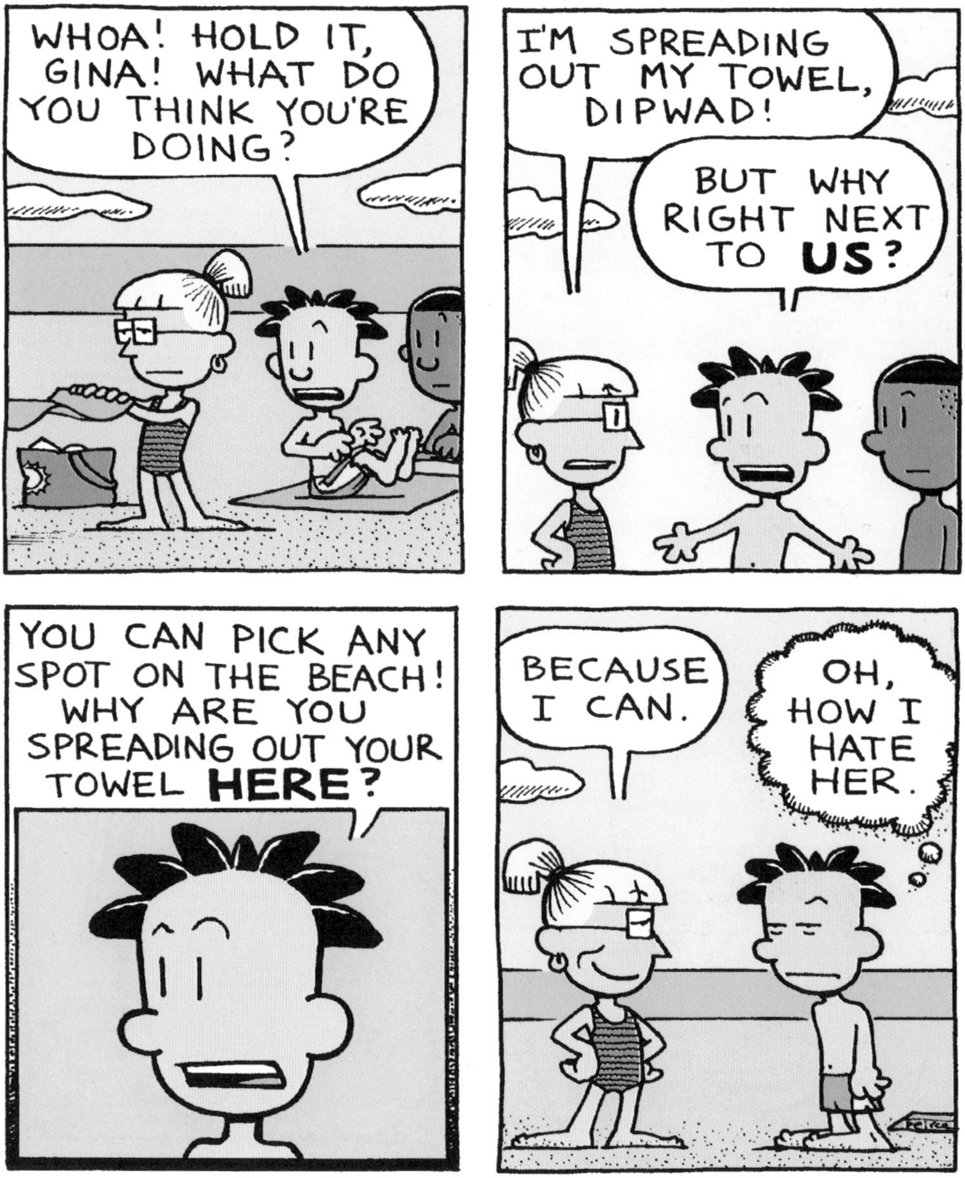
WHOA! HOLD IT, GINA! WHAT DO YOU THINK YOU'RE DOING?
I'M SPREADING OUT MY TOWEL, DIPWAD!
BUT WHY RIGHT NEXT TO **US**?
YOU CAN PICK ANY SPOT ON THE BEACH! WHY ARE YOU SPREADING OUT YOUR TOWEL **HERE**?
BECAUSE I CAN.
OH, HOW I HATE HER.

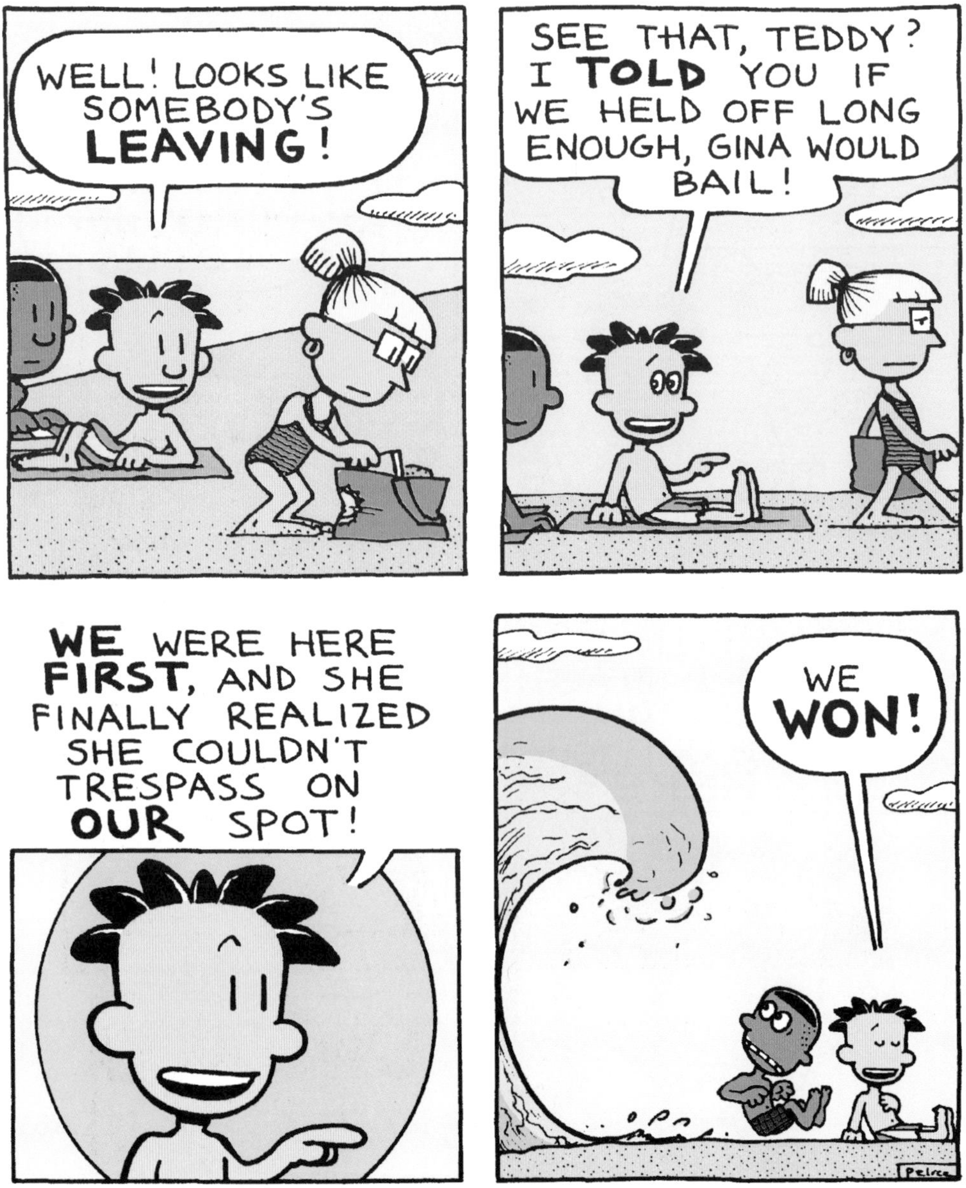
WELL! LOOKS LIKE SOMEBODY'S **LEAVING**!
SEE THAT, TEDDY? I **TOLD** YOU IF WE HELD OFF LONG ENOUGH, GINA WOULD BAIL!
WE WERE HERE **FIRST**, AND SHE FINALLY REALIZED SHE COULDN'T TRESPASS ON **OUR** SPOT!
WE **WON**!
Peirce

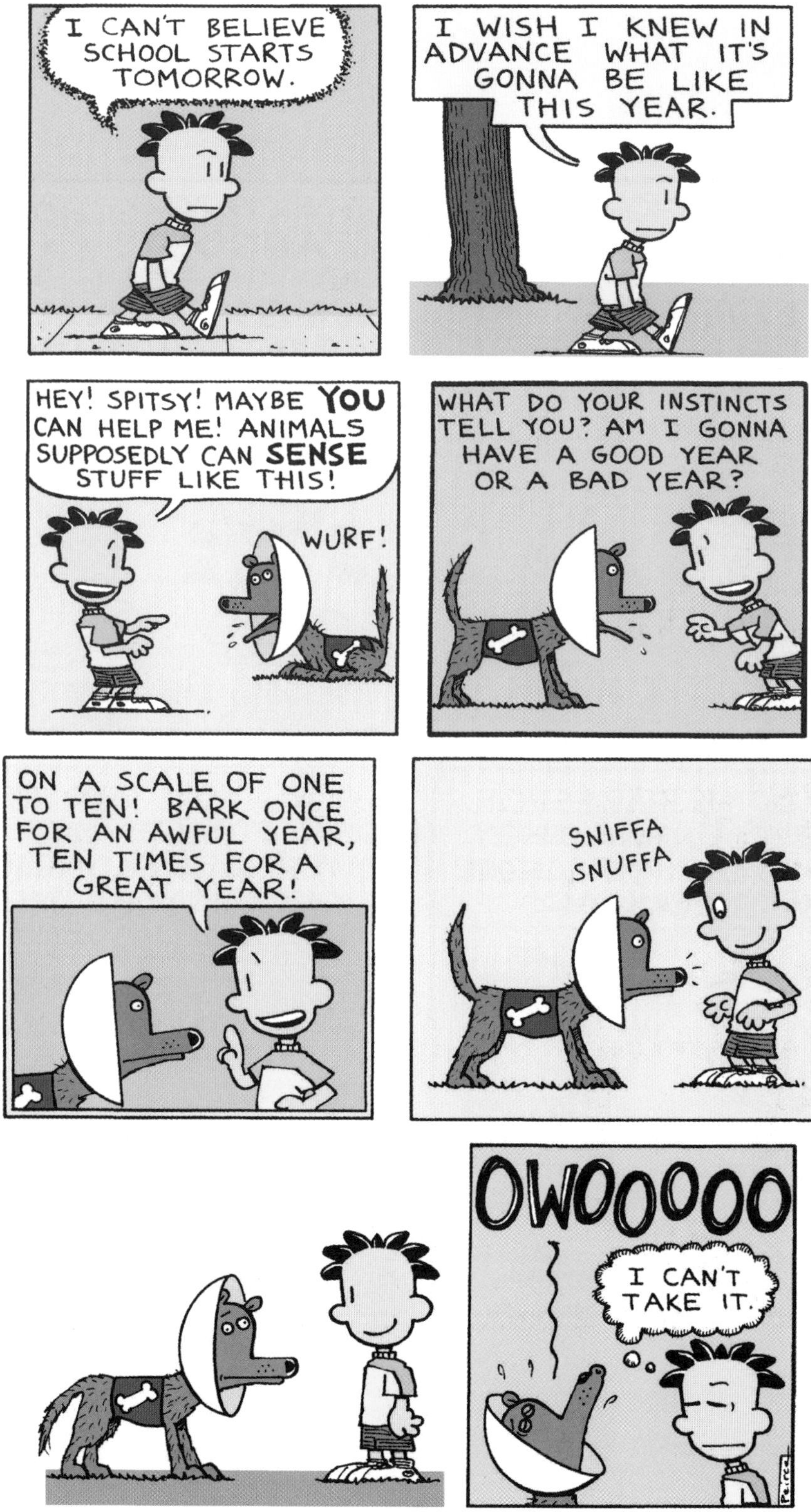
I CAN'T BELIEVE SCHOOL STARTS TOMORROW.
I WISH I KNEW IN ADVANCE WHAT IT'S GONNA BE LIKE THIS YEAR.
HEY! SPITSY! MAYBE YOU CAN HELP ME! ANIMALS SUPPOSEDLY CAN SENSE STUFF LIKE THIS!
WURF!
WHAT DO YOUR INSTINCTS TELL YOU? AM I GONNA HAVE A GOOD YEAR OR A BAD YEAR?
ON A SCALE OF ONE TO TEN! BARK ONCE FOR AN AWFUL YEAR, TEN TIMES FOR A GREAT YEAR!
SNIFFA SNUFFA
OWOOOOO
I CAN'T TAKE IT.
Peirce

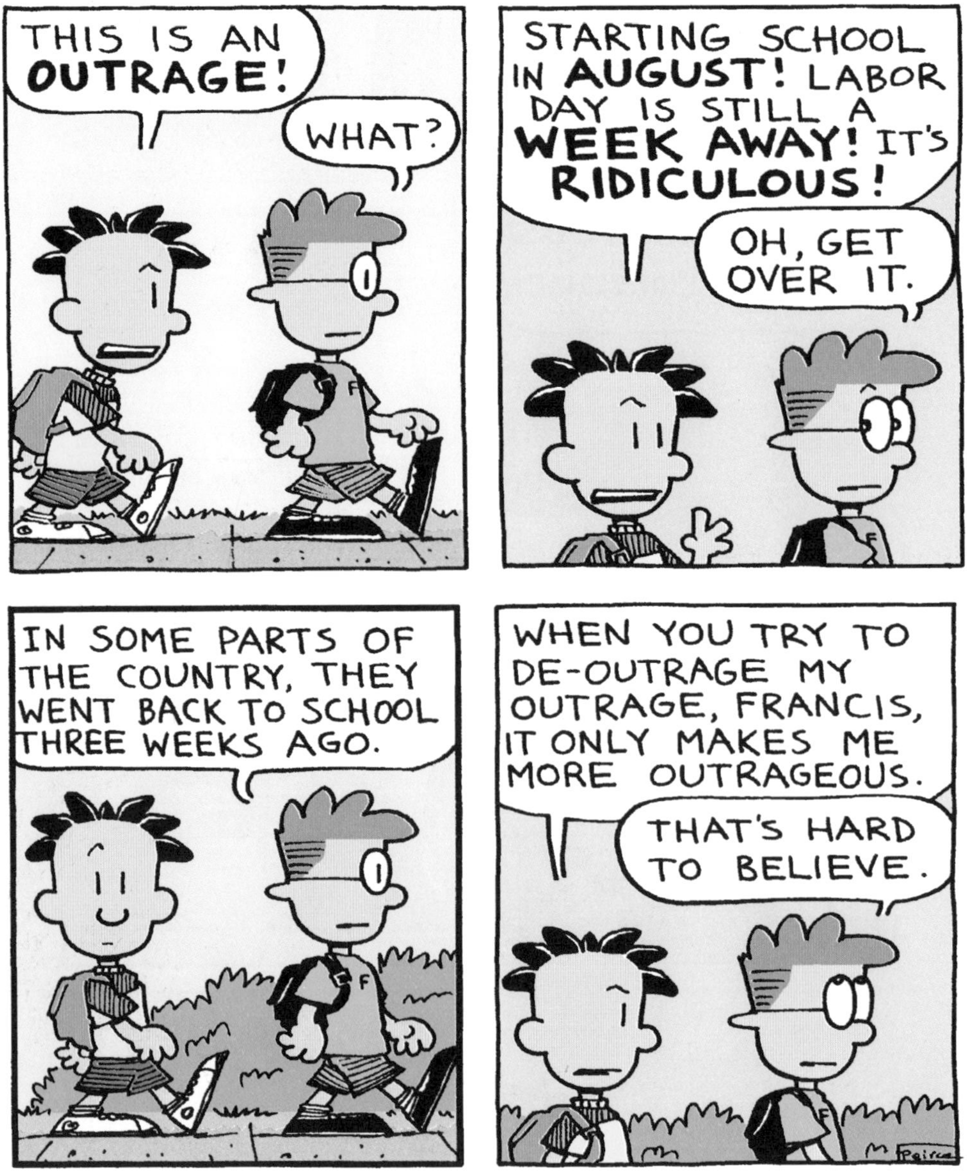
THIS IS AN OUTRAGE!
WHAT?
STARTING SCHOOL IN AUGUST! LABOR DAY IS STILL A WEEK AWAY! IT'S RIDICULOUS!
OH, GET OVER IT.
IN SOME PARTS OF THE COUNTRY, THEY WENT BACK TO SCHOOL THREE WEEKS AGO.
WHEN YOU TRY TO DE-OUTRAGE MY OUTRAGE, FRANCIS, IT ONLY MAKES ME MORE OUTRAGEOUS.
THAT'S HARD TO BELIEVE.
M. Peirce

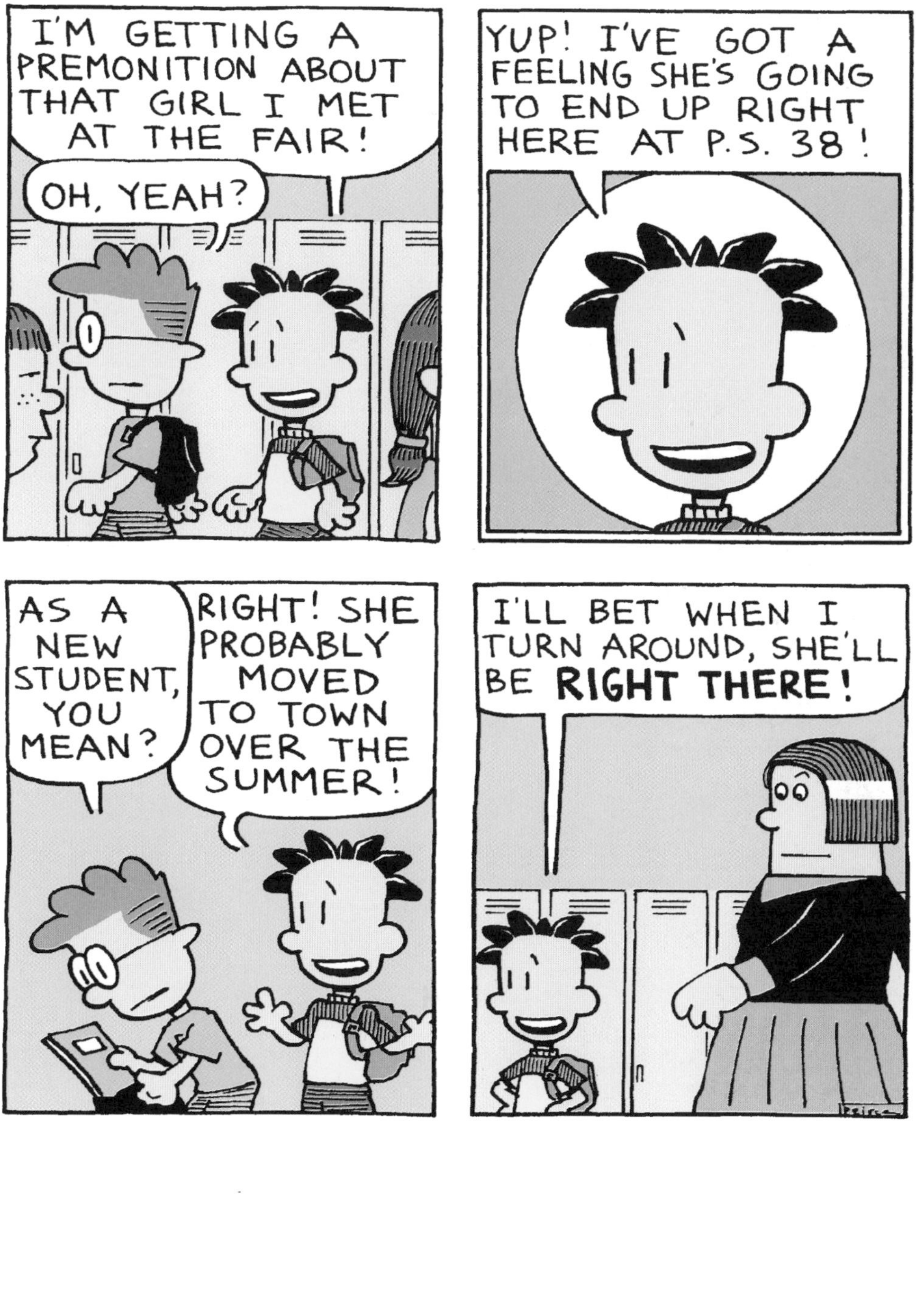
I'M GETTING A PREMONITION ABOUT THAT GIRL I MET AT THE FAIR!
OH, YEAH?
YUP! I'VE GOT A FEELING SHE'S GOING TO END UP RIGHT HERE AT P.S. 38!
AS A NEW STUDENT, YOU MEAN?
RIGHT! SHE PROBABLY MOVED TO TOWN OVER THE SUMMER!
I'LL BET WHEN I TURN AROUND, SHE'LL BE **RIGHT THERE**!

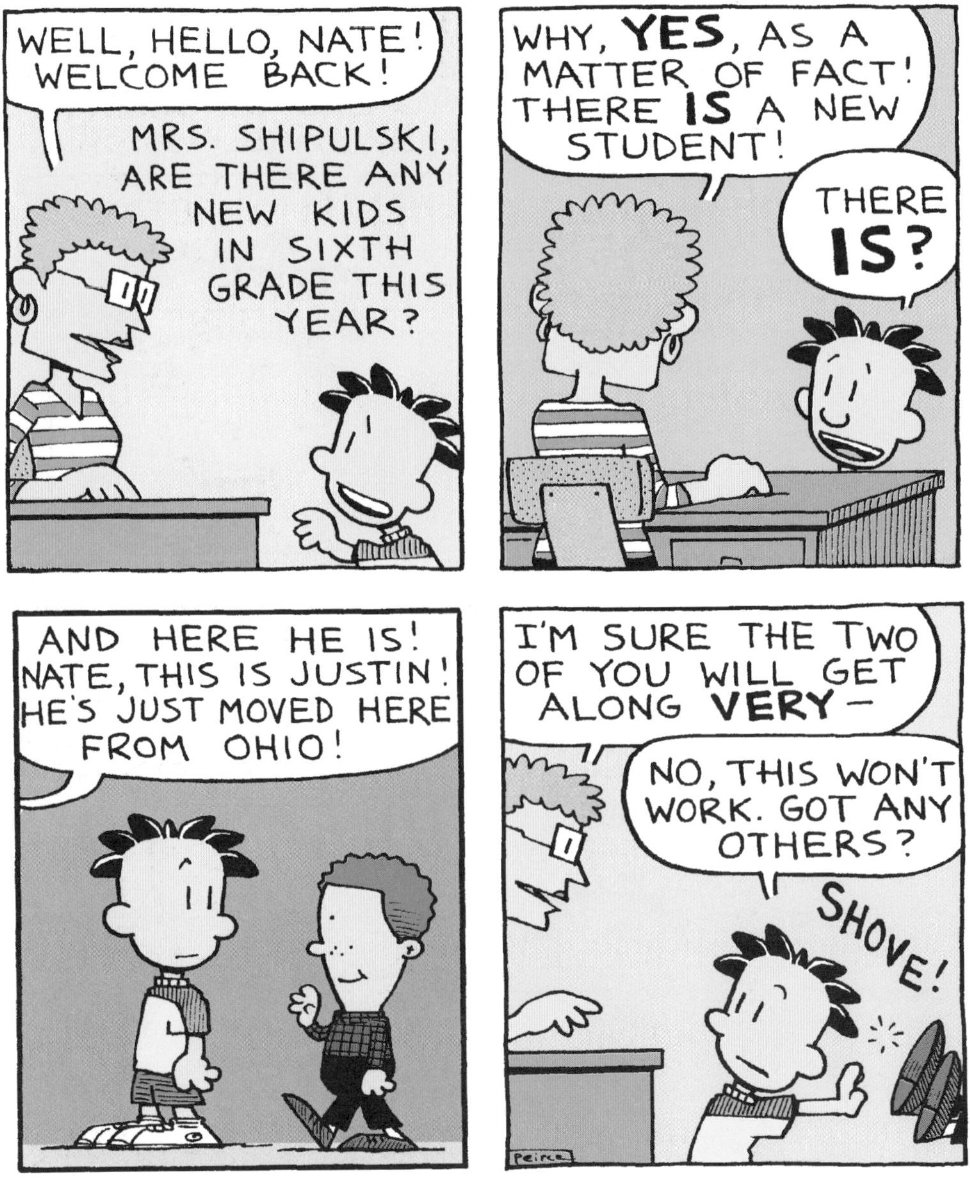
WELL, HELLO, NATE! WELCOME BACK!
MRS. SHIPULSKI, ARE THERE ANY NEW KIDS IN SIXTH GRADE THIS YEAR?
WHY, YES, AS A MATTER OF FACT! THERE IS A NEW STUDENT!
THERE IS?
AND HERE HE IS! NATE, THIS IS JUSTIN! HE'S JUST MOVED HERE FROM OHIO!
I'M SURE THE TWO OF YOU WILL GET ALONG VERY–
NO, THIS WON'T WORK. GOT ANY OTHERS?
SHOVE!
Peirce

...AND WHEN I RODE THE FLAMETHROWER, I ENDED UP SITTING NEXT TO THIS GIRL! I DIDN'T KNOW HER, BUT SHE WAS CUTE! **WICKED** CUTE!

AND WE GOT ALONG **GREAT!** I MEAN, THE RIDE ONLY LASTED A COUPLE MINUTES, BUT THERE WAS **CHEMISTRY** BETWEEN US! I COULD **FEEL** IT!

THEN THE RIDE ENDED, AND I LOST HER IN THE CROWD! SHE DISAPPEARED BEFORE I COULD EVEN FIND OUT HER **NAME!**

SO I SAID TO MY- SELF: I'M GOING TO TRACK HER DOWN IF IT'S THE LAST THING I ... ...

ALL I ASKED WAS "HOW WAS YOUR SUMMER?"

YAK YAK YAK YAK YAK YAK YAK YAK YAK YAK

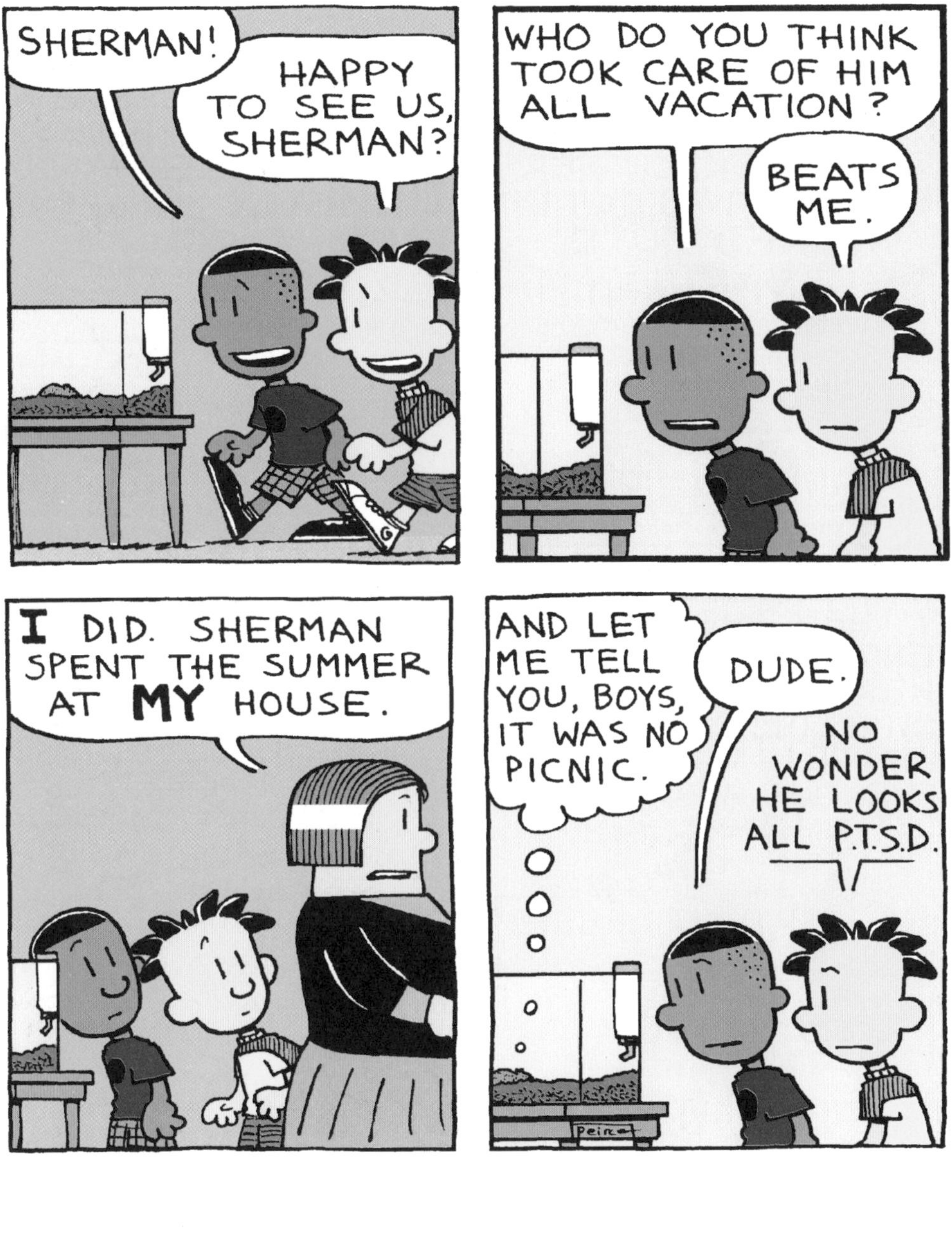
SHERMAN!
HAPPY TO SEE US, SHERMAN?
WHO DO YOU THINK TOOK CARE OF HIM ALL VACATION?
BEATS ME.
I DID. SHERMAN SPENT THE SUMMER AT MY HOUSE.
AND LET ME TELL YOU, BOYS, IT WAS NO PICNIC.
DUDE.
NO WONDER HE LOOKS ALL P.T.S.D.
Peirce

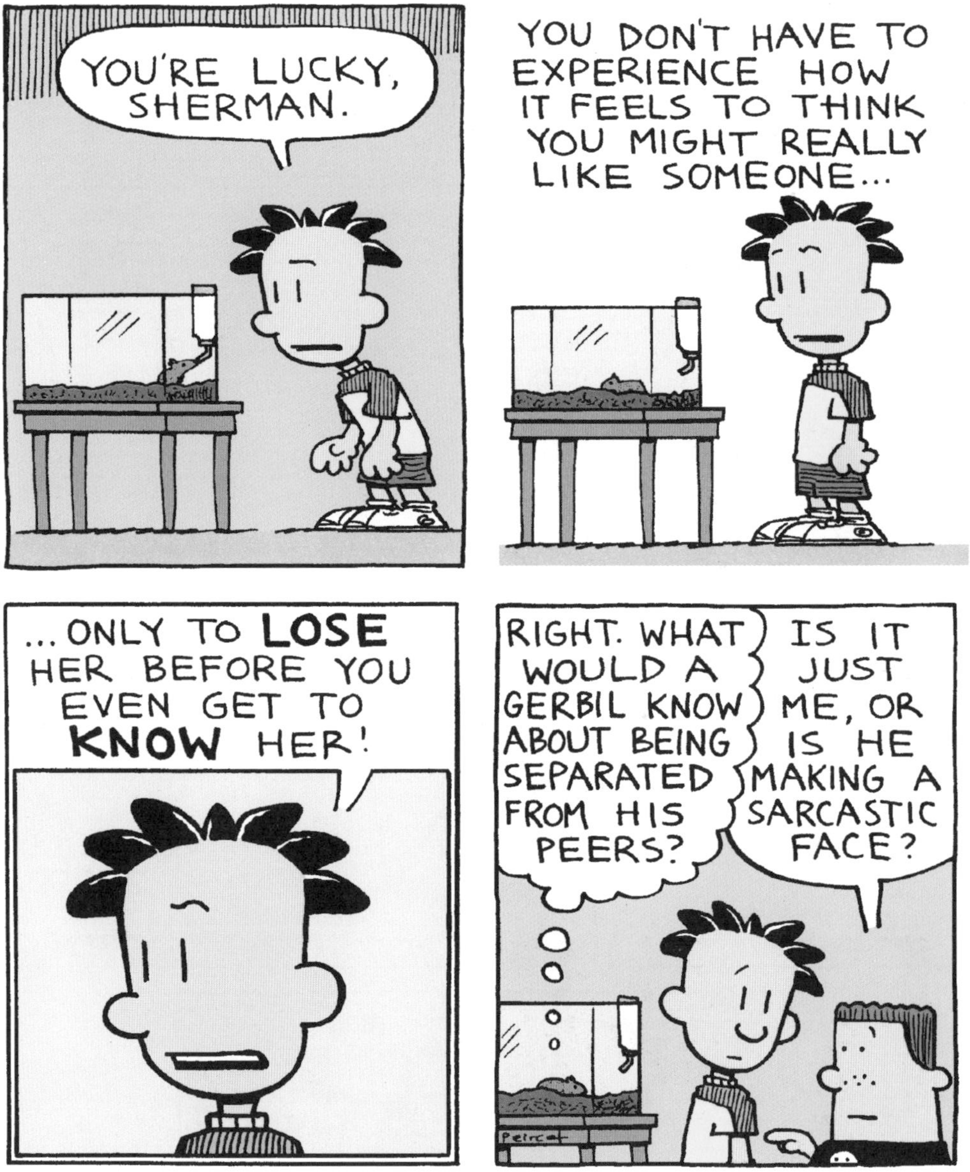
YOU'RE LUCKY, SHERMAN.
YOU DON'T HAVE TO EXPERIENCE HOW IT FEELS TO THINK YOU MIGHT REALLY LIKE SOMEONE...
...ONLY TO LOSE HER BEFORE YOU EVEN GET TO KNOW HER!
RIGHT. WHAT WOULD A GERBIL KNOW ABOUT BEING SEPARATED FROM HIS PEERS?
IS IT JUST ME, OR IS HE MAKING A SARCASTIC FACE?
Peirce

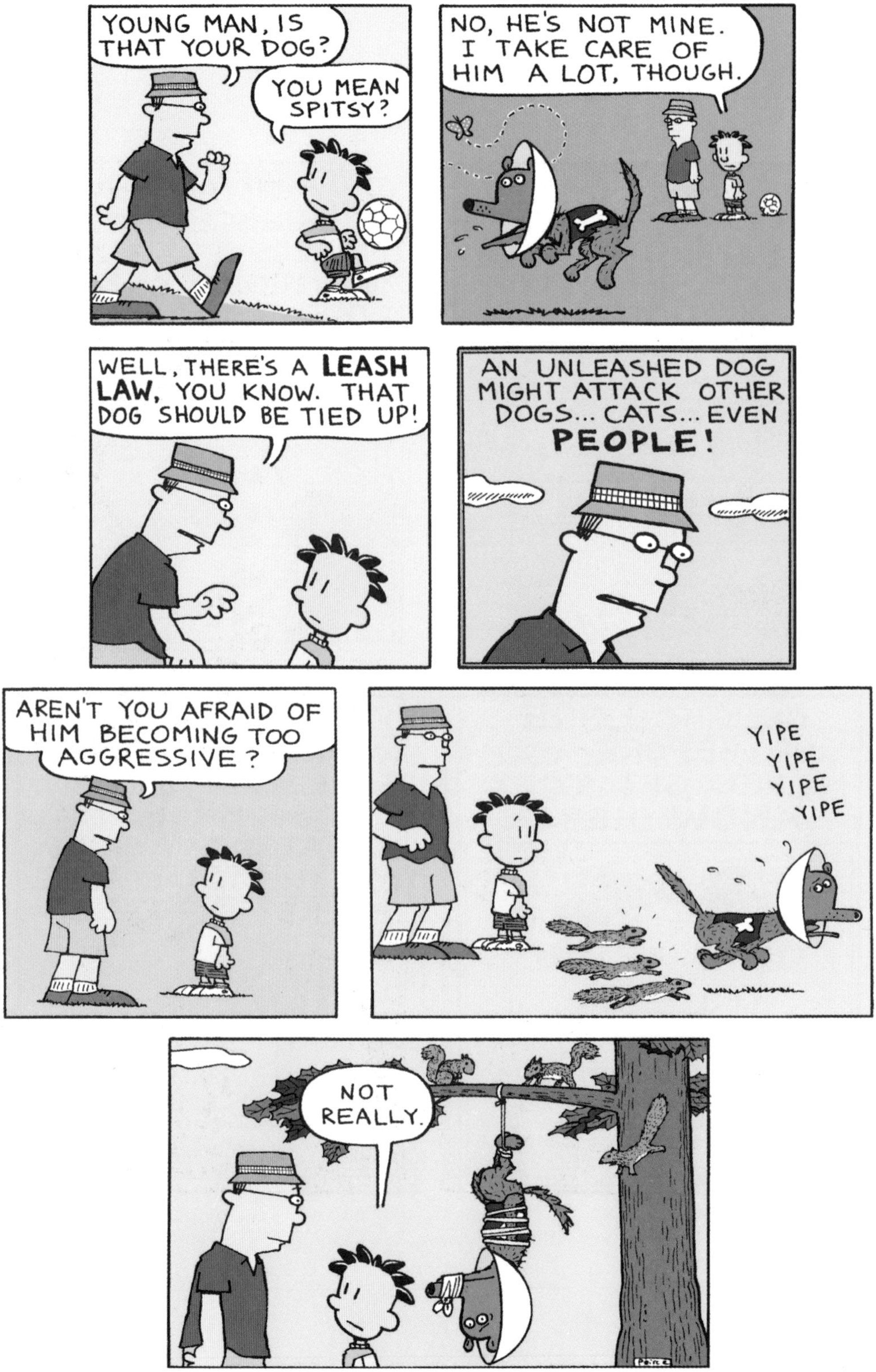
YOUNG MAN, IS THAT YOUR DOG?
YOU MEAN SPITSY?
NO, HE'S NOT MINE. I TAKE CARE OF HIM A LOT, THOUGH.
WELL, THERE'S A LEASH LAW, YOU KNOW. THAT DOG SHOULD BE TIED UP!
AN UNLEASHED DOG MIGHT ATTACK OTHER DOGS... CATS... EVEN PEOPLE!
AREN'T YOU AFRAID OF HIM BECOMING TOO AGGRESSIVE?
YIPE
YIPE
YIPE
YIPE
NOT REALLY.

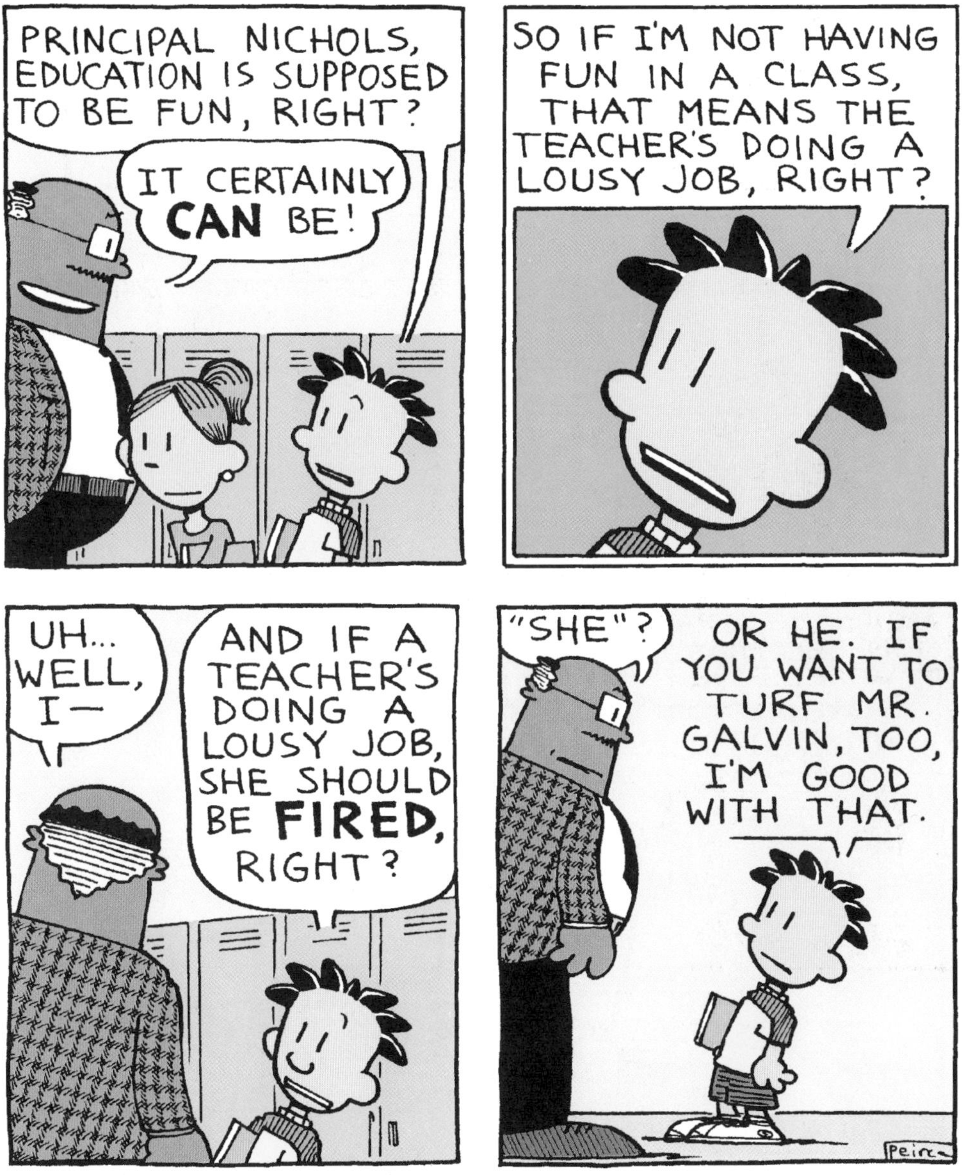
PRINCIPAL NICHOLS, EDUCATION IS SUPPOSED TO BE FUN, RIGHT?
IT CERTAINLY **CAN** BE!
SO IF I'M NOT HAVING FUN IN A CLASS, THAT MEANS THE TEACHER'S DOING A LOUSY JOB, RIGHT?
UH... WELL, I—
AND IF A TEACHER'S DOING A LOUSY JOB, SHE SHOULD BE **FIRED**, RIGHT?
"SHE"?
OR HE. IF YOU WANT TO TURF MR. GALVIN, TOO, I'M GOOD WITH THAT.
Peirce

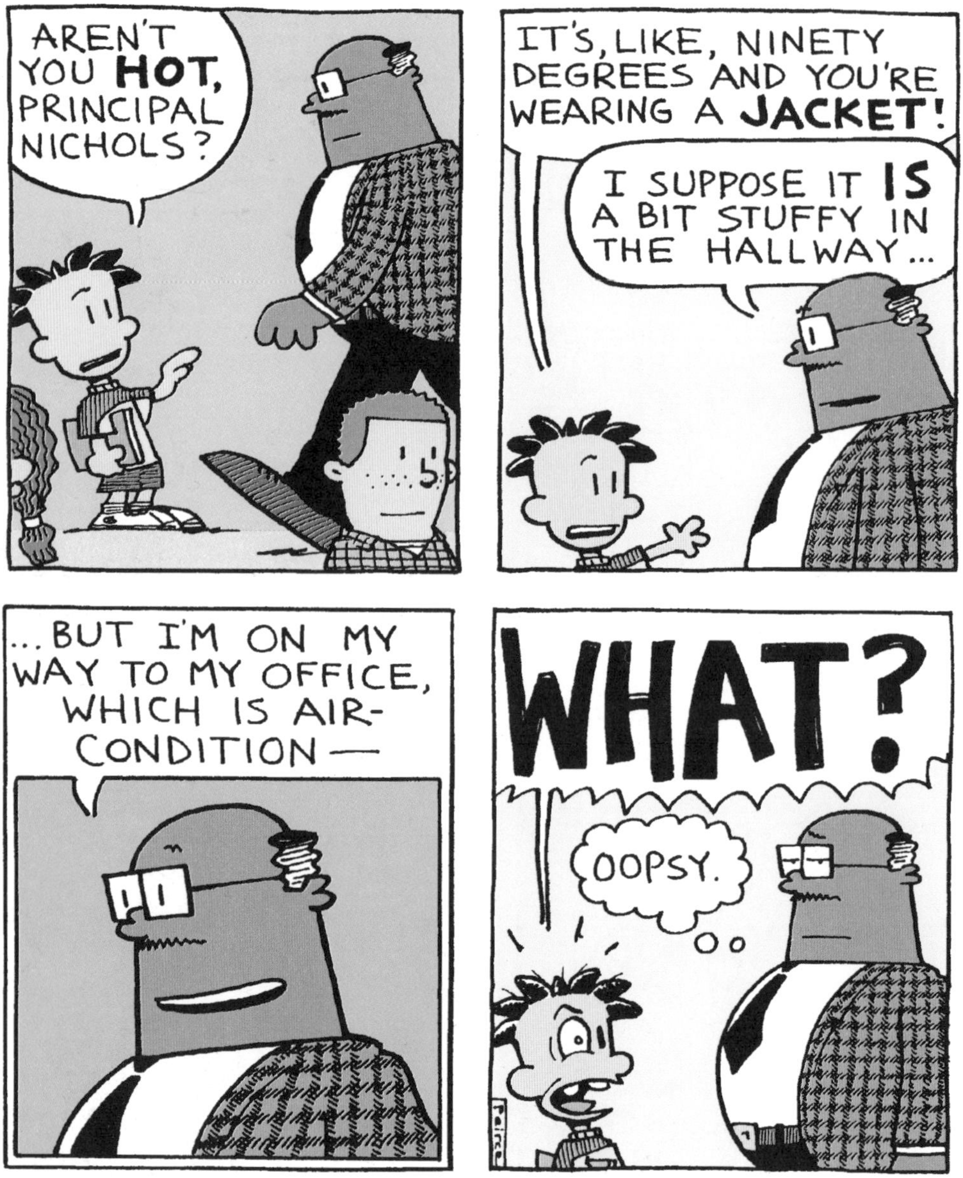
AREN'T YOU HOT, PRINCIPAL NICHOLS?
IT'S, LIKE, NINETY DEGREES AND YOU'RE WEARING A JACKET!
I SUPPOSE IT IS A BIT STUFFY IN THE HALLWAY...
...BUT I'M ON MY WAY TO MY OFFICE, WHICH IS AIR-CONDITION—
WHAT?
OOPSY.
Peirce

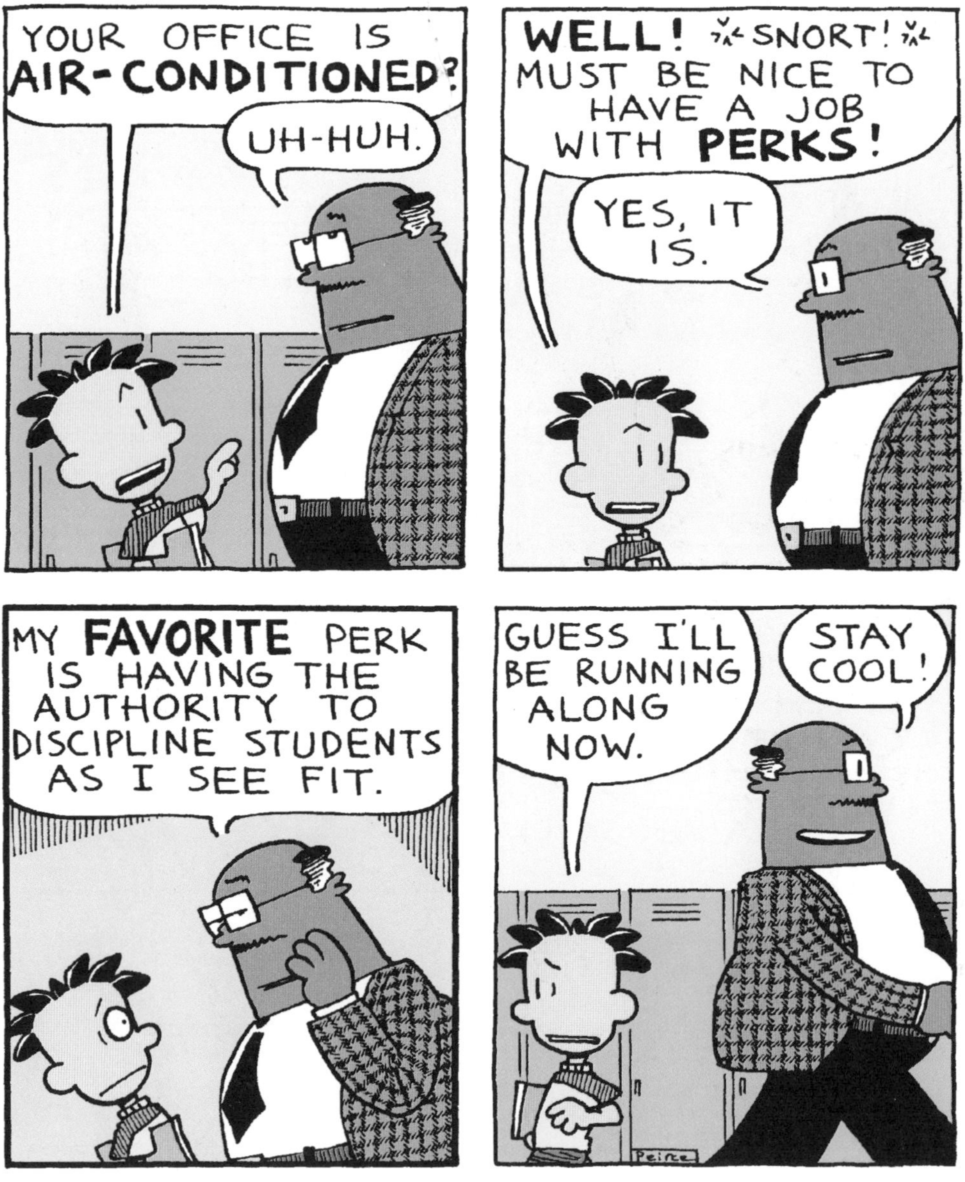
YOUR OFFICE IS **AIR-CONDITIONED**?
UH-HUH.
WELL! SNORT! MUST BE NICE TO HAVE A JOB WITH **PERKS**!
YES, IT IS.
MY **FAVORITE** PERK IS HAVING THE AUTHORITY TO DISCIPLINE STUDENTS AS I SEE FIT.
GUESS I'LL BE RUNNING ALONG NOW.
STAY COOL!
Peirce

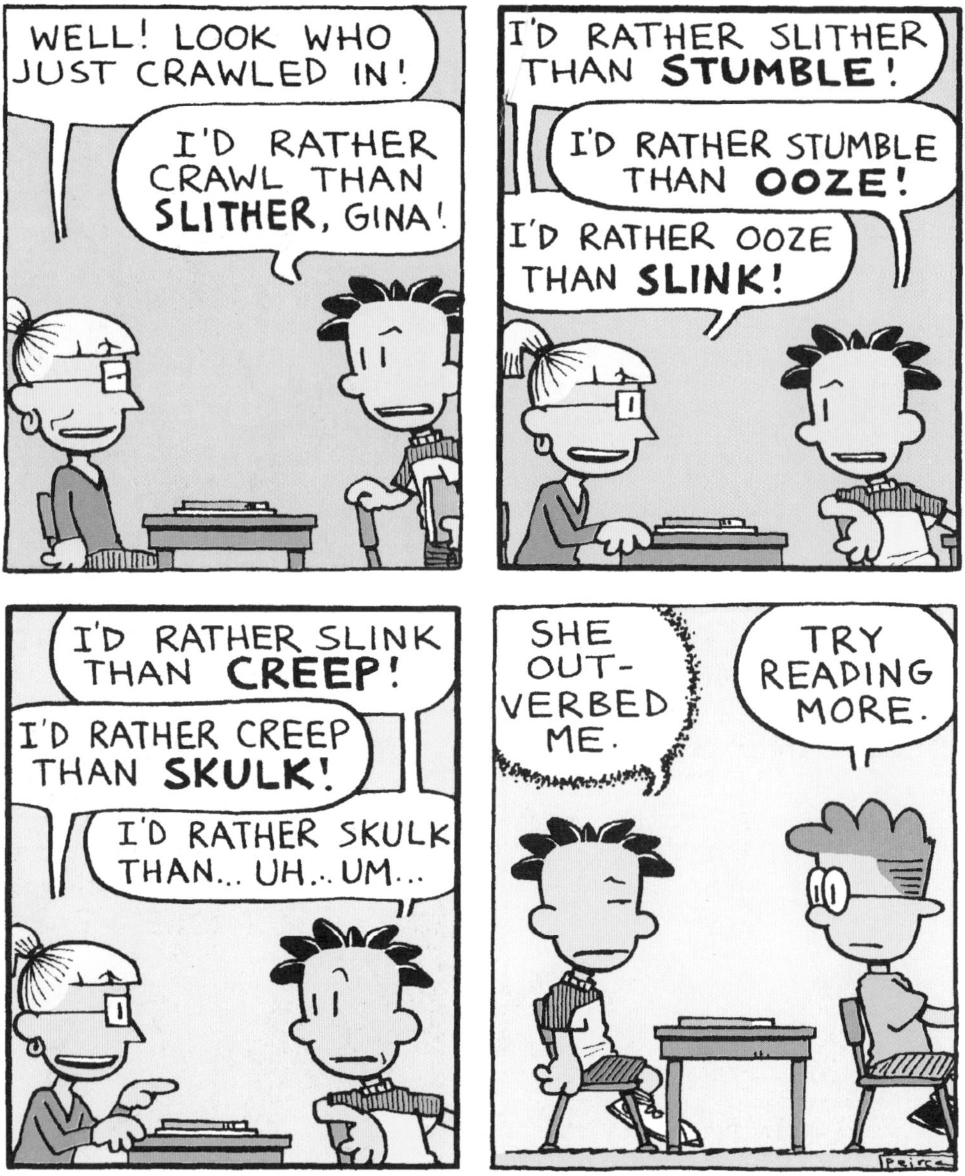
WELL! LOOK WHO JUST CRAWLED IN!
I'D RATHER CRAWL THAN **SLITHER**, GINA!
I'D RATHER SLITHER THAN **STUMBLE**!
I'D RATHER STUMBLE THAN **OOZE**!
I'D RATHER OOZE THAN **SLINK**!
I'D RATHER SLINK THAN **CREEP**!
I'D RATHER CREEP THAN **SKULK**!
I'D RATHER SKULK THAN... UH... UM...
SHE OUT-VERBED ME.
TRY READING MORE.
Peirce

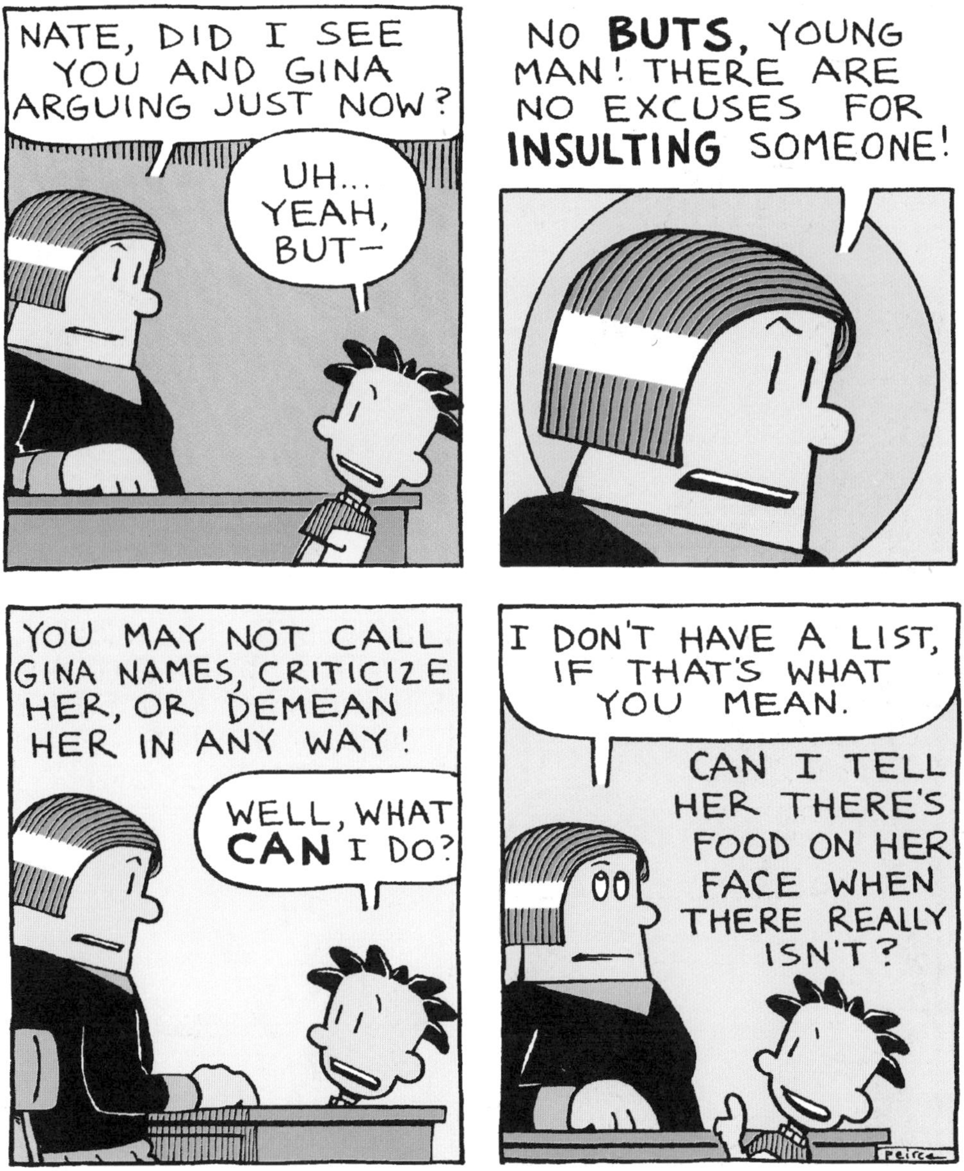
NATE, DID I SEE YOU AND GINA ARGUING JUST NOW?
UH... YEAH, BUT—
NO **BUTS**, YOUNG MAN! THERE ARE NO EXCUSES FOR **INSULTING** SOMEONE!
YOU MAY NOT CALL GINA NAMES, CRITICIZE HER, OR DEMEAN HER IN ANY WAY!
WELL, WHAT **CAN** I DO?
I DON'T HAVE A LIST, IF THAT'S WHAT YOU MEAN.
CAN I TELL HER THERE'S FOOD ON HER FACE WHEN THERE REALLY ISN'T?
peirce

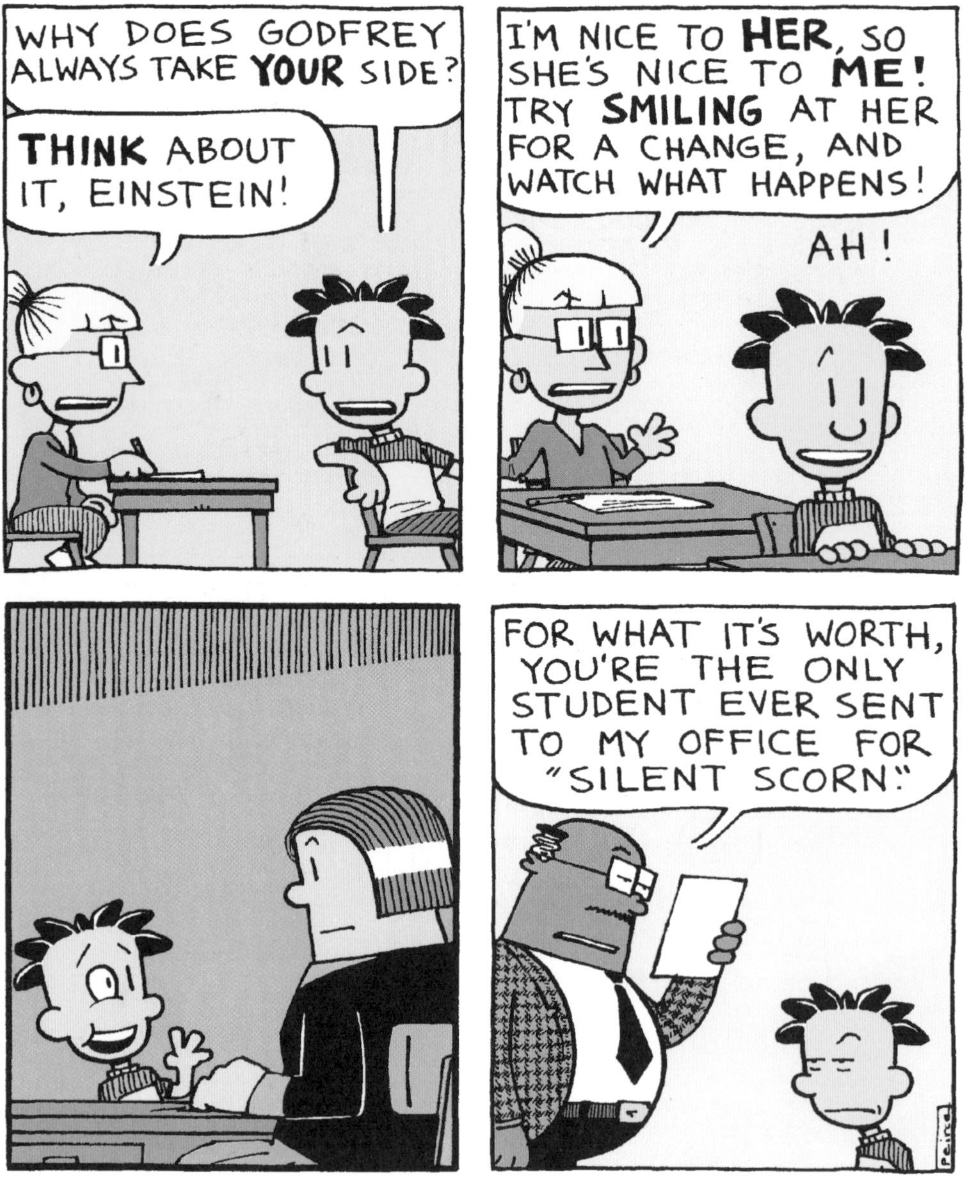
WHY DOES GODFREY ALWAYS TAKE YOUR SIDE?
THINK ABOUT IT, EINSTEIN!
I'M NICE TO HER, SO SHE'S NICE TO ME! TRY SMILING AT HER FOR A CHANGE, AND WATCH WHAT HAPPENS!
AH!
FOR WHAT IT'S WORTH, YOU'RE THE ONLY STUDENT EVER SENT TO MY OFFICE FOR "SILENT SCORN."
Peirce

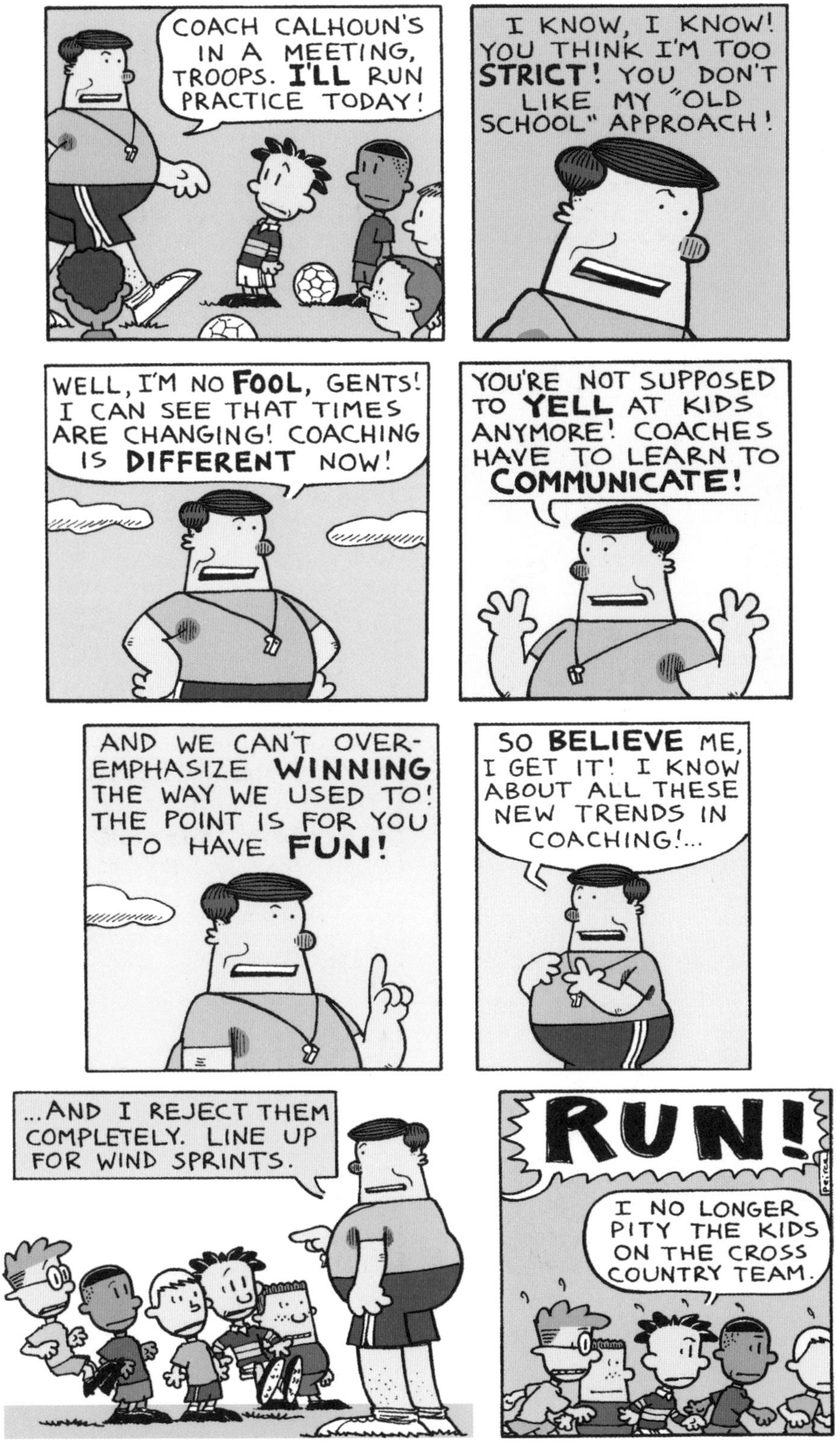
COACH CALHOUN'S IN A MEETING, TROOPS. I'LL RUN PRACTICE TODAY!
I KNOW, I KNOW! YOU THINK I'M TOO STRICT! YOU DON'T LIKE MY "OLD SCHOOL" APPROACH!
WELL, I'M NO FOOL, GENTS! I CAN SEE THAT TIMES ARE CHANGING! COACHING IS DIFFERENT NOW!
YOU'RE NOT SUPPOSED TO YELL AT KIDS ANYMORE! COACHES HAVE TO LEARN TO COMMUNICATE!
AND WE CAN'T OVER-EMPHASIZE WINNING THE WAY WE USED TO! THE POINT IS FOR YOU TO HAVE FUN!
SO BELIEVE ME, I GET IT! I KNOW ABOUT ALL THESE NEW TRENDS IN COACHING!...
...AND I REJECT THEM COMPLETELY. LINE UP FOR WIND SPRINTS.
RUN!
I NO LONGER PITY THE KIDS ON THE CROSS COUNTRY TEAM.